# Need You Now

**Books by Nicole Helm**

Mile High Romances
*Need You Now*
*Mess With Me*
*Want You More*

Gallagher & Ivy Romances
*So Wrong It Must Be Right*
*So Bad It Must Be Good*

# Need You Now

## NICOLE HELM

ZEBRA BOOKS
KENSINGTON PUBLISHING CORP.
http://www.kensingtonbooks.com

ZEBRA BOOKS are published by

Kensington Publishing Corp.
119 West 40th Street
New York, NY 10018

All Kensington titles, imprints, and distributed lines are
available at special quantity discounts for bulk purchases
for sales promotion, premiums, fund-raising, educational,
or institutional use.

Special book excerpts or customized printings can also
be created to fit specific needs. For details, write or phone
the office of the Kensington Sales Manager: Attn.: Sales
Department. Kensington Publishing Corp., 119 West 40th
Street, New York, NY 10018. Phone: 1-800-221-2647.

Zebra and the Z logo Reg. U.S. Pat. & TM Off.

First Printing: June 2017
ISBN-13: 978-1-4201-4276-1
ISBN-10: 1-4201-4276-3

eISBN-13: 978-1-4201-4277-8
eISBN-10: 1-4201-4277-1

10 9 8 7 6 5 4 3 2 1

Printed in the United States of America

*To Maisey, Helen, and Wendy.*
*Mile High exists because of your belief in it.*
*I'm forever grateful.*

# Chapter One

Brandon Evans stood on the porch of his office and stared at the world below him, a kaleidoscope of browns and greens and grays, all the way down the mountain until the rooftops of Gracely, Colorado, dotted into view.

Across the valley, up the other side of jagged stone, the deserted Evans Mining Corporation buildings stood, like ghosts—haunting him and his name. A glaring reminder of the destruction he'd wrought while trying to do the right thing.

He wished it were a cloudy day so he couldn't see the damn things, but he'd built the headquarters of *his* company in view simply so he could remind himself what he was fighting for. What was right.

"Are you over there being broody?"

Brandon looked down at his mug of coffee balanced on the porch railing, not bothering to glance at his brother. He *was* brooding. They were outvoting him and he didn't like it. He took a sip of coffee, now cool from the chilled spring air.

He leveled a gaze at his brother, Will, and their

business partner, Sam. This was his best *I'm a leader* look, and it usually worked.

Why the hell wasn't it working today?

"Hiring a PR consultant goes against everything we're trying to do." Of course, he'd already explained that and he'd still been outvoted.

"We need help. The town isn't going to grow to forgive us. We can do all the good in the world, but without someone actually making inroads—we're not getting anywhere. We can't even find a receptionist from Gracely. No one will acknowledge we *exist*."

"We have Skeet."

"Skeet is not a receptionist. He's a . . . a . . . Help me out here, Sam?"

"His name is *Skeet*," Sam replied, as if that explained everything.

The grizzled old man who answered their phones for their outdoor adventure excursion company and refused to use a computer *was* a bit of a problem, but he worked for cheap and he was a local. Brandon had been adamant about hiring only locals.

Of course, Skeet was a local that everyone shunned, and he seemed to only speak in grunts, but they'd yet to lose an interested customer.

That they knew of, Will liked to point out.

Brandon set the offensive cold coffee down on the railing of the deck. He needed to do something with his hands. He couldn't sit still—he was too frustrated that they were standing around arguing instead of Sam and Will jumping to do his bidding.

Why had he thought to make them all equal partners?

"She's local. Great experience with a firm in Denver. She can be the bridge we need to turn the tide." Will ticked off the points they'd already been over, patient as ever.

"She's recently local—not native—and she can't change our last name."

"Well, even lifer townies working every second at Mile High can't do that."

"Can we cut the circuitous bullshit?" Sam interrupted with a mutter. "You were outvoted, Brandon. She's hired. Now, I've got to go."

"You don't have a group to guide until two."

Sam was already inside the cabin that acted as their office, the words probably never reaching him. Apparently his time-around-other-humans allotment was up for the morning. Not that shocking. The fact they'd lured him from his hermit mountain cabin before a guided hike was unusual.

Brandon turned his stare to his brother. They were twins. Born five minutes apart, but the five minutes had always felt like years. He'd been George Bailey born-older, and any time Sam sided with Will, Brandon couldn't help but get his nose a little out of joint.

He was the responsible, business-minded one, not the in-for-a-good-time playboy. They should listen to him regardless, not Will. Brandon had spearheaded Mile High. It was his baby, his penance, his hope of offering Gracely some healing in the wake of his father's mess of an impact. The fact that Will and Sam sometimes disagreed with him about the best way to do that filled him with a dark energy, and he'd need to do something physical to burn it off.

"Go chop some wood. Build a birdhouse. Climb a mountain for all I care. She'll be here at ten. Be back by then," Will ordered.

"You know I'd as soon throat punch you as do what you tell me to do."

Will grinned. "Oh, brother, if I kept my mouth shut

every time you wanted to throat punch me, I'd never speak."

"Uh-huh."

Will's expression went grave, which was always a bad sign. They both dealt with weighty things and emotion differently—Brandon acted like a dick and Will acted like nothing mattered. If Will was acting like something was important . . .

Well, shit.

"Don't think we don't take it seriously," Will said, far too quietly for Brandon's comfort. "Trust, every once in a while, we know as well or better than you."

"My ass," Brandon grumbled, feeling at least a little shamed.

"She'll be here at ten. I have that spring break group at ten-thirty, and you, lucky man, don't have anything on your plate today. Which means, you get to be in charge of paper—"

"Don't say it."

"—work and orientation!" Will concluded all too jovially.

"I could probably throw you off the mountain and no one would ask any questions."

"Ah, but then who would take the bachelorette party guides since you and Sam refuse?" Will clapped him on the shoulder. "You'll like her. She's got that business-tunnel-vision thing down that you do so well."

Brandon took a page out of Skeet's book and merely grunted, which Will—thank Christ—took as a cue to leave.

Regardless of whether he'd like this Lilly Preston, Brandon didn't see the usefulness or point in hiring a PR consultant. What was that going to accomplish when the town already hated them?

If even Will's personality couldn't win people over,

they were toast in that department. The only thing that was going to sway people's minds was an economically booming town. Mile High had a long way to go to make Gracely that. And they needed Gracely's help.

Hiring someone who had only cursory knowledge of Gracely lore, who couldn't possibly understand what they were trying to do, wasn't the answer. Worse, it reeked of something his father would have done when he was trying to hide all the shady business practices he'd instituted at Evans Mining.

Brandon glanced back over at the empty buildings. If he wanted to, he could will away the memories, the images in his mind. The pristine hallways, the steady buzz of phones and conversation. How much he'd wanted that to be *his* one day.

But then he'd told his father he knew what was going on, and if Dad didn't change, Brandon would have no choice but to go to the authorities.

The fallout had been the Evans Mining headquarters leaving Gracely after over a century of being the heart of the town, his father's subsequent heart attack and death, Mom shutting them out, and everything about his life as the golden child and heir apparent to the corporation imploding before his very eyes.

A lot of consequences for one tiny little domino he'd flicked when his conscience couldn't take the possible outcomes of his father's shady practices.

So much work to do to make it right. He forced his gaze away from those buildings into the mountains all around him. He took a deep breath of the thin air scented with heavy pine. He rubbed his palms over the rough wood of the porch railing.

It was the center—these mountains, this place. He believed he could bring this town back to life not just because he owed it to the residents who'd treated him like a king growing up, but because there was something . . . elemental about these mountains, this sky, the river tributaries, and the animals that lived within it all.

Untouched, ethereal, and while he didn't exactly believe in magic and ghostly legends of Gracely's healing power, he did believe in these mountains and this air. He was going to give his all to fix the damage he'd caused, and he was going to give his all to making Mile High Adventures everything it could be.

So, he'd put up with this unwanted PR woman for the few weeks it would take to prove that Will and Sam were wrong. Once they admitted he was right, they could move on to the next thing, and the next thing, until they got exactly what they wanted.

Lilly took a deep, cleansing breath of the mountain air. The altitude was much higher up here than in the little valley Gracely was nestled into, but even aside from that, the office of Mile High Adventures was breathtaking.

It was like something out of a brochure—which would make her job rather easy. A cabin nestled into the side of a mountain. All dark logs and green trimmed roof, with a snow-peaked top of a mountain settled right behind to complete the look of cozy mountain getaway. The porches were almost as big as the cabin itself. She'd suggest some colorful deck chairs, a few fire pits to complete the look, but it took no imagination at all to picture groups of people and mugs of hot chocolate and colorful plaid blankets.

The sign next to the door that read MILE HIGH ADVENTURES was carved into a wood plank that matched the logs of the cabin.

If it weren't for the men who ran this company, she'd be crying with relief and excitement. She *needed* a job that would allow her to stay in Gracely, and this one would pay enough that she could still support her sister and nephew even with Cora's dwindling waitress hours and low tips.

Cora and Micah were doing so well, finally moving on from the abusive nightmare that had been Stephen. Lilly couldn't uproot them, and she couldn't leave them. They needed her, but her Denver-based PR company had refused to let her continue to work remotely when they'd merged with another company and kept only those willing to relocate to Denver.

So, here she was, about to agree to work for the kind of men she couldn't stand. Rich, entitled, charming. The kind of men who'd hurt her mother, her sister, her nephew.

Lilly forced her feet forward. This was work, not romance, so it didn't matter. She'd do her job, take their money, do her best to improve the light in which their business was seen in Gracely, and not let any of these rich and powerful men touch her.

Shoulders back, she walked up the stairs of the porch. There was a sign on the door, hung from a nail and string. It read *Come On In!* in flowing script. She imagined if she flipped the sign there'd be some kind of WE'RE CLOSED phrase on the back.

Impressive detail for a group of three, from what she could tell, burly mountain men hated by the town at large.

Her stomach jittered, cramped. She really didn't want to do this. She *loved* Gracely. Even for all its problems, it was charming and . . . calming. She felt cozy and comfortable here. More than she'd ever felt in Denver, where she'd grown up.

Working for Mile High would keep her here, but would it still be cozy and comfortable if the town looked at her with contempt? If they considered her tainted by association with these men she'd never heard a good word about?

Well, as long as Cora and Micah still needed her, it didn't matter. Couldn't.

She blew out a breath and lifted a steady hand. She opened the door. Will *had* instructed her to come on in, and the sign said as much.

Upon stepping into what was an open area that seemed designed as both lobby and living room, she wasn't surprised to find more wood, a crackling fire in the fireplace, warm and worn brown leather couches pushed around the hearth. The walls were mostly bare, but there was a deer head over the mantel, a few framed graphics with quotes about going to the mountains and the wilderness.

A grunt caused Lilly to jerk her attention to the big desk opposite the entryway. She wasn't sure what she'd expected of the other employees of Mile High, but she'd assumed they'd all be like Will. Young, athletic, charming, and handsome.

The man sitting behind the desk was *none* of those things. He was small and old with a white beard and a white ponytail. A bit of a Willie Nelson/*Dirty Santa*-looking character in a stained Marine Corps sweatshirt.

Not what she expected of a receptionist . . . any-where.

"Hello. My name is Lilly Preston. I'm supposed to be meeting Will Evans and his broth—"

The man grunted again, a sound that was a gravelly huff and seemed to shake his entire small frame.

What on earth was happening?

"Ah, Lilly!" Will appeared from some hallway in

the back. "Skeet, you're not scaring off our newest employee, are you?"

The man—Skeet, good Lord—grunted again. Maybe he was their . . . grandfather or something.

She returned her attention and polite business smile to Will and the man behind him. It wasn't any stretch to realize this was Will's brother, Brandon Evans. There were a lot of similarities in their height, the dark brown hair—though Brandon's was short and Will's was long enough to have a bit of a wave to it. They both sported varying levels of beard, hazel eyes, and the kind of angular, masculine face one would definitely associate with men who climbed mountains and kayaked rivers.

There were some key differences—mainly, Will was smiling, all straight white teeth. Brandon's mouth was formed in something a half inch away from a scowl.

Well. She forced her smile to go wider and more pleasant. She wasn't a novice at dealing with cranky or difficult men. About seventy-five percent of her career thus far had included dealing with obstinate and opinionated business owners. The Evans brothers might be different, but they weren't unique.

"You have an absolutely lovely office. I'm so impressed."

Will gestured her toward the couches around the fireplace. There were rugs over the hardwood floor, patterns of dark red and green and brown. It was no lie, she *was* impressed.

"Have a seat, Lilly. I have a group to guide rock climbing shortly, so Brandon will conduct most of your orientation. We've got the necessary paperwork." He placed a stack of papers on the rough-hewn wood coffee table. It looked like it had probably come from Annie's—the furniture shop in Gracely. Furnishing and decorating from local vendors would be smart.

Smart, rich men with charming smiles and handsome scowls. It didn't get much more dangerous than that, but Lilly never let her smile falter.

"Once we've done that, Brandon will show you around, show you your desk, and you can ask any questions."

"Of course." She leaned forward to take the paperwork, but Brandon's hand all but slapped on top of the stack.

"One thing first."

Will muttered something that sounded like an expletive.

The stomach jittering/cramping combo was back, but she refused to let it show on her face. Nerves were normal, and the way she always dealt was to ignore them through the pleasantest smiles and friendliest chitchat she could manage until they went away.

"I'm at your disposal, Mr. Evans," she said, letting her hand fall away from the papers as she settled comfortably into the couch. At least she hoped she was exuding the appearance of comfort.

His expression, which hadn't been all that friendly or welcoming, darkened even further. "You will call me Brandon. You will call him Will. There are no misters here."

Ah, so he was one of those. Determined to be an everyman. She resisted an eye roll.

He leaned forward, hazel eyes blazing into hers. "Do you believe in the legend, Ms. Preston?"

"The . . . legend?" This was not what she'd expected. At all. She quickly glanced at the door in her periphery. Maybe she should bolt.

"You've lived here how long? Surely you've heard the legend of Gracely."

"You mean . . ." She hesitated because she didn't

know where he was trying to lead her, and she didn't like going into unchartered territory. But, he seemed adamant, so she continued. "The one about those who choose Gracely as their home will find the healing their heart desires?"

"Are there others?"

Lilly had to tense to keep the pleasant smile on her face. She didn't like the way this Evans brother spoke to her. Like he was an interrogating detective. Like she'd done something wrong, when Will had been the one to convince her to take this job.

Because working with the Evanses was going to put a big red X on her back in town, and she didn't trust men like them with their centuries of good name and money.

But she needed a job. She needed to stay in Gracely. So, she had to ignore the way his tone put her back up and smile pleasantly and pretend he wasn't a giant asshat.

"So, Ms. Preston." Oh she hated the way he *drawled* her name. "The question is: do you believe in the legend?"

This was a test, a blatant one at that, and yet . . . she didn't know the right answer. Would he ridicule her for believing in fairy tales if she said she believed the first settlers of Gracely were magically healed when they settled here and all the stories that had been built up into legend since? Would he take issue with her being cynical and hard if she said there was no way?

The biggest problem was her answer existed somewhere in between the two. Half of her thought it was foolishness. Losing her job and having to take this one hardly seemed like healing or good luck, but her sister and nephew had flourished here in the past year and, well, healing was possible. Magic? Maybe—maybe not. But possible.

So, maybe it was best to focus on the good, the possibility. "Yes." She met his penetrating hazel gaze, keeping her expression the picture-perfect blank slate of professional politeness.

"And what do you think is the source of that legend? What makes it true?"

"True?" She looked at Will, tried to catch his gaze, but he looked at the ceiling. She might not trust Will, but at least he was polite. Apparently also a giant coward.

"Yes, if you believe Gracely can heal, what do you believe *causes* that ability?"

She flicked her gaze back to his. It had never wavered. There was a fierceness to his expression that made her nervous. He was a big man. Tall, broad. Though he wore a thick sweater and heavy work pants and boots, it was fairly obvious beneath all those layers was the type of man who could probably crush her with one arm.

She suddenly felt very small and very vulnerable. Weak and at a disadvantage.

Which was just the kind of thing she wouldn't show them. Powerful men got off on causing fear and vulnerability. She'd seen her nephew's father do that enough to have built a mask against it, and she'd worked with and for plenty of men who'd wanted to intimidate her for a variety of reasons.

She could handle whatever this was. Chin up. Spine straight. A practiced down-the-nose look. "Do legends need a cause? A scientific explanation? Or are they simply . . . magic? Do I need to analyze *why* I believe in it, or can I simply believe it happened and continues to? And, more, what on earth does it have to do with my work here?"

"If you're going to work here," he said, his voice low and . . . fierce to match his face, "you will need to understand what *we* believe about the legend. Because it has everything to do with why we built Mile High Adventures."

"That's not what I heard," she muttered before she could stop herself. Okay, maybe remote consulting *had* dulled some of her instincts if she let things like that slip.

"Oh, and what did you hear, Ms. Preston? That we're the evil spawn of Satan setting out to crush Gracely even deeper into the earth? That we're bringing in an influx of out-of-towners, not to *help* the businesses of Gracely, but to piss off the natives? Because if you think we don't know what this town thinks of us, you don't understand why you're here."

"I know what the town thinks of you *and* I know why I'm here." She took a deep breath, masked with a smile, of course. "I'm here because I think this is an excellent opportunity." *To sell my soul briefly so I can stay where I want.* "I do believe in the legend, and I think it would be imperative you do too if you expect to sell the town on you being part of its salvation."

His eyes narrowed and she knew she was skating on thin ice. He was one of those control freaks who didn't like to be told what to do, only unlike most of the men she'd worked with like that, he wasn't placated by sweet smiles or politeness.

She'd have to find a new tactic.

"I believe, Ms. Preston"—that damn conceited drawl again—"in these mountains. In this *air*. I believe that, if people choose to look, they can find themselves here. I believe in this town, and that it can be more than what it's become. You'll need to believe that too if you want to work here."

"We've already hired her, Brandon," Will said, *finally* inserting something into the conversation. *After* letting this man act as though she were . . . well, unwelcome, unwanted.

Typical.

"*You* hired her."

"Did I walk into the middle of something, gentlemen? I can just as soon come back at another time when you're ready and willing to be in agreement." She even stood, picking up her bag to slide over her shoulder. Because she might be desperate, but she wasn't going to sell half her soul *and* be treated poorly.

That was not what she'd signed up for. She'd as soon move back to Denver. It would kill her to leave Cora and Micah, but she had some pride she couldn't swallow.

"Have a seat, Ms. Preston."

When she raised an eyebrow at Brandon the Bastard, he pressed his lips together, then released a sigh. "If you would, please." All said through gritted teeth.

Ugh. Men.

She took a seat. One more chance. He had *one* more chance.

"I apologize if I've come off . . ."

"Harsh. Douchey. Asshole spectacular."

Brandon glared at his brother, who was grinning. She didn't want to find it humorous. They were both being asshole spectaculars as far as she was concerned, just in different ways.

"This business and what it stands for is everything to me, so I don't take it lightly."

She met his gaze. Just as she didn't want to find them amusing, she didn't want to soften, but she realized in simple, gravely uttered sentence, that he wasn't much as . . .

Passionate.

She met his gaze with that realization and her stomach did something other than the alternating jittery cramps. Her chest seemed to expand—something flipped, like when Cora drove them too fast down a mountain road.

She couldn't put her finger on that. The cause, what it was, and more, she didn't think she wanted to. If she was going to survive working for the Evans brothers, it was probably best to keep her polite smile in place and ignore any and all *feelings*.

# Chapter Two

Lilly Preston was gorgeous. Brandon hated it. Hated. It. Will had not mentioned that, and considering his brother mentioned just about anything to do with the female population both before, during, and in the aftermath of his failing marriage, Brandon had been a little . . . taken aback.

Which was stupid, which was why he hated it. This whole thing.

He'd now spent an entire week with her underfoot, and she kept . . . being there, asking him questions, looking . . . gorgeous. He'd escaped her with the excuse that he had to chop wood so many times they probably had enough wood to get them through two winters.

It wasn't his finest collection of moments, but there was something about the way looking at Lilly made his chest feel tight that could bring absolutely nothing good to his life. So, he ignored it. He walked away from it. He went to the woods and chopped it to hell.

"Brandon?"

If he didn't think she'd hear him, he would have said, "For fuck's sake," or roared, or pounded his head against the logs of the woodshed. Instead, he glanced her way. Warily. She made him constantly wary.

She picked her way down the porch stairs and across the hardscrabble ground of their mountain plateau yard. Every day, regardless of morning or afternoon, she had that shiny PR look about her. Silky shirts with intricate, fussy ties at the neck, and black pants that skimmed the long, lean lines of her legs without hugging too tight. Boots that went up to mid-calf, sometimes with a heel, but most of the time without.

Her hair was always glossy and styled, some indistinguishable color made up of blondes and browns and even hints of red. Her makeup was always subtle except for her mouth, which, more often than not, was painted some bright shade of pink or red.

Always polished, always the right outfit, hairdo, whatever for the right situation. It reminded him of Evans Mining more than he wanted to admit.

Because there were days he *missed* Evans Mining. The efficiency, the clean lines, and the professionalism. The confidence and comfort in knowing you were working for a company that not only had your name in the title, but had been around for as long as anyone could remember.

An institution. Revered. Maybe a little feared. But that had been before Brandon had found out that everything Evans was built on was lies, manipulation, greed, and corrupt choices.

She reminded him of the good times, the shiny glow of a facade, and he didn't like that at all.

He was tempted to growl, *What do you want?* Or possibly grunt at her like Skeet did. Apparently Skeet was just as unnerved by Lilly as Bran because the old man found as many excuses as he did to avoid her whirlwind of polite, professional suggestions.

Only, the way Lilly Preston gave a suggestion was more like a general barking an order wrapped in silk. It *sounded* sweet and nice, but it was a hard-edged *you better do this* underneath.

It was fascinating.

Another thing he hated.

She waited, a good few feet away from him, while he internally warred with himself about the appropriate business greeting. She clasped her hands on the tablet she was always carrying, fixed that pleasant smile on her face, and just *waited*.

He wanted to groan. Instead, he sighed. "What can I do for you, Ms. Preston?"

She pursed her lips, presumably because he refused to call her Lilly even though he insisted she call him Brandon. He knew it was a weird upper-hand thing, but he had not changed his mind about her uselessness, so he would have the upper hand even if it was—as Will had said the other day—asshole spectacular.

"I've set up a meeting with Corbin Finley of the—"

"Gracely Lodge," he finished for her, hating the way she had to *explain* everything to him. He knew who these people were. He'd grown up in Gracely. He'd come back to Gracely after six years of college and getting his MBA in Boulder with the express purpose of taking over Evans Mining. His only other long-term absence was when he'd had to deal with Dad's affairs after he'd died so suddenly.

But that was it. Gracely was his home, his soul. The people may not like him, but he knew them. And what he didn't know, he made sure to find out because he was trying to win them over.

"Why does it always seem there are approximately five arguments going on in your head at once while not one word exits your mouth?" she asked, her tone exasperated, her knuckles white on the little tablet she held to her chest.

"Arguments might not be the right word for it."

Her brightly painted, pressed-together mouth almost, *almost* quirked upward, but it was quickly schooled back into that placid PR smile.

He was beginning to really hate that smile.

"Anyway, I set up a meeting with him tomorrow, but I thought it might be good if you or Will or Sam could come along. I think Will might be the best option, but if I'm reading Skeet's handwritten schedule correctly, you're the only one available."

"I do love to be the runner-up."

"Actually, I haven't met Sam, but I think you'd be my third choice if I were given one."

It was his mouth's turn to quirk, before he pressed it back down. Every once in a while, Ms. Prim and PR let a little bit of her real personality shine through, and it invariably amused him.

He had zero interest in being amused, attracted, affected.

A meeting with Corbin. It wasn't half bad for a week on the job. Not that it meant they needed her. Even if he'd been trying to schedule a meeting with Corbin for, well, years.

"Obviously you have many talents," she said as gently as one might to a child who'd just peed his pants in front of the class. "Perhaps . . . charm isn't one of them?" She said it so sweetly one could almost miss it was an insult.

Or worse, a dare. He *could* be charming, damn it, but he didn't want to be. Not with her. He didn't use charm on his employees. He wasn't his father, manipulating the women employed by him at will.

So Lilly could be all attractive, amusing, et cetera, but he could not afford, by any means, to be *affected*.

She sighed, tapping purple fingertips against her tablet. "Are you really that bent out of shape over the truth?"

"No."

"Good, then you'll attend the meeting? Or switch with Will and guide his bachelorette party so he can?"

Her tone was so hopeful, Brandon matched it with certainty. "*I* will attend the meeting."

She frowned, the arches of her light eyebrows flattening. "I just want what's best."

"Then you don't want to bring the man who everyone knows took Corbin Finley's daughter's virginity in Corbin Finley's fishing cabin, that Corbin Finley promptly sold after he found out said deed was done."

It took her a minute to connect all those dots, but when she did, her mouth parted slightly. "Oh," was all she managed.

"Will may be more charming than me, I'll give you that, but you might want to check with me before you parade him to the town proper. He pissed off more than one dad back in the day, and they haven't forgotten."

"Ah, yes. Well." Something in her expression changed, though he couldn't read it. She seemed almost deflated by this. Disappointed.

Maybe she had a thing for Will. Oh, for fuck's sake. It wouldn't be the first time, but he'd thought a little better of Ms. Preston and her businesslike demeanor. Best to nip this in the bud right here and now.

"If you're harboring any fantasies about Will, we have a strict no-fraternization policy, and . . ." But before he could add the fact Will was still technically married, she barked out a laugh.

Then her eyes narrowed, before she shook her head and laughed again. And laughed. And laughed.

Why the hell was she laughing?

"Is something funny?"

She shook her head as she turned and started walking toward the cabin, *still* laughing. "The meeting is at two tomorrow," she said between little bursts of laughter. "I'll drive."

"Why are you laughing?" he called after her, irritated that he didn't just want to know, he was desperate to know.

But she didn't answer. She gave him a little wave as she walked up the porch stairs and into the cabin.

He scowled at where she'd disappeared, then back at the remaining cords of wood that in no way needed to be chopped.

He pulled on his work gloves, picked up his ax, and proceeded to chop the hell out of every last piece.

Lilly alternated between laughing and fuming. *Harboring any fantasies* for Will Evans. Like hell. As if that was simply the default. Women couldn't help but fall all over men like the Evans brothers.

Strict no-fraternizing policy. Ha! As if she needed some policy? Her. Her of all people. The idea was ludicrous and invariably insulting. No wonder Gracely hated the Evans brothers. For all their "passion for mountains" crap, they were arrogant jerks who didn't have an ounce of sense in their head.

She frowned at the cozy interior of the cabin. Okay, they had *some* sense, somewhere deep, deep down. Enough sense to put this perfect little place together. But that was all she would credit them with.

Harboring fantasies for any of them. Ugh, the nerve. She'd as soon throw herself at . . . a bear. At . . . Skeet!

Speaking of, the man was sitting at the reception desk, handset of the old-fashioned phone to his ear, writing something onto a wrinkled legal pad in his illegible chicken scratch.

Lilly stood with her hands on her hips watching him interact with whoever was on the other side of the phone. Every response was a grunt or one word. Grunt. "Number." Grunt. "Two-thirty." Grunt. "Hiking boots." Then *slam,* he hung up the receiver.

It wasn't her place to chastise Skeet's phone courtesy, but it was so hard to bite her tongue. How could they employ someone so . . . so . . . *Skeet?*

For as hostile and wary Brandon was of her questions and ideas, you'd think he'd have something to say about Skeet's demeanor and way of doing things.

But *nooo.* Probably because they wouldn't suspect Skeet had "harbored fantasies" for one of them.

Lilly wandered closer to the reception desk. She looked longingly at the computer that probably hadn't ever been turned on, as covered in dust as the monitor was. It would make her setting up meetings with vendors and business owners so much easier if she could read the schedule. And plan the meetings when Brandon was busy.

For all his oh-so-pleasant knowledge of the townspeople and who Will might have . . . done things with, public relations needed a certain charm. Brandon's fierceness—be it passion or being an ass—didn't translate into, *Forgive us our sins, for we are contrite.*

If he had any hope of winning the town over, *that's* what she needed from one of them. *That* Will could do. And possibly the as-yet-to-be-seen Sam. Brandon? She'd bet her house he didn't have it in him to be anything other than foul. He might be handsome, but he may as well look like Skeet with his personality.

She surreptitiously looked over the desk, trying to read any one word of the squiggles Skeet had jotted down.

"Good afternoon, Skeet. How's your day going?"

*Grunt.*

*Ughhhh.* "It sounded like you set up another guide," Lilly continued as cheerfully as she could force. She tapped his scribbles. "What does this say?"

*Grunt.*

Lilly frowned. She was tired of grunts being used as communicators. Skeet eyed the door, then the hallway back to the kitchenette and the rooms that acted as offices, but she had him pretty well blocked in. All exits were behind her.

He'd have to go through her to escape.

Her smile became a little more genuine. "You know, I would really love to be able to read the schedule. Perhaps be able to add to it? Maybe I could show you how to use—"

"How old do you think I am?"

"S-sorry?" He'd finally spoken words, a raspy, sharp demand. About his age. She was more than a little taken aback.

"How old do you think I am?" he repeated, milky blue eyes boring into her.

"Uh, well . . ." She blinked a few times, tried to take an inventory of the signs of age on his face. He was full of wrinkles and well, there was the white hair, the milky eyes that spoke of perhaps cataracts. She glanced at his hands, which rested on his knees. His knuckles were large, swelled bumps of arthritis from the looks of it.

Still, she couldn't exactly guess what she wanted. *One hundred?* No, that wouldn't do at all. "Perhaps . . .

in your . . . sixties?" she said instead, smiling brightly. *An invincible troll?*

"Flattery!" He slapped his knee and she flinched. "Bullshit! Tell me the truth." He waved a finger at her.

"All right, perhaps . . . seventy . . . five."

He narrowed his eyes at her, leaning forward in his chair. It was only her determination to be kind and professional that kept her from taking a step back.

"I am eighty-damn-three years old and I'll shit into a bag before I learn how to use one of them damn machines."

Shit into a bag. Dear Lord.

"All right." She kept her smile in place, gave a perfunctory little nod. "What about if *I* took over handling the schedule? Or entering it into the computer? Maybe we can make little printouts." She didn't particularly like to take on work that wasn't her own, but if it would *help* her end of things, she'd suck it up and do—

"I don't like women."

She was taken completely aback at this bold, rude statement. So much so that she didn't even have a response, couldn't even force a smile because all she felt was a blow of shock. "Oh."

"But I don't like men much either."

"Well." Maybe he *was* a troll. Some sort of fictional, evil being sprung from a mountain spring.

"I like mountains, dogs, and bacon. End of list."

"I see." She didn't even begin to see. Why that would be his list or why he was sharing it with her. Or why he couldn't learn to use a computer or be kind or any darn thing that would be of any use to her.

"I don't change the way I do things for nothing that ain't those three things. So." He made a shooing motion.

For a moment, a brief moment, temper washed

through her, a violent hot wave that no doubt made her face red and her eyes blaze, if Skeet's careful leaning back—away from her—was any indication.

She breathed through it, forced her mouth to curve over gritted teeth. The haze around her vision slowly began to fade. She was in public relations because she *could* swallow down that anger, that furious righteousness over being treated like something he could *shoo*.

"Skeet," she said gently, though the tone did nothing to stop his gradual recline away from her. "I hope in time you'll change your mind. Perhaps, if the computer is too much of a trial, you can develop a system of *symbols* that I can understand." And before she could add anything else snarky or he could try to shoo her again, she turned on a heel and walked out of the front room and back to the little kitchenette.

She breathed in through her nose, out through her mouth, pictured Micah's face when she told him she could afford to get him the ridiculously priced basketball shoes he so desperately wanted. Pictured Cora's face when she told her she didn't have to worry about begging for more hours, because this job was going to allow Lilly to keep them all afloat. Happy and settled.

She breathed in and out a few more times and then set out to make some tea. It would calm her frayed patience, as would sitting in her office this afternoon making more phone calls and setting up more meetings.

The things she could handle, schedule, maneuver—those were the things she excelled at. The things that calmed her. Boorish, arrogant, jackass men aside, she had work to do and she was going to do it.

It would be best for Mile High if she knew everyone's schedule. It would be best for Mile High if they sent the most personable member with her to meet with business-owners in the town. It would be *best* if the men of Mile High treated her as something other than an annoyance.

But she wasn't here for Mile High. Not for Gracely's legend or Brandon's passionate speeches about mountains.

She was here for her and her family. So, if she didn't get all the support she needed to be the best at her job, that would not be her fault.

She sighed and pressed her palms into the counter. She couldn't stand it. Shrugging and saying she was doing the best she could with what they gave her just wasn't in her. She couldn't shift the blame or back off. She needed to succeed. It would eat at her until she did just that.

She had not gotten to where she was, she had not gotten Cora and Micah out of a volatile situation, by shrugging her shoulders and letting things go. She had maybe failed Cora a little bit in those teenage years when Mom had been working two jobs and Lilly simply hadn't been firm enough or inventive enough to keep Cora out of trouble.

But she had learned from her mistakes, and to simply wash her hands of a situation wasn't in her. She'd been in charge and taking care of her family for too long to simply let a responsibility roll off her shoulders. She was needed, and she would not sidestep that need.

The back door creaked open and Lilly straightened, peeking around the opening of the kitchenette. A man walked through the hall toward the front, but it wasn't Will or Brandon, which meant the dark-haired, very bearded, tall and burly man must be Sam.

He gave her a polite nod, and then strode past.

She opened her mouth to speak, but he was gone into the front room before she could get the "good afternoon" out of her mouth.

She glared after him, tired of every last *man* associated with this business. "You're all a bunch of obnoxious bastards," she muttered into the quiet of the kitchenette.

A cackle caused her to jump and let out an embarrassing shriek. Apparently her muttering had been overheard. By Skeet, who was now standing at the opening between the hall and the front room. So, she glared at him too.

He cackled more, showing off a missing tooth in the top right of his mouth. "Watch out!" he said, waggling his gnarled fingers at her. "I may learn to tolerate you yet."

It was undignified, impolite, and completely unbusinesslike, but it took everything in her power to keep from sticking out her tongue at him or flipping him the bird. She wanted to stomp to her office and slam the door.

She let herself picture doing all of those things, and then blew the bad thoughts out with a deep exhale.

Then, she did what she always did when she wanted to strangle someone. She smiled. Because no one could mess with her self-control.

No. One.

# Chapter Three

Brandon stared at the door that was slightly ajar with all the gravity one might approach a gravestone.

He didn't want to go in there. He really, really didn't want to go in there. He hadn't been in there since Lilly had taken it over as an office. Just walking down the hallway, you could smell it. Her. It. Whatever perfume she wore.

It wasn't pleasant. Well, the smell was, but the meaning wasn't. Sure, it reminded him of the sweet note of clover in the air during summer, but this wasn't like a date's promising perfume. This was a woman's mark slowly encroaching upon his life, his business. In a less enterprising woman, it might not be so off-putting.

In Lilly Preston, he had the irrational fear she'd sweep through and somehow make Mile High hers. He had never in his life encountered someone so damn determined and unshakeable in her resolve to accomplish things.

Unless he counted knowing himself, which was not a comforting thought at all.

*Suck it up and be a man, Evans.* He shook off the heavy cloak of dread. He would not be intimidated by a public relations specialist. Or anyone. Period. Not when he had things to accomplish.

He rapped his fist on the door—too hard. Unwarrantably hard. Where had all his poise and control disappeared to?

"Come in."

That sweet voice of hers was one hell of a false advertisement.

She raised her eyebrows at him as he ducked into the small room. The doorway was just a hair too short for him, and his body all but filled up the frame. Which meant, unfortunately, he had to plant both feet completely inside the room.

She glanced at her computer, presumably to discern the time. "I don't think we need to leave for another fifteen minutes yet."

"No, we don't, but we should talk about our plan."

"*Our* plan?" Sweet tone. *Are you fucking with me right now?* meaning.

"You were the one who wanted me to go." Which was a good idea, he could grudgingly admit. Silently. To himself. "Do you expect me to sit in the meeting silently without some sort of plan of attack?"

"Well . . ." She tapped a fingernail on the keyboard of her computer. "Let's put it this way. . . . There's a saying that PR is a little like sex. Most people think they're good at it. Few really are. Maybe you should leave PR to the experts?"

The word sex short-circuited his brain for a second, and his eyes took a tour of her body before his brain gave any kind of permission. She was *not* talking about sex for sex's sake, so . . .

He wrenched his gaze from her and focused on her desk to recalibrate the jumble that little . . . unexpected turn had caused. The long dark-wood table was sparse and minimal, but on the little filing cabinet next to the desk, she had a framed photo of herself, another woman, and a little boy.

It struck him suddenly that he knew nothing about her. Was that *her* little boy? Who was the woman? Mother? Sister? Partner?

As much as he didn't want to get to know Lilly, he didn't want to be his father either. Treating his employees like machines that didn't have lives outside of his company, or worse—like sex objects at his bidding. No, he'd promised himself some things about how to run a business and he needed not to forget them just because he hadn't expressly approved of her hiring.

She was hired. She was an employee, and whether or not she made herself useful enough to remain employed didn't matter. He owed her some courtesy, some humanity. And absolutely no sex thoughts.

Proof the Evans name didn't have to be synonymous with cruel, heartless, immoral. He'd given that to Evans Mining Corporation; he was damn well going to give it to Mile High Adventures.

"Is that your son?" The boy looked like her, but then so did the woman. The indistinguishable hair color, the little dent of a dimple in all their right cheeks.

Her face softened. "No, my nephew and my sister."

"They live nearby?" Damn, he was not usually so bad at small talk. He'd been up on this mountain too long, shutting himself away from Gracely in some attempt to win them over simply by not making waves.

Things needed to change. Mile High had hit a rut, and they needed to reach out.

"With me, in fact," she said. The softness of her expression was gone, and the warm note of clear family love in her voice disappeared with it. Her eyes were slightly narrowed and she was looking at him as if he were a creepy stranger who'd just offered to buy her a drink. "Why are you asking me this?"

"I was curious."

Her suspicious eyes narrowed more. "Why?"

Christ, she exhausted him. "Courtesy? Surely you've heard of it."

She unfurled from her office chair, stood between him and the picture frame as if she needed to create some buffer. *Keep your Evans curse away from my family*, her demeanor all but yelled.

"I appreciate the . . . attempt, but let's agree that we don't need to be friends. My family is my business."

If he didn't understand the way familial protectiveness worked, and sometimes swept over you at the strangest times, he might have been offended, but as it was, he understood all too well.

For a brief moment, he wondered if her family appreciated the protection, or if they shunned her as easily as his mother shunned his efforts.

*Not the time.* Right. They had business to accomplish, and what else mattered? "I'd like to do most of the speaking."

Her mouth dropped, and then she did the laughing thing. Where she laughed and laughed, endlessly, just like after he'd accused her of harboring fantasies for Will.

Apparently he was quite a comedian to her.

"I'm serious."

"I know. That's what's so funny. Did you set up the meeting?"

"No, but—"

She crossed her arms over her chest, a direct contrast to the fake casualness of her voice. "Has Corbin Finley allowed you to even suggest a meeting in the past almost five years you've been in business?"

"No, but—"

"Did you read my resume, my references? Did you see how much experience I have doing this and all that I've accomplished?"

"Yes," he said through gritted teeth. He was always gritting his teeth around her. She had a way of poking at his temper, at his frustration, that almost made him wish he had a little more of his father in him.

He'd seen his father lay into an employee. He knew how to do it. There'd been a time he'd looked forward to having that kind of power, but pride and his personal code of conduct kept him from the outburst.

"You've hired me," she said more gently. "Whether you were of the yes vote or the no vote, you've hired me. Now, I need you to let me do my job the best I am able."

Since it was the same thought he'd had not that long ago, he couldn't argue. It didn't stop him from being pissed and frustrated, but he couldn't argue.

"We should go," he said, gesturing toward the door, knowing he'd failed at making that anything but a demand.

Her lips firmed, but she didn't shoot off some witty comeback. She went to her desk, gathered her tablet and some folders, and shoved them—with a little more force than necessary—into her bag.

She gave him a pointed look. "My raincoat is hanging on the back of the door."

Which meant he either needed to move farther into the office so she could get to the back of the door, or step out into the hallway.

For one fleeting, bizarre moment, something about the silvery threads of blue in her eyes, or her shoulders-back, chin-up stance, something about *her* made him want to step forward. Closer.

He didn't. He stepped into the hallway, trying to

eradicate whatever weirdness was buzzing along his skin. Much like the way his arms felt after turning off a chainsaw. No more vibrations, but he could still feel them, echoing through his body.

She closed the door, then opened it after a few seconds, the silky polka-dot top now covered with a midnight-blue jacket that reminded him of dusk. Reminded him of the color of her eyes.

There was seriously something wrong with him.

He turned abruptly from her and walked through the hall in silence. He could hear the sounds of Will entertaining his bachelorette party group in the front room. Will had a way of laying down the guidelines and instructions while simultaneously making every woman wearing a plastic penis crown feel like he was flirting directly with them.

Brandon had never understood Will's skill at that. Had never wanted to. He had seen the way Dad's charm had worked, and while Will's was good-natured underneath, like everything Will was, the charm made Brandon uncomfortable.

It made him itch. Any instinct that reminded him of his father made him itch, worry, tense. *Am I like him? Deep down?* Because he'd wanted that once, to be just like him.

Now, he was quite determined to be the opposite, because this was his life. He'd made his choices. Now, he got to dig himself out of the consequences of those choices. *And some of Dad's consequences, too.*

He shoved away the thought as he pushed open the back door to the little gravel lot where they parked their vehicles. "I'll drive," he said into the quiet afternoon.

"I prefer to drive," she returned pleasantly.

"So do I."

"Well, how problematic."

"Yes, you are," he couldn't stop himself from saying.

She stopped halfway across the lot. "This is my meeting that I set up, with absolutely no help from you. So, I will be in charge. I will drive and I will run this meeting. I know you think my services aren't necessary or important, or maybe you simply think I don't get your mission. I get it. I'm ready to sell it. Are you?" She arched a brow at him, making so much sense he wanted to yell. Or chop more wood.

Neither option was available to him right now. "I'm driving," he reiterated, knowing it was small, but also knowing if she didn't give him something, he wasn't going to be able to give her anything, and they somehow needed to be in accord, on some even ground. If this was going to work, and it needed to.

"Mr. Evans," she said pointedly, purposefully. She knew he didn't like her calling him that and she was throwing down the gauntlet. "I am trying so very hard not to *harbor any fantasies* of pushing you off this mountain, but quite honestly you're driving me to it. Grunt by grunt, order by order, obnoxious silence by obnoxious silence."

He blinked at her, and then blinked again when the peachy rose of her cheeks blotched a bit pink.

"If you'll forgive me for being so blunt," she added. She pressed her perfectly maintained fingers to her forehead. "I don't know why or how you always seem to bring the worst out in me. It's like I'm living my very own *You've Got Mail* without the love story or Meg Ryan's hair."

He followed that sentence for maybe five words. She really was a baffling woman. "I . . . literally have no idea what you're talking about."

She sighed. "Of course you don't." She shook her

head. "We need to go before we're late, and that isn't the impression I want to give."

But, much to his relief, instead of heading for her car, she stalked over to his truck.

Finally, a point for him.

Mr. Finley wasn't happy, and she'd known he wouldn't be with an Evans brother sitting next to her, but he didn't kick them out of his office, which meant Lilly had a shot to work her magic.

If Brandon Evans would keep his obnoxious bastard mouth shut. "It is so gracious of you to take time out of your day to see us, Mr. Finley."

"I took time out of my day to see you, Ms. Preston."

Pointed. She couldn't blame him, but she merely smiled serenely and handed him a folder, which he reluctantly took. She'd only needed a cursory look around the room to understand that Mr. Finley would prefer paper over tablet.

Everything in the office was a little dated, even the computer. Which at least he used, unlike a certain someone who'd rather "shit in a bag."

Sometimes she really couldn't believe what she'd gotten herself into.

But here she was, at the only hotel left in Gracely, and hotels were exactly the kind of partnerships Mile High needed. Sure, some of their activities included overnight camping and backpacking, but they did a lot of day-trip-only guides as well, and having a deal with the local hotel would help keep people in Gracely— which was good PR—and allow them to go back to Mile High the next day—good business.

"I put together some information on Mile High Adventures. I think of most interest to you will be the sheer number of people they have coming into Gracely every weekend throughout the year. People who would probably love to have somewhere nice to stay at the end of a hard hike or camping trip."

"As I'm the only game left in town"—he flicked an accusatory glance at Brandon—"I imagine those people already come to me."

"Actually, I conducted a survey, which you'll find is the third sheet in your folder."

She waited while Mr. Finley shuffled through the papers, waited for the reaction she knew would come. A slight eyebrow raise, eyes widening just a pinch, followed by consideration.

Lilly had to press her lips together to keep from smiling too broadly.

"I appreciate this . . ." He fluttered the page in the air dismissively, and yet his eyes stayed glued to that spot at the bottom. The number of people who said they chose to go to a nearby town with more "modern" and "cozy" amenities. ". . . survey," he finally finished. "But how do I know these aren't simply numbers you made up?"

"Well, I suppose you don't," she said, nodding as gravely as she could manage. "Of course, there's my word, but I don't expect you to take that. Not knowing me all that well."

He placed the paper back down on his desk, looking at it even now. A thoughtful look, but there was a lot of anger and prejudice that ran through whatever had gone down. She didn't quite understand it, why the moving of Evans Mining headquarters had hit the town so hard, or so . . . emotionally.

But that was neither here nor there, because at some point, the people with businesses left had to look at numbers. They might not look at them when an Evans was bugging them to do it, but when *she* was at the helm?

She was going to make this work.

"You have a nice view," Brandon said conversationally, pointing toward the large window behind Mr. Finley. His office was in the back of his cozy mountain lodge, so his window was mainly mountain face and evergreens and whatever other things grew out of rock.

To Lilly, in comparison to all the other views out there—all the views from Mile High, for starters—it was utterly bland.

Oh, God, she hoped he wasn't going to point that out.

"You think so?"

"There are few things more inspiring than the middle of a mountain, don't you think? I know, people like the snow-peaked caps. Everyone wants to get a good look at the view below, get to those vistas and take those wall-worthy pictures. As they should. It's . . . spiritual, really." He waved a hand at the view of mountain wall, and she had never seen him seem so . . . calm, easy.

What on earth was he up to?

"But this? This right here." He leaned toward the window and Mr. Finley peered behind him at the view. "This is the real view," Brandon said, almost reverently. It was like a speech, and he was an excellent orator, all things told. Considering she too was leaning forward, staring at the grey and green.

"This is a symbol of a man who has worked hard. Like those mountains. You've built over time and you've sustained. I remember those campfires you used to have in

the summer for guests and townspeople. It was such a
good idea."

Lilly had to close her eyes in hopes he wouldn't
point out that Mile High did that sort of thing now. The
last thing they needed was Mr. Finley accusing them of
stealing an idea.

"Not very cost-effective *now*." He glared.

"No, no. Of course not. But you had a lot of great
ideas, Mr. Finley. Ones that capitalized on the visitors to
Gracely. I can't help but think that, if we worked together at least a little bit, Mile High could help you
cater to the type of clientele we have so you could . . .
make use of these extra out-of-town visitors' dollars."

Mr. Finley grunted and Lilly wanted to scream. What
was it about these men that grunting was their preferred mode of communication?

"What exactly are you proposing?"

Brandon glanced at her, a clear *you're up*. It surprised
her he would pass the baton. It surprised her that the
chest-expanding, driving-down-a-dip feeling from that
first day returned when his eyes met hers.

It was when he let go of that condescension and con-
trolling obstinance that she couldn't catch a full breath,
and her heart sometimes thundered too loud in her
ears. Such a . . . strange thing.

She needed to figure out a way to eradicate it. He
cleared his throat and nodded toward Mr. Finley.

Right. Business. That was what she was here for. She
went over her proposed plan with Mr. Finley. Coupons
and cross-promotion and events sponsored by both of
them. He didn't agree to anything, but as they walked
out of the cozy if outdated Gracely Lodge, she knew
he'd think about it much harder than he would have if
Brandon hadn't given his little speech.

She remembered what she'd thought yesterday. That she'd bet her house he couldn't be anything but foul.

He hadn't been foul or stiff or cranky or stupid. He'd been calm and brilliant and impassioned.

"I owe you my house," she muttered, somewhat distractedly. He'd done it. He'd charmed Mr. Finley with that speech. He'd charmed . . . her. Damn it.

"Owe me your . . . what?"

She waved him off, irritated it had slipped out. Irritated he had more to him than she'd thought. Irritated, because she'd been nearly as rapt as Corbin Finley, and that wasn't her.

"I told you. This isn't a game. It isn't even about me. This business is my everything, and I will do whatever it takes to build it, to make it the foundation of this town. If I have to trot out some charm and goodwill to do so . . ." His gaze drifted to beyond her. Up the mountain slope, opposite of Mile High.

She looked over her shoulder at where his gaze had gone, but she saw nothing other than some old buildings. "What are you looking at?"

His gaze flicked back to hers as she turned her head back to him. He shrugged. "Mountains."

But it was a lie. She'd seen him stare at the mountains outside of Mile High. It was when his face looked most handsome. Awed. Every time she cornered him outside to talk about some piece of business, his eyes sought those mountains like a man might seek a cross at church or a drink in the desert.

This look was not that look. Whatever he'd looked at or seen in those mountains opposite the Mile High offices had caused his mouth to firm, his expression to go as granite as the stone that shot up into the bright blue sky. That fierceness he had in him. The thing that drove him to talk about saving the town and giving back.

All hidden under this wall of rock, the reasoning, the motivation. Sure, he prettied it up in magic mountain talk, but based on that look, it wasn't what drove him.

Well, she was determined to figure out what it was. Brandon Evans's rock facade had nothing on her sheer tenacity.

# Chapter Four

She was staying. Brandon sat on the couch sandwiched between his brother and Sam, watching Lilly give her little presentation on what she and Corbin had agreed upon for cross-promotion, and all Brandon could truly focus on was the fact she was staying.

There'd be no cause to get rid of her now. After five years of getting nowhere with the town proper, Lilly had been at work for two weeks and made a deal with one of the biggest businesses still in Gracely.

There were coupons, possibly events, flyers. She had it all worked out. She had Corbin Finley's *support*. Brandon couldn't fully wrap his head around it. The only thing that kept ringing in his head was the fact he was screwed. Screwed into Lilly Preston being part of his business. For the long run, if she wanted to be.

Damn.

Lilly stood before them, eyes wide and expectant. "Well, aren't you three going to *say* something? This is huge!"

"I think we're in . . . collective shock," Will offered. "You got Corbin to agree to *all* this."

"He was really very rational," Lilly replied. Her excited smile dimmed. "Brandon was very persuasive when we met with Mr. Finley, and I think Mr. Finley understood it would be bad business to turn you down."

"Turn us down *again*. Because he has turned us down. Repeatedly. For years," Will said. "So, I'll have to call BS on Brandon having anything to do with it."

"I got us in the door. Brandon sealed the deal," Lilly said firmly.

Brandon wished she'd take all the credit. He didn't want Sam and Will's shocked gazes glued to him any more than he wanted her matter-of-fact hat tip.

It shouldn't be shocking he could sell a guy on a concept. He'd sold Will and Sam on making their college dream a reality. On starting it in Gracely. He'd sold a lot of people on this mission of his. He was just finally making inroads with the Gracely-ites.

"All that matters is we made the deal. Good for us. Pat on the back. Lilly will work on the details and make sure we're aware of anything that affects our jobs. Correct?"

Lilly nodded.

Brandon pushed off the couch. "Then that's that and we can go back to actual work."

"I'll put a rundown in your mailboxes and make up the flyers. Would you all like approval before I have them printed?"

Brandon stopped his quick retreat. "Mailboxes?"

"Well, I notice none of you check your email with any regularity, so I made little mailboxes. They're in the mudroom, so you can always check them before you leave." She smiled sweetly, one of those orders wrapped in silk. Still an order.

It grated.

"Bran checks his email constantly," Will offered.

Lilly raised one of those perfectly arched eyebrows at him. "Funny. He never responds to mine."

Damn it. Brandon scowled at Will, irrationally feeling as if he were ten again and having his misdeeds repeated to his mother by his younger twin.

"So, Brandon ignores my emails," Lilly said crisply, crossing her arms over her chest. "What are you two's excuses?"

Will grinned. "I'm not much of an email guy. You know, trying to filter through all that stuff. I'm more of a doer."

Lilly pressed her lips into an even firmer line and Will's charming smile wilted.

"And you?" she said, pointing at Sam.

"I . . ." Sam cleared his rarely used throat. "I don't have Internet at my cabin."

Lilly blinked at Sam as though he'd just admitted to killing puppies. "You don't . . ."

"No cell service either. No smartphone," Sam added. "I . . ."

"If you need to faint, try to fall toward the couch," Brandon muttered. "The rest of us have *work* to do. Will, the canoe? Sam, your gear?"

"Gentlemen, the communication around here is going to need to run more smoothly," Lilly said as if Brandon hadn't spoken at all. "Now, if you don't want to do it in a modern convenience sort of way, I'll adapt. But we will communicate, and well. So, pick your way. You will either read and *answer* my emails . . ." Blue eyes flashed to his, accusing, and revealing some other emotion Brandon didn't feel much like analyzing.

"*Or* you will check physical mailboxes. But, if I'm going to keep doing what I'm doing—bringing you business *and* helping your reputation in town, you will not *ignore* me. You can't afford to."

She marched around the couch and stood in front of the reception desk, pointing an intimidating finger at Skeet. "And that goes for you, too."

Skeet grunted.

Brandon watched, very nearly fascinated at the way anger flashed in those dark blue depths, something like silver, or a very lethal spark. She took a deep breath that stretched the buttons of her denim dress thing at her chest.

He very purposefully looked away from that, back to her face, where she smiled sweetly as she let out the breath. All of that anger seeming to evaporate.

Or was she just extremely adept at hiding it? Interesting.

*No, not interesting. Nothing about* her *can be interesting.*

"I've also made a grunt jar."

"A what?" Will and Brandon asked in unison.

She turned to face them, and even though she was still smiling happily, there was an edge to the way she turned toward them. Something forbidding and very nearly threatening.

"Yes, every time one of you *grunts* at me in that manner when I am asking you a question that requires an answer with *actual* words, you will put a dollar in that jar." She pointed to a giant jar that must have once held full-sized pickles or industrial quantities of mayonnaise.

There was a label stuck to the front and in pretty, flowing script the words *Grunt Jar* were written in pink.

"Once the jar is full, we will donate it to the school or some other local charitable organization of your choice. Understood?" She pinned each of them with one of those cool blue gazes that irritated him because it was the exact look he gave Will and Sam when they weren't cooperating.

"Good. Now, you're free to go." She walked over to the coffee table, where she'd left her tablet, and began gathering up everything she'd used during her presentation.

Sam and Will and Skeet dispersed like contrite children. Brandon would not be so easily dismissed. *He* was the boss here. She might be a new addition. She might be good. She might even be staying, but she was not in control.

It was time she learned that.

She turned to him and offered another one of those faux-pleasant smiles. "Do you have something to add, Mr. Evans?"

He forced a fake smile of his own as the idea took shape. He was stuck with her, so . . . "Tomorrow, wear pants. Jeans. And boots—real boots, not those things. A winter coat, gloves. Probably a hat. Still supposed to be cold in the upper altitudes."

Her lip curled and she pulled her head back. "Excuse me?"

"You've proved you've got a place here. Now you're going to have to learn what that really means."

"Learn what *what* really means?" she repeated, a crease popping up between her eyebrows.

"What it means to have a Mile High Adventure." He looked down at her fashion boots, the dress she was wearing over dark-colored tights. He genuinely grinned, couldn't help it.

Yeah, he might be stuck with Lilly, but that didn't mean it had to be *all* annoyance. Watching her perfect facade get a little mussed would be something of an enjoyment.

Especially if she hated it.


Lilly tried to curl her toes in the uncomfortable hiking boots. They were half a size too small, but they were all she'd been able to find on such short notice. She pouted. They weren't even cute.

At least she had the rest of her prescribed outfit for the day. She adjusted the sunny yellow knit cap on her head, fluffing the little puff on the top. The prospect of Brandon showing her what a *Mile High Adventure* really was filled her with dread, so she'd at least look colorfully cheerful while she did it. Her scarf matched the hat, a pretty contrast to the midnight blue of her winter coat.

She'd even grabbed a pair of green fuzzy socks with little forest animals on them. Oh, they were hidden under the ugly brown boots, but *she* knew they were there, so that was all that mattered.

She'd been tempted to ignore Brandon's obnoxiously barked order about what to wear, but in the end she'd wanted to prove to him she was up for anything he could throw at her. Not just up for it, up for it with a *smile.* And a cute hat.

She walked up the stairs to the offices, and then took a moment to do what she'd done every morning since coming to work here.

She stopped. She breathed. She looked around.

The men inside were frustrating, grunting jerks, all things considered, but this place . . . it was a joy to work here. Starting each day driving up the craggy face of the mountain, watching the peaks get closer, being nearly blinded by a sky so blue it looked fake—it was like wiping every annoyance and aggravation from the day prior away and starting with a blank slate.

Spring up here was different from spring in the valley. The air was colder, and snow still dotted the landscape and the green trees. The peaks were full white farther up. It looked so much like Christmas she didn't even mind being cold.

For as many things as she and Brandon didn't agree on, those simple words he'd said that first day had stuck with her, lodging into her consciousness every morning.

*I believe in these mountains. In this air. I believe that, if people choose to look, they can find themselves here.*

She was in no need of finding herself considering she knew exactly who and what she was, but she did believe in the mountains, in the air. She wanted to believe in that magic.

*Of course, believing in magic is what got your mother and sister into their past messes, isn't it?*

That was the one problem with this place: she forgot how easily magic could swoop in and make you stupid. Well, she had not been stupid for nearly thirty years of her life. She would not start now.

The front door swung open and Brandon stepped out onto the porch. The shimmer of magic faded in the shadow of his big body, the bulky black coat, and equally black stocking cap.

She wanted him to look boring in all that drab lack of color, but those hazel eyes were lit with a mischief she didn't trust. And for the first time in two weeks, Brandon greeted her with a smile.

It had a very unwelcome effect somewhere in the center of her chest. An odd fluttering sensation that almost, *almost* had her smiling back.

"Ms. Preston." He surveyed her outfit. "You listened."

Any impulse to smile was gone. "Some of us are good at following instructions, Mr. Evans." She placed her bag inside the doorway, then shoved her hands into her coat pockets to make sure she had her cell phone.

"We're going to be in each other's pockets a bit today. I'd suggest using Brandon if you want me to go easy on you."

"I assure you, Mr. Evans, you needn't go easy on me." She tried to relax, mostly so she didn't keep sounding like some prim Jane Austen character. "I don't consider your insistence I use your first name charming, equalizing, impressive, or whatever it is you're trying to prove. So, let's leave it as is." Argh. Why couldn't she bite down her temper around him?

"I'm not trying to prove anything, *Lilly*. But I'm not my father, and I'd like not to be reminded of him."

His words were flat with such an icy chill, Lilly had no snappy comeback for that. Apparently he had some . . . issues. Bigger ones than she'd given him credit for.

*Familiar ones, right? Daddy issues.*

Ha! As if she let her worthless father run her life. She'd built a life for her and her sister that rivaled everything he'd ever promised and failed to deliver.

"Ready?" Brandon asked gruffly, all the usual tension back in his demeanor, all the usual simmering frustration in his expression.

The last thing she wanted to do was go on a hike with him. She didn't . . . trust him. He was so hard to read, and she usually had no problems reading people. Though she felt guilty for getting the name thing wrong. She forced that equitable tone to her voice, and the ice out of her words. "You know, I do have actual work to do." Okay, maybe not *all* the ice.

"And you should understand our *actual* work as you work to public relations it to death." He handed her a brochure—one she recognized as Mile High's easiest guided hike. She'd already read and studied all their brochures cover to cover. They weren't terrible, though she had a few suggestions for them.

That she'd put in an email. That Brandon had ignored.

"You know, if you moved the information about—"

"For every excursion you survive, you have carte blanche to redo the brochures *and* the website section as you see fit. But you have to survive first."

"I hardly need to go on a hike to understand the appeal enough to do my job. And it is my job. Why should I have to jump through hoops to do my job?" Her voice was getting increasingly shrill, but he was so aggravating. And he made no sense.

Brandon shrugged, walking down the stairs. "My company. My rules."

His company was a pain in her butt. "It's hardly legal to force me."

"So, quit." He never stopped walking, long strides eating up the sidewalk that wound around the office cabin and to the trailheads in the back.

Irritated, she hurried after him, wincing a little at the pinch of her boots. "You've seen what good I can do."

"And you've seen what a contrary asshole I am."

Touché. "If your plan is to kill me via mysterious fall down a mountain, I can assure you my sister will know it's not an accident."

"The only way you fall off a mountain is if you don't listen to me and do something stupid. This is a hike. Our shortest and least strenuous offering."

"Then why do you look like a pack mule?"

He turned to face her at the trailhead, adjusting the straps of his backpack. "I didn't say it was *easy*, I just said it was the least strenuous. Besides, prissy as you are, I have no idea how long this will take. You should be thanking me for carrying water and snacks for you."

"Prissy!"

His generous mouth curved, just on one side. As though his mouth weren't sure what to do with a genuine smile.

Her chest fluttered. Why did he have to be handsome? It wasn't fair she should feel any kind of affected by his smile. But it didn't matter. Her body might occasionally *react*, but her brain was driving this train.

"Your cheeks get all red when you're really angry."

"I'm well aware. I must be a veritable apple every time you're around."

"Near enough. Can we get started?"

Lilly took a deep breath. He thought she was prissy and couldn't do this, which meant she'd be bruised and bloody before she admitted to him or herself that he was right. She'd hike as long and as fast as him.

And he could take his smug, charming smiles elsewhere after that.

"I expect you to have me back by lunch so I can at least get a half day of work in."

He shrugged, stepping forward on the trail that led into the trees. "If you can keep up, we will be."

"Oh. I can damn well keep up," she muttered. She trailed her finger along the trailhead sign. SOLACE FALLS TRAILHEAD. Well, she could certainly use some solace.

She took a step onto the dirt path, which was covered

in pine needles and bits of snow that hadn't melted. She didn't think she was going to find any of *that* here, but she'd at least find something to throw in Brandon's arrogant face. And that would be all the solace she needed.

# Chapter Five

Brandon waited at one of the slab benches they'd installed for people exactly like Lilly. Prissy and too confident for their own good.

He'd be lucky if they got back to the cabin by dinnertime.

She finally huffed into view, leaning heavily on a stick she'd found along the way. Her cheeks were red with exertion instead of anger, or maybe there was some of both. Most of her hair had fallen out of its band and hung around her face and in her eyes. Every once in a while, she'd blow at the loose strands irritably.

He'd say she was out of shape, but her shape was just fine. Quite unfortunately. He'd walked behind her for a while, a gallant attempt to let her set the pace.

But her ass in those jeans had been in his face. No matter how slow he'd tried to go, every time he'd looked up . . . there it had been. Her coat ended right at the top of her jeans, so he'd found himself wondering—more than once—how that subtle curve might feel underneath his palms.

Naked.

It was his turn to blow out a breath. He had to push his unfortunately overzealous imagination about the shape or feel of her *anything* far, far away.

He wasn't his father. He *wouldn't* be his father.

She finally reached him.

"I hate you," she said between huffed breaths.

That at least cheered him a little. "You won't soon enough."

She snorted, slumping onto the bench. "Unless there is a giant hot fudge sundae and a hot, muscle-bound man to carry me *down* this mountain while I eat said hot fudge sundae, I will still hate you."

"You have quite the imagination."

"We've been walking for hours and you've said maybe two words. What the heck else am I supposed to do with my time?"

Brandon handed her the water he'd previously dug out of his pack. She gulped it down and he got off the bench. She'd shown up with bright pink lipstick this morning, but it'd all worn off.

Unfortunately, when she wrapped said lips around the water bottle, it didn't particularly matter how bright or not bright they were.

He stared at the trees that lined the path, tried to focus on counting individual pine needles rather than think about her mouth around anything. Her mouth, period.

"What time is it?" she asked. No, not just asked. *Whined.* He glanced at his watch. "We've only been at it an hour."

"That's it?"

"Come on. If you sit there much longer you're never going to want to get up."

"I already don't want to get up."

"Don't be a child."

"No, being a child would be calling you a giant butt, which is what I'm doing in my head."

"A giant . . . butt." He couldn't help but laugh. It was a *baffled* laugh that escaped him, but it was a laugh nonetheless. "You're sitting there calling me a *butt.*"

She put the water bottle down and tugged the band out of her hair, the riot of colors cascading over her shoulders and obscuring her face. "Yup. I live with my ten-year-old nephew. You're lucky I'm not calling you a poop fudge sundae."

"I . . ." He laughed again, because what on earth was one supposed to do when his very prim and proper employee referenced *poop*?

In quick, efficient movements, she pulled all her hair back into its band. Somehow, the messy tangle looked chic and alluring. Why was every damn thing about her *alluring*?

"Is it so very difficult?" she asked gravely.

Could she read his mind or something? "Is what difficult?"

"Smiling. Laughing. Normal positive human emotion." She pushed off the bench and took a deep breath, motioning for him to lead the way up the remainder of the trail.

"I'm a serious guy, with serious plans," he grumbled, feeling moderately shamed that he'd been . . . *so* grumpy with her. It wasn't fair. It wasn't her fault she was distracting and he had about eight million reasons not to be distracted.

It wasn't her fault Will and Sam had overruled him to hire her, and it wasn't exactly her fault that it irritated him she was so good at her job.

"I have serious plans myself, but I've never forgone laughter and enjoyment for them."

"Then you've never had to atone for a sin." They reached the last hurdle before the view of the falls, and Brandon had the sinking feeling he was going to have to help her up the rock face. He climbed up the little rock wall in three easy steps, then crouched and offered her his hand.

But she was staring at him. "What sin?"

He shook his head, because he wasn't going into it. Not with her. Not with anyone who didn't already know. "Doesn't matter. But this does. Take my hand. Let's go."

She hesitated another minute, then nudged her foot onto a good rock and grabbed his hand. He helped her up the steep if short climb, and then stepped ahead to pull back the bough that was blocking the path. He motioned her forward, ignoring the fact she was still watching him with that considering gaze.

Finally, she took careful steps onto the craggy precipice, and then her breath went out in a whoosh. "Brandon." She said his name with a kind of awed reverence that sent an unnamable feeling through him. Something heavy and potent.

But it wasn't for him. It was for the view.

She took another few careful steps closer to the edge, where a valley between mountains stretched out, Solace Falls a roaring column of water across the way. It'd be more breathtaking once spring went all out. Right now, the lake below was as grey as the mountains that surrounded it, as clear as the water that cascaded a few yards down. Only the green of the pines and the blue of the sky offered any color.

But that didn't make it less amazing. The sheer size

of the mountains, the crystalline sheen to the water, the way the air was fresh and thin.

"It's the most beautiful thing I've ever seen," she said, her voice some wavering thing he wouldn't have ever attributed to Lilly Preston if he hadn't seen and heard it with his own eyes and ears.

"Worth the climb?"

She gave him a sideways glance, and as much as the smirk was just that—a smirk—some of that wonder was still in her expression, in her eyes, and he kind of lost the impulse to be a dick.

"I suppose," she replied primly, her blue eyes returning to the view in front of them.

He watched her, he couldn't help it. No matter how often he told himself to look at the view, to look at the trail back, his gaze kept drifting to the reverent way she looked at the mountains, at the falls. The way she pressed her gloved fingers to her mouth.

He didn't want to interrupt it. He wanted to let her drink it in for as long as she wanted. And if he drank in a little bit of *her,* it was just . . . research in a way. Part of this business was understanding what other people were searching for, even when they didn't know it themselves.

So, he would file Lilly's reaction away with those of all the other people he'd watched be awed by this view. For . . . business reasons.

She let out an audible breath, then pulled her cell phone from her pocket. "Take a picture of me. Frame it nicely so you can see me and the falls and the lake if possible." She held out her phone.

He grimaced at her outstretched phone. "What for?"

"So I can prove to my sister I climbed a mountain," she said with a bright smile.

"You didn't exactly—"

She slapped the phone into his hand, her gloved hands forcing his to curl around the phone.

"Take the picture, Brandon," she ordered.

He grunted, but took a few steps back so he could frame both her and the background in the picture. She shook her hair back, settled her hand on her hip, and smiled brightly.

She was like a damn catalogue with that ridiculous yellow fluffy hat and cheesy pose.

"Take your hand off your hip," he instructed.

She frowned. "It's flattering."

"You don't need flattering. You're standing in front of the most beautiful thing you've ever seen."

She dropped her hand, but gave him a doleful look, which is when he decided to click the button on her phone to take the picture.

"Take one of me smiling!"

Click. She was pointing her finger at him and the camera, looking very irritated.

"Brandon!"

Click. Scowling. He grinned.

Finally, she laughed, a genuine, non-posed laugh, and he had a bad feeling that this picture of her pretty smile and bright eyes and one of his favorite places was going to haunt him for a very, very long time.

"There," he grunted, handing the phone back to her.

She surveyed the pictures, pressing her lips together as she usually did when she was irritated, but there was a curve at the corner. A hint of a smile.

He needed to stop noticing any *hints* of anything when it came to her.

"What's the most beautiful thing you've ever seen?" she asked, her eyes still glued to her phone screen.

The question caught him off guard, but it wasn't so hard to answer when her attention was on her phone.

"I do this as a night hike sometimes. Not often—have to have the right group. But . . . on a clear night . . . it's like nothing I've seen anywhere else. The stars make up the entire sky—you can see the Milky Way, everything. You can hear the waterfall, the steady hum of life in the trees and mountains. And around it all is this big shadow of mountain, and you know without a shadow of a doubt you are in the presence of something greater than yourself."

Her blue eyes met his, dark and none of that silvery thread of anger he was so used to. No, something in her expression was soft, and it hit him with the force of a punch.

"I'd like to do that sometime," she said, her voice little more than a whisper.

"Sure. You're going to have to pass a few more tests," he managed through a tight throat. He didn't understand her effect on him, but he wasn't about to try to.

She slid her phone in her pocket, looking back over the view. "Well, I have lots more ideas for the brochure and the website. And we need to really push this one at Gracely Lodge. Something easy people can do, then stay at the lodge for a nice dinner. It'll be quite the weekend package."

It would be. It had been his plan for years, but he hadn't been able to get Corbin to agree. Until her.

He hated feeling like he owed her something when she irritated him so damn much, but . . . "You did a good job with Corbin."

She raised an eyebrow. "I know."

He chuckled. Unfortunately, he appreciated the little thread of ego. He liked people who were easily confident in their abilities. They were easier to work with than people who needed constant reassurance or who let their egos run wild.

"You know," she said lightly. "You could be this way all the time. Pleasant. Responsive."

He grunted.

"You better put a dollar in the jar when we get back."

He rolled his eyes. "So I'm not a pleasant, responsive guy. It's not exactly a necessity for the business I'm in." Exactly. There were times he had to pour on the charm, but *she* was not one of them.

"Will doesn't seem to struggle. So unless you and Sam are harboring secret erotic feelings for one another by being broody, I don't understand why you can't be *nice*."

"As much as that would make a very successful movie, Sam does not have the equipment I would prefer in an *erotic feelings* partner."

He officially had no idea how they had gotten on the subject of anything erotic. "Ready to go?" Because the last thing they needed was to linger in *that* atmosphere.

Lilly gave one last look to the falls, then nodded. "I'll follow you."

Lilly's feet hurt so badly she wanted to cry, but she knew they were close to the office, and she wouldn't give Brandon the satisfaction. As much as some of their conversation seemed to have shown an actual human, decent side to Brandon, she didn't plan on giving him any ammunition. She would rise to every challenge he lay at her feet. If it meant she had to get in better shape, so be it. Maybe it would end up being good for her.

If her feet survived. She was pretty sure her blisters

had blisters, and she nearly whimpered when her foot slid a little on the path and she narrowly held herself upright.

"Be careful going downhill here. There are a lot of loose rocks."

How did he make it look so easy? He strode down the slope with no problem, but just about every time she took a ginger step, she slid a little.

"You're overthinking it. Too many halting steps and you're going to—"

Something burst from the trees, a blur of fur and scattering rocks. Lilly screeched, took a step back, but her ankle gave out on the uneven patch of earth. She tried to grab on to something to break her fall, but there was only air.

And then ground. Hard, unrelenting *painful* ground. She closed her eyes against it, trying to figure out just how she'd gotten onto her back. Oh, it hurt. Her back, her arm, her ankle simply throbbed.

She groaned, nearly afraid to move her body and assess the damage the fall had caused.

Then something was touching her arm, a warm, sturdy grasp. When she opened her eyes, concerned hazel eyes were way too close to hers. "Does anything feel broken?" Brandon asked, his voice grave and no-nonsense.

She groaned again, pushing herself into a sitting position; then she swore. Profusely, because, damn it, she'd been proving just how much she could handle and then she'd taken a tumble down the trail. "Nothing's broken. Except my pride. And possibly my phone."

"So, nothing important."

She glared at him.

His lips almost curved. "I don't think I've ever

heard . . . anyone swear like that. And I've known a lot of people with filthy mouths." Some of his amusement dimmed. "You're going to have to let me touch your leg."

She tried not to grimace, or scoot away, but the thought of him . . . touching her. Ack. It filled her with a very particular kind of nerves. A very particular kind she refused to name. "Why?"

"Believe it or not, I'm trained in a lot of first-aid things in case of emergency. Let me feel around. It looked like your ankle took a nasty turn before you fell. Just stretch it forward."

She stretched her leg forward, forgetting about her trepidation over Brandon touching her as a bolt of pain went through her. She bit back the whimper, but barely.

Brandon pulled off his gloves with his teeth. Oh, that was . . that was not hot. She would keep telling herself. Until she believed it.

Then that big, ungloved hand wrapped around her ankle. Lord, his fingers could make a complete circle around it, and his hand was so warm. Lucky for her unruly thoughts, her ankle really, *really* hurt and she gave a little yelp when he pushed under it.

"That's about what I thought," he said, gravely.

"What?"

"Nasty sprain. We're going to have to get you to the cabin. You'll probably need X-rays to make sure you didn't really damage anything."

"X-rays?" She stared up at him as he got to his feet. "How . . . how am I going to get back?"

"It's only a little ways. I'll . . ." He grimaced and let out a breath. "I'll carry you."

"What?"

"I'm going to carry you."

"What if *you* fall?"

"I won't." He said it so simply, so matter-of-factly she wanted to . . . she didn't know. Certainly not trust him. She would *never* trust him.

"Great. Just great." She swallowed down tears, more at the humiliation than at the pain. Though the pain sucked.

Brandon crouched next to her, and she did her best to maneuver onto her good side and get at least a little upright so he could help her down. Surely he wasn't actually going to carry—

Then she was being swung up into his arms, all very Rhett Butler on the stairs, except she didn't feel near as graceful as Scarlett. She scrambled to latch her arms around Brandon's neck, while somehow also keeping her breasts from grazing his chest.

She failed. She was failing at just about everything, because as he began to walk, easily, without a slip or extra pant of breath, she simply couldn't remain unaffected.

She was being carried down a mountain by a very handsome, strong—*strong*—grumpy, bearded man. She had her arms around him, he had one arm under her knees, and one hand around her back.

She was basically living Cora's current fantasy, and was rendered completely mute by it. *Okay, Cora, you win. Beardy lumberjack types* are *hot.*

She would tell Brandon any of that never. Ever. Never ever. Even as her stomach did that little jitter of teenage foolishness. She refused to accept what it was, what it meant.

"Don't feel so bad. Will dislocated his shoulder just about the same place," he said, and she knew he was trying to be . . . kind and comforting. Which made her even *more* uncomfortable.

Brandon being kind and comforting? Why didn't he

just undo her completely? She closed her eyes, but that only made it worse.

She could smell his soap; she could feel the hard wall of muscle against her side and under her legs with even more *clarity*. Like closing her eyes made the sense of touch that much stronger.

Which was ridiculous. She opened her eyes, focused on the trees, on how close they were getting to the office. She wanted to squirm, but she was afraid that would put her into contact with more hard, intriguing parts of him.

"I-if it's that dangerous that you've had multiple accidents, why do you take people on it?"

Somehow, he shrugged. He was *carrying* her down a *mountain* and he shrugged as though it were nothing. "He was drunk. And you were all but attacked by a vicious . . . bunny."

She stiffened in his arms. "I didn't know what it was! I just heard something jump out at me."

"A bunny. A tiny, fluffy bunny. Barely bigger than the little puffball on your hat." His lips curved, that mischievous glint to his hazel eyes wreaking havoc with her ability to catch her next breath.

So, she focused on the irritation. On the fact this was all his fault. "I could hit you right in the junk."

"So we can both fall?"

"You're lucky I can out-rationalize my anger. Very, very lucky."

"I can't believe you threatened to junk punch your boss."

"I can't believe it takes me *injuring* myself for you to show a sense of humor."

They reached the trailhead, and he walked easily and

*still* without any outward signs of exertion toward the office. "I was being nice to you before you fell."

"Nice." She snorted. "You were being . . . polite at best." But he had a point. The Brandon on top of the mountain was a different Brandon from the one she'd known up to this point.

Oh, that was dangerous. This whole thing was one heaping pile of danger.

*You are stronger than Mom. Than Cora.* Or so she'd told herself for years, but didn't that all stem from her fear that making herself stupid over a man or becoming a victim to a man was just in her genes? Unstoppable.

Brandon stomped up the stairs, easily turning the knob and kicking the door open. "We'll get you bandaged up, then I'll drive you to the ER."

"All the way in Benson?"

"What happened?"

"Two words from you, Skeet. Why, that is a record," Lilly said. The throbbing pain in her ankle seemed to make any of the threadbare patience she'd had with all of them completely disappear.

She needed to get her control back. She needed to breathe and center herself and remember this was her job, and sprained ankle or no, she had an image to project.

Of course, then Brandon gently set her on the couch and began to untie the boot on her hurt leg, and she just felt . . .

Warm and fuzzy. Grateful. Foolishly mesmerized by his big hands deftly and carefully removing the boot from her foot.

"Skeet, go get the first-aid kit, yeah?"

"On it, boss."

"He didn't even grunt," Lilly muttered. "I should have caused myself bodily harm earlier."

Brandon's laugh was low, and it caused a shiver to go up her spine. And not one of those creepy shivers. No, this was warm and nice and . . .

She groaned and let her head fall back. Why, oh why, was she *this* stupid?

# Chapter Six

In the end, Will had somehow charmed the new doctor in town into taking a look at Lilly in her clinic instead of making them go to the ER in Benson.

Not somehow. Will had flirted with Dr. Frost until she'd overlooked the fact her boss would *hate* her doing a favor for an Evans.

"You could stop pacing," Will offered from his spot in one of the waiting room chairs.

"I hate these places," Brandon muttered. Which, sure, it was true, but it wasn't the source of the edgy, antsy feeling dogging him.

Maybe Lilly falling hadn't been his fault, but if she'd seriously hurt her ankle, he'd feel like a grade-A tool.

A door down the hall squeaked open, and Lilly and Dr. Frost emerged, Lilly slowly and on crutches that looked a few inches too big to be comfortable.

"You can return the crutches when you're feeling up to walking on your own *or* if you find a better-sized pair. Otherwise, ice, elevation, and if the pain is bothering you, ibuprofen should cover it."

"Thank you. I appreciate it."

"Any time." Dr. Frost turned to Will. Her smile went sly. "I'll see you about six, Will?"

Will grinned back. "Yes, ma'am."

She nodded at him, then Lilly, and went back down the hall they'd appeared from.

They helped Lilly out the door.

"You didn't need to take her out to dinner on my account," she said, sounding about as tired as she looked.

"Aren't you supposed to not date until the divorce is final?" Brandon added, opening the truck door for Lilly.

But she whipped her head around. "You're married?"

"I *was* married. And the divorce *is* final. Why?" He winked at Lilly. "Interested?"

Brandon was torn between concern over the fact that Will hadn't mentioned his divorce had gone through—and what that meant about Will's mental state—and the need to punch his brother in the nose for flirting with Lilly.

Because they would not be his father. Not for any reason.

"Shouldn't you only flirt with one woman at a time?"

"I'm newly divorced. I like to spread the flirting around." Will helped Lilly close the door, avoiding Brandon's gaze.

"We need to talk about that," Brandon said before opening the driver's-side door.

Will merely grunted and walked around the car to climb in the passenger seat. Brandon gave himself a second to breathe before he got in the car with someone who irritated him and someone who . . .

Well, crap, he felt guilty about Lilly and didn't he have enough guilt issues? He sighed and climbed into the driver's seat.

"Well, Lilly, we'll get you home, and—"

"Home! I haven't worked for one minute today." She rapped him on the shoulder with the papers the doctor had given her. "You're taking me back to Mile High."

"Lilly, honey," Will said, that overfamiliar *honey* causing Brandon to grit his teeth. "You're not coming to work all banged up. You heard the doctor. Ice. Elevate."

"Rest," Brandon added, his tone much less gentle than his brother's, which also irritated him.

"All things that can be done at the office. I'll work from the couch, foot elevated, with ice on my ankle. I suppose one of you will have to drive me home, but I need to get some work done today, and I don't have any of my things at home."

Brandon and Will shared a glance. One that said, *You argue with her.* Which Brandon realized meant they were both beat, and maybe a little whipped by their PR consultant.

But it *was* his fault she was in this position. Maybe he hadn't caused her to fall, but if he'd just left her alone, she wouldn't have been on the trail *to* fall.

Damn.

"Fine," Brandon muttered, backing out of the parking lot and driving through the main street of Gracely. There were too many empty storefronts, too many FOR SALE signs. Too much emptiness.

And quite a few stares that were anything but empty.

"I really don't understand why they hate you so much," Lilly said, and when Brandon glanced in the rearview mirror at her, she had her forehead pressed to the window. Watching the few people on the streets follow them with nasty glares.

"It's irrational, sure," Will said, his voice low and serious, that thread of dissatisfaction that worried Brandon more than he liked to admit. "But one minute this was a booming, peaceful tight-knit community, and then . . ."

"Then what?" Lilly pressed.

"Without Evans Mining to employ half the town, people had to look for jobs elsewhere. People had to move. Businesses failed and *more* people had to move. Maybe it isn't rational to blame us, but we're part of the root cause."

"What, like you were the ones who moved the mining company?"

Brandon stiffened, but when Will didn't answer, Brandon knew he needed to. "I was part of the reason."

"But why?"

She sounded as baffled and hurt as all the people he'd tried to explain it to back then. It didn't matter he'd done the right thing. It didn't matter he'd stood up to greed and corruption, maybe even saved some miners' lives; he'd cost them their jobs and their town.

"Business decision," he muttered, ignoring Will's disapproving glare.

But he wasn't rehashing all that ancient history with Lilly. She hadn't lived here; she didn't deserve any explanation. More, it didn't matter. It didn't matter to the townspeople of Gracely—why should it matter to her?

Everyone was silent for the rest of the drive up to the office. Brandon parked and Will helped Lilly out and onto her crutches. Will cracked some joke and Lilly laughed, and Brandon trailed behind, hating what he knew he needed to do.

But, he had a code, and it was a little hard to follow when it came to Lilly because . . . well, because she . . .

He rubbed his hand over his beard. He hated having to admit it to himself, but Lilly was a *temptation*. Being rude or hard on her though, it wasn't right. He'd promised himself he'd be a much better boss than his father had ever been, even when the town had loved him.

Which meant Brandon had to go out of his way to be less of a dick, and more of the man he'd promised himself he'd be.

"Lilly." He took a breath, feeling like an idiot. But he was an honorable idiot, damn it. "I'm sorry."

She stopped in the doorway, giving him a quizzical look. "For what?"

"Forcing you into a hike. I should have let things be."

Her eyebrows drew together, creating that deep crease between her eyes. "I'll be back to full mobility in a few weeks. I bet it's even prettier with spring things blooming, and I expect you to take me back."

"You do?"

"Yes, and we had a deal. Every excursion I survive, I get to fix the brochures. So, I expect more than just a measly hike. After all, I did survive."

"Barely."

She rolled her eyes. "As though you've never gotten hurt doing all your adventure stuff."

"Not for a long time." Because it had been a long time since he'd felt invincible and stupid.

"Well, I'll consider it a badge of honor. I don't want apologies for stupid things that aren't really your fault. You *can* apologize for being grumpy, but an accident— I'll pass on the guilt, thank you."

He didn't have anything to say to *that*. Maybe it wasn't his fault, and maybe he shouldn't feel bad, but he wouldn't be him if he didn't take responsibility for events he set in motion. So, whether she passed on the guilt or not, it was there.

"Oh, and don't forget to put a dollar in the grunt jar." She swung herself inside, somehow still managing to make the move look easy and graceful.

Brandon blew out a breath. Maybe there was some more wood to cut, somewhere in the world.

\* \* \*

Lilly wanted to stomp in frustration. Except she couldn't stomp because of her hurt ankle, and it was driving her crazy not being able to pop up off the couch and get what she needed. It was driving her crazy that Skeet of all people kept asking if she needed anything.

When he brought her yet another mug of tea, with a little plate of cookies, she simply could not hold her temper. "Stop mothering me."

"Being helpful."

"I don't need help! I don't need . . . cookies. I . . ." She took a deep breath and closed her eyes. She hated being nasty to people when they didn't deserve it. Skeet was being nice—she shouldn't snarl. Even if that's all she felt like doing to anyone.

She reached out and took a cookie. "Oh, of course I need cookies. Thank you."

He grunted, but it was so darn sweet she didn't even demand he put a dollar in the jar. Instead, she bit into the cookie and returned her attention to the brochure she was redoing on her tablet.

She'd rewritten most of the copy during her afternoon of couch captivity. She was still debating overall design and what images to include.

She reached over to the coffee table and grabbed her phone, scrolling through the pictures she'd taken, the pictures Brandon had taken of her, and then the picture of Brandon he had no idea she'd taken. He'd probably hate having it on the brochure, but . . .

It was perfect. You could *see* the awe on his face as he looked out at the valley, and you didn't have to see a picture of the view that couldn't possibly do it justice.

You could see how *amazing* it was in his eyes, in the way he seemed to be cloaked in peace.

Solace.

Add to that the fact he looked all mountain-man chic. The scuffed hiking boots, the rugged pack on his back, the well-kept beard.

He made a handsome picture. One that would make women want him to be their guide and men interested in seeing where he could take them.

Yes, Brandon would hate it, but he *had* given her carte blanche, and as much as she didn't blame him for her tumble, he blamed himself. She could use that.

Which was terrible, but it was for the good of *his* company.

The front door opened and Will stepped in, tugging off his hat and shaking out the waves of his hair. It was fascinating how much he *looked* like Brandon, and how completely differently he acted.

Like smiling at her immediately. "How you holding up, champ?"

She wanted to be nice back, but she was too achy and surly to try and put on the PR face and smile things away. Besides, she'd proven her worth here; she didn't need to suck up. They'd be idiots to get rid of her now. "I didn't know injuring myself would turn you all into a bunch of over-concerned smotherers."

But Will's smile never died. "Skeet been doctoring you up then? The old troll's got a soft heart under all that . . . well, that." Will gestured to Skeet's desk, where he was grunting on the phone.

"It's very sweet. I'm just not . . . very good at being fussed over." Possibly because never in her life had she been . . . taken care of. For as long as she could remember, she was the woman who took care of business, whether she wanted to or not. "I broke my arm years ago and no one made me tea. Especially not grumpy old men who'd rather 'shit in a bag' than learn how to use a computer."

Will settled himself on the arm of the couch next to where her hurt ankle was propped up. "And how did you break your arm?" he asked with that easy smile.

Oh, why couldn't this one be the Evans brother who made her all . . . tingly? Actually, no, it was good. Good that the one she was physically attracted to was the one she kind of wanted to throttle. It would make resisting temptation that much easier. If she got all . . . weird over Will *and* he was nice and personable, well . . .

"I was trying to put up a Christmas tree. I got kind of tripped up in the tree and the ladder, and snap. Nice clean break." She'd still done everything she could for Mom and Cora with that cast on her arm for weeks.

Mom had been too busy working to do any fussing and Cora had been . . . well, Cora.

"How many years ago was that?"

"Oh, about fifteen."

"Fifteen? You can't even be knocking on thirty's door. How old were you?"

"Twelve. So, I guess seventeen years ago." It felt like a lifetime, really. When she'd still been a scared little girl with no idea how she was going to keep everything going, everyone happy.

She'd learned. It had taken some failures, but look at all she'd done for Cora and Micah since Mom had given up on them.

"Why were *you* putting up the tree by yourself?"

Lilly looked down at her tablet. How had they gotten here? Those places in her past she hadn't built armor over. The sore spots. The little things she didn't want anyone to know about her.

She took a deep breath, trying to blow out all those

old hurts and fears with it. "Mom worked three jobs. If I hadn't done it, it wouldn't have gotten done." That year, it hadn't gotten done. But she'd made sure Mom and Cora had pretty presents under the tree. She'd baked cookies one-handed.

She had learned from that injury and that Christmas that she could overcome just about anything. And she'd stopped hoping someone might help or fuss over her. She'd finally given up the dream of her father's promises.

It was good, all in all.

When she looked back up, determined to be strong and certain, she didn't meet Will's eyes. She met Brandon's.

He was standing a few feet behind Will. Apparently she'd missed his entrance, and for some reason, she immediately looked down. She had a bad feeling Brandon would see through her a lot more easily than Will ever would.

"Will." Brandon's voice was all gruff, bossy order. "I need to talk to you."

Will smiled, but there was an edginess to the way they surveyed each other. Like there had been outside the car when Brandon had seemed surprised to hear Will's marriage was officially over. "Talk away."

"In our office."

She only had a sister, so she couldn't speak to how brothers communicated, but it was so much more stilted and weighted than how she talked to her own sister. Which was why it was fascinating.

Far more fascinating than her own family issues.

Will let out a gusty sigh, gave her good foot a little pat, and then followed Brandon down the hall.

Lilly tried to go back to work. She did. But work would be so much easier if she had a few files from her office. And she had to use the restroom. If that meant she *happened* to walk by Brandon and Will's office, well, who could help it?

She reached for her crutches and Skeet immediately popped up next to her, clucking his tongue. "Whatcha need, girl?"

"I don't need help. Just have to use the bathroom and grab something from my office. Unfortunately, you can't make my bathroom trips for me."

He grunted, helping her with her crutches. And . . . oh, darn it all, it *was* nice to be fussed over. As nice as she'd always imagined. She leaned over and kissed his whiskered, grizzled cheek. "Thank you for being so sweet."

He grunted and then stomped back to his desk, grumbling about women.

Lilly couldn't help but smile. The old troll was growing on her. She started toward the hallway. The crutches were taking some getting used to, but she managed her way toward the bathroom without making much noise.

She paused. Since the bathroom door was at the end of the hall beyond Will and Brandon's office, she couldn't go inside without them noticing. So, she . . . stopped.

It was wrong. It was absolutely wrong to eavesdrop, but . . . well, they weren't exactly being quiet, and the door was only halfway closed. She couldn't even see them.

"No one liked it when I married her. I don't get why anyone's upset we're getting divorced," Will said, and Lilly imagined he was trying very hard to seem casual and unaffected.

In her estimation, it was a failure.

"I'm . . . concerned that you're not telling me these things."

"It was a formality. I don't get why you're being so weird about this."

"Maybe because you *aren't* being weird about getting divorced after seven years."

It was interesting to hear the note of concern in Brandon's voice. It was a very big brother tone. The same tone she'd used with Cora more times than she could count.

"It was barely seven, and we were barely married. Don't act like you don't know that. She never spent more than a few days in Gracely before she had to gallivant off somewhere more exciting."

"Have you . . . told Tori?"

The door swung open, and she squeaked and jumped as Will's face popped out, looking as angry as she'd ever seen it.

"Would you like to join us, Lilly?"

Then she yelped when the jump caused her to put some weight on her ankle. "I . . . I . . ."

Brandon's face joined Will's in the doorway, looking confused and concerned, and . . . she was an *idiot*.

"I was just going to the bathroom," she managed, her cheeks absolutely on fire with embarrassment. She scooted into the bathroom, closing the door behind her, then leaning her forehead against it.

"Idiot, idiot, idiot," she muttered.

# Chapter Seven

Brandon finished putting away the canoe gear after making his annual spring check of the equipment. Lilly would likely want to go home soon, and as Will had already left for his date with Dr. Frost, and Sam tried not to set foot in Gracely proper if he could help it, Brandon knew the chore fell to him.

It was fine. He'd make a big to-do about eating a big dinner at the Gracely Café. He'd tip whomever his waitress was some obscene amount. Maybe it hadn't worked the first one hundred times he'd done it, but he'd keep trying.

Just that reminder—that the sum of the past five years could be boiled down to *keep trying* and *infinitesimal change can happen*—strengthened him. Centered him.

He would not give up or in, because that would make everything he'd stood up to his father for worthless. Pointless.

Brandon locked up the shed and walked slowly to the office. He always tried to walk *slowly* here, to take in what was around him, what he'd built at the center of it. He'd always figured part of his father's problem—

even when he'd still idolized his father—was that he didn't stop and take stock. He didn't appreciate.

He'd been driven by the need for more. Bigger. Brandon hadn't wanted that, even when he'd wanted his father's life. He'd wanted to be the head of Evans, he'd wanted that power, that . . . deference the town had paid his family.

But he hadn't needed more money or a bigger company. He'd just wanted Evans as it was, Gracely as it was.

He wanted what his father had never been able to find. *Contentment.* Even when this place drove him crazy, when the town poked at every insecurity and exposed nerve, even when Lilly made him want to tear his hair out . . .

He really was . . . content. He was slowly carving out exactly what he'd set out to do, and something about it being *hard* appealed to him. He'd grown up with easy, and he was done with it.

The front door opened as he came around the corner, Lilly's bright purple bag coming into view before she did. Then her crutches. Her hair obscured her face, but something in his gut stirred.

Something in his *contentedness* changed, opened up a little. As if to insinuate something was missing. As if to whisper somewhere inside of him that a *place* was not enough.

But that was ridiculous. Because he had more than a place. He had Will and Sam and . . . Skeet. That was enough. That was more than enough.

Any whispers inside of him were clearly his underused libido trying to make a case for female companionship.

Which wasn't such a terrible idea, as long as it wasn't Lilly. Or any Gracely-ite who might gain more reason to hate him. So, a good idea in theory. In practice, his too-long celibate streak needed to continue.

Lucky him.

Irritated with that line of thought, he strode up the porch steps. "I'll carry your bag." He reached for the unreasonably huge thing. Why on earth did she carry around so much junk?

"You don't have"—she reached for it the same time he did, the long strands of her hair brushing his cheek, his chin just barely grazing her shoulder—"to." Blue eyes met his, and it was as though her sharp intake of breath stole his. Or someone had reached inside and squeezed all the air out of his lungs.

"Let me," he managed, his voice sounding oddly cottony to his own ears.

"A-all right."

He grabbed her bag and slung it over his shoulder, moving out of that too-close proximity to her eyes. To her. "Do you need help on the stairs?"

"No." She maneuvered to the top of the stairs, then frowned at the three slabs of wood.

Yeah, that couldn't be easy on crutches, especially for someone without a lot of upper body strength and with crutches that were a hair too big. He doubted if she'd appreciate him pointing that out, so he grunted instead.

"Just . . . just hold on." He stepped to the bottom of the stairs; then, steeling himself for any kind of unrelenting bodily response, he placed his hands on her waist, gave her a quick, easy lift down to the bottom.

She was soft. She smelled damn good. Why the hell was he always *touching* her today?

"Um, well, that's one way of doing it." She balanced on her good leg and crutches and he released her, stepping back.

This was a one-off. One random day where he was forced to put his hands on her, but that didn't mean he had to enjoy it. Or be haunted by it.

They walked to his truck in silence. He should help her up. It couldn't be easy to clamber into the thing with a bum leg. Still, he hesitated.

A man could only take so much innocent touching before his brain started making things not so innocent.

Before his conscience could get the better of him, she opened the door, propped her crutches against the truck, then pulled herself up and in. Easily, she pulled the crutches up next to her, then closed the door.

Brandon let out a sigh of relief. Then he skirted the back of the truck and climbed into his own seat. He swung her bag into the back.

"You look good with a purple bag. You should consider investing in one."

"I think green is more my color."

She laughed, a sound that caused him way, way too much stupid pleasure. So she laughed at his joke? What was he? Thirteen? *Not* her boss?

He pulled out of the Mile High lot and noticed the usually calm and collected Lilly was fidgety.

"So . . ." She sighed and looked out the window, then shook her head and turned her gaze to him.

He watched the curvy mountain road in front of him.

"I already apologized to Will, but I wanted to apologize to you. I . . . didn't exactly mean to eavesdrop this afternoon, but . . . I should have stopped myself."

"We're not used to having other people around, I guess." Certainly not used to prying eyes and ears in their place of business.

"I am sorry," she said, sounding sincere and contrite.

But then she asked a question that ruined it all. "Who's Tori?"

Something about her asking bothered him—and not for the reasons it should. It *should* bother him because not only had she eavesdropped, but now she was asking questions about things she'd heard. Personal business between him and his brother.

But it actually bothered him because it was a question that pointed to a particular kind of interest. Would Lilly care about some stranger's name in Will's past if it weren't the name of a woman? He doubted it.

"Just because Will is divorced doesn't mean—"

"If you insinuate I'm *harboring any fantasies* for Will one more time, I'm going to . . ."

"Junk punch me?"

She blew out a breath. "I only said that because I was . . ." She gestured toward her leg. "Hurt and out of sorts."

Silence followed, so he took the opportunity to change the subject. Away from his brother and junk interaction of any kind. "Where do you live?"

"Corner of Aspen and Hope," she replied.

He gave a nod. He was a little surprised she lived on the old mining workers' strip, but he supposed that was where the most affordable real estate in Gracely existed. Not that there was much unaffordable in a dying town.

"Brandon. To be clear. I'm not . . . I have no interest in Will. I just find you both a little fascinating. The question was an innocent one. I don't quite understand why you take everything I say about your brother to mean something else, but . . . it's unnecessary. I seem to be immune to Will's many charms. So, please. Take my word and stop irritating me over it."

That shouldn't soothe him. He shouldn't *need* to be

soothed, but Lilly Preston was really screwing with his *should* and *would*. Also with his determination not to give anything away.

But, just like he didn't like the idea of Will following in Dad's footsteps no matter how innocently, he didn't want her thinking he looked at her as the possible downfall of anyone. It wasn't *her*, or even his opinion on women. This was all his baggage.

"My father . . . was not a particularly *good* person." He already hated himself for starting this line of conversation.

"I think I've deduced that."

"He took advantage of his employees. Particularly the . . . female ones."

"Oh. Well."

"There were some lawsuits, but mainly . . . he got away with things. He manipulated people, and he had enough power to get away with it. The point is, I'm not trying to be . . . It isn't about *you*."

"Well, you should understand that regardless of *your* baggage, I have my own. And it includes a very strict personal code. The three of you are completely off limits to me."

Which was . . . good. They were both on the same page. And hell if he didn't get far away from this line of conversation. "Don't you mean four?"

She cracked a smile. "I don't know. Skeet might be an exception to the rule. He did bring me a plate of cookies today."

"Well, cookies. Who can resist that?"

"Precisely." She pointed to a little green house on the corner. "That's me."

He pulled into the narrow drive—his truck barely fitting on the concrete strip. The house itself was a little run-down, which surprised him, but colorful pots lined the stoop and brightly patterned curtains hung in the windows. Obviously Lilly had tried to make her mark.

He reached back to grab her bag. "I'll help you inside."

"That won't be necessary," she said primly, holding out her arm as if she could maneuver her giant bag and crutches all while climbing out of his truck.

"I'm going to sit here and watch you struggle with crutches and your giant bag?"

She met his incredulous gaze with a chin-raised, ice-queen kind of look. One that brooked no argument. "No, you're going to drive away."

Oh, he was going to brook a damn argument. "Like hell," he returned, grabbing the bag and hopping out of the truck before she had another opportunity to argue. When he got to the passenger side, she'd pushed the door open and was working to get her crutches situated in a way that would allow her to get out alone.

She was failing. He could tell by the irritated look on her face.

"Let me help," he said, or, more accurately, growled.

She frowned down at him, eyebrows drawing together in frustration. "I'm . . . I'm not used to that."

"Find a way to get used to it," he returned, grabbing the crutches and leaning them on the ground against the truck. He held out his hand. "Now, come on."

"It's not like you're going to follow me around lifting me up and down every set of stairs for the next few weeks."

"Maybe not, but that doesn't mean I won't help when I *am* around."

She grunted, and if she hadn't slid her hand into his in that moment, he might have had the presence of mind to tell her she owed a dollar to the grunt jar.

But her palm was soft and her fingers . . . dainty in

his oversized, calloused ones. She was so polished and pretty, even not at her PR best. It reminded him of all those things he'd walked away from, all those things he missed.

*All the things that turned out to be a lie.*

She planted her good foot on the step of the truck, and then she let go of his hand and he wound his arm around her waist to help her down.

He forced himself to focus on the patchy grass at his feet. Count the scuffs on his boots. Anything but pay any mind to how soft and silky she felt. How floral and feminine she smelled.

He could try to argue it away, he could not want it—and he definitely did not—but there was a spark of attraction there, some thread of interest. Though that didn't mean it had to get the better of him.

He settled her on the ground and she took her crutches.

"I can get my bag."

"Don't make me—"

The door flung open and a redheaded woman burst out like a bright little bullet. "Lilly! Oh my gosh! What happened?"

Her sister, obviously. There wasn't a lot of similarity in how they looked, except the riot of colors in their hair, and the cool blue eyes that assessed him with distrust and irritation. Yes, that reminded him one hundred percent of Lilly.

"I took a little tumble on a trail and sprained my ankle," Lilly said easily. "Brandon, this is my sister, Cora. Cora, this is my boss, Brandon. Will you take my bag from him?"

Cora all but yanked the bag from his shoulder. Clearly Lilly had been sharing some not-so-flattering stories of him at home.

He probably deserved that.

"Good-bye, Brandon. I'll see you tomorrow."

"Tomorrow? But you should—"

"I may be a little late, but I will be in the office," she interrupted, already swinging herself on the crutches toward her house. "Thank you for the ride."

With one last suspicious look from her sister, the two disappeared inside.

And Brandon decided he could use a stiff drink.


Lilly sank into the couch, chastising herself for . . . pretty much everything. For prying. For being so snotty. For being so damn affected by . . . him. All of him. His help. His touch. His stupid pretty eyes.

His stupid big muscles.

It had been a long time since her . . . whatever this was—loneliness? Lust? Crazy hormonal imbalance?—had been . . . potent.

She'd been kind of stiff and snotty to him when he'd *helped* her, and . . .

Ugh. Why did things have to be so hard? Complicated? Why did she always have to want the absolute *wrong* guy? Some Preston family trait? Like blue eyes and skinny ankles?

"You'd tell me if something was wrong, right?"

Lilly forced herself to open her eyes and smile at Cora. "Of course. All that's wrong right now is a swollen ankle and being irritated I can't drive myself places. Do you have a shift tomorrow, or can you play chauffeur?"

"Nope. I'm off for the next two days and at your beck and call." Cora stood in front of the couch, pulling on her bottom lip, eyebrows drawn together in concern. "It was an accident, right?"

"Of course it was!"

"Well, just everyone in town acts like you've made a pact with the devil by working for them. I just wanted to make sure . . ."

"Honey, I promise. This was an unfortunate accident. You know I'd be straight with you." She couldn't blame Cora for being worried. Not after what she'd been through. Lilly had been careful not to complain about Brandon or the frustrating men of Mile High at home, where Cora might construe it as something Lilly was sacrificing for the good of her and Micah.

Even if that was the one and only reason she'd agreed to the job. But, now she was glad she had. So. It was all a . . . moot point.

Cora plopped next to her on the couch. "Why were *you* on a trail?"

"We thought it'd be a good idea if I saw some of the things they did firsthand so I could write up really clear, truthful copy." If she told her sister Brandon had been the one to think of it, she'd only be more suspicious.

"He's . . ."

"He's a complete professional." He really was. If a little condescending. If a little . . . gruff do-gooder. Why was *that* the undoing of her normal sense?

"I was going to say ridiculously hot."

Lilly let out a small laugh. It wasn't funny, in the least, but damn if it wasn't true. "You should see the rest of them."

"Work surrounded by hot, rugged mountain men. Oh, the sacrifices you make, Lil."

"Worse, they seem . . . nice. Decent."

"Or you've finally succumbed to the Preston curse of thinking that of any guy with a hot smile and a few dollars in his pocket."

"Or that." She didn't really believe it of the Evans

brothers. They weren't . . . the same. But maybe that was just faulty thinking. "Where's Micah?"

"Oh, we had a fun 'don't you dare leave that room until your homework is done' fight right before you got home."

Well, that was a surprise. Usually Cora was far too easy on Micah. Maybe the joint therapy really was helping.

Cora chewed on her lip. "Do you think I should apologize?"

"You're setting a good, strong precedent. He's been through hell. I know you feel guilty for it, but that doesn't mean you stop parenting. You owe it to him to be his parent more than his friend."

"Now you sound like the therapist." Cora pouted.

Lilly's stomach rumbled, and she grabbed her crutches. No one was apt to bring her tea and cookies in this house. So, it would be up to her to get dinner on the table.

How hard could it be? Surely she just needed a day or two to get used to the crutches. They really couldn't be *this* inhibiting. She kept telling herself if she just kept all weight off the hurt ankle for a few days, she'd heal so much faster than the doctor anticipated.

Lilly tried to grab everything she would need to do a simple little stir fry, but bending over putting all her weight on one leg was a chore, and trying to carry stuff from refrigerator to counter was irritating and taxing.

She was even breathing a little heavily as she grabbed yet another thing from the fridge and half limped, half hopped her way over to the counter with it.

Cora was still brooding on the couch, looking at the stairs that led to Micah's bedroom. Lilly sympathized, she really did. Cora's sole purpose and focus lately was trying to get Micah back on track with school before the end of the year.

But her ankle hurt and she was trying to cook dinner for two able-bodied people. It . . . grated. It shouldn't, but it did. "Do you think you could help me with dinner?"

Cora brightened, just as she'd done as a little girl when Lilly had unexpectedly included her in something. "Of course!"

Maybe Brandon was right—horror of all horrors—and she needed to get used to *help*.

# Chapter Eight

"Fold," Sam said, disgustedly tossing his cards on the coffee table. "Will's still adept at cheating at cards I see."

"I never cheat, Sammy boy. Just way luckier than you."

Sam grunted and Brandon laughed as Will tossed another chip into the pile.

Brandon surveyed his cards with a bloom of satisfaction. Will *was* luckier than either of them, but that didn't mean Brandon didn't come out on top every once in a while.

It had been a genius idea really, although anything would seem genius after the amount of alcohol he'd ingested. But they hadn't done this in too long. Relaxed. Done something completely pointless and unrelated to business. His own fault, but it was good to take a breath and remember.

The business was important, but the reason they even had one was because they liked each other. Because they could have fun together—even as different as the three of them were. Easy to lose sight of in his one-track mind, but that wasn't any good.

"Call." He spread his cards out across the table, and when Will grinned, he swore. "You did not win again."

"Afraid so, gentlemen. What a lot in life to be so good at poker." He pulled the change that was acting as chips toward him on the table.

"Good, my ass," Sam muttered.

Will got up off the floor and headed for the kitchenette, whistling cheerfully. "Who needs another?"

"Me. And bring that bag of chips—we're nearly out."

"Quick. Tell me something he's bad at before I have to punch him when he walks back in here. Wait, the date." Sam turned and pointed at Will in the kitchenette. "You were back way early."

"Dr. Frost immune to your charms then?" Brandon couldn't say he disliked the idea of his brother striking out. Not just because he didn't like the idea of Will screwing things up with any locals who might be open to supporting them, but because obviously Will hadn't fully dealt with any of his issues about ending his marriage.

And didn't want to.

Will returned with a bottle of scotch, which he thumped onto the table before tossing the bag of chips at Brandon.

"She was not immune."

"And yet you were home in, what, an hour?"

"Something . . . came up." Will poured himself a big glass of the liquor. "Who's dealer?"

"What came up?" Brandon pressed. "You didn't—"

"No, I didn't piss your potential Gracely ally off, Brandon. Thank you for being more concerned about your business than anything else. It never fails to warm my heart."

"She must have dropped you hard," Sam replied, an easy attempt to diffuse the tension Will had uncharacteristically injected into the room. "You're not usually this much of a dick. That's Brandon's department."

"So talkative today, Sam. To what do we owe the annoyance?"

"Alcohol, apparently. What happened with the doctor?" Sam gestured with his beer bottle. "I'm curious how Will Evans strikes out first time at it in a few years. Skills rusty? Getting too old?"

Will took a big gulp of his drink. "I did *not* strike out. It was me. I just . . . Strangest thing. I thought I saw . . ." He shook his head. "I was having a hallucination."

"A hallucination of what?" Brandon pressed, popping the top of his beer.

"Sarge."

That got both Brandon and Sam's undivided attention. Brandon leaned forward. "Tori's dog?"

"Yeah, but look. It's nothing." The way Will glared at the glass full of scotch said otherwise. "You brought her up the other day. There was an old German shepherd outside the café. It was dumb to think . . ." Will downed the rest of his glass. "That dog's gotta be dead anyway."

"You know, it's been something like seven years," Sam pointed out. "You could tell us what happened there."

Will shuffled the cards, meeting no one's gaze. "Nothing happened there."

"My ass," Sam grumbled. "One minute, there were four of us ready to run this place; the next minute, you're married and Tori's gone."

"You two making conspiracy theories is a bunch of girly bullshit. Are we going to play poker, or are we going to get our panties in a twist about dates and women?

Because if it's the latter . . ." Will looked up, that easy grin back on his face. "We should talk about Lilly."

Brandon scowled, not at all liking the way his brother was looking at him. "What about Lilly?"

"She's hot."

It was Brandon's turn to look down at the cards. "She's a pain in the ass."

"Agreed. On both counts," Sam offered.

Brandon glared at him. "You two were the ones who wanted to hire her. Why are we discussing what she looks like?"

"Because it's *there*. And pain in the ass or not, she's making progress. You kind of owe us an apology. It was a brilliant hire," Will said.

"So, she's good at her job. You were right for once. Congratulations."

"She's more than good. Corbin Finley hated me *before* everything happened with Evans. She got him to work with us. She's a damn miracle worker." Will studied his cards, trying to hide his shit-eating grin behind them. "And looks damn fine in one of those tight office skirts."

"Knock it off, asshole."

Will didn't stop grinning. "Why? Marking your territory?"

Brandon snorted. "Not on your life."

"She *is* your type," Sam added, discarding a few cards and replacing them.

"I do not have a type."

Sam and Will exchanged a glance that irritated Brandon. He did *not* have a type. Because he'd been all but celibate for five damn years. He stared at his cards, trying to think about strategy over Lilly damn Preston.

"Okay, let's pretend like you don't—even though we all know you do. You *argue* with her. Nearly constantly."

"Because, as I said, she's a pain in the ass."

"Or, it's the 'thou dost protest too much' thing. You argue so you don't pay attention to how attracted you are to her."

"Are you sure we shared the same womb? Did I get all the brains and you just have a bunch of useless nuts and bolts bouncing around in that hard head of yours?"

Will's amusement flickered into something else. Something Brandon didn't trust at all.

"You know it wouldn't be the same, right?"

Brandon glared at his brother. "What wouldn't be the same?" he demanded, because he might know what Will was getting at, but he wasn't going to discuss it if Will couldn't even say the words.

"Your grand attempt to be the polar opposite of Dad. Just by . . . *wanting* that, you aren't him. So, you don't have to be dick extraordinaire to her. You two have chemistry."

"Now who's talking about girly bullshit?" Sam muttered.

It was Brandon's turn to walk away from the table in search of some other kind of snack or liquor that would somehow make this less annoying.

"It's different for you." Will hadn't been groomed to take Dad's place. He hadn't been settled and ready to take over that role, that life. He didn't understand how powerful the urge sometimes was. To be that larger-than-life, perfect-to-the-outside-world flash and swagger his father had been. Brandon had wanted that.

So much that, even knowing how fake it all was, how crooked and warped it turned out to be, he could still miss it.

"Yes, I know. Five minutes younger, the useless second son." Will pretended to yawn. "It didn't affect me at all."

"I didn't say—"

"If you two are going to argue about family drama, I'm out. You're already pushing my limits for human interaction."

"Shut up and bet," Brandon said without any heat, returning to the table empty-handed. They were *not* arguing about drama. Or Lilly. Or anything.

They were getting drunk and playing poker. The end.


"You're not going to let me come in and see?" Cora pouted as she helped Lilly out of the car and onto her crutches.

"You don't want to see. You want to flirt."

"That *involves* seeing."

"I'll sign you up for an excursion."

"As long as excursion in this context means sitting on that porch under a blanket with some hot cocoa, looking at the stars. Enjoying attractive male company."

"Go home, Cora."

"Meanie."

"Just keeping you sane, little girl. Go home. Look into those online courses. For me. Please."

"I can't afford—"

"You figure out what you need, and then I will decide what *we* can afford."

"You can't play mom to me forever, Lil," Cora said, seeming more sad than peevish. Which, in turn, made Lilly sad. As far as Cora had come emotionally, she was still at loose ends.

And too bright and vibrant and antsy for sitting around with a part-time job to be *any* good for her.

"Why not?"

"Because you're my sister? Because I'm an adult? With a nearly middle-school-aged child of my own."

"And you're my favorite sister," Lilly said, putting her hand on Cora's cheek and giving it a little pinch like she used to do when they were younger.

Cora slapped her hand away. "Oh, stop trying to soften me up. You have to let me spread my wings a little."

"Spread them on the way to signing up for an online class, please." Lilly adjusted the backpack on her shoulders. It was butt ugly, but much like the hiking boots from yesterday, it would serve the purpose.

No one had to carry her bag or help her, unless she wanted them to. She was sort of resigned to asking Cora for help now because, much to her surprise, Cora had jumped at the chance.

Oh, Cora needed some direction and occasionally *re*direction, but she seemed to enjoy the opportunity to . . . spread her wings, so to speak.

But the last thing Lilly wanted to do today was ask Brandon for help. It certainly wasn't his place as her boss to be driving her around or carrying her bag. There had to be clear lines. For her sanity. For her own protection.

"Make dinner if you think of it," she told Cora, pushing the car door shut. "Have Micah help you. He really likes playing sous chef."

"Yes, ma'am."

"And pick me up at five-thirty."

"As you wish, master," Cora returned with a dramatic bow.

Lilly rolled her eyes and moved up the stairs. Since Cora was still starting the car and backing away, she didn't take her normal time to enjoy the view. She stepped inside.

She stopped right in front of Skeet's desk, then had to blink to make sure she was seeing things right. Skeet was sitting behind the front desk like he always did, but instead of the pristine living room she had worked most of the day in yesterday, there were three burly men in various states of disarray lying across the couches and chairs that made up the living area.

Sam was slumped in one chair, a bag of chips on his lap, many beer bottles on the table by his side. Will was curled up on the rug, also surrounded by chip crumbs and beer bottles, as well as a bottle of some kind of hard liquor that looked mostly gone.

Brandon was on the couch, arms crossed over his face and a scattering of playing cards all over his body. They were all snoring. Had she slipped into some dimension where this was a frat house instead of a place of business?

"What the hell happened here?" she demanded of Skeet.

He only grunted, but before she could point to the grunt jar, he added a word: "Dunno."

"And you didn't think to wake them up? You didn't think to ask them what was going on? When—"

"There ain't no expeditions until noon. And they're grown men. I don't care what's going on, and I'm sure they'll be up in time to get ready for work."

This was ridiculous, but Lilly knew better than to argue with Skeet over that. She walked with her crutches over to where the three men were sprawled out. The whole room smelled of beer and salt.

It wasn't her business to do anything. It wasn't her business to wake them up, to make sure they were ready for their jobs. Yet, she couldn't just walk away from the scene. Her job was public relations. Her job was making sure they looked good.

This did not look good. If the *public* came in off the street and saw this scene, they wouldn't want to be guided through the woods by these three dopes.

So, it *was* sort of her job to wake them up. To make sure they cleaned up this horrible mess before anyone happened to stop by. It was rare, but it was *possible*.

She could start with Sam or Will; they were both closer. But Brandon was the head of this company. He was the boss, even if all three of them had a say in things. It was obvious Brandon ran the show.

So, she swung herself over to the couch and leaned on her good leg. She lifted her crutch and poked him in the stomach with it. He grunted and pushed at the crutch, but did not wake up.

"Brandon. Wake up." She moved the crutch higher, so it was now poking him in the chest. He pushed at it again, and the movement caused her to lose her balance a little bit.

Oh, damn this stupid ankle. If she fell on him . . .

Before she could poke him again, his hand closed around the crutch, eyes still closed, and he gave it a little jerk. "Leave me the hell alone," he muttered, this time dropping the crutch with a force that did completely have her losing her balance.

And falling right on top of him. Chest to chest. His very hard, hard chest. He was only wearing a thin T-shirt, but luckily she had on her light jacket. She could only sort of make out the impression of . . . *hard muscle*.

Lord.

Of course, the coat didn't help when she pressed her palms to his chest to push herself up. Then she could feel not just *hard*, but each little ridge of muscle under her hands.

She managed to get her chest off his by pushing upward, but her hands were still on his chest. She tried to push off him and back onto her good leg, but his eyes opened and then she was kind of . . . frozen there. Her hands on his chest, her mouth way, way, way too close to his.

He didn't say anything, simply stared at her. Why was she suddenly having a hard time taking in a breath? Why had her heartbeat accelerated as though she'd just run a mile?

*Fear. Just being startled from falling. That's all.*

"You . . . you grabbed my crutch," she managed breathlessly.

"Sorry," he muttered, those hazel eyes sleepy and something else. Something that made her even more breathless, and made her completely forget about getting to her feet.

Then something cleared. He narrowed his eyes and looked at where her hands were, then back up at her. "Wait . . . what did you say?"

"You grabbed my crutch," she repeated dumbly, wondering why she couldn't get her body to work the way she needed it to. *Probably because your wants are in direct opposition with your needs.*

"Crutch." He blew out a breath, his hand curling around her wrist as if he was going to help her up. But then it just . . . held her there.

She merely squeaked. He had to feel her pulse thumping erratically, which only made it jump against her wrist harder. She managed a breath, tried to sound completely unaffected when she spoke. "Yes, crutch. What did you think I—" *Oh.* Yeah, no, none of that kind of grabbing.

Her cheeks had to be flaming red by now. She gave a little tug on the arm he still had those long, strong fingers around. "You have to let go of my arm." When he did, like he'd been holding on to some hot, burning thing—which was more than a little possible—she managed to scramble back onto her other crutch and disperse her weight between it and her good foot.

"Right. Sorry." His voice was all sleep rasp, and he looked incredibly rumpled, and Lilly had to work very hard to focus on anything but how appealing all that was.

He looked around the room blearily. "Where the hell . . ." He sat up, wincing and grumbling and running his hands over his face. "Damn. What time is it?"

"Nine," she replied primly. "And while I realize you don't have any groups coming until noon, I'm not sure this is the kind of image you want to send to the world."

"No, it isn't." He rubbed his hands over his face again, then reached back and stretched.

Lilly very nearly squeaked again.

She hadn't really seen his arms before. Forearms, yes, when he had his sleeves rolled up, but somehow the T-shirt was different. She could see almost his whole arms. As he stretched them out and back, she could watch each muscle contact and move, and he was just . . . muscle. Curves and dips and . . .

She could make out a distinct shape and movement of all parts of his upper body under the thin fabric. Even though she knew he was strong from the fact he'd *carried her down a mountain*, this was visual proof. Now she had the visual, *and* what it felt like to be hefted by those arms and . . .

*Not. Good.*

She tried to speak—to say she was going to make herself some tea or go to her office or anything—but it was a strange, strangled sound that actually escaped her mouth.

If he noticed, he pretended not to. "I'll get these two

lumps out of your way and we'll get it cleaned up. I'm sure it'll be more comfortable to work out here."

"My office is fine."

"We want you healed up good and fast. What can I do to help make your office comfortable?"

She gave him a skeptical look. She was pretty sure his hotness hadn't completely fried her brain and he was acting weird. Nice and accommodating without an ounce of grunting gruffness. "Why are you being weird?"

"I'm not being weird. I'm being nice." When she only continued to look at him skeptically, he crossed his arms over his chest. "I can be nice," he insisted.

She did not trust his nice, but she decided to keep that to herself. Besides, she was just the tiniest bit distracted at the curve of his bicep, the way he looked all intimidating lumberjack. But sexy intimidating, not creepy intimidating.

She nearly groaned at her own idiocy.

His eyes kind of narrowed and he studied her face for a second, giving the impression he knew *exactly* where her thoughts had been for ninety-five percent of this conversation. Okay, maybe ninety-eight percent.

But then he turned toward the mess and started cleaning up, and Lilly did what she should have done all along.

She disappeared into her office.

# Chapter Nine

Brandon tried to wade through the mess that was his desk. Spring was fully springing its ass off, and they'd been packed the past few days. Which meant paperwork needed to be filed, and bills needed to be dug out of the mail, and he had the energy to deal with none of it.

"Brandon?"

He tensed even farther. For the past two weeks, he'd done everything in his power to be polite, friendly, and completely . . . bland to Lilly. No arguments. No being irritated. Because he was damn well going to prove to *somebody* that she was *not* his type and there was *no* abnormal amount of protesting when it came to that.

"Come in," he said, putting every last effort into it not being a growl. He'd rather face the pile of mail than Lilly in his office.

She was off her crutches, though she was still supposed to limit the time on her feet. She'd worn distracting nearly knee-high boots for the past three days because she said it was the only "cute" shoe she had that was comfortable and covered up the "ugly bandage." Which seemed to mean nothing but skintight pants and long sweaters or dresses, which he guessed were supposed to cover her ass in said overly tight pants, but all they did was draw his gaze to wherever the bright piece of fabric ended.

Which meant all too often he found himself staring directly at her ass and all but drooling like an idiot.

Luckily, as far as he could tell, she'd been too busy to notice. She'd been obsessively working on the little brochure for Solace Falls Trail, in between meetings with Patty at the Gracely Café and incessant emails with Corbin over the details of their cross-promotions.

It gave Brandon a headache just thinking about it. As did her perfume infiltrating all the air in *his* office as she stepped toward his desk.

"Here, I've got the brochure mock-up. I wanted to make sure I didn't miss anything important or put in any wrong information about the hike and the area before I order a bunch of copies."

"All right." He took the outstretched piece of paper, then forgot all about all his "polite" attempts when he saw the first page. "What the hell is this?" He stared at his own damn likeness under the SOLACE FALLS DAY HIKE header. "Where did you get that picture?" It had been taken at the overlook, but . . . how?

"I took it," she said, with an easy shrug. "The day we hiked it."

"When the . . . How . . . Why . . . ?" He had to resist crumpling the brochure mock-up into a little ball. She'd taken a picture of him on their hike and now she was . . . "No."

But her fake sweet smile never faltered. She merely inclined her head. "You said carte blanche, don't you recall?"

"That doesn't mean you can use a picture of me that you took without me knowing!"

"But you're the face of Mile High. Or one of them. Most of your customers aren't Gracely natives, so it won't hurt your business any to put your face on the front."

"This is a hike locals could do. Easily. And I'm trying to get them to like me, to see we're *supporting* Gracely, and want them to work *with* us. The last thing I need them thinking is that I'm some kind of . . . of . . ."

"Attractive, capable trail guide?"

He looked at her, hovering over his desk like some kind of evil fairy. Beautiful evil fairy. Who had just called him . . . attractive. Not that *that* mattered. He slid the brochure paper back to her, determined to keep his tone and expression flat and neutral. "This isn't about me."

"But, it doesn't hurt to use you. It's more eye-catching if there's a person in the picture, especially if it's trying to appeal to locals. They've grown up with this view. They know what mountain vistas look like." She tapped the picture of him. "But with you at the center—a person—it evokes an emotion, a feeling. A *longing*."

Okay, she really had to stop saying shit like *longing*.

"How's your ankle?" he asked in an attempt to change the subject. Because he was being polite. Calm. He would not be prodded into arguing with her.

She looked down at her foot. "Fine. I got one of those little pedometer things to keep track of how many steps I take each day so I don't overdo. I'm determined to be one hundred percent pain free by Monday. Why? Do you have my next challenge ready?"

He was going to do his level best to do zero more challenges with her. "You're going to have to be better than fine before you can take on anything else. And considering you injured yourself on our easiest thing—"

"Perhaps I needed a better guide." She said it so sweetly he couldn't swallow down his growled frustration.

"Take my face off the brochure."

"No."

He stood so he could have some height on her. "Yes."

"How about we take a vote?" She grabbed the brochure and turned toward the door. "I'll ask Sam and Will and Skeet and—"

"If you show that to anyone else, I'll . . ."

"You'll what?" she asked in that fake, saccharine PR way, turning on him yet again with one of those smiles.

He would do almost anything to wipe it off her face. *Almost.* "This is my company and—"

"*And* you gave me carte blanche to handle the brochure if I did the hike. The hike was completed. I have carte blanche, which includes your—"

"Completely unauthorized photograph."

"Yes. It includes that. And, if you'd take five seconds to *think* rather than *react,* you would see that, once again, I am more than a little right."

"You are the most giant pain in my ass, and I work with my twin brother."

"And you know I'm right," she repeated.

Damn it. "Have Will take some ridiculous selfie of himself. He'd make a better face of the company anyway."

"He refused to work with me on the Instagram account, which is a mistake, FYI. You're building not just a business, but a brand. And part of your brand, if you're smart, is young, buff lumbersexual types."

"Lumber-what?" He had to sit down. She was giving him a headache.

"Flannel. Beards. Belief in mountain healing. It's a thing. A thing you could exploit to your advantage if anyone in this godforsaken place would *listen to me.* Or keep your word. You gave me carte blanche. You said those words. Would you like me to define that phrase for you?"

"You're getting pricklier as time goes on." He wished he didn't admire that about her.

"And you've finally given up on being Mr. Nicey Nice Boss. Thank God, really. It was getting creepy."

He looked at her, leaning precariously on her good leg, and knew he had to find some inner strength to get back to being Mr. Nicey Nice Boss. Creepy or not, it was his best shot at being who he wanted to be. "You shouldn't be on your feet."

"Why are you being so difficult about this? Are you, like, in the witness protection program?"

"No."

She tapped his picture again. "Think about it. Think about what this looks like without a person. It's just a run-of-the-mill picture of a mountain and a valley and one of a million pretty waterfalls out here. It's something probably everyone has seen some version of. What makes this picture and this brochure stand out is that face. You can see the difference. You have to be able to see the difference."

He did. She was right. It seemed she was always right. But that didn't mean he wanted his face on the cover of any brochure. He didn't want his face anywhere. But there was no way of explaining that to her in a way that made any sense.

At least not without getting to the heart of things. Why did she always have to demand and poke until she got to the heart of things? He liked keeping all those motivations and knee-jerk reactions deep under the surface. Where he didn't have to examine them too closely.

But he was being Mr. Nice Boss. He was being Mr. Unaffected-by-Lilly's-Charms Boss. Which meant he had to give her the heart of things, without acting like that's what they were.

"Do you have time for a little field trip? No hiking," he amended quickly when she looked at her foot.

"Is it going to be worth my while?"

"If you want to understand all of this." She wouldn't understand all of it, not really. But maybe if she saw some of what made him tick, some of why this business was so much of his belief in what was right, they could reach some even ground where he could always maintain a polite boss-like demeanor. She could stop pushing him toward being the man he was afraid lurked beneath.

"Well, then, yes. Let's go. I'll go get my bag."

"I figured as much," he grumbled. He might know it was the best answer. Possibly the only answer. But that didn't mean he had to like it.

Lilly sat in the passenger side of Brandon's truck. Again. It was strange how often he had driven her places in the past month of working for Mile High. Strange that it had been a month. It seemed like shorter and longer at the same time.

In truth, she could've driven herself, but she hadn't felt like fighting with him when he seemed to be giving her an inch—and he would fight her if she argued for the right to drive. There was just something about the way he didn't quite meet her gaze, something about the way he'd been acting the past few weeks after the unfortunate crutch-grabbing incident, that made this feel like it was important.

Getting to understand Brandon better was probably not the best way to go when she all too often found herself fantasizing about the way his chest had felt under her palms that morning, how his muscles had looked as they'd moved and rippled in a stretch.

How he infused every part of his business with this thing he believed in so deeply. She admired that about him, and, yes, that was dangerous.

He was dangerous. But she had to live with it. Maybe if she understood, she could find some way to resist it.

It took her a while to realize where he was taking her. They'd driven down through town and back up again. This road wasn't nearly as curving or windy as the road up to Mile High. This one was straight, and there were guardrails that looked like they might have been in good shape not too terribly long ago.

They pulled closer and closer to the cluster of buildings Brandon had been looking at that day they'd met with Corbin. Yes, she was sure these were the buildings he'd stared at so intently from Mile High's parking lot.

Something granite and a little mean in his expression then and now. If she chose to look away, like any smart woman with an ounce of self-preservation, she might have missed the hint of something else underneath. Something soft, maybe a little vulnerable.

*Crap.*

He shoved the truck into PARK and reached across the space between them to the glove compartment in front of her. Without sparing her a glance, or bothering to explain himself, he pulled out a set of keys. She had to chew on the inside of her mouth to keep from asking a dozen questions. Okay, *hundreds* of questions.

"You're okay to walk?"

"I've got three thousand steps left for today."

He gave a curt nod and then climbed out of the truck. She knew that he would come around to her side to help her out, so she made sure she had the door open and she was putting her feet onto the ground before he got there. Her ankle *was* better, and even though it irritated her with every fiber of her being not to push, she was being careful with it.

He gave her one of those disapproving looks, but he didn't say anything. He simply started walking toward the main building. Slow, steady strides, looking like the weight of the world had situated itself on his shoulders.

So, Lilly followed him. Though everything looked deserted and in some disrepair, it was easy to see that it had once been a pretty impressive place.

"Welcome to Evans Mining Corporation," Brandon said, gesturing to the whole of the buildings. "Established 1858. Crumbled out of existence over the past ten years." He shoved a key in the lock and pushed open the door.

Lilly wasn't quite sure what to expect, or what he was trying to show her. She followed, though, because she wanted to know—against all her better reasoning.

"We were only in the process of moving the offices to Denver when . . . well, the mines were closed, officially. The business imploded. A lot of the valuables here were sold off, but in the end, these deserted offices became the last of our worries."

He explained it in the way a bored history teacher might discuss the facts of the Civil War for the hundredth time in his career. A certain practiced distance from the reality of it.

But did he feel that underneath?

She followed him down the grungy hallway that had probably been a pristine white once. It was weird to see things simply . . . abandoned. There were a few random chairs, tables, and magazines, and even framed pictures on the wall.

As they walked, Lilly noticed a pattern to the contents

of the frames. In just about every picture—whether it was about mining safety or the company itself—the same man was featured. A man who looked an awful lot like Brandon himself.

She didn't quite understand why this meant Brandon would want to avoid his face on things, but she knew this was what he'd meant to show her. He had said that his father wasn't a very good man, so maybe this was all about not being that man.

"He plastered his face over everything. His name—our name. He tried to make it *his* instead of this town's." Brandon stopped next to one of the posters that looked particularly like him. She'd never seen him in a suit with that businessman smile, but the likeness was there. It was obvious.

"It never should have been like that. It never should have become more about what he could make, and what he could be, than about the realities of mining, the changing face of environmentalism. The health of this town and the people who worked for him in good faith." Brandon shook his head. "I don't want my business to be like his. I won't let us fall into the same trap. I'm not the *face* of Mile High, Lilly—neither should Will or Sam be. Mile High is about the *mountains*. It's about the experience. It isn't about me."

"It isn't the same," she said, surprised to find her voice small. Even knowing he was ignoring specifics and details about what exactly had derailed Evans Mining, she saw—just like on that first day—that this meant something to him. That it was important.

"People tell me that, Lilly. And I appreciate it, I do, but there's a slippery slope. And I refuse to slip."

She understood that well—too well, maybe. But that didn't mean she was beat. "What about a dog?"

He turned his gaze from the man in the poster to her, some of that fierceness chased away by sheer bafflement.

"What *about* a dog?"

"I'll Photoshop a dog in your place. On the brochure. It might not have the same effect, but it's still better than just the waterfall."

He let out an odd breath, something that might have been a laugh deep, deep down. He took one last look at the poster. His father. This man he was trying so hard not to be.

It shouldn't soften her. It *wouldn't*. The course of her life had been run by not-good men, and she couldn't possibly trust another. Even if he didn't want to be *like* his father, it didn't mean . . .

Those hazel eyes met hers, all that intensity and fierceness there and directed right at her. She swallowed, surprised at the little trickle of fear.

"I won't let anything turn me into him. Not anything."

He said it like a threat, and—even though she hadn't done anything wrong, anything worthy of being *threatened*—she felt each word like one. A threat. A promise. Something *against* her.

"Who you turn into isn't any of my business," she managed to return.

He gave a little nod toward the door. "So, you'll take my likeness off the brochure."

"Sure," she said easily, forcing herself to shrug and move as though she weren't . . . affected by any of this. Affected by him. "Consider yourself replaced."

This time, when he laughed, it was an actual laugh, but it was a dark thing. A little bit scary.

But she would not be scared or intimidated, because now she understood something. A little something, but a something nonetheless, and if she worked hard—

really, really hard—maybe it would serve as a reminder that Brandon Evans was far more complicated than he appeared, and just as dangerous as she'd always expected.

*Uh-huh. Sure, it will.*

# Chapter Ten

"Here is my doctor's note. Now, what brochure excursion do I get next?"

Brandon stared over at Lilly, constant thorn in his side, as he aired out the tent from last night's overnight excursion. It had been good to get away for a day, to spend the night under the stars. He'd woken up feeling more relaxed than he had in a while, and packing up the campsite and getting everyone back hadn't dulled that sense of satisfaction.

Until Lilly popped out of the office. Less like a thorn and more like a splinter, really. Small and sharp and digging harder and deeper until he wanted to cut his whole damn finger off. And she was holding out a piece of paper. She had actually gotten a doctor's note.

"If you didn't notice, I'm kind of busy," he muttered, gesturing toward the tent. He really didn't want to think about taking her on another excursion. More one-on-one time. Not in his plans any time soon. Not after the trip to the old offices last week.

"That doesn't mean we can't discuss my next excursion. I'll want to be more prepared this time. Those brochures need work, and I am ready to do the work."

"Lilly." He looked at the tent he'd stretched out over the chairs. He was sorely tempted to tell her to forget the challenges, and just work on the brochures without doing the excursions. But he was a little afraid that made him a coward.

Besides, he wanted her to understand what she was writing about. Maybe she couldn't do all of the excursions, but the ones she could do—it would be a benefit for her to understand them. Even someone as un-outdoorsy as Lilly could see the impact of nature, could feel that change. He'd seen that in her on the day they'd had their hike.

"If you're that dead set on it, I think you could probably handle the Ice Lake canoe trip. I'll check my schedule to see where I can fit you in." Maybe in a few weeks, when he felt a little less prone to spilling his guts around her.

"Great!" She stood there, as if expecting him to jump right into checking his schedule.

"When I'm done with this," he added, pointing at the tent and all the paraphernalia that went with it.

He made the mistake of looking at her then. Her pink-painted mouth spread into a wide grin, and he couldn't help but grin back. "Do you really have a doctor's note?" he asked, unable to help himself.

"Oh, yes." She took two dangerous steps toward him, holding out the piece of paper.

He took it because he had no other choice. The note was on a piece of Gracely Clinic's stationery, written in careful print: *Please consider Lilly Preston completely healed and ready to take on whatever duties her job requires.* Dr. Frost's scrawled signature was underneath.

"Is this for real?"

"What? You think I'm lying?"

"I'm not sure what to think." Why on earth had she gotten an actual doctor's note? Why did he *care*?

"Well, I certainly didn't trust you to take my word for it. So I thought the safest option would be to get Dr. Frost to write me a little note."

"You certainly do cover all your bases."

"And I pride myself on that." She remained there, too close, watching him work over the tent.

He tried to ignore her presence. Maybe she was curious how they packed up the equipment. Maybe she was working up to saying something. It didn't matter to him. She would not be a distraction.

He grabbed the bag of stakes and somehow upended the whole thing. "Damn it," he muttered. When had he turned into such a clumsy dumb ass? He'd resisted plenty of women. What was different about Lilly Preston?

*Not a damn thing.*

"So . . ." she said, handing him a stake that had rolled over to her feet.

He took it with a grunt. "So?"

She fidgeted, that rare sign of uncertainty. "I have a meeting with Patty Waters. The owner of—"

"I'm well aware what Patty is the owner of." *Get it together, Evans. You're not barking at her anymore, remember?*

"Right. Well." She clasped her hands together. "Will is the only one who's available for the time Patty wanted to meet, and I just wanted to make sure . . ."

"He didn't do any deflowering of her offspring?" Lilly grimaced and Brandon couldn't help but laugh. "What offends you—the thought of Patty having offspring or Will deflowering them?"

"I think it's the actual word 'deflowering,' quite honestly. I just wanted to make sure there was no . . . personal history that I should be aware of."

"Why don't you ask him?" Brandon might know most of Will's exploits, but he doubted he knew everything that had happened when they'd been teens. He certainly didn't know much of what happened those years in Boulder and after.

Brandon's life had always been business—high school, college, and beyond. Every relationship or *exploit* he'd had as a teen had been with an eye toward making sure it would suit the history and reputation of Evans Mining.

What a joke *that* had been.

"*You* were the one who warned me about Corbin's history with him," Lilly said. "I'm not sure it's appropriate for me to go ask Will for a list of people who might hate him due to any . . . deflowering."

Brandon glanced at Lilly, and though he didn't want to be amused, she could be so utterly obvious sometimes. "You thought about it though, didn't you?"

She scowled at him. "Maybe I did. And, I wouldn't be opposed if you all gave me a list of anyone you should be avoiding. It *would* make my job easier. I think you underestimate how much of my job is people and relationships."

He bundled up the tent stakes and shoved them into their bag. "You want a list of all the women in town we've slept with?"

She rolled her eyes, but her cheeks turned a little pink. "It's not about who you've slept with. It's about who you all have pissed off on a personal level. And if your slept-with list is the same as your pissed-off list, well, you need to work on yourself, Brandon."

"Ha. You might want to talk to Will about all *that*. No one in town hates me for . . . that." Wait. Why were they talking about . . . ? How . . . ?

Lilly seemed to sense they'd walked into weird territory as well. She pushed her hair behind her ears and looked away. "Well. Anyway. Will's okay to meet with Patty with me?"

"When did she want to meet?"

"Tomorrow morning. Ten."

"Sam's out for the next three days on the backcountry pack hike, and I have . . . the businessman's fishing trip?"

Lilly nodded in confirmation.

"I'll get Will to switch and I'll go."

"So Will *did* deflower someone she's related to?"

Brandon laughed, checking the tent to make sure it was dry before starting the folding process. "No, Patty and Will get along well enough as far as I know, but I'd like to go."

"Because you don't trust Will? Or me?"

He stopped his folding and frowned at her. "It has nothing to do with trust."

"Oh, right, you're a control freak."

His frown morphed into a scowl. "Will's a charming guy. Without even trying. I don't want . . . It's great for customer service and customer relations, but I don't want that being a part of how we get business partnerships."

Lilly picked up the other end of the tent, stepping toward him in an effort to help him fold. "Does he know that?" she asked gently.

He met Lilly in the middle, their fingers brushing as she passed her material off to him. It made no sense that even that simple touch could feel like electricity— could be completely un-simple. No one had ever . . . felt so complicated.

Which was a good reminder she was to be avoided as much as possible.

Her blue eyes studied him carefully, and it was odd to

want to explain to her. All the ways he was careful with Will, the ways he maneuvered him without explaining.

But it wasn't any of her business. "I'll trade the excursion with him. Plan on me going to meet with Patty." He wasn't proud of the icy, dismissive note in his voice, but . . .

She let out a gusty sigh. "Remember a few weeks ago when I said you all needed to work on communication?"

"How could I forget one of your many tirades against our ways of doing business?"

She narrowed her eyes at him, apparently undeterred by the acid in his tone. "Believe it or not, silence can be as bad as a lie, Brandon. Be careful with that."

Then she turned and walked away, her words echoing in his head loud enough he forgot to stop himself from watching her go.

Lilly decided to work from home that next morning and meet Brandon at the café for their meeting with Patty. She hadn't been in the mood to share another ride with him.

Something about yesterday morning's conversation had rubbed her the wrong way. As though she'd had one of those little plastic tags stuck in her shirt all day and couldn't find the source.

It was none of her business how Brandon handled Will. As much as she'd claimed her input was about their communication as business partners, she knew herself well enough to know that she cared more about them as people than as businessmen.

It hit close to home, unfortunately. That way of handling things that didn't give anyone around them the idea they were being handled. Making sure you were needed, that you were in charge.

Yes, she knew that well, and she didn't like seeing it in someone else. Didn't like seeing it in a negative light when she did it all the time.

So, she'd made it about something else. She shouldn't have said anything, that she knew. But she was a woman who firmly believed that silence was as bad as a lie, because she had lived with both. Her father had been the liar, and her mother had been the one who had kept every truth from them.

On a sigh, she parallel parked her car in front of Gracely Café.

Just because she'd lived with it didn't mean that it was her business. It certainly didn't mean Will had to be affected by it in the same way. Maybe he agreed with Brandon's estimation. Maybe it really didn't matter.

It was none of her business, and she really needed to let well enough alone. She certainly needed to stop poking into Brandon's psyche. She was all . . . connected enough, quite frankly.

Brandon was already there, of course. She'd had no doubt that he would not just be on time, but that he'd be early. That was Brandon.

His truck was parked a few spaces ahead of her, but he stood next to a streetlight post. He was waiting for her, and there was no reason that she should feel . . . anything. There should be no rapid heartbeat; there should be no fluttery feeling in her stomach. Everything should be as bland and disconnected as things with any other coworker had ever been.

But he wasn't. And she was a moron.

"Good morning," Brandon offered.

"Good morning," she returned, doing her best not to take in what he was wearing, or how good he looked in the morning light. Yup, she was an idiot, but at least she *knew* it so she could manage it. "Are you ready?"

"As I'll ever be." He glanced up at the sign for GRACELY CAFÉ. It looked old, like it could have been around since before he was born. The letters were faded, and whatever design was next to the text was indistinguishable.

He didn't linger though. After that brief glance at the sign, he moved to the door and opened it and gestured her inside.

Lilly stepped inside the café, and looked around for Patty. It wasn't a surprise to see her waiting tables herself. Her staff was bare-bones at best, and the crowd was nearly nonexistent. It wasn't a busy time of day, but that didn't mean business was good during meal times either.

"Lilly! So glad you're here. I hope that business with your sister won't interfere with our meeting. Sit. Sit." She ushered Lilly to a table, and Brandon followed despite Patty acting like she didn't even see him.

But Lilly couldn't think about Brandon for a moment. "What happened with Cora?"

"She . . . she didn't tell you?" Patty squeezed her eyes shut and wrung her hands together. "Oh, now I feel even worse for having spilled the beans."

"What happened with Cora?" Lilly repeated holding on to the back of a well-worn chair. It couldn't be a dire situation or Patty would be acting more upset, but that didn't mean it wasn't important.

"Well, I . . . It's just that I couldn't afford her anymore. When she needed so much time off. I can barely afford to pay the staff I have who come in all the time." With that statement, she finally acknowledged Brandon's existence. With a glare. As though everything were his fault directly.

But Lilly couldn't concern herself with that right now. "You fired her?"

"Lilly, she's a sweet girl but . . ." Patty shook her head. "She's a downright terrible waitress, an even worse busser. The only thing that I could trust her with was cashiering, and I just don't have enough money or customers to keep someone on who's only good for one thing."

Lilly swallowed, completely blindsided by the whole situation. "When did this happen?"

Patty shook her head sadly. "Last week, honey."

Lilly had to close her eyes and breathe. She couldn't believe Cora hadn't told her. But this was not what she was here for. She had to focus on the fact that she was here as the PR consultant for Mile High Adventures, not as the sister who knew nothing apparently.

"Thank you for telling me, Patty," Lilly managed to say without giving away too much of her emotional state. "I'm sure you did what you had to do. Now, let's talk about something that might be able to help you with that lack-of-customers problem."

"Oh, I do like you, Lilly. What can I get you? Tea? Coffee?"

"I'll take some coffee." Lilly looked back at Brandon to make sure he ordered the same easy thing she did.

But he shook his head before nodding toward Patty—who had already left for the kitchen. "She's not asking me."

Lilly gaped a little at Patty's disappearing back. Though she was still out of sorts from the Cora bombshell, she couldn't believe that this town really treated the Evans brothers like this. It was insanity.

Which meant she had her work cut out for her. She couldn't be thinking about Cora or Micah or even the fact that Cora had kept something from her. She had to be thinking about Mile High Adventures and winning over Patty.

She lowered herself into the chair.

Patty returned from the kitchen with a large coffeepot. With a small smile, Lilly flipped the overturned mug on the table so that Patty could pour the coffee. Brandon didn't flip his mug, and Lilly didn't know if that was just because he knew Patty wouldn't pour him coffee, or because he didn't want any.

It didn't matter. Not really. She was here to do business, not worry about Brandon's hurt feelings, or Cora's apparent firing that no one had deemed necessary to tell her about until now.

"Well, Patty, I want to thank you for meeting with us today," Lilly said with so much forced cheer in her tone she had to dial it down a notch. "I know that it seems on the surface as though the Gracely Café can't benefit from Mile High Adventures, but on the occasion that you do have an out-of-towner come to your establishment, what is it that you notice about them?"

Patty furrowed her brow and crossed her arms over her chest as she sat across from Lilly, still pretending Brandon wasn't there. "Well, most times it's old folks. Every once in a while, it's them trendy types."

"The exact kind of trendy type that makes up the majority of Mile High's clientele. They're the kind of people who like non-chain restaurants. They're the kind of people who want something kind of old-fashioned and kitsch. The café is exactly the kind of thing they like discovering, but they can't discover it if they're not *in* Gracely. We can send people to Main Street, or they can bypass it altogether and just come up to Mile High. We'd prefer to work with Gracely. We can send people to the café. We can encourage customers to visit the heart of the town. Incentives make that all the more appealing. We're in our busy season. Do you know we've had twenty-four out-of-town people in our office just this week?"

"When you say incentives, you mean discounts." The way Patty said discounts was the way some people said rat infestation.

"Yes, discounts or coupons. Although the type of discount that you want to offer is completely up to you. The discount is to bring people to you—it doesn't matter what it's offering."

Patty changed her piercing, unmoved gaze to Brandon. Her eye twitched as she did it. "And what do you have to say about all this?"

"I agree with everything Lilly's said."

"First time I heard something intelligent come out of your mouth in the past five years," Patty muttered.

Brandon didn't bite or flinch. He didn't really react at all. His lips may have actually curved upward just the tiniest bit.

"So, you just want me to give you coupons? You'll hand them to those twenty-some people that are coming out to you when they take one of your hikes?"

"To start." Lilly pulled her folder out of her bag so that she could show Patty what she'd done for Gracely Lodge.

"I don't want to see your paperwork, girl. I want that boy to tell me—after everything his father and that company did to me and this town—why I should agree to do anything for him."

"Patty, I—"

"I want him to talk. Only him." Patty waved a thick finger in the air between her and Brandon. "What do you have to say for yourself?"

Lilly knew she couldn't say anything, and she was surprised at how much she wanted to step in the middle of this. She wanted to tell Brandon he didn't have to explain. Why would anyone blame him? It wasn't fair, and she really hated sitting here pretending like it was.

But she didn't have a choice, because this was what Patty wanted.

Brandon casually linked his fingers together on the table in front of him. He made eye contact with Patty, not one ounce of irritation or frustration showing in his expression or in his voice when he spoke. "Patty, I love this town. I grew up here. I ate breakfast in this very café as a kid with my grandmother, who was your friend, if you recall."

"Oh, I recall," Patty said bitterly.

"I believed that I was a part of the fabric of Gracely— I still believe that, Patty. The Evans name gave me something, some duty to the land and the people here. I can't speak for my father. Not only is he dead, but he was a liar and a cheat. And once I found that out, I never stood by him."

"And we all paid."

Brandon took a deep breath and Lilly took it with him, because the vehemence in Patty's tone, in her expression, in her demeanor . . . it was vicious. Brandon and Will had been right when they'd told her that it didn't have to make sense—people *felt* betrayed, and that didn't have to be fair to be true.

But Brandon never broke eye contact with Patty. "You're right. You all paid. I can't change that. If I had known what would happen, would I have done things differently? Probably. But it could have killed this town either way. If I had let things go, the things that were happening in that mine could have killed everyone in this town—not just their businesses, Patty. Killed them."

Patty showed absolutely zero signs of softening even as Lilly's heart twisted painfully.

"So you say."

"So I say. You don't have to believe me. I don't expect anyone in this town to believe me after what my father did. The lies he told. The Evans name doesn't mean much here anymore, and I get that. I do. But I can't change my last name, and what's more—I won't. Because I have learned something from the terrible example of the people that ran the company into the ground. I said it before and I'll say it until I die. I love this town. It is a part of me. You don't have to agree to work with me. Corbin Finley did, though. And you know how much he hates me and my brother especially. But he cared about his business succeeding and being able to stay in this town more than he cared about some vendetta against the Evans."

"You think I give a shit about what Corbin Finley does?"

Then, for the first time, Brandon smiled. A real smile. A knowing smile. "Yes, Patty. I think you care very deeply what Corbin Finley thinks."

And Patty, large, intimidating, no-nonsense Patty, blushed all the way to the grey roots of her dark hair.

Lilly had to close her eyes because embarrassing Patty was so not the way to go here. How could he say something that would make her blush? When he'd been so moving and honest? Striking out at her was the absolute wrong tactic and—

"Well, boy, you surprise me." Patty sounded . . . amused? "Got balls, you do. Your daddy didn't have a one when push came to shove."

"I'm not him. I may not be the man you want to do business with, but I am not my father."

Patty studied him, nothing about her suspicious expression changing. "All right, Lilly. Show me your folder. We'll go from there."

Lilly stared open-mouthed for a few seconds before her brain engaged. "Of course!" She pulled the folder out, glancing at Brandon.

His smile was self-satisfied, but when he caught her gaze, he merely shrugged.

The man was a miracle worker.

# Chapter Eleven

Lilly and Patty pored over the paperwork Lilly had brought. Examples of the coupons Corbin had agreed to, potential mock-ups for the flyers they could post on the Mile High bulletin board.

Brandon didn't have to add much after his little speech, though he was a little overly pleased his gamble to mention Patty and Corbin's secret affair had worked in his favor. The whole discussion had been more than he'd wanted to give Patty, but remembering that she had been friends with his grandmother once upon a time softened him. She'd slipped him extra whipped cream on his pancakes and made him feel special when he was a kid. He'd forgotten all about that until he'd sat across from her and *felt* her anger, her hurt.

He was starting to realize that making inroads in Gracely was always going to mean giving more than he wanted to. Which meant he had to come to accept it rather than fight it. That was going to take a little bit of time. But it was for Mile High. He'd decided long ago he would do whatever it took. He just hadn't expected leaving his heart on the table to be one of those things, but such was life.

Patty got up from the table. "I'll have Hayley come wait on you two. Lunch is on me. . . . 'long as you choose something from the value menu."

"Thank you, Patty. That's very kind," Lilly said, in that voice that always amazed Brandon. She made everything sound so damn *genuine.*

"Yeah, yeah," Patty muttered. She disappeared into the back.

"Just for the record, I am paying for lunch. The last thing I need around town is Patty telling everyone that I cheated her out of money."

"It's a nice gesture."

"An incredibly nice gesture. And it will be an even nicer gesture when I pay her for the meal that we eat."

Lilly kind of shook her head, but in the end she didn't have much of an argument for him. A young woman with an apron and a pad of paper came over to their table. "What can I get you guys?" she asked cheerfully.

Lilly ordered some froofy salad and he debated between heeding Patty's order to choose off the value menu and getting what he really wanted.

"I'll have . . ." He glanced up at the waitress to find her staring at him like she'd seen a ghost. Or a monster. "Are you all right?"

She nodded overemphatically and he tried to place her face. He didn't think he knew her, but she was obviously younger than him. Maybe he'd known her as a kid.

"What did you want?" she asked, her eyes immediately going to her little pad of paper.

"Um, just a burger. Thanks."

"Be right back," she said, hurrying off before he could order something to drink.

"What was that about?" Lilly asked.

"I have no idea."

"I tell you what, I've never gone to a meal with some-body who produced such a . . . *response* from people." She lifted her refilled mug of coffee to her lips and sipped. "It's like dating a celebrity." Her cheeks imme-diately flushed red and she put the mug down with a click. "I didn't mean that. . . ."

"No, I know. I know."

"Good. Because that would be . . . dumb." She laughed awkwardly and fiddled with her silverware, looking toward the door to the kitchen as if willing her food to come out.

"Right. Dumb," he echoed.

Silence settled over them. Really awkward silence. But how did he fix that? How did he think of something new to talk about when all he could do was wonder what exactly she meant by "dumb."

The waitress came out with their food, studiously avoiding any eye contact with him. She scurried away again before he could ask for water or figure out why she was so jumpy around him.

Honestly? With the stories circulating around town about how he was the reason for Gracely's ruin, he shouldn't be surprised if some of the younger genera-tion who were left looked at him as though he were the big bad wolf.

He turned his attention back to Lilly. She looked tense and miserable, and that wasn't their . . . usual. The awkward-tense thing. Angry tense, sure. Awkward was new. . . .

He was a total bastard, because he kind of enjoyed her discomfort. She was always so in control, such a facade of cheerfulness. It was comforting to see her rattled.

He shouldn't rattle her further, but . . . "So . . . what exactly would be dumb about it?"

She froze with a bite of salad halfway to her mouth. Slowly, very slowly, she put the fork back in the bowl. He had to work really hard not to smile.

She cleared her throat. "About . . . being on a date?"

He nodded, working on his best innocently interested expression.

"We . . . work together. You're my . . . boss."

"Right." He nodded, lifting his hamburger. "But that's it, right?"

She cocked her head, and either she finally grasped that he was teasing—at least partially teasing—or she was prepared to tease him back regardless.

"Are you asking me if I'd be interested in you if it weren't a potential moral misstep?"

"No," he said gravely.

"Okay, good." She got the lettuce on her fork again, and he waited for her to bring it to her mouth. Of course, he got a little sidetracked by her mouth, the way it managed to keep whatever bright color she painted on it most days.

"But, you know, would you be?" he asked, falling a little past the teasing he'd intended. A little.

She let out a shocked laugh.

"I *am* joking," he managed to say, sounding very . . . certain. Far more certain than he was.

"Good, because I'm not answering that question," she replied primly, the bite of salad finally making its way into her mouth.

"Sam and Will think you're my type." The words tumbled out of their own accord, probably because she'd licked a little drop of dressing off the corner of her mouth and suddenly he'd had no idea what they were talking about.

"Have you three been spending a lot of time talking about me?"

"*They* have."

"Let me guess, while you grunt and stomp around?"

"Something like that." He had a really bad feeling they were flirting, and he should stop that.

But what could be the harm? They were in a public place. What was a little innocent flirting? *Slippery slope.* Maybe, but much like the camping trip, and the poker night . . . he hadn't been having much fun lately, and didn't he deserve some?

They ate, and maybe they even flirted a little. When the jumpy waitress came by with the check, he tried to see her face better, but she darted away.

"You really don't know her?" Lilly asked, her gaze following the young girl.

"I don't think so. It's possible she's just the jumpy sort and heard all sorts of monstrous stories about me."

He slid the appropriate amount of money, plus a generous tip, into the little envelope. When he glanced up, Lilly was studying him with drawn-together eyebrows.

"I just don't understand why *you* took the fall for *everything.*"

He didn't *want* to tell her, but someday someone would. Someone would explain his every misdeed to her from some other point of view, and he realized he didn't want that. He wanted her to hear his side first.

"My father was doing all sorts of shady things to keep the EPA from finding out about some of the illegal practices he was using. I found out when I was being groomed to take over, and I told him if he didn't fix it, I would turn him in."

Lilly's jaw dropped. "That . . . couldn't have been an easy decision."

Funny, very few people ever thought of it that way.

From *his* position. They thought of it from theirs. He supposed Lilly could simply because it affected her in no way whatsoever, whereas everyone he knew and everyone here was tied to it in some way.

"No, it wasn't. And, in the end, Dad outmaneuvered me. He kept his illegal practices up, and was in the process of moving our headquarters to Denver, making sure anyone who asked was told *I* wanted the move. That didn't last for long, because the EPA was figuring out Dad's pattern, and the heart attack happened soon after."

"So, how can they still blame you?"

"Because if I'd kept my mouth shut, they'd still have their mine and their jobs, Lilly. Their businesses died. They had to leave or get used to a much harder way of life. Me? I still had a trust fund, a fancy degree, connections everywhere. I didn't suffer at all."

"I wouldn't say you didn't suffer at *all.*"

He smiled, because even though he didn't agree, it was nice someone thought it. Nice that *she* in particular thought it. "Funny, when people are struggling to make ends meet, when they've lost everything they loved, they don't much care for the poor rich kid's emotional discomfort."

"You lost, too."

"And then I gained."

"It's still not fair they blame *you.*"

"Fair? No. But . . . it's understandable. It doesn't bother me. I mean, it does, but I get it, too, you know? Anyway. Let's head out, huh?"

Lilly nodded and stood, slipping her bag onto her shoulder. They walked through the nearly empty dining room, but a woman's small voice stopped him.

"Mr. Evans?"

The waitress stood by the table, holding the money he'd left for payment and tip. There *was* something eerily familiar about her, but he couldn't for the life of him place it. Not in any context. He took a step back toward her. "Do I know you?"

"No." She said it with complete certainty; he didn't know how it could be a lie. But she just stood there and stared at him.

"Hayley! Get back here!" The waitress glanced back to Patty's booming voice. She gave him once last glance he couldn't read. "Thanks for the tip." She shoved the money in her pocket and hurried back to the kitchen.

Brandon wasn't sure how long he stood there trying to work it all out.

"You okay?" Lilly asked.

"Something about her was familiar," he said, still staring at where she'd disappeared. But no matter how he worked it, he couldn't put his finger on it. "Growing-up-in-a-small-town curse, I guess." He wanted to believe that's all it was.

But he couldn't quite get himself there.


Brandon walked with Lilly toward her car, even though his truck was a few steps in the other direction. He looked confused and maybe a little shell-shocked. She couldn't blame him. A lot had happened in there.

Which reminded her, she needed to figure out how to bring up to Cora that she knew she'd lost her job at the café.

But first, she had to work. And she had . . . Brandon. *Be careful where you walk. You have three mouths to feed.* She stopped her walking and turned to face Brandon.

She had the overwhelming urge to touch him—just something simple and gentle. An arm brush, a hand pat.

She kept her arms firmly at her sides. "Are you sure you're all right?"

"She said she didn't know me."

"She seemed very certain she didn't," Lilly reassured. "I could ask Patty for her full name for you."

"No. It's fine." He shook his head. "I'm sure I'm just Gracely's equivalent of the boogeyman. I'll see you back up at the office?"

She managed a smile and a nod. She was tempted to stop in at home and see if Cora was there and if she had an explanation for not having a job anymore, but a phone call would have to suffice.

She got into her car and dialed Cora's number before pulling out onto Main Street.

"Hey, Lilly," Cora answered, music blaring somewhere behind her. "What's up?"

"You gotta turn down the music. I can barely hear you."

"Sorry!" The music went down and Cora breathed heavily into the receiver. "I was doing this dance workout thing I found online. So fun. What's up?"

So fun. Cora was home having fun dance workouts and Lilly was working her ass off. *Not fair. You know that's not fair.* "Cora, why didn't you tell me?"

"Tell you what?"

"I had a meeting at Gracely Café today. Patty happened to mention she let you go." Which was a much nicer way of saying fired. Because Cora could act like the café just didn't need her, but based on the way Patty talked . . . yeah, Lilly knew Cora hadn't made herself a very important cog in the machine. "You should have told me."

"I didn't want to disappoint you." Cora blew a breath into the receiver. "I know you wanted me to have something, but there's just . . . nothing I'm any good at. Can't we talk about this later? I want to finish—"

"Please. Just . . . please tell me you looked at those classes." She gripped the steering wheel, her brain a constant wheel of *please, please, please* in Cora's silence.

"It's all pointless, Lil. And your job is keeping us afloat. You said I didn't have to worry."

That old familiar mix of anger and guilt wound through her chest. Anger because Cora expected her to handle it, to take care of everything. To be the financial provider, the bad guy to Micah when he needed punishment.

Guilt because Lilly had been the one to raise her, and she hadn't done a particularly great job at it. She *had* told Cora not to worry, but she hadn't meant it quite . . . like this.

Lilly had to remind herself that Cora was still healing from everything Stephen had put her through. It hadn't just been the physical abuse; it had been verbal as well, along with a lovely dose of emotional manipulation. Lilly had to be patient and understanding—besides, what would she do if Cora didn't need her?

She just didn't know why her sister couldn't do something *productive* while Lilly was being oh so patient and understanding. "You're good at a lot of things. You'll never find something if you don't try."

"Can we talk about this later? Please? Don't you have work to do?"

Lilly stared at the winding road ahead of her, Brandon's truck easily chugging up the rugged curves. She did have work to do. She'd always had work to do and a sister to care for, and now a nephew.

*Both of whom have been through a hell of a lot worse things than you have.* Right. Maybe they should talk about it later when she had more reserves to listen to that sensible voice inside her head. The last thing she wanted to do was lose her temper and yell. That would be truly wrong and unfair to Cora.

"Yeah, we'll talk later. But can you please at least—"

"Okay, bye!" Cora said, hanging up before Lilly could harangue her about the classes one more time.

Lilly tried to breathe through the frustration, the fear, the guilt. All the emotions that swirled inside of her when she had to face the fact she had failed Cora, time and time again. She hadn't ever been able to give her little sister what she needed.

A tear spilled over and she tossed her cell into her passenger seat, trying to swallow down any sobs. If she could just get through this moment without crying, she could cry . . .

When? When Cora and Micah were around? When she had to feed them and make sure Micah did his homework and went to bed instead of playing video games all night? While she was at work with all those *men* around with their grunts and their grand plans to win over the town?

There was *no* time to cry, and that realization of course only made the tears fall faster. Because she was always working so hard for everyone else, and the minute she thought things were finally on the right track, that maybe—just maybe—she could focus on herself for a bit . . .

"Not fair," she said aloud into the quiet of the car as she pulled into the Mile High lot. Cora and Micah had been through *hell*, and Mom had always worked so hard to provide for them . . . at least until Cora had gotten herself in trouble.

Lilly pushed her car into PARK and pressed her forehead to the steering wheel, taking a deep, steadying breath. She'd made it this far. Cora and Micah were alive and safe, and she'd gotten them to this place where Cora didn't have to worry—not about money or Stephen or anything.

So, she was fine. It was fine. Hell, what would her life be without Cora and Micah in it? No need for tears or feeling like she was being buried alive. Everything was *great*.

She swallowed at the lump in her throat and collected her bag. She could see Brandon getting out of his truck so she didn't have time to reapply her makeup. She did her best to wipe away any traces of tears with her fingers before stepping out.

She closed the door and then just stood there. She felt empty and frail, and she didn't know how to *move* feeling like that.

"Are you okay?" Brandon's voice asked from somewhere on the other side of her car.

"Yeah. I just . . . talked to my sister." She blew out a breath.

"Oh, about the job thing?"

His voice was closer now so Lilly nodded, trying to hide the fact she'd been crying. She didn't know if she'd succeeded, but he at least acted as though he didn't notice.

"Well, this has been a shit morning, huh?" he asked, shoving his hands into his pockets.

"Oh, boy, has it," she muttered, trying to surreptitiously wipe under her eyes in case her mascara had run.

He looked up at the mountain peak behind the

office building. "I'll see if we can't do that canoe trip tomorrow. Sound good?"

She nodded wordlessly. He was trying to . . . comfort her. Himself too, she thought, but he was extending that courtesy to her. She should reject that.

"Tomorrow sounds good." She'd worry about being stronger another day.

# Chapter Twelve

Brandon double-checked the contents of his pack for the canoe trip as Will looked on. He didn't know why his brother was looming over him this morning, but he wasn't about to ask.

"You know, I could take Lilly out on some of these. It doesn't have to be all you."

"I'm not sure we'll be back before your rock climbing thing, and Lilly wanted to do it in the morning." Brandon replied, zipping up the bag one final time. They'd have to take a little hike down to the lake and the dock, get the canoe. He had most of the supplies they'd need, and snacks. "It's fine."

"Oh, I bet it is *just* fine." Will drew out the word just as any high school girl might.

Brandon wanted to respond—preferably with a middle finger, but in the end all it would do was fan the flames of this particular fire. So, he slipped the bag onto his shoulder and moved to set it by the front door.

"We can always amend our policy on inter-office—"

"Do you know a young woman by the name of Hayley who works at the Gracely Café?" He'd been back and forth on bringing it up to Will for the past day, and if it got the heat off Lilly talk, well . . . so be it.

"No. Is that supposed to be a change in subject to make me think you *don't* have a thing for Lilly? It's not going to work. Waitresses named Hayley are not your type."

"No, she's too young. If I had to guess, I'd say she's barely twenty. She waited on Lilly and me at the café yesterday. And acted very, very weird."

Will scraped a hand over his jaw. "And you didn't recognize her?"

"No. I didn't get her last name. Though I could ask Patty. It could be as simple as all the gossip about us being the devil incarnate, but . . . I swear she looked familiar." Brandon shrugged. He had no idea why the woman's behavior had bothered him into today. He kept trying to put it out of his head . . . but it stuck.

"Well, we do get a lot of weird in town."

"Yeah, we do." Stupid to be fixated on it.

The door swung open and Lilly stepped in, a bright whirl of color and cheerful smiles and greetings.

He didn't realize he was smiling back until Will nudged him with a wink and a smug, knowing grin.

"Bite me," Brandon grumbled, scowling.

Lilly placed her bag on a hook by the door. "Now, Brandon, I know what you're going to say about my outfit, but—"

"You cannot wear those boots."

She huffed out an irritated breath and fisted her hands on her hips. "But, the original brochure said waterproof footwear. These *are* waterproof." She kicked out a leg to show off the ridiculous rubber rain boots on her feet. They were pink with little white hearts dotted all over.

"Yes, it also mentioned the half-mile hike down to

the dock, which requires footwear that is, oh, I don't know, suitable for walking. And not covered in hearts."

"The design on my boots hardly determines their . . . usefulness."

"They're ungainly. You fall out of the canoe, they'll just fill up with water and sink you right to the bottom."

"There's a chance of falling out?" She chewed on her bottom lip, then moved her gaze to Will. "Is he being honest?"

"Afraid so. Both about those boots being a bad choice and about the possibility of falling in. Maybe not the sinking to the bottom. You can swim, right?"

She frowned and patted her hair. "I can. I don't particularly *want* to."

Brandon gave a defiant *so not my type* smirk to Will before looking back at Lilly. "Well, if you change your shoes and listen to directions, you won't."

"I knew you were going to say that," she grumbled, grabbing her bag again. "I have my hiking boots in my office. I need to check a few emails, and then we'll head out around . . ." She glanced at the phone in her hand. "Nine?"

Brandon gave a slight nod, and Lilly walked past. He didn't even notice himself turning to watch her walk down the hallway. It was like she entered a room and his brain went dead and his body acted of its own accord.

"You keep fighting it, and you keep sinking deeper and deeper. She's like quicksand to you, bro."

"I don't know what you're talking about," Brandon grumbled.

Skeet cackled from his seat over at the front desk, and Brandon turned his glare on the old man. Not that any glares ever affected Skeet.

"You know," Will said, far too casually, gripping Brandon's shoulder hard enough that Brandon would have to fight to get away. "No one would blame you if you went for it."

Brandon could grunt that off, but it seemed the whole too-much-honesty thing was like an epidemic and the truth came out instead. "*I* would blame me."

Will's grip loosened. "You're too hard on yourself. Just like I'm too easy on myself. Maybe someday we'll meet in the middle."

"I won't hold my breath."

Lilly popped her head out of her office, her feet now in hiking boots—though they weren't laced. "Oh, and I forgot to tell you. Last night, I asked my sister if she knew that waitress from yesterday. She didn't know much about her, but she said her last name is Winthrop."

It wasn't immediate, but the last name and the waitress's familiar face—it didn't take long to connect the dots. He looked back at Will, and Will nodded grimly.

"Ms. Winthrop. She was Dad's secretary for how long?"

"Five years, at least," Brandon replied, trying to think back to that time. He'd been in elementary school so not part of the business then, but he'd always loved going over there, and Dad had loved parading him about. "What was her first name? Vanessa?"

"I think so. I guess I'll be doing some researching before my rock climbing, huh?"

"Did you want to cancel?" Lilly interrupted, looking perplexed and—if he wasn't kidding himself—a little disappointed. "We could reschedule."

"No, it's fine. The waitress probably just heard horror stories about Evanses growing up." But something settled in his gut. Uncomfortably. The way that girl had looked at him—the connection she had to Evans Mining, no matter how loose.

Something was off there, and Brandon had a bad

feeling it was another wrong he was going to have to right.


"I have to take a picture!" Lilly pulled her phone out of the little Ziploc bag she'd secured it into. Brandon's offhand remark about falling in had forced her to take some precautions before stepping foot in a canoe.

"Keep me out of it," Brandon grumbled.

"You have *no* vision, Brandon," she teased, framing the picture so he wasn't in it. The crystal-clear lake reflecting a deep blue sky and the red canoe on the rocky shore were pretty enough to be used in the brochure. Having people in the photograph *would* be better, but you could get a sense of the *peace* in the pictures she was taking. The quiet and the breathtaking beauty.

She set the phone down and simply *looked*, taking a deep breath of fresh, piney air. It really was magical. But she wasn't here for peace or magic. She was here for her job. "You know, we should hire a photographer. Someone to go on a few excursions with actual customers who are willing to be photographed."

"Your list of 'we shoulds' gets longer and longer, and more and more expensive."

"Public relations is all about reaching the public, and you're doing well enough to invest in that. Or you wouldn't have hired me."

"I wasn't complaining exactly. Just commenting. You're very good at what you do or we wouldn't keep investing in you." He dropped his backpack into the canoe, then did a bunch of official-looking things to all the doohickeys inside of it.

She waited for him to say something annoying or teasing, but he'd simply said she was good at her job and moved on.

Yesterday morning must be weighing on his mind. It was certainly weighing on hers. The fact the waitress was a relative to someone who had worked for Brandon's father and acted so . . . strangely was certainly odd enough to keep wondering about.

Lilly hadn't been able to get it out of her head last night, if only because focusing on that woman's weirdness kept her from lashing out at her sister, who was bound and determined to remain "not good at anything!"

Which simply wasn't true.

So, she'd thought about Hayley the waitress and wondered what might cause her to react differently from Corbin or Patty. Or any of the other townspeople Lilly had encountered on behalf of Mile High Adventures. They'd all been very clear in their hatred and mistrust of Brandon and his business.

Hayley had been different. Skittish.

"Your carriage awaits," Brandon said, motioning her toward the canoe. "Go sit on the far bench. I'll push us in and we can start."

Lilly placed her phone back in the Ziploc bag and did as she was told. She did her best to climb in the canoe without looking like some hapless monkey, though she was sure she failed. She felt clumsy and fat-fingered, and that was not something she was used to feeling.

But Brandon didn't tease her or make fun of her at all. He simply pushed the canoe out into the lake and stepped in easily and efficiently, grabbing the ends of the oars that were locked into the sides of the canoe.

She had not exactly anticipated or thought about the fact he would be *rowing* them places, and even in the long-sleeved henley he wore, his . . . form was on complete display.

Crap.

"So, you think you know the waitress from yesterday?" she asked, far too cheerfully and brightly for the situation. But she *had* to somehow make conversation so she wasn't tempted to ogle. Ogling led to uncomfortable dreams, and uncomfortable dreams led to wondering if reality lived up to them.

She had the time and inclination for neither.

"No. I don't think we know each other, but she has the same last name and looks a lot like a woman who was my father's secretary. I would have only been in . . . fourth or fifth grade when she was replaced. And I can't remember why. But . . ."

"It's concerning."

"Yeah. It is," he agreed, his eyes trained on the lake behind her as he rowed them farther and farther from shore. "But Will's got an hour or so before his excursion, maybe he'll have found something by the time we get back."

"I hope so." Her eyes drifted to the easy movement of his arms twisting the oars in mesmerizing circles, every distracting muscle engaged whether the oar was cutting through the water or poised midair.

Crap. She really needed to keep her mouth moving.

"So, tell me about this excursion. Oh, does this place have a history? Something we could put into the brochure? An ancient legend? Maybe a ghost? All the information you guys advertise right now is about canoeing—not about the location."

"Did you say ghost?"

"Sure. There's a huge segment of people who would do anything for the chance at seeing a ghost. I'd think you'd even have a lot of overlap between that type and the outdoorsy adventure type. People who like a good thrill."

He gave her one of those looks that seemed to imply she'd lost her mind, but she was right—whether he wanted to see it or not. Some people would do anything for the chance to see a ghost, or step inside an ancient legend. The healing legend was the only reason Gracely remained afloat, she was certain.

"I don't know of any ghost stories. Skeet might better know some legend or another about the lake in general. But let's avoid ghosts, please."

"Are you afraid of ghosts?" Lilly asked with mock grave concern.

He offered her a scowling eye roll, but then his gaze shifted to something in the bottom of the boat.

"How'd that little bastard get in here," Brandon said without much heat, letting go of the oars and leaning forward. When Lilly saw what Brandon was referring to—a wriggling, scaly snake—she didn't think, didn't breathe. She simply *panicked*, and jumped up and out of the canoe in one move.

She managed not to fall completely into the lake, landing upright and on her feet in the water. Luckily, they were still shallow enough the water only came up to her waist, though it splashed up and onto her face.

She wiped it with the sleeve of her shirt, then glanced back at the canoe. It was completely upside down. "Oh, shit." She took a step toward the capsized boat, but it flipped upright and Brandon resurfaced, completely soaked.

Oh no. Oh *no*. "Are you all right?"

"All right?" He shook his head—not to say no, but to rid himself of excess water, the drops flying off his face and scattering along the rippling surface of the lake. "I've survived worse."

"I'm so sorry. I just saw the snake and . . . panicked."

She tried to walk toward him, but he was already pushing the canoe toward more shallow water.

"It was just a garter snake."

"Well, how was I supposed to know that?"

He fixed her with a glare. "Maybe if you hadn't *leapt* out of the boat, I might have had a chance to explain it to you."

"I don't like snakes!"

"Most people don't. And yet I've never had someone jump out of the boat because there was a snake in it."

"Have you ever had a snake in your canoe before?" she asked, her teeth beginning to chatter. The sun above was warm, but goodness, the water was icy.

"Ye—"

"Before you claim you have, let me r-r-rephrase. Have you ever had a snake in a canoe when you were with a group of customers?"

"No."

"I r-r-rest my c-c-case."

"Push the canoe to the shore and sit in the sun. I have to try to find the bag you just lost me."

She reached for the canoe and curled her hand around the wet edge. She felt foolish for jumping at the sight of the snake, and even more foolish that the jump had caused the problem. She wanted to help him find it, but her whole body was shivering now.

She walked toward shore, pulling the canoe along. With some trepidation, she glanced over into the boat to check and make sure there were no little snakes wriggling about. It appeared to be clear, so she pulled the canoe up onto the rocky beach.

Even with her pants plastered to her legs and her shoes slushy with water, the sun immediately began to warm the coldness of the water away. She glanced out to where Brandon was surfacing again. Water dripped off of the ends of his hair, the tip of his nose, the end of his beard; rivulets slid down the wet gray henley that now clung to every muscle.

*Oh boy.*

He pulled the pack from the water as well, sliding it onto his shoulder as he walked toward the shore. The water went from being thigh high, to knee high, to calf high, every inch of his clothing now plastered to him as he moved.

She shivered. She wanted to blame it on the water, but watching him was like having an out-of-body experience. Or being in a romantic comedy. Or something a little more . . . erotic.

He tossed the bag onto the rocky shore with an oath. "Luckily, I do prepare for accidents so almost everything in there is waterproof."

"I am sorry," she offered, trying to keep her gaze on the backpack and not on the way his jeans now molded to his thighs. She'd never gotten that good of a glimpse at what might lie underneath his usual uniform of heavy work pants though, so it was quite the feat to look away from . . . *his muscular, powerful thighs. Yum.*

Heaven help her.

"You do realize I cannot take you on any more of these things," he said, shaking his head, water still dripping from the ends of his hair. From the tips of his long, blunt fingers. From the crotch of his pants.

*Really, Lilly, get a grip.*

"Someone is likely to die. Or maybe you'll set a wildfire that takes out all of Colorado."

"That makes me sound like some clumsy, quirky movie character. I'm not clumsy. And I'm not quirky."

Brandon looked at her dolefully. "Are you sure about the quirky part?"

"Yes. I'm sure," she retorted, knowing she sounded prim.

"If you say so."

"So, you won't take me out any farther? The brochure says you have to get to the end of the canoe trip to see the bottom of Solace Falls, and I wanted a good picture from that angle."

"Lilly, look. I get you're not the outdoorsy type. You don't have to force yourself to be. We'll hire a photographer to get all the angles."

"I love the outdoors." When he gave her another condescendingly disbelieving look, she fisted her hands on her hips. "I do! Maybe I don't love all living things equally. Maybe I am not the most athletic person. But this is beautiful. And as long as there aren't any creepy crawlies in the canoe, it's actually quite relaxing." She could use some relaxing. Some time just to . . . to just be, as stupid as that sounded.

Brandon situated himself on a large rock directly in the path of the sun. It teased out the golden glints in his dark hair, made his skin glow like he was some kind of outdoorsy Greek god.

It wasn't fair. If she'd fallen in, she'd look like a drowned rat with scraggly hair and no makeup.

"Let's take a little break here and try to dry off," he said, stretching his legs out in front of him. "It might be a nice day here, but the breeze will still be awfully cold while we're wet if we really get going in the current. We'll dry off, see if there's any snacks to be salvaged, and then we'll go a little further out. But maybe we can avoid doing the entire excursion."

"I want to see the bottom of the falls. Besides, how can I learn to be outdoorsy if I never get any practice?"

"Maybe your practice shouldn't happen during work hours," he retorted.

"You're being mean." Mean was maybe harsh, but she hated that he was punishing her for . . . well, sucking at this. She never sucked at things! She just needed more time to learn.

He turned and looked over at her. She was still standing on the rocky shore, but he was sitting on that rock lounging like some big, knowing, powerful supernatural being. She scowled at him.

"I'm not being mean. I'm being realistic. If I was being mean," he said on a grumble, "I'd throw you in that lake."

She gave a haughty laugh. "You'd have to catch me."

He raised an eyebrow, his lip curving slightly with it. "Is that . . . is that a challenge?"

At the all too competitive glint in his eyes, she found herself stumbling to backtrack. "Well, no. I . . ."

He stood from the rock, and she had the worst feeling that she was about to be thrown in the lake. She edged away from him. "Brandon, that's not what I . . ."

He took a step toward her. And then another. She tried to scurry to the side. "Don't . . . You can't . . . Don't you dare!"

But he kept walking toward her, and that usual scowl on his face quickly and easily curved more and more upward until it was a full-on grin, and he was full-on chasing her.

She ran up the shore trying to tell him to stop, but all she could do was laugh and run and try not to trip on a rock. Her breath came in puffs. This was as much physical activity as she'd done since her twisted ankle. She hadn't even gotten back on her normal treadmill running schedule.

It didn't help that she was laughing hysterically as she ran from her boss across the rocky shore because he was acting as though he was actually going to throw her in a lake.

What on earth was happening with her life?

She stopped, taking a deep breath to try and get her lungs back on track. "This is ridiculous. You're not going to throw me in the lake."

He stood just a few paces away from her, still grinning, still unfairly gorgeous. Not breathing hard at all. "I'm not?"

"No, you're not. Because we're not teenagers. We're coworkers. It would be childish and unnecessary for you to throw me in the lake. Especially when you getting wet was simply an accident."

"It's a shame for you, Lilly," he said, his voice surprisingly low and seductive. Combined with that grin, it was nearly lethal to everything south of the border. "But I feel a little bit like being unnecessary and childish today." He took another step toward her.

"You can't. You can't." But her "can't" ended on a laugh, and those big, muscular arms came around her waist. He hauled her up and over his shoulder in one all-too-easy movement.

She gasped because she couldn't believe what was happening. How did every excursion involve him carrying her? Could she make sure every excursion continued to? Because there was a lot to say for being carted around by a big, strong man.

He walked steadily back toward the lake, and she remembered his intent with this particular carrying. Not to get her to safety. "You have to stop. This isn't funny. You're not going to throw me in."

"You know, I've never really been fond of people telling me what I can't do. And considering you dumped me into the lake because you saw a snake—a completely harmless snake—I think you deserve a dunking."

"Brandon, I'm warning you—" But suddenly she was in the air and even more suddenly she hit the cold wet surface of the lake. Because of how he tossed her off his shoulder, she landed butt first, completely submerged in the water. When she scrambled into a standing position, sputtering water out of her mouth, she wasn't surprised to find him standing on the shore laughing.

The bastard. Oh, he was going to pay.

"There," he said still chuckling. "Now we're both completely wet, and even."

"Oh, I do not believe we're remotely even." She stalked toward him. He was taller, he was stronger, he knew what the hell he was doing. But that didn't mean she couldn't get him back. Especially when he only grinned at her advancing form.

"What are you going to do?" He crossed those impressive arms over his distractingly broad chest. "Are you going to throw me over your shoulder?"

"I wouldn't dream of it," she said sweetly. She reached the edge of the shore, still standing in the cold water. It *was* freezing, but something was keeping her warm. She didn't know how to name that feeling, but the frigid ice of the snowmelt-filled lake just didn't penetrate it. She bent over and, using both of her hands, she splashed as much water onto the front of his body as she could.

He stood there, still with arms crossed over his chest, water once again dripping down his body. "So this is how it's going to be?"

"*Now* we're even."

"I do not think so." He charged toward her and she had nowhere to go except back into the deeper water, so she waded back in. Until it was waist high, and then she had to swim, but Brandon just kept advancing on her until his arms were around her.

She kicked and pushed, but his grip was too strong, and he was laughing. Which in turn made her laugh. Deep in the lake, holding on to each other laughing ridiculously. It was not exactly what she'd predicted for the day.

Even with the cold of the water, Brandon's body was close and warm. And they both laughed like idiots. It felt good. Crazy, but good.

"All right. I think that's enough. Truce?" He looked down at her with hazel eyes that reminded her of the woods, his hair darker from being completely wet. There were drops of water on his golden eyelashes and multiple ones hanging from the edges of his beard. She wanted to brush them away or lick them off.

Heat curled in her belly, some nameless . . . *want* taking up residence there. "How is it fair that you just look like some kind of male model fresh from a photo shoot in the ocean, and I look like . . ." She waved a hand at herself, one of her hands curling into his shoulder for balance.

*Yeah, balance.*

"You look fine, Lilly." His voice had gone soft, maybe a little rough, and she was suddenly aware of the way his big hands spanned her waist, keeping her afloat since she couldn't quite touch ground. It sent a surprising startle of electricity through her, and when their eyes met, she could barely suck in a breath.

Because they might be in the water—cold, *cold* water. But their arms had wound around each other, and their bodies were brushing as they bobbed there—Brandon steady on his feet, and her sort of swaying at his mercy.

The laughter was gone. His gaze was . . . hot. Searing. She couldn't look away. "Fine?" she asked on a hushed whisper.

He didn't respond to that, but she noticed that his

breathing had become as labored as hers. That either he or the water had drawn her closer and there was almost no space between them. She felt as though maybe she'd slipped completely under the surface, and this was some other reality where only the warmth of his body and the point where brown and green met in his eyes mattered.

*And where does that kind of losing yourself end? Same place it ended for Mom and Cora.*

She needed to get away. She needed to have some sense and swim back to shore. They couldn't keep holding on to each other and staring at each other and breathing heavily in the middle of a *lake*.

It would only end in disaster. She did not have time for disaster. Too much was riding on her, and she'd spent too much of her life avoiding making this mistake. It might gild gold here, but outside the water it would be what it always was for women like her.

Pain. Hardship. Disaster.

But her body didn't listen, no matter how insistent her brain was. Because when his mouth lowered closer to hers, she didn't pull away. She didn't let him go or wiggle out of his grasp.

She leaned into it. Moth to a flame, magnet to metal, some invisible force drawing her close and closer to . . .

Well, complete ruin probably.

# Chapter Thirteen

Kissing Lilly would be worse than any mistake Brandon had ever made. He didn't even need to think through all those many mistakes to know this would top the list. It was against everything he'd built his life to stand for.

He kept trying to get that *fact* through to his arms, through to his mouth and maybe even hers. Both were hovering perilously close to one another.

In this freezing lake, with her not even at a place that she could put her feet on the ground. He was a complete tool. She was at a disadvantage and he was just *holding* her there.

"We should get back to shore," he said, his voice sounding strained even in his own ears. But for the first time in his life, reason *was* a strain. Something he had to grapple for and hold on to as tightly as possible. Something that kept slipping through the cracks.

"Yes. Yes, that is what we should do." But her grip on his shoulder didn't loosen, and those dark blue eyes that never failed to get him lost didn't break eye contact. So he didn't move. He didn't know how to move.

She made a little squeaking sound and looked behind

her, which, unfortunately for him, pressed her even more flush with his body. "I think something just brushed my leg."

"It was probably me."

"But what if it was the snake?" She looked back at him, smiling sheepishly. "You're going to tell me snakes can't swim."

He laughed, couldn't help it. "I'm going to tell you it wasn't the snake." But—thank God—whatever it was broke the weird fog in his brain enough for him to move his feet a few paces back toward shore. Which brought her closer to a place where she could at least touch the ground with her toes.

He felt a little shudder go through her body, and as much as he wanted that to be something—he wanted it to be nothing even more. Shuddering couldn't be anything to do with *him*, even if he was fighting some shuddering of his own. Among other things. A lot of other things.

He was not his father's son who would be undone by simple . . . physical connection. So he was attracted to her? That didn't have to matter. It wouldn't matter. He would not give in to the raging need inside of him.

That was the black part of him that he'd never release. The thing that *enjoyed* keeping her in that place she couldn't touch the ground. That wanted to press that advantage. Will could say no one would blame him, but that's what Will didn't understand.

He felt it. Those urges and that coldness inside of him. He could *imagine* how easy it would be to turn into Phillip Conroy Evans. Like that hideous middle name they shared linked them to this dark, egomaniacal, power-driven center.

The only difference was Brandon refused to succumb to it. No matter how strong it urged. It *was* wrong. It was wrong to fool around with your employees. It was too complicated, with too many power differentials. It had the potential to burn everything to the ground.

He wouldn't do it. He was not going to do that, no matter how tempting it might be. And if he kept taking safe step after slow step toward the shore, eventually all of this crazy would fizzle out. He would be able to think all of those things and feel all of those things and know what to do without a hint of doubt or Will's voice or Lilly's eyes trying to change his mind.

"If you . . . I can walk now," Lilly said, her voice possibly as timid as he'd ever heard it.

He let her go. What an idiot he was. Because he didn't want her timid and he didn't want her confused and he didn't want this look from her like she . . . thought he had some answer.

There was no answer for this.

He'd never felt temptation this strong, and it scared him to his bones.

They finally got to shore, dripping with water. Lilly's cheeks were flushed, her hair a sopping mess of tangles, and he could see the outline of every sweet curve of her body. Nipples pebbled with cold, the soft swell of her breasts, and he actually had to curl his fingers into fists to fight off the need to touch her.

It wasn't need, just a dangerous want that disguised itself as need. Thinking it was a need was selfish, destructive behavior.

"We should get back in the boat," he managed to say, though his breath felt oddly raw and overused.

"Yes. Great idea," she said, sounding so relieved he thought maybe she was on the same idiotic precipice he was. Trying so hard to ignore that current between them that seemed closer and closer to taking them under.

He forced his legs to take him over to the pack, and he checked on the contents, shaking off anything especially waterlogged. Lilly crawled back to her spot on the canoe, the sun glittering against her wet hair—the water somehow making it one golden color.

He'd been in long-term relationships before, thinking about the possibility of marriage, and he'd thought about those women less. Noticed them less. Certainly never paid attention to the color of their hair or the sweep of their eyelashes on pale cheeks. Something about Lilly wasn't just mesmerizing or hypnotizing; it was all-encompassing.

He didn't know how he was going to survive this. Her. But he didn't have a choice. He had to survive.

He gave the canoe a push back into the lake, then hopped on to his seat. "Let's try to stay out of the water and actually dry off this time, huh?"

She managed a small smile and nodded, though he noticed the way her eyes drifted down his chest. He looked down too, but all he saw was his shirt plastered to him.

The bolt of arousal was unfair. That just her simple *notice* of him could make his dick stir. But . . . that's what that look was. Notice. Appreciation.

This thing that danced between them, or all but bound them, was mutual. It wasn't all him.

Mutual was so much worse. It gave way to little excuses, possibilities, chances. *If she wants it too . . .*

*Doesn't matter. Dad made plenty of women believe they were willing.*

Right. So, he had to pretend he didn't notice. It was easier when he could focus all his energy on moving the paddles through the water swiftly and efficiently, getting them to the falls as quickly as possible. No more stops. No more smiles. Definitely no more touches.

He was not a slave to some *physical* desire. And Lilly wasn't a slave to hers, obviously, because she had pulled away as much as he had. This was a mutual pulling away, and therefore . . . things would be fine.

Just fucking fantastic.

Lilly wanted to enjoy the awe of being at the bottom of the falls. It *was* beautiful, and kind of amazing to be close enough to occasionally feel a drop of the spray from waterfall hitting lake below.

The mountains seemed even more towering here than they did in town. It was as if there were nothing else in the world but mountains on all sides and big, blue sky way, way up there. She felt small and isolated and . . .

She blew out a breath. No matter how she tried to grab on to some kind of awe-inspired peace, her gaze kept going back to Brandon.

His expression was grave and fierce, and it did nothing to abate this stupid overexcited heartbeat and nervy feeling in her chest.

She didn't know how to deal with this. No man had ever tested her determined resolve to stay away from powerful, savvy businessmen before. Certainly no man had ever seemed like he might be worth it.

It was lowering to admit that she'd considered herself somehow . . . above Mom and Cora. She hadn't swanned about acting better than them; she'd simply believed something in her was stronger or maybe even a little smarter than the women in her life who'd been manipulated and used and lied to and then thrown out like they were no better than garbage.

She was *shamed.* Because she hadn't realized such an arrogant thought had existed in her heart, but more because it simply wasn't true. She wasn't stronger or better.

She'd wanted to kiss Brandon, in the middle of that lake. She'd *liked* feeling a little bit at his mercy. There had been an excitement in him being so much bigger, holding her above the surface of the water. Power and control could be thrilling coming from a man, and oh damn, she did not need to *experience* that.

But even with her brain functioning again, she still wanted that and liked that, and she didn't know how to eradicate that piece of herself. It was exhausting.

"Aren't you going to take a picture?"

"Oh, right." She didn't much feel like taking a picture. She didn't feel like memorializing this particular moment, because she was pretty sure every time she saw any picture she took now, it would remind her what had happened before this moment. She wouldn't be awed by the view—not the falls, not the beauty—and she wouldn't recall the peace. She would relive that almost kiss in the cold water.

But, because it would be weird if she didn't, she pulled her phone out of her pocket, undid the Ziploc bag, and dutifully took a slew of pictures of the falls, of the amazing mountains above, of that huge blue sky that was simply breathtaking no matter how exhaustingly emotionally stupid she was.

She plopped the phone back into the Ziploc bag and closed it. "That should be good for the brochure."

"I could take a picture of you to put on it."

"Ha ha."

"Not a joke. You're the one talking about how we need a person in the pictures, and how they should be emoting something. I'd think someone who has seen this for the first time would be *very* emotive."

She had to look away when he said *emotive*, because she was pretty sure she was emoting all over the damn place. *I'm attracted to you. I want to kiss you. I have very little self-control left.*

But, he was talking about work. And work she would talk about. Somehow, someway. "I'm not the one guiding people on these excursions. You are. Sam is. Will is. It should be someone who's always going to be a part of Mile High Adventures. It's not just about the look— it's about who is behind all this. I know you took me to the old Evans offices to prove some point about how you don't want to be your father, and have your name and face plastered everywhere. But this company is about you, whether you meant it to be or not. It's built on this thing that you feel. I think that's quite a bit different from your father inserting himself in every mining poster ever."

Brandon was silent, and she knew she'd taken her little tirade too far, but she was passionate about this topic. She wanted to be passionate about a topic way more than she wanted to be passionate about a man.

"Ready to head back?" he finally said.

"I'll take that as a cease and desist," she replied, giving him an arch look.

He shrugged. "Take it however you wish." But there was the tiniest hint of an upward curve to his lips.

"Can I help paddle back?"

He stopped reaching for the oars and looked at her like she'd lost her mind. "You want to help paddle back?"

"Yes. I think it would be a good experience to know how much effort goes into all that movement. Besides, I'm curious."

Brandon's mouth curved into a full-blown smile for the first time since they'd gotten back in the boat. "Should we take bets on how long you last?"

"Rude," she replied, with an injured sniff. "I may not be the most outdoorsy of types, but I do have a gym membership."

"What gym?"

"That cute one on Main Street. Next to the bakery."

"You mean the one that closed like three months ago? Because it was next to the bakery and people went to get cupcakes after they worked out, which completely negated the purpose of the working out."

"It closed? Oh, gosh, those cupcakes are really good."

Brandon laughed, and the sound did *not* flow over her like a warm ray of sun. That was just the actual sun.

She glanced up at the sky, but the sun was covered by a big, puffy white cloud. Damn it.

Brandon pulled the oars toward him. They sliced through the water with amazing ease, and she knew she would never in a million years be able to duplicate his movements. But she didn't want to duplicate them. She wanted to learn something. Maybe she'd never be as good as Brandon or Will or Sam. But that didn't mean that she couldn't do it.

She wanted to learn something new—maybe needed to keep her brain occupied. But more than that, maybe if she did learn this new thing, maybe if she proved that she could take on this completely different and out-of-character task that wasn't exactly in her wheelhouse, she could prove to Cora that there were so many opportunities for her to do something. Something other than sit around at home thinking Lilly would take care of everything.

"I want to try." She held out her hands for him to pass over the oars.

"All right. Don't overdo it. It's very strenuous, and you want to be able to move your arms tomorrow." He passed her the handles, and then his big, callused hands positioned her small, about-to-be-callused hands in what she assumed was the correct position for oaring.

Not that she was noticing. It did not matter that he had big hands. It didn't matter that they were touching her. Because she . . . she was over all of that. She had moved on. Mind over matter.

Of course, then she looked up at him, his hazel eyes steady on hers. He wasn't smiling or even scowling, but he was . . . studying her. As if he were trying to solve some puzzle that was all the same color.

It seemed the more he looked, the more times she met his gaze, the harder her breath would catch, the louder her heart would beat in her ears. She didn't understand why or how someone could just swoop in and day by day steal a little bit more of her control.

Or maybe, day by day, she liked him a little better. Day by day, she understood he was no soulless enemy. She understood him better, and it wasn't working in her favor like getting to know a guy usually did.

What did she do with that? There wasn't anything she *could* do. As long as she didn't jump him, she supposed she would be okay. Probably.

"You're going to want to move your arms in a broad circle. You don't want to try too hard. You want the movement to be smooth. Even when you're going through the water, you're not pushing—you're not pulling. The whole time, you're just making a circular movement with your arms."

Lilly listened to the instructions and tried her best to follow them. But how was she supposed to not push or pull when it was really hard? The canoe was heavy. The water wasn't air—it was hard to pull the oar through.

She had to use every last ounce of strength just to make one rotation.

"You're trying too hard," he admonished.

"I *have* to try hard. I don't have any muscles!"

He laughed again and, carefully and barely rocking the boat at all, moved to the center bench, which was narrower than the one he'd been sitting on. It didn't seem to matter to him. He perched himself on it, mostly dry now from their rest in the sunny cove at the end of the falls.

Which meant his clothes were no longer plastered to his skin, and she couldn't make out every ridge of muscle. Which was a shame. A darn . . . no, it was a blessing. *Remember that, Lilly.*

Then his fingers closed over hers and she forgot all about blessings.

"Here. We'll work together. Steady."

He moved her arms for her, steadily pushing and pulling so that they were working together. Holding hands. Basically.

This was so not a good idea. Especially when he glanced at her and they were touching and looking at each other, and why did she feel like a fifteen-year-old who couldn't control her hormones?

"This was . . ." Brandon cleared his throat, and though his hands didn't leave hers, his gaze did. He shook his head. "This was a bad idea, wasn't it?"

"Just terrible," she agreed emphatically.

And then he smiled, which was even worse. Because she smiled back, and he was so handsome.

"I don't know why this is so . . ." How did she finish this sentence? Potent? Hard? Oh, she could bet a lot of things on him were hard. *Get a hold of yourself, girl.*

"Yeah. Me either." And he did look as conflicted as

she felt. Which helped, actually, knowing she wasn't alone in this stupidity.

"But we can't. We're coworkers. There can be nothing like . . . this. We have to be sensible, rational adults."

"Yes! Exactly. Both reasonable, responsible, sensible adults. We can control this. We don't want it, so we can completely control it. Right?"

She didn't know if the question was for agreement or reassurance, but she was ready to offer both. She leaned forward, excited that he agreed with her. Surely, if they felt the same way, nothing could happen. "Right. In fact, we can take measures to make sure that we're not in situations like this where we might be tempted to . . . well."

"Exactly. No more excursions together. Definitely no more excursions. Sam or Will should take you."

"Yes," she agreed, ignoring the little pinch in her chest. Because she liked these excursions and him, but that was the point. Avoiding that like. "And no more meetings where you drive me places. We can do like what we did with the café meeting. We'll schedule them in the morning and I'll meet you there in a separate car."

"Right, and we'll look at the schedule more closely to make sure that we aren't in the office alone."

"This is a great start. And reasonable. I don't know why we didn't think of it before."

"Me either," he said, still smiling at her. Still causing all those fluttery, longing feelings neither of them wanted.

Lilly glanced down at where their hands were joined on the oars. He'd made considerable progress—and she did have to give him almost all the credit. But maybe that meant they should stop . . . touching. "You should, uh, do all the rowing right now."

"Oh, yeah, sorry." He released her hands and then took over with the oars as she clasped her hands in her lap.

She didn't exactly *never* look at him and his muscles moving the little boat they were in on the way back. But having a plan in place made that totally okay. The occasional glance at his attractive features wasn't going to hurt because they were both on the same this-isn't-going-to-happen page.

Everything was just great. Super, wonderfully great. She'd convince herself of that at some point.

# Chapter Fourteen

It started raining the second they reached the shore. Brandon had to hurry up and flip the canoe in its place. "You better run for it," he said, nodding his chin toward the trail. "I'll be right behind you."

"I can help. Let me help," Lilly replied, moving closer to where he was struggling with the toolshed where they kept the oars and the canoe cover.

"Okay. Then help me latch this. Take these and hang them up while I get the cover on."

He pulled open the door and shoved his key into his pockets. Lilly jumped to work hanging the oars exactly where they needed to be, and Brandon grabbed the canoe cover.

He worked to cover it, and Lilly returned from the toolshed, quickly making a move to help get the other side attached.

The thing about Lilly was—no matter how out of her element she was with all this outdoorsy stuff, no matter how little physical strength she had—she was always game to try. He admired that about her. He liked that about her. He needed to stop thinking about all the things he liked about her.

It was such a good thing that they had agreed to avoid each other. Sure, it made him some kind of a coward, but he was sure as hell going to choose coward over screwing something up.

Once they had the cover attached and the toolshed locked up, he gestured Lilly up the trail so that they could make a run for the office. It was all uphill so it wouldn't be a fun run, and they were probably just going to get soaked anyway, but the faster they got back to the office, the faster they could get dry for the eight millionth time that day.

A flash of lightning cracked across the sky, immediately followed by a rumbly boom that shook the air around them. They had to hurry—it definitely wasn't safe being out in a storm like this.

The rain intensified as they tried to run up the trail, the lightning and thunder getting worse. Quickly, everything was becoming slippery with wet and mud. Brandon had to lock arms with Lilly to help her up the last incline.

"Maybe I shouldn't do any more excursions," she yelled above the din of pelting rain and booming thunder. "It seems to be unlucky every single time."

They reached the open yard of Mile High's office and hurried up the stairs to the porch. "You do seem to have a certain kind of luck in this area." Really bad luck.

They stepped into the office and out of the rain. He was dripping, and so was she. He quickly looked away because he could still remember this morning clear enough and he wanted nothing else reminding him of . . . wet.

This woman was nothing but bad luck.

"Where is everybody?" Lilly asked.

Brandon was surprised to realize the office was completely silent and dark. Skeet was not behind the front desk, and Will and Sam—who should both be back from their excursions—were nowhere to be found. "I have no idea," he said, not wanting to look further since he was still dripping.

"Oh, there's a note." Lilly tugged off her boots, then her socks. She pulled off her T-shirt, leaving her in a tank top, and rung her hair out on the discarded shirt.

*Stop watching her, you idiot.*

But without the T-shirt—he wrenched his gaze away as Lilly stepped toward the desk. He would dutifully look for his cell in the pack, not stare at her breasts like some kind of perv.

"It's from Will. He sent Skeet home because of the storm. Sam's back and everything's packed up, so he's at home too. Will took some clients down into town since they were going to be rained out."

So. Brandon was here alone with Lilly. In the office. In the middle of a storm. Soaking wet. Brandon did everything in his power not to look at Lilly. "So, we should get out of these wet clothes. . . ." He squeezed his eyes shut, because that came out all wrong. "I mean, change our clothes. Separately." Christ, he was a moron. "Do you have any clothes here, or would you need to borrow something?"

The phone ringing cut off any answer Lilly might give. Thank God. The last thing he needed to think about was her and clothes and wet and naked and . . . He grabbed the phone with more force than necessary. "Mile High Adventures," he muttered into the receiver.

"Hey, you made it back. Thank God. Thought I was going to have to send out a search party in all this." Will's voice crackled in the storm static.

"We, uh, just got back. Where are you? Still in town?"

"Yeah. I was trying to get back, but the road's closed about a mile away from the office. Completely washed

out due to some sort of rock avalanche with all the
water. They're saying they can't even open one lane
until tomorrow morning at the earliest."

"Tomorrow *morning*?" Brandon glanced at Lilly, who
was spreading out the wet layers she'd shed.

"That's what the construction guy said when I tried
to get back. Lilly with you?"

Brandon swallowed. "Yeah. She's here."

"Tell her she can't go home. Aside from the road,
the storm's supposed to be nasty for a while. Bad lightning, wind. You should stay put too. You don't want to
get your truck stuck in the road up to the house."

"So, you're saying . . . Lilly and I should stay in the
office building all night. Together."

Lilly immediately straightened and turned to face
him, her cheeks already tinged pink.

Will's chuckle crackled across the connection. "Well,
when you put it that way . . . I think that is what I'm
saying. Enjoy each other's company."

Brandon turned from Lilly's panicked gaze. "This
isn't a joke, Will," he muttered into the receiver.

"I'm not joking. You two really should stay put. If you
don't believe me, check the weather station. Call Gracely
Road Division. Do what you gotta do, but if you want to
be safe—if you want Lilly to be safe—you're going to
have to stay put."

"And what are you going to do tonight if you can't
get up to the house?"

"Oh, I'll figure something out."

"That better not mean what I think it means."

"I bet Dr. Frost has an extra room for my use. A
couch I could crash on."

"But you struck out there."

"Will Evans does not strike out, big brother."

"Whatever. Just, if you hear anything about the road being fixed early, let me know so I can get Lilly home."

"Aw, come on. There's no rush on that."

Brandon gripped the receiver tighter. "Yes, there is." He hit the end button—hard—then dropped the phone on the desk. On a weary sigh, he mustered the nerve to look at Lilly. She was standing there looking wet and gorgeous, and this was some sort of karmic punishment for all the things he had done wrong in his life. Like every last one of them.

"The road down to Gracely is washed out. There is no way for you to get home right now."

Her jaw dropped, even though she had to have heard at least his side of the conversation with Will. "There's no way to get home," she repeated, sounding shell-shocked.

He might say shell-shocked was a little extreme if he weren't filled with complete dread himself.

"Will said there was a sort of rock avalanche and the road is washed out and they don't think they can have it fixed until tomorrow morning."

"Tomorrow morning," she echoed, clasping her hands together and looking worriedly down at them. "So we're stuck here until tomorrow."

"That is how it appears."

She nodded, as if getting ready to brave battle. "I guess I should call Cora and tell her that I'm stuck here." She rummaged around for her bagged-up phone. "All night. With you," she added on a mutter.

"You know, it's not so bad. It's . . . not. We're lucky that we made it back. That storm sounds terrible."

"You're right. Of course." She held on to the phone like it was her anchor.

"We can still keep our distance. You can be in your office and I can be in mine. We don't even have to talk."

"I don't have any clothes to change into," she said softly, a note he couldn't read in her voice.

"Yeah, I'll see what I can scrounge up." He tugged off his boots and his socks, much the way she had when she'd gone to read the note. If he were alone, he would have stripped out of his shirt and pants completely. But, he wasn't alone. Lilly was here. With him. All night.

It was fine. They were going to be fine. Why did this feel so dire when they were two adults with a brain between them at least? It was fine.

He stalked back to his office, where he kept all manner of extras. It wasn't uncommon for him to spend the night in the office. Sometimes he didn't feel like driving to the little house he and Will shared.

He could likely find a T-shirt and maybe some sweatpants or something with a tie for Lilly to wear while her clothes dried. And she could keep them forever, because he would never want them back knowing that she had worn them. Because he was screwy in the head.

He went to his office and rummaged through his closet of odds and ends. He chose the smallest things he had that he held no personal attachment to. When he returned to the front desk, she was standing there, running a comb through her hair.

She looked . . . different. All the makeup washed off of her, her hair a mess, everything about her a mess really. He liked her polish—he couldn't ignore that—but there was something about seeing her without it that felt . . .

Intimate.

Great. Just what he needed. "Here's some stuff that should work. I'll start a fire. Because it will dry our things faster than just sitting out. But, in the meantime, you can take these and change in your office or the bathroom. And I will . . . start a fire." And not think about her changing clothes.

"Brandon . . ."

He stopped on his way to the fireplace, surprised that she was looking at him with a frown and that line between her eyebrows.

"It isn't always going to be . . . weird between us, is it?"

"No," he said, knee-jerk, because he didn't want it to be weird. He certainly didn't want it to be like this. "No, I don't think so. I think it's just a little weird because it's new and we admitted it to one another. But, it'll be . . . fine." Why did he keep saying that damn word? "We just have to get over this initial awkward hump of awkwardness."

She smiled, a small, not-at-all-comforting smile. "Okay, because I don't want it to always be like this."

"Me neither." He meant that. More than he should.

"Good."

"Yes, good."

She shook her head. "I'll go change and you will start a fire. And this is normal. And we are fine. And . . ."

Brandon let out a long breath. "You know what? It's not fine. We're totally fucked."

Lilly gripped the clothes she held tightly and laughed. "So *very* fucked." She chewed on her lip for a second, her hands fiddling with the clothes. "We should probably not say that word."

Christ.

"I'm going to go change," she said in a squeaky voice.

"Yup." He stared at the fireplace and tried to find enough brain cells to remember how to start a fire.

\* \* \*

Lilly stared at the door of her office. She was starving. Just *starving*, but if she left her office, she might run into Brandon. And her mouth might fall on his mouth.

Or lower.

She closed her eyes and groaned and narrowly resisted banging her head against her desk. Was there some sort of crazy sex vibe in the thin air up here? Like . . . people came up to these mountains and then suddenly couldn't keep it in their pants?

Was that the secret behind Mile High Adventures? You hiked around in the clean air and took in the gorgeous views and then turned into a sex-crazed moron who fantasized about screwing her boss on her desk, against a wall, on the floor next to the fire he'd started. Anywhere. Everywhere.

It was the *only* explanation. Because this was not her. She was not this woman. She didn't even read Cora's romance novels—always thinking they were just a little *too* racy with the shirtless men on the covers.

Now, she wondered what was *in* those books—when she wasn't wondering about what was in Brandon's pants.

She felt as if she'd tumbled down that trail a few weeks ago and somehow forgotten a blow to the head she'd taken. Because here she was, in Brandon's clothes, fantasizing about all those things while her stomach rumbled and her blood pounded with some unspoken, thwarted want.

Calling Cora to explain her absence hadn't helped any. Not when Cora kept drawing out the words *okay* and *sure* as if Lilly could somehow *make up* the terrible storm outside.

The weathermen were predicting flooding and mudslides and all manner of apocalyptic emergencies, and Cora had the nerve to not believe her.

Which should make Lilly that much more committed
to avoiding Brandon and his . . . pants.

Her stomach rumbled loud enough to rival the thunder. Okay, so she had to eat something, but she could
just tiptoe into the kitchen, scrounge something together, then tiptoe back to her office and focus on all
the work she hadn't been able to focus on for the past
two hours because she was . . .

"Ridiculous. You are ridiculous, Lilly Preston, and
you need to get a hold of yourself." She stood and faced
the door—shoulders back because she had gotten this
far in life by braving her way through things and being
determined to beat every odd stacked against her.

She had made herself into a successful business-
woman. She had done everything in her power to get
her sister and nephew out of a physically abusive situation and give them a new life. She could face down an
attractive man without losing that part of herself. She
had for nearly thirty years.

*Except none of them affected you like this one.*

So, the challenge was getting more . . . challenging.
Didn't mean it would beat her. Besides, a girl had to eat.
Bottom line. So, she grabbed her doorknob, turned,
and opened the door. Determined to—"oof."

She glanced up at the big, hard wall of person she'd
just bumped into, his hands immediately reaching out
and steadying her so she didn't fall backwards from the
force of nearly bouncing off him.

She blinked up at him, trying to remember what on
earth she'd been doing, but all she could think about
was how easy it would be for him to simply pick her up
by the arms. He was that strong, and he always seemed
to be picking her up.

And if he picked her up, just a few inches, their

mouths could meet—that easily. Or he could lean down and . . .

She dropped her gaze, determined to find some sense, but that just put her eye level with his chest, which looked like an awfully nice place to lean, to . . .

Brandon should rethink his belief that the mountains could heal. She was now certain mountains could turn you into a sex-obsessed nut. It might be a good PR angle, all in all.

He uncurled his fingers from her arms in what felt like slow motion. He cleared his throat and took a step backward in that tight hallway. "I was just about to knock and check to see if you wanted some dinner. We have a few staples in the kitchenette."

"That's . . . actually what I was coming out for."

He gave a tight smile. "Great. Then we can . . . make something."

"Great," she echoed with as much dread in her voice as had been in his.

He waved his hand down the hall. "After you."

On less than steady legs, Lilly walked down the hall and into the kitchenette. Would he expect her to eat with him now? As much as she was still hungry, her stomach was all twisted in nervous knots and she didn't know how she'd swallow a bite with him sucking up all the air in the room.

"We have cans of soup, I know. Or maybe . . ."

"Cans of soup is fine."

"Great."

Yeah, great. Everything was super great and wonderful. *Fine.* That was certainly why they kept repeating that inane word.

Brandon opened a cupboard and pulled out two cans of soup, then rummaged around in another cupboard and pulled out a pot.

Lilly stood in the corner of the kitchenette feeling stupid and useless. There were few things she hated more. She was pretty sure the feelings were tied in hateland with all this lust. "Is there anything I can do?" she asked desperately.

"Unfortunately, heating up soup doesn't take a lot of help."

"Right." Lightning flashed outside the kitchenette window. Thunder boomed immediately in time with it, rattling the panes of glass. It startled Lilly to the point she let out a little screech and jumped. The entire office went dark and oddly silent. The only light in the room was now from the flickering fireplace and the occasional burst of lightning.

Brandon was only a shadow. "Well, there goes the electricity. It's all right. I've got a grate I can put on the fireplace and we can heat up the soup like that. Will you grab me a flashlight from the emergency drawer, and then light some of the candles in there? If we set the candles on the coffee table, between that and the fire, we should have enough light to eat dinner by."

A candlelit dinner in front of a cozy fire. Yes, that was *so* what this day was missing.

But what choice did she have? She went to the drawer and grabbed him a flashlight, then collected the fat utilitarian candles and a box of matches and took them to the living room.

The wind raged outside and rain pelted the roof and the windows as she lit candles around the fireplace. Thunder boomed and lightning flashed at such a rapid rate she felt jumpy.

She'd never been scared of storms before. She hadn't been able to be scared of much of anything because she had always had to comfort Cora. But this was a little . . . ominous. Overwhelming.

"What would you like to drink?" Brandon asked from the kitchenette.

"Oh, um." A bottle of wine. Maybe some kind of drug that would knock her out until she could escape this poised-for-sex cabin. "I guess I'll have some water."

After a few moments, Brandon came into the living room and set a bowl of soup and a glass of water on the coffee table next to her. Before he went back to the kitchen, he glanced at her and seemed to take in her clasped fingers and worried glances at the windows.

"This is probably the worst storm we've ever had up here. But at least we're not down below where there's flooding."

"You mean down below where my sister and nephew and your brother are currently?"

Brandon grimaced, the fire and candlelight somehow softening the harsh angles of his face, the rugged lines usually around his eyes. Everything about him looked warm and golden and . . . inviting.

"Okay, I've never been any good at comforting people. But everything will be fine. Mother Nature can be an incredibly scary thing, but she can't really . . . Okay I don't have any reassuring words. This is concerning. I've never seen this much rain. Not in my entire lifetime here."

"Brandon, please stop talking and trying to make me feel better because this so does not."

"Sorry. I'll go get my soup and shut up."

"Great idea," she muttered into her soup.

He disappeared into the kitchenette and fiddled around in there for a while before he returned and placed his soup on the coffee table edge opposite h⸻

It was weird to be in the office without the b⸻ electricity. She'd never really noticed the way ⸻ and the lights sort of buzzed and had a life⸻

Sure, it wasn't silent because of the rain pounding outside, but it certainly wasn't the same as when the lights had been on.

Everything felt eerie and otherworldly. But she ate her soup and drank her water and tried to focus on the fact that they were fine. Safe. Everyone she knew was somewhere in shelter, and that was something to be thankful for and not at all scared over.

"Everyone will be fine," Brandon said in a low, certain voice. She knew he was trying to make her feel better, and that was really sweet. The last thing she needed from him right now was more sweetness.

"Yeah, I know. I'm not . . . You have to understand, I raised my sister and I have practically raised Micah for the most part, and it's very strange to be away from them when something kind of scary is going down. I'm sure that Cora has it handled. I'm sure they're fine. But it's hard not being there." Because what would it mean if they *were* fine? That they didn't need her?

*Of course they need you. You're their meal ticket.* An incredibly gross and unfair thought that felt awfully close to the truth.

"How much younger is your sister than you?" Brandon asked, bringing a spoonful of soup to his mouth.

She could not look at his mouth, so she looked at her own spoon. "Only two years. But my mom had to work a lot of jobs to keep us afloat. So, for as long as I can remember, I have been in charge of keeping Cora safe and out of trouble. Which was a full-time job and I failed that pretty miserably. But everything's good now. I mean aside from the fact she doesn't have a job."

"She hasn't found anything yet? What's her background? Maybe I know of an opening somewhere. Or is there anything here she could do?"

Lilly looked at Brandon, her mouth probably slightly

ajar because she couldn't believe he was basically offering her sister a job. "Why . . . why would you want to hire her? You don't even know her."

"But I know you, and if you vouch for her, and there's something around here she'd be qualified to do, I don't see what the harm would be."

"No, I didn't want you to offer this. I mean . . ." She didn't know why, but the offer scared her. Not just because she hated the idea of them both being at the whims of Mile High Adventures' success—because as much as she believed Mile High would continue to be successful, she didn't want something to happen where she and Cora would both be out of a job. But that wasn't what was bothering her. She wished that were it, but the real reason was something else.

She had a bad feeling what bothered her was the fact that she didn't want her sister encroaching on her space here. She didn't want the possibility that Cora would come in here and make this mistake Lilly was desperately trying not to make.

Which was a nasty, insidious thought, but there it was.

"I meant it as a friendly 'I trust your opinion' sort of thing. I'm sorry if that . . . offended you in some way?"

"No. It didn't." No offense, just her being a terrible person. "It's just complicated. Cora's never really done anything aside from waitressing and I know she doesn't want to be a waitress, but she doesn't have a college degree, I barely managed to convince her to get her GED, and she hasn't really built any skills. I've tried so hard to push her into finding *something*. I love her and I want to give her everything, and I feel so horrible saying this, but I don't know what she could do here." Lilly frowned into her soup. It was true. That was . . . honesty. Why was she being honest with him? It was none of his business.

"I don't think you need to feel terrible about that."

"She's my sister and I basically said she's useless."

"No, you said she hasn't figured out what she's good at yet, and she's resisting doing that. You know her best and I think it's better to be honest about what she can and can't do than lie. Look, Will and I are twins, but I was the oldest. I came out first, so that was how it went. And growing up in my family, which was very sort of old-money traditional, we all had roles to play. Will struggled to figure out who he was and what he wanted to do, and I was looked at to be the next president of Evans Mining. There were no choices."

Brandon idly stirred his soup and she realized this was the most he'd really talked about growing up. He'd talked about Mile High, he'd talked about Evans, but he hadn't talked about him and Will as people. Kids.

"I think, for a while there, he felt like he didn't have a place. I think there's two ways that people deal with that feeling. One is to go out on their complete own, find a completely different passion. And another is to act like they don't have one at all and pretend that that's fine with them."

"So, what you're saying is that because I was so responsible and had such a clear place in our family being her caretaker, that she has reacted by finding no place for herself?"

"Well, no, not exactly. If you think that doesn't sound right, you would know better than me. I'm just saying that in my experience, that's what I saw."

"That theory is . . . annoyingly accurate."

"Annoyingly?" he asked, with a slight curve of his mouth. The light flickered around him, soft and romantic, and he was very nearly smiling and her heart did some weird flipping thing in her chest and this was just awful.

He was right *and* hot. "Yes, it's annoying when

someone tells me something about my life I should know, but didn't, because I was so wrapped up in myself. *Annoyingly.*"

His mouth curved wider and she looked down at her soup because this was getting worse and worse. Smart and funny and nice and handsome. This conversation felt like they had some sort of camaraderie, and she just couldn't keep walking away from this.

This thing she'd never had. That was the bottom line—she'd never had someone to tell her concerns about Cora to, and she'd never had someone to pick her up when she fell or take her to the doctor. She'd always had to do everything on her own, and Brandon seemed so infinitely capable of swooping in and taking care of some of the things she simply couldn't.

It was scary that she wanted that. It was wrong. And yet she couldn't ignore the way that want grew inside of her like a vine curling tighter and tighter until she didn't think she'd have any air left.

"Listen," Brandon said, getting quiet for a minute. "I think the rain is letting up."

Lilly was silent and let the sound wash over her. It was still going pretty steady in her estimation, but maybe it was letting up a little bit, and the lightning had certainly stopped flashing so much.

"It should keep tapering off from here. That was the last storm cell in our area from what I looked at before we lost power."

"Hopefully."

"I have a bed in my office for the occasional times Will or I want to spend the night, but you can use it tonight. Alone, obviously." He winced a little at his own terrible assumption. "Fresh sheets. It's . . . you can use it."

"Where will you sleep?" Which was not the right thing to ask. It did not matter where he would sleep.

It was very kind of him to offer her his bed to sleep in— alone. She did not need to know his sleeping arrangements.

"I'll just sleep on the couch like I did the other night."

"What exactly were you three doing the other night?"

"We had a little bit of a poker game. It had been a while since we relaxed and did something as friends instead of constantly doing work things as coworkers."

"Well, next time you should invite me."

"You?"

"I'm a coworker."

"But . . . you're a girl."

She let out a little laugh. *Girl.* As if. "So?"

"So, we give Will a hard time about his reputation with women, we give Sam shit for being a hermit. It's a very manly affair."

"Obviously," she said with mock seriousness that made him chuckle. "You should invite me next time. I may not be a *man*, but I am part of this business and you said yourself that I'm a *valuable* part of the business. I should be part of the camaraderie aspect as well." A self-consciousness she rarely felt or identified swamped her. Because . . . she wanted to be a part of *this*. Not just work for it.

She forced herself to bulldoze her way through and meet his gaze. "I'd like to be friends with you all." It was surprising how hard it was to admit. She'd never asked to be a part of something. She'd always been so busy just trying to get by. She still *was* just trying to get by, but something about the Evans brothers and Sam and Skeet and this place made her want to be a part of it. A real part of it, not just that woman who got everything accomplished. The woman you went to when you had a problem. She wanted to be more than that. She wanted to be friends.

"Okay. Next time we have a poker night, consider yourself officially invited."

She couldn't read his expression, which was just as well. The less she could *read* him, the better. "Good. Well . . ."

"Well . . ."

It was stupid to be sitting across from him, feeling breathless and swoony just from a little extended eye contact and meaningful conversation. Stupid. "We should clean this up and . . . retire to our rooms." *Retire to our rooms.* Honestly.

Brandon got to his feet with a nod. "Yes, that is what we should do."

They gathered their dishes and took them into the tiny kitchenette, where they couldn't seem to help but bump into each other again and again as they tried to avoid each other and clean out the bowls and carry around candles and flashlights at the same time.

An arm brush, a hip bump, and then somehow, hands empty, they were standing face-to-face, very nearly chest-to-chest.

Lilly knew she should move. She should get out of his way and he would simply walk out of the kitchenette. Because he was likely trying to walk back to his office and she was in his way. She should move. She had to move. Why would her feet *not* move?

"Lilly." His voice sounded rough. He cleared his throat and she had to *move* or say something at least. Not just . . . look at him and breathe heavily like some kind of statuesque fish.

"I'm headed to my office," she said even though her feet were still firmly planted and she was still completely one hundred percent in his way.

"Right, and I'm going to grab a few things from my

office and then it's all yours to sleep in whenever you're ready for that."

Alone. Sleep in his office alone. She did want to sleep alone. *You honestly have to sleep alone, Lilly. You have to want that.*

God help her, she didn't want to be alone and she didn't want to pretend this thing between them was some figment of her imagination. She didn't want to think or beat it. She wanted to *give in to it.* And hard.

*You can't. You can't. You have worked too hard to be this weak woman.*

"Lilly . . ."

"Yeah?" Her voice was a whisper, her gaze mesmerized by the flecks of green in his eyes, the way they dropped their attention to her mouth. Where she wanted *his* mouth.

He cleared his throat again and stood there staring at her like she was something that he wanted. Something that he needed, and she knew she was probably making that up. It was all in her head—need and want. It was mixed up with a million other things and yet she could not stop herself from leaning forward. She couldn't stop herself from leaning in, and he did the same.

They met—just their bodies brushing up against each other, their arms still at their sides. Their mouths somehow still inches apart.

But they were touching. Their chests were brushing. Electricity seemed to tinge the air, not the storm outside. No, them. This *thing.* This thing that was . . . what was the point in pretending it didn't exist?

It existed like the storm, like the lightning and thunder. Like the rain washing away everything man had built.

Lust was erasing everything she'd ever built for herself, and she couldn't fight Mother Nature, so why should she think she could fight lust?

"I'm going to kiss you," he said, his voice a tight, low, *painful*-sounding thing.

She knew that was his warning. He was giving her a chance to move. A chance to back out. A chance to be the reasonable, sensible adults they both kept claiming that they were.

But she didn't want to be that person. Not right now. So, she looked him in the eye and said, "Okay."

She didn't have a second to take a breath before Brandon's mouth was on hers, before his hands were diving into her hair and she was crushed against him. His mouth was on hers, soft and insistent, his beard rough against her face, his hands strong and absolute at the base of her skull.

It was the most glorious feeling in the world and she didn't care that it was wrong. She didn't care that she was failing or doing all the things she'd promised herself she would never do. It didn't matter when she could taste lightning. Experience thunder.

It didn't matter when the storm inside of her raged darker and more powerful than any storm outside. She'd ride it out.

And finally get what she wanted out of it.

# Chapter Fifteen

Brandon rejected any arguments his brain was trying to make. Why would he listen to an argument when Lilly's mouth was under his? Eager and sweet. Her arms winding around his neck.

Somehow, she tasted exactly as he would have thought. Bright and fresh and sweet. It was just a mouth, the same as any mouth he'd ever kissed, but it wasn't. No matter how much reason dictated it should be—she was everything unique and new.

Her hair was silk and her breasts were soft crushed to his chest. She was this strong, determined woman, but she'd melted against him like wax and he wouldn't deny the thrill that gave him.

Later, much later, he could worry about all that psychological crap. For now, it was only her. The way he could span her back with his two hands, taking the entire landscape that existed under the thin fabric of his old T-shirt.

She always walked around like she held the world capably on those narrow shoulders, and it was easy to forget how much bigger he was than her. He liked that she could be both, a complex, fascinating, maddening mix of all manner of polar opposites.

Her fingers trailed up his neck and into his hair, her satisfied sigh against his mouth sending a sharp dart of possession through him. He wanted that satisfaction—to be the cause of it. Only him.

His hands stopped at her waist, because he needed something to hold on to, and he could get a grip there. She arched against him, everything about her reaction proving that whatever he was feeling—she felt it equally.

Maybe it was complicated, but they were on equal ground. Equal ground that somehow wasn't close enough. He needed more of her against him; that gentle arching of her back wasn't nearly enough.

He moved her backwards, until she was against the wall, until he could press his entire body against hers. Her knees, her thighs, her stomach—everything was against him, under him. *For him.*

He broke the kiss at that, because . . . this thing lighting a fire inside of him was new and, he could admit in the comfort of his own mind, more than a little concerning. Okay, fine, *frightening*. It was this thing he'd skillfully avoided for years, purposefully, hoping it would never grab him by the throat like this.

But here it was. Her hands might not be around his throat, but her fingers were in his hair and her body was pressed to his, and that was enough for him to want to toss every promise he'd ever made himself in the fire.

Her eyes fluttered open, meeting his gaze. In the faint fire and candlelight, her eyes seemed like some kind of liquid silver, mesmerizing and something he could drown in.

"We can stop." He *would* stop, because he was a better man than his father *somewhere*.

She smiled at him—smiled—and even if he'd tried

to come up with an argument now, a rational, reasonable cease and desist, it'd be impossible. He was in some fog made up of her smile, and those smoky blue eyes, and the warmth and softness of her skin.

It was all he wanted.

"No. No, we shouldn't stop," she said, her voice hushed, her arms curling around his neck, soft but somehow with a strong, tight grip. "We just started."

His lips curved in return to her smile, always she was coaxing reactions out of him he didn't want to give, let alone thought he *had* to give. Yet they were here, easy and effortless when she was smiling up at him.

"We're two very reasonable, responsible people, aren't we?" she asked, her hands unlinking from around his neck and skimming down his chest.

"I suppose we are," he managed to return even though most of his brain was focused on the trajectory of her hands.

"I'm so *exhausted*," she said, her fingers curling in the hem of his shirt and lifting the fabric up. "Exhausted with being the one who always has to do the right thing." She lifted the shirt higher and higher until he had to release his grip on her waist and lift his arms up.

"Tired of always being the one who has to have all the answers, but the minute you're wrong, or not even one hundred percent right, it's thrown in your face?"

She jerked the rest of his shirt off, gaze firmly on his. "Exactly that." Then her eyes dropped to his chest and her fingertips followed her gaze, pressing into his chest like little brands. Brands that—in the moment—felt like they might always be there. The heat of her fingertips, the electricity of her touch.

"We deserve this," he said, his voice hoarse as he mimicked her previous movements and curled his fingers under the hem of *his* T-shirt, which she wore.

"We deserve a lot of this," she returned, slowly raising her arms above her head, the power of those silver-threaded blue eyes holding him captive as he lifted the shirt.

"A lot of this," he repeated, his gaze only dropping once the shirt obscured her face. She wasn't wearing a bra. *Christ.* He dropped the shirt without consciously thinking about it.

Even though he'd seen her clothes plastered to her, even though he'd too often caught himself staring at the way her sweaters clung to that soft curve, the reality of it was something else entirely.

The pale expanse of skin, the light crescent-shaped birthmark between her breasts, small pink nipples tightened into points. Points he wanted to touch, or put his mouth to, and yet all he could seem to manage was to place the palms of his hands—big and rough compared to the soft delicateness of her skin—on her abdomen, spreading his fingers wide. But not wide enough to touch what had been bared to him.

It was the strangest thing, as if it were some last line to cross, as if there were no going back. Stupid. There was always going back, but his hands stayed on her stomach, and she shivered underneath him.

"Oh, for heaven's sake, touch me."

"I *am* touching you," he replied, meeting her impatient gaze.

"Brandon," she nearly growled.

It made him grin. "Well, I am."

She tugged his wrists upward. "You know what I—" Her words ended on a moan as he slid his hands up her torso to cover the soft swells of her breasts, the rough skin of his palms catching on the hard buds of her nipples.

And then he groaned too. He lowered his mouth to

her neck, trailing his mouth across her jaw as he absorbed the weight of her, the silky warmth of her skin, and the hint of that floral scent she always wore—stronger there, under her jaw, where she must have dabbed some perfume this morning. How had the lake and the rain not washed it away?

She arched against him again, this time a slow curl up, and then down, drawing against the hard length of his dick with each move. He dropped his mouth to her shoulder, using his thumbs to circle a path across her chest.

When he scraped his teeth over the curve of her shoulder in time with running the pad of his thumbs over her nipples, she arched again, that long, hot slide of her against him. And he thrust into it this time, enjoying the painfully desperate ache building there.

"W-wait," she said, her hands clutching his shoulders.

"Wait?" He cupped one breast, bringing his mouth closer and closer, and when she never said what to wait for, he drew her into his mouth. He used his tongue to tease her nipple, enjoying the way she shuddered against him, a breathless laugh escaped her before ending somewhere closer to a moan.

"But, wait. I mean . . ." She sighed when he moved to her other breast, her fingers threading through his hair.

"Brandon. Let me think."

He released her nipple and smiled up at her. "That's kind of the opposite of the point here."

She smiled in return. "The occasional thinking is necessary. Do you have a condom or anything?"

He stood to his full height. "Well, we have the condom bucket."

She scrunched up her nose and pushed him back a step. "You have the *what?*"

"Will has kind of made a name for himself doing

bachelorette parties—float trips or hikes or whatever. Those women put condoms and penises on everything. Veils. Cups. Goody bags. They're constantly leaving a trail of glitter and condoms in their wake. The penises get tossed, but it seems a crime to waste a condom." He shrugged.

"Some would say it's a crime to waste a penis," she said, looking very grave for approximately a second before her mouth curved into a grin.

"Is that an . . . actual saying?"

She shrugged and laughed, and he didn't know why it was different with her. But he'd never stood laughing over penis jokes with a woman, especially a half naked one.

"Come on." He grabbed the flashlight off the counter and linked fingers with her and led her down the hall to the linen closet, where they kept a random mix of extras. On the top shelf, in the back corner, was a bucket. He pulled it out and shone the light toward the contents.

"Take your pick."

She peered into the bucket, which held somewhere around twenty condoms of varying types. Then she looked back up at him, that line between her eyes that never failed to make him want to smile.

Smiling. Grinning. He was starting to feel downright jovial around her.

She shook her head, then pulled a black packet out of the pile. "Oh my God, it says, 'glow in the dark.'"

"I'll pass."

"But I'm curious now. Does it really glow in the dark? Is that somehow optimal? I have so many questions." She looked up at him, her face a mix of light and shadows from the single beam of the flashlight.

Since his hands were full of condom bucket and

flashlight, he leaned forward and took her mouth. Not a kiss, he *took* her mouth with his. Because it was his, and whatever lingering discomfort he'd had at that thought, that feeling was dead or silent or too quiet to acknowledge.

He pulled her bottom lip between his teeth and heard the condom packet fall back into the bucket as Lilly swayed toward him.

When he pulled away, her eyes were on his, her breath coming in shallow little bursts. She didn't even look back down at the bucket; she just shoved her hand in and grabbed a condom.

"Okay, this'll do." She took the bucket out of his grip and placed it carefully on the floor. Then she grabbed his hand and led him to his office.

He enthusiastically followed.

Lilly had never *pulled* a man to bed before, and she couldn't even bring herself to be bothered by it. She wanted him with a need that was so big she didn't even feel scared of it anymore. Not after she'd felt what he could do with his mouth.

To her mouth, to her neck, to her breasts. She shivered again as she dropped his hand and turned to face him. There was no light in his room except for the beam of the flashlight and the weakest grey glow from the window.

It was a shame to do this in the dark, when he looked like he did. When she wanted to memorize every last inch of him. But it would be more of a shame to wait until the lights came on. More of a shame to wait, period.

"Hold on for one second," he said in that low, gravelly

voice that spoke of restraint and want all at the same time.

She *loved* that voice, the way it could make her nerve endings dance with something giddy and light. The ecstatic possibility in what might happen when he dropped some of that finely tuned control.

He rummaged around in the big dresser that seemed to hold both office supplies and who knew what all. He retrieved a candle, struck a match, and lit it. It wasn't much light, but then he lit another, and then another.

She could make out the shape of the bed, the shape of *him*, and that was enough.

"There," he said, turning to her. She couldn't make out the exact shade of his eyes or every line of his abs—*abs*—but she could make out the *intent* in his gaze. She could feel that like a heavy, rough touch.

And oh, she wanted his heavy, rough touch, even as he stood on the opposite side of the room, simply staring at her.

All that laughter from before, the simple *enjoyment,* that nervy, giddy *"Should we do this? We should do this"* was now replaced by one thing.

Desperation.

She didn't want to explore or savor; she wanted to take and be filled and race to that end. Which was not her in the least, but she was realizing Brandon made her someone else. Tomorrow, maybe she'd worry about that, dissect it, admit her mistake, and move on.

For tonight—she wanted him.

"Brandon." Her voice was a raspy thing, someone else's voice. Someone passionate and sensual and impulsive. Words she would have never used to describe herself in her entire life, but they were used now. She wouldn't turn it away. For tonight, she'd revel in it. Allow herself something she'd denied for always.

Enjoyment. Pleasure. Maybe a little recklessness. It was her turn. *Hers.*

"Lilly." He didn't move, just said her name just as she'd said his.

She pushed out an impatient breath. "Come here."

He was silent for a stretching movement, not moving. Not taking even one step toward her. "I've never really been one for taking orders."

"Me either." She fisted her hand on her hip, made a grand sweeping gesture down the length of her leg. "But I'm not wearing any underwear under these."

His gaze dropped, then returned, the candlelight flickering to somehow make that curve of his mouth both amused and dangerous. "Hmm." He took a step then, and then another, closer and closer until she could barely take a breath.

It felt like the air was nothing but flame, and yet she didn't want to run. She wanted to burn in it, to lose herself to this completely different world. But she couldn't *do* that if he just *stood* there, not touching her.

"*Bran.*" She couldn't even say his entire name. It felt too formal and weighty with his gaze taking in every inch of her naked skin. Her skin felt too weighty in the air of the room, her breasts heavy and her nipples hard. Everything in her stomach was pulled painfully tight. Every cell in her being waiting for him to touch her again, to light her aflame again.

He reached his hand out and brushed a thumb across her jaw. "Bran." His mouth quirked. "I like that from you."

It warmed her in some ridiculous way it shouldn't, melted a pinch of that coiled tightness inside of her. Yeah, she was all too pleased that he *liked* anything from her. *So this is what it's like to be completely stupid over a guy.* Well, if the payoff was half as good as the little make-out session in the hallway, it'd probably be worth it.

His fingers, somehow so completely light against her jaw despite the fact they were so big and strong and rough, kept tracing—across her chin, then down her neck, her side, until his fingers hooked in the waistband of the drawstring athletic pants he'd given her earlier.

His gaze flicked to her face briefly, watching her in the seconds his fingers followed the path of the waistband until he found the string. Then his gaze dropped again and he didn't tug or pull the pants off. Instead, his fingers deftly untied the string, his knuckles occasionally brushing against her abdomen.

She wasn't cold, but she kept shivering nonetheless. She was nothing but goose bumps and electricity. And want. She was completely saturated in a desperate wanting that had never, ever gripped her before. No person, no thing, no achievement had reduced her to this quivering mass of *feeling.*

All he had to do was touch her in the lightest, slightest way, and she shivered, shuddered, vibrated from the inside out. He was magic, and she didn't even care how fanciful that sounded.

In the end, he didn't have to tug her pants, because once he untied them, they simply fell off her hips and pooled at her feet.

She stood in front of him completely naked. At least candlelight was flattering. It couldn't make up for the modest-at-best size of her breasts, but Brandon didn't seem to mind. He didn't seem to mind anything about her. In fact, he looked downright rapt, which did some things for her ego.

But he still wasn't touching her.

So she touched him instead. She placed an index

finger at the center of his chest and then followed the trail of hair down his center, slowly touching his chest with each of her other fingers as she went down. He was warm and soft, the gentle scrape of his chest hair against her fingers reminding her just how damn *manly* he was.

Her very own sexy lumberjack, with the mind of a businessman, the heart of a poet. Oh, she couldn't be thinking about all the things he was, all the ways he tugged at her heart.

So she focused on him. The ridge of each muscle, the way he jumped and tensed the closer her fingers traveled to his obvious erection. When she got to the waistband of his pants, she *did* tug and pull, until his cock sprang free.

And what a glorious cock it was. She really hadn't seen all that many. She'd been very, very selective in her choice of lovers. She had a firm five-date rule before she even let a man cop a feel. As for sex, a man had to last at least three months, all without getting bent out of shape about it.

Not many had risen to her stringent standards. And she supposed that's why she'd had them.

If she wanted to justify this, well, she and Brandon had been on something like dates. The excursions. The drives to their meetings or to Evans. She'd been with Mile High for almost two months now.

But the bottom line was Brandon was not her boyfriend. This wasn't that kind of relationship, and she'd never had sex with someone without being in a relationship.

She was really curious if that made it better. If spontaneity and complete boldness could make it hotter. Because so far, this experience was way hotter than anything she had ever done in her life. Possibly hotter than anything she'd *dreamed* of doing.

When she glanced up at him, his eyes were on her hands and where they now rested at his hips. She drew her fingers closer to center, watching as his face turned to granite the closer her fingers trailed to his erection.

Meanwhile, he wasn't touching her at all, but she found she liked that right now. She liked that she was the one with all the power. The power was in her fingertips. The power was in the torturous trail she was taking to touch him. His gaze was rapt on her fingers. Her fingers were in charge.

Yes, this was a completely different experience from anything with any other man in her entire life.

Slowly, her eyes never leaving his face, watching as his jaw tensed harder and tighter, she curled her fingers around the hard length of him. They both groaned.

His skin was hot and smooth, and he was so hard under her palm. Her gaze dropped to where she held him, needing to see it. Needing to sear into her memory what it looked like holding Brandon's hard, impressive erection in her hand.

She stroked once, but then his fingers curled around her wrist. She met his fierce stare. But he didn't stop her stroke—at first, he simply held her wrist as she slid her palm down to the base of him.

But then his grip loosened and he trailed his fingers up her arm, over her shoulder, along her neck, and then into her hair. He fisted his fingers deep into her tangled mess of hair and her breath caught at the fissure of excitement that went down her spine.

She stroked him again and his other hand slid up her waist, her stomach, up to her breast, where he drew his thumb across her nipple, back and forth. She stroked more quickly, letting her palm absorb the shape of him, the weight of him, the length of him. All the while, his hand was in her hair, gripping her there, and her heart kept beating impossibly fast, excitement building impossibly sharp in her stomach.

He took a step toward her so that with every stroke she could feel her own hand hit her stomach. So close she could smell that faint, piney scent she figured must be deodorant or soap because she only ever smelled it when she was pressed up against him. He was so much like those mountains he loved so much, and it made her feel like she knew him somehow. Understood him.

Which wasn't what this was supposed to be about, and luckily she could push it out of her mind when his hand loosened from her hair and followed the same trail back down as it had gone up. But it didn't stop at her waist. He traced the curve of her hip, trailed his fingers across her thigh, and then slowly, with careful gentle pressure, those long, blunt fingers drew across her inner thigh and nudged her legs a little farther apart.

For a moment, she was so absorbed in the sparkling pleasure, the giddy hint at what was to come, she stopped stroking him. She was intent on his fingers, on where they would go, on what aches they might ease.

"Don't stop."

She swallowed at the rusty order. She moved her palm down the length of him again as his fingers danced closer and closer to the aching hot center of her. When his index finger slid between her folds, she squeezed him, needing something to anchor her. Why not that?

Brandon was not a man who simply touched. He didn't merely stroke. No, his hands explored, they invaded. She felt the pressure of his touch everywhere, even though his fingers were concentrated at the center-most part of her.

Without setting out to do it, every time his finger slid

inside of her, she drew her hand down to the base of him and then back, matching his rhythm stroke for stroke, invasion for invasion. And every time his finger slid deeper and his palm pressed against the outside part of her, her breathing became more and more labored because the pleasure coiled in her stomach and her chest, where his other hand was still teasing her nipple.

She tried to swallow, but she couldn't because all there was was this heat, and need. She needed to follow that edge, and she didn't know how, but with each stroke of his finger, she got closer. Each time he moaned from the way she touched him, she stepped farther on to that precipice, that edge.

It all seemed so dreamlike, the world around her fuzzy and dim, every atom of her being focused on where he touched her, where she touched him. An ache that seemed to have been hiding inside of her for years yawning open wider and wider.

When he slid another finger inside of her and pressed his palm hard against her, the orgasm rushed over her, through her, a blinding wave of pleasure that pulsed with heat and satisfaction. Her legs shook and she cried out, cried into that release.

His arm hooked under her to hold her weight and then somehow, just as he'd done multiple times in the past two weeks, he swept her into his arms, and then onto the bed. She didn't even have time to be breathless or enjoy it because the orgasm was still rattling her brain and making her insides nothing but air and pleasure.

In less than a second, he was on top of her, pressing her into the mattress, and it was the most glorious thing in the world to be overpowered. To be gloriously powerless and feel as though someone else was running this show. She didn't want any of the power from before now; she wanted him to have it. She wanted him to use it to give them both the end they sought.

"The condom?"

She'd forgotten about it, but he glanced at the floor they'd been standing on. For a brief second, his weight left her and she felt surprisingly chilled and alone even with the aftereffects of the first orgasms still blasting through her.

But then he was on top of her again, already rolling the condom on to protect himself. But he didn't immediately enter her. He held himself above her, his arms locked, his gaze intent and intense. She could barely breathe under the weight of it, under the fierceness of it.

How had she resisted him this long? How had she not immediately surrendered to this feeling that coursed through her? How, when he looked at her like that? "Bran . . ."

"I've never wanted anyone like this." It was a grave admission, and she knew that it cost him something. She knew he was offering her this piece of himself, and she knew that because she felt it too. That nothing else had taken away her control and taken away all those things she prided herself on.

In the beginning, it had been scary. In the here and now, with him so close to making love to her, she could only glory in it. "Me neither."

His gaze blazed a trail of warmth and pleasure down her chest and stomach, and she followed it, seeing herself, and seeing him above her. Then they both watched as he slowly pressed himself into her entrance.

It shouldn't be a shock. She had done this before, with more than one partner, and she knew what to expect.

Still, he was bigger and more intense, and somehow this was shocking. This experience was *so* big. It was like nothing that had ever come before, and it swamped her. The emotion of it, the brightness of it. How could his sliding inside of her feel so right?

She knew it was wrong—this thing they were giving in to. She had been resisting it for weeks, and yet this was the most whole she had felt in all of those weeks. Him on top of her. His mouth gently touching hers.

It was a strange thing to be on fire with desire and need and want and yet still be able to enjoy that gentle kiss. Just a little brush of mouths. It was meaningful. She didn't know what to do with meaning. She didn't know what to do with the way this all roiled inside of her.

But she knew she wanted more. She arched to take him deeper and he groaned, thrusting to meet that arch. He pulled away and she watched the impressive tense and pull of the muscles of his arms before he thrust again. She arched to meet him again because every moment he completely filled her was like no other pleasure or moment she'd ever known. She wanted that feeling to last. She wanted that feeling again and again, so she met him every time, moving so that she could be at just the right angle for building the orgasm higher and higher, closer and closer.

She trailed her fingernails down his chest and he clamped one hand on her hip, somehow pushing deeper and harder, and it was even more powerful than she could have ever imagined. In all of her wildest fantasies and dreams. This was so much more than everything.

It wasn't just sex. It was bigger than that. It was a connection that she didn't know how to describe, and she wasn't quite sure where it came from. It was deeper than two people liking each other. It was soulful.

When his gaze met hers, she held it, offering herself to him, chasing that orgasm again. She didn't look away or close her eyes when she tumbled over, though she wanted to. But it was a pleasure to watch him watch her. It somehow added to the waves of fulfillment, that deep exhale of satisfaction.

She wanted to see him fall too. So she watched him until his thrusts became more and more frantic and he pushed deep and hard one last time, that heavy, fierce gaze never blinking, never leaving hers.

Even though she watched him, it took a few minutes to come back to herself. To realize how heavily she was breathing, and how heavily he was breathing. To realize how hard his hand was gripping her hip and how deep her fingernails had dug into his shoulders. Still she didn't look away. His hand uncurled from her hip, but it didn't leave her. Instead he raised it, pushing a few strands of hair off her forehead and behind her ear.

She tried to swallow at the weird lump in her throat, tried to breathe through the odd tightness in her chest. She wasn't sad, but it felt like everything inside of her was so big and so out of control and she didn't know how to handle that, how to process it.

She couldn't organize it away, or power through it. It overtook her, but she wouldn't cry in front of him, even if that was exactly what she wanted to do. Instead, she forced herself to smile. "I guess that was okay."

He choked out a laugh. "Yeah, it was all right." He rolled off of her, but he didn't go far. He lay right next to her, his shoulder pressing to hers, his fingers tracing up and down her own. They lay there and she stared at the ceiling, finding it strangely intimate the way their breathing came back to normal together, the way they didn't speak but they touched.

"Lilly?"

"Yeah?"

"I think I'm dead."

It was her turn to huff out a laugh, and she turned to face him. His lips were curved in that sort of easy way that made something in her heart pinch, because he was so rarely cheerful or easy. So much of what she knew of him was serious and stern. But how often had she seen him laugh or smile in the past few weeks? How often had she seen him react to her in a way that wasn't at all serious or stern?

Quite a bit, really. He liked her. And she . . . she had to admit she liked him. It was a sharp pain to realize that there really couldn't be more to it. That all the liking in the world, all the attraction, all the amazing sex didn't change the fact they were ruled by very strict personal codes.

Personal codes that had to categorize this as a mistake. Maybe not this second, but in the morning at the very least.

So this was it. This was all they had and it was a terrible, terrible feeling. But what could she do?

"I know we're not . . ." Brandon let out a sigh, touching the stray strands of her hair again, those featherlight touches so at odds with the size of him, and the strength of him. Those beautiful contrasts she couldn't give her heart to, even though she wanted to.

Why was her heart involved?

"This can't go anywhere. I think we're on the same page with that, right?"

She nodded because of course they were on the same page. She couldn't keep sleeping with her boss, and he couldn't keep sleeping with an employee. For a million reasons, they just couldn't do this.

But she couldn't speak past the lump in her throat. She couldn't get over the way sadness and pain snuffed out any last pangs of pleasure.

"But it could go a few more places until morning, don't you think?" He grinned, and she couldn't fight a laugh.

"That depends just what you mean by 'places.'"

His grin only grew. "Why don't I get the condom bucket and show you?"

And it was possibly the strangest combination of words ever said to her, but also *exactly* what she wanted.

# Chapter Sixteen

Brandon woke up to the warmth and brightness of sun on his face. Which was weird considering his room had a west-facing win—

His thoughts stopped immediately. Because the floral scent that seemed to be a part of him was Lilly. Only ever Lilly. The warmth of her pressed against him rivaled the ray of sun on his face. Those soft curves pressed to his side, and he had never wanted reality not to call him so badly as he did in this moment.

There'd been a lot of moments in his life when he'd wished that reality would stop, but Lilly . . . she was something . . . something he could not have again. As much as his dick might be trying to argue with him, as much as his brain was already thinking of ways they could do it just one more time, he knew last night had to be a one-off, an aberration.

It had been a long time since he'd felt a loss this deep, and it didn't make sense. It shouldn't make sense. She was just a woman, and she was a very nice woman, an incredible woman, really, but just a woman. There were one million of them out there who could do the same things she had done with him last night.

Not one of them appealed to him. He could think of nothing but her and the sounds she'd made and the way she'd felt under his palms. He'd tasted her, and all he could think about was wanting more.

A weaker man would make excuses. A weaker man— like his father—would give in to the yawning emptiness at the prospect of not having her like this again.

He was not his father. He was not a man who took advantage. As much as last night had been equal ground and consensual, he was still her boss. The potential for problem areas and power differentials was too big.

It was too important to him not to be that person, not to blur any lines. He was a better man than that. Had to be.

He might have a whole town to save, but Lilly had her sister and nephew to support, and she didn't want to be in a weird position anymore than he wanted to put her in one. She was their sole provider right now.

Getting more involved with her, while she was working for him . . . it was ethically wrong.

He wouldn't bend those strict codes he'd made for himself, and more, he cared too much about her. Because if he let this grow, and become something bigger than it already was, the business could suffer. And the relationship could suffer because of business or vice versa and he didn't want to put either of them in the middle of that.

He wouldn't be the kind of man who made things difficult and expected everyone else to deal with it or clean up the mess. He had to accept the fact no matter how his entire body screamed rebellion against the idea that last night had been a mistake

The most wonderful, amazing mistake of his life. But a mistake nonetheless.

It helped that she knew it too. He knew she wouldn't

want to risk her job any more than he would want to risk his code of honor. They were the same, really. They both had this strict edict to be the responsible adults life deemed they had to be. He wouldn't jeopardize that for her.

*How much longer are you going to lie here and try to rationalize?* Well, he wouldn't mind lying here until she woke up. Surely it couldn't be that late. He shifted a little to try and see if he could get a glimpse at the clock.

But the door swung open, Will stepping inside. "Hey, Bran . . ." He glanced up, saw the lump that was quite obviously Lilly. His eyes widened and he immediately took a step right back out, closing the door behind him.

Brandon squeezed his eyes shut. Oh, *shit.*

"Please tell me that wasn't what I thought it was." Lilly's voice was soft with sleep, but when he looked at her, her eyes were squeezed closed, her nose all scrunched up.

"Well, what did you think it was?"

Her eyes opened, that blue somehow darker and deeper in the morning. He wanted to see how they changed over the course of a day, what made them thread silver or smoke. What . . .

*Get a hold of yourself, Evans.*

"Will saw me, didn't he?" She sat up in bed, taking the sheet along with her to cover her chest. Pity.

No, he couldn't be thinking like that anymore. They had had their one night of forgetting about responsibility and sense, and that was it. Now it was over and they had to go back to the plan they'd decided on during the canoe excursion.

Stay away from each other. Avoid being alone with each other. Because they so clearly could not handle it.

"So, I don't suppose there's an explanation we could feed to Will that he'd believe? Like, our clothes were stolen by bears and we had to sleep in the same bed naked together for . . . warmth?"

"I mean, you're welcome to offer that explanation to him. As long as I can be in the room to watch his expression when you do."

"Bran." Her voice was exasperated, but he couldn't get over . . . There weren't very many people in his life comfortable enough to shorten his name. It shouldn't mean anything, really. She was around the two people who did it most, so it would make sense she would pick up on it.

But it felt like a gift. Like some reward for doing something right. Just that one syllable in her cool, clipped voice that made him think about clear lakes and blue skies.

Obviously having sex after such a long period of time had somehow turned his brain into a useless lump of melting snow.

She touched a finger to the corner of his mouth, and there was such a weighty wistfulness in her expression his chest ached. Physically, painfully ached as though he'd fallen off a mountain cliff onto nothing but hard rock below.

Her finger dropped and she sighed heavily. "I should get dressed. *We* should get dressed and see if we can avoid *everyone* walking in here to get a good look. If the road is fixed, I need to call Cora."

"I . . . can't promise Will won't tell Sam. I can't even promise he won't tell Skeet. Will gets some enjoyment out of seeing me squirm."

She straightened her shoulders, chin jutting forward as her fingers tightened on the sheet she held to her chest. "Well, that's just fine. I, for one, refuse to squirm, considering we did what any two attractive, consenting adults would do."

"Any?"

"Surely we aren't the only people who can't keep it in their pants." She grimaced. "In fact, I know we're not."

"I suppose I meant I don't think I would have done it with anyone else."

She slowly turned her head to look at him, something like shock on her face. "No, I don't suppose I would have either," she said after a few humming seconds of staring.

That painful knot in his chest seemed to pull tighter, but Lilly shook her head and looked away. "I have to get dressed."

From anyone else, that might have been a brushoff, but he could hear his own feelings in the tone of her voice, read them in the way her posture slumped.

This . . . hurt. He didn't get why, and he wasn't particularly *pleased* with the emotion, but it hurt.

There was no way around the fact it couldn't happen again, or the fact it'd probably keep hurting.

Lilly slid out of bed and then pressed her fingertips to her forehead, still clutching the sheet to cover her with the other hand. "I don't have a shirt. Or underwear. My clothes are all strewn out in front of the fire. Well, except the underwear."

"Where's your underwear?"

"I hung it in the closet in my office. We were trying *not* to tempt one another, remember?"

"Just what kind of underwear were you wearing?"

"Bran." She shook her head and there was that pain again. He didn't understand how it could be so easily erased, only to return with a vengeance. And he really didn't know why . . . why it was only her. He couldn't think of anyone else who'd ever tied him in such painful, unfortunate knots.

"Put on one of my shirts, and the pants you had on last night. I'll go get your clothes and bring them to you in your office."

She nodded, still clutching the sheet to her chest as he got out of bed. He handed her her pants and then went in search of his boxers.

"Um, I think they're over here."

She pointed to a lump of fabric next to her when he turned. Her cheeks were a little pink, her eyes decidedly lower than his gaze.

"Are you checking me out?"

"Well . . . it's right there." She waved toward what was becoming a rather unfortunate erection.

He shook his head and pulled on his boxers, but he was grinning again because she let out a kind of wistful sigh that he thought meant she might miss the view.

"When you put on the shirt, can you do it like in slow motion?" she asked, finally looking up at him, her smile mischievous and fun.

"Only if you lose the sheet, sweetheart."

She chuckled, but then her smile died and his did too. Because this had to stop. Joking and enjoying. This was the end of that particular road.

He returned to his closet and pulled down two shirts. One for her and one for him, and when he held hers out to her, she'd already pulled on and tied the pants from last night.

"Well . . . aren't you going to turn around?" she asked, and if there wasn't a faint upward curve to her beautiful mouth, he might have.

"No. I'm good."

She rolled her eyes and held the sheet with one hand while trying to wiggle her other arm into the fabric of the shirt. She struggled and bent this way and that without quite managing it.

He shook his head and then stepped close. He didn't miss the way her breath caught, the way she stilled, the way those blue eyes that might haunt him damn near forever slowly rose to meet his.

"Let me," he said gently, and took the shirt, putting it over her head and pulling it down, protecting her modesty though it was the absolute last thing he wanted to do.

"Thank you," she said in nothing more than a whisper.

"You're welcome." He sighed, close enough to ruffle her tousled hair. He'd seen her fall down a mountain trail and sail over a clear lake, and yet she'd still somehow looked like an untouchable, graceful thing.

But here in his office, in his clothes, her hair a mess from rain and sex and sleep . . . she was a mess. A beautiful, amazing mess.

*That is not yours to have.*

He should step away. Go get her clothes. Move this morning along. Will knew they were in here, and Sam would likely be in soon. Even if Will *did* tell everyone, that didn't mean everyone had to see the walk of shame. He could handle it, but Lilly didn't deserve it. So, he should move. Walk away. Step away. Christ, anything but stand here hovering perilously close to her mouth.

He was talking himself out of kissing her because he had to. Because they both knew what they were doing and walking away was the only option. It was. It *was*.

But then her mouth brushed his, soft and sweet, and not nearly long enough. "Thanks," she said, taking a very distinct step back and away as she did. "I'll be in my office."

"Yeah, I'll . . . get your things."

He let her go first, surprised that he had to keep his

fingers clenched in fists to keep himself from reaching out, to keep himself from stopping her and keeping her here and doing a lot more than *brushing* lips.

But that wasn't an option. Not an option. He had to go get her clothes, bring them to her, and keep his damn hands to himself.

Brandon steeled himself for walking into the living room and whatever Will's response was going to be. Jokes. Lectures. I told you sos. He would take whatever. He deserved it. This would be his due.

But when he stepped into the living room, Will was huddled with Skeet over the front desk and what Brandon could only assume was the handwritten schedule.

Will looked up, his face completely inscrutable. "Probably going to have to do some canceling and rescheduling due to the rain. Want me to make the calls?"

Not a word about Lilly. Not a grin. Nothing. Brandon didn't trust it, not for a second, but he'd go with the flow for now. "Give me ten."

Will nodded and turned back to Skeet. Brandon grabbed Lilly's clothes from the hearth, not missing the way Will stood in such a way that Skeet couldn't see what he was doing.

So, he'd definitely be hearing about it later, just maybe not in front of Skeet. Which, for inexplicable reasons, made Brandon feel like some kind of slimy dick.

Which probably wasn't too far from the truth.


Lilly sat in her desk chair feeling about as out of sorts and mussed and utterly *messy* as she ever had in her whole life. She'd put her underwear on, but then she'd had to put Brandon's extra clothes back on over it while she waited for him to return with her clothes.

She had felt conflicted a lot of times in her life. So many times with Cora, she hadn't known if she was doing the right thing or if there was a right thing. But this was different somehow. Not weightier or bigger, but . . . different. She couldn't work out why or how or what it meant.

She leaned forward and rested her forehead on her desk. Oh, this was bad. Worse because Will knew. She wanted to be that strong person who didn't care. The person who made her choice and could live with it—head held high.

But she wasn't that person. She was going to agonize and obsess and freak out over this. . . .

She couldn't even make her brain think it was a mistake even though she knew it was. It *had* to be a mistake. More than anything, she hadn't wanted to just *brush* a kiss across his mouth and thank him. She'd wanted to kiss him and hold him. She'd wanted to be with him.

That couldn't happen. So, she had to get it out of her head. Angst and freak-out aside, in the light of morning she was making the right decisions.

The door creaked open and Brandon stepped in with her clothes neatly folded in his hands.

"Here you go."

His gaze didn't quite meet hers as he held the clothes in his outstretched arms. She thought about just having him put them on the desk. Because she didn't want to accidentally touch fingers and feel that electric connection that jumped between them. But she wasn't a coward, and more, she knew it was there so she could handle it. She had to be able to handle it.

She took the clothes, and made sure that their

hands were nowhere near each other when she did. "Thank you."

He cleared his throat, shoving his hands in his pockets. "Obviously you can take as much time off as you need today."

Oh hey, this was where it got weird not just in a general way, but in a *he is your boss* way. Fantastic.

She forced a smile, paltry as it might be. "Thanks. I just need to head home and take a shower and change. I'll be back after lunch." She didn't look at him because she didn't know how to make this normal. She didn't know how to make it feel less weird that her job was in his hands and she had slept with him.

It wasn't like he was two different people, but somehow it felt like that. The Brandon she'd experienced during those excursions, who could smile and laugh and enjoy himself. Who carried her down a mountain or tossed her in a lake. She liked that Brandon. The one she'd had fun with and slept with against all her very strict rules for herself.

But then there was the Brandon who ran this business and had been against hiring her in the beginning. The one who almost never smiled, and took everything so gravely seriously. Because he needed to save this town to assuage some guilt he felt.

They felt like two different people, but they weren't. They were the same person and she had to deal with that. The reality of that.

"Whatever time you need." He took a step back toward the door, but he hesitated there for a few seconds. He didn't say anything, and neither did she. What could be said?

In the end, he just walked out.

She wasn't bereft or hurt because that was what had to be done. She was alone in her office and needed to put on clothes that had been through . . . quite a bit in the past twenty-four hours. She needed to go home. She needed to figure out her life from this very big ignoble fall.

Trying not to berate herself, she got dressed. She gathered everything she needed and she steeled herself for whatever would greet her when she stepped outside the safety of her office walls.

But when she stepped into the living room area and looked around, there was no one there. Brandon must be in his office and maybe Will was too, or outside seeing to something. Skeet sat at the front office desk, but he was on the phone, grunting.

She didn't have the energy to tell him to put money in the grunt jar, because all she needed to do right now was leave. She needed to get out of here and screw her head back on straight.

She gave Skeet a little nod, and he barely glanced in her direction as she walked out the door. She went to her car and headed down the mountain.

She passed where the road had washed away and where they were slowly working to fix it to make it two lanes again. As she drove down the curving road, she could see the cabin of Mile High Adventures peeking through the trees. She couldn't help but wonder if it would always be ruined for her now. It wouldn't be that breath of fresh air, not after what she'd done.

"Ugh."

She drove through town and then parked in the little narrow space in front of her house. She could hope and wish that Cora wasn't home, but she knew better. Even if Micah had basketball camp, Cora would be home from dropping him off by now.

Somehow, Lilly had to make sure that she had her game face on. Had to make sure Cora couldn't read into anything that happened yesterday. She might suspect things, but Lilly couldn't give her the confirmation. As nice as it would be to have someone to confide in or talk to, she couldn't let Cora know she had made this mistake. Not after all the lecturing and anger and fights they'd had over Cora's string of boyfriends before Stephen.

When Lilly stepped inside, Micah was curled up on the couch playing on some sort of video game thing she'd never seen him with before.

"No basketball camp?" Lilly asked, trying to make her voice sound light and easy. Micah would be good practice for that game face.

"No, there's some flooding out by the school so they canceled it today."

"Too bad." She walked over to the couch, tapping the top of the little video game thing he held. "What's this?"

"Video game," Micah said in a grunt that would have made her point to the grunt jar at work.

"But where'd you get it?" She and Cora had talked endlessly last Christmas about whether or not to allow Micah to have a handheld video game thing. In the end, they'd decided against it.

"Dad."

Lilly's entire body went cold. She'd been gone and . . . "What?" She must be misunderstanding something. *Please God.*

"He sent Mom a big package thing yesterday." Micah lifted the device a little, his fingers never stopping their clicking and his eyes never leaving the screen. "This was for me."

Lilly kept herself very still. Micah was too old not to understand what had happened with Stephen. The boy knew exactly what his father was capable of. He'd witnessed it. He'd experienced it. But as young as he was, and as much as he probably didn't quite understand that a gift from his father was problematic, this had to affect him in some way.

"And you're okay with that?" Lilly asked lightly. She'd learned long ago not to let Micah think she was treating anything too seriously, lest he withdraw farther.

Micah shrugged. His eyes never left the device, but Lilly had been a part of his life from the very beginning, and she knew, when he was quiet and focused on something, that was usually when he was working through something hard.

She would press on that point, but she would give him some space first. Not to mention she had to figure out what the hell was going on with Cora. What she was feeling, and what she was thinking letting Micah have something from Stephen.

"Where's your mom, sweetie?"

Micah shrugged. She would've chastised him for that non-answer any other time, but she didn't have it in her right now. Maybe he needed some time to deal. And maybe she needed to make sure Cora got him an appointment with the therapist so he could discuss this with her.

Lilly gave him a pat on the head like she had been doing since he'd been a baby. Her little nephew, just another person she got to take care of and protect. Just another person she'd failed.

But now was not the time to be morbid and self-pitying. She had to fix this. She had to find a way to make this okay. Because she hadn't been here yesterday, because she'd lost her ever-loving mind.

When Lilly got to the top of the stairs, Cora's door

was closed, so Lilly knocked on it and then pushed it open without waiting for an answer. Cora was sitting cross-legged on her bed, a shiny new laptop on her lap.

"Hey, Lil." She smiled, but Lilly could read Cora's little shift of uncertainty. "Didn't expect you back so soon."

"The road was fixed enough to let traffic through, so I came home to shower and change." She swallowed and did her best not to look disapproving. "What's that?"

Cora fiddled with the corners of the laptop, uncrossed, then recrossed her legs. "Well . . . we got a package yesterday."

"From who?" Her eyes burned and her chest squeezed so tight it was nearly impossible to breathe. Guilt and anger and frustration and fear working their way through her gut. One misstep into irresponsibility and enjoyment and . . . this happened.

Well, if it wasn't a clear sign from the universe, Lilly didn't know what was.

"Okay, so, before you totally flip out and make accusations and call Dr. Grove and everything, just hear me out, okay?"

"Hear you out about what?"

"Lilly, promise me. Five minutes. You don't speak."

Oh, Lilly hated when Cora pulled that out. Five entire minutes of not responding was torture, but Lilly steeled herself to do it. To offer Cora this thing in the face of anything to do with Stephen. "All right," she managed between gritted teeth.

"So, all Stephen did was send a package. It had a little note that he was feeling bad for how things went and he wanted us to have some stuff."

Lilly opened her mouth, but Cora glared and Lilly

bit back the words. She'd made a promise to let Cora get it out; she could abide by that.

"It's not like he showed up or broke the court order. He missed Micah's birthday and—"

"He's always—" Lilly snapped her mouth shut.

"It was a short note, saying we deserved these things. He didn't ask to visit or talk. Maybe it's guilt. Maybe he just feels . . . bad. And, sure, none of this stuff makes up for it, but don't me and Micah deserve some nice things you didn't have to pay for?"

When Lilly didn't answer, Cora rolled her eyes and flopped back into bed. "You can talk now."

"Why does he have our address?"

"I don't know, Lilly, but it can't be that hard to find."

Not when you were rich and had endless access to endless things. "Honey—"

Cora sat up, anger sharpening her features. Instead of looking young—like Lilly so often still saw her—she looked fierce. Just as she'd looked when she'd finally determined she had to cut Stephen out of their lives for good.

"Don't 'honey' me, and don't patronize me! Why shouldn't I have something nice from him? After everything he did to me. To *us*. Why shouldn't I get a nice computer out of the deal?"

"Because you know him and what he's capable of. You know he doesn't give things without strings. You *know* if he's reaching out to you, that isn't where it ends."

"He didn't ask to meet. He didn't even ask to call."

"You know better than this."

Cora shoved the computer off her lap and got to her feet. "No, I clearly don't. Because here the laptop is, and there downstairs Micah is playing with the video game. So, I *don't* know better. God, sometimes you remind me of *him*."

Perhaps, on another day, Lilly could have parsed that hurt a little better. In a better personal place, maybe she could duck that blow a little easier, brush it off as Cora being scared and hurt and manipulated.

But this morning, after everything she'd done last night, and then walked away from this morning, she didn't have the strength to fight the tears that sprung in her eyes. She tried to swallow at the lump in her throat.

"I am trying to . . ." She had to swallow again when her voice cracked. "I love you, and I have never thought you were stupid. But I know he hurt you, and I know that—"

"I'm a grown woman. I know things, too. You still treat me like a child. You have always treated me like I'm stupid, just like he did. He was right, though. Look at me. I'm worthless. No job. No skills, and I know you want me to go to school, but for *what*?"

"So you don't feel that way anymore! So you take some responsibility for your life! Maybe I'm tired of constantly dragging you through." Then whatever last thread of control she had on the tears ended because, oh, what a horrible thing to say. How could she have . . .

She scrubbed her hands over her face trying to wipe away the tears, trying to find the calm and with-it-ness she usually had. She had always saved breakdowns and harsh words for late-night cry sessions by herself.

Never to Cora. Never . . . like this. When she was only trying to help. Trying to make things right. It was all she'd ever tried to do and . . . no one seemed to give a rotten damn. "I've only ever tried to help. I only want him to never be able to hurt you or Micah again."

Cora's arms came around her, strong and sturdier than Lilly would have given her credit for. "Shh. I know. I shouldn't have said it."

"I shouldn't have said what I said either." Her arms came around Cora, but even as heartfelt as both apologies were, all Lilly felt was hurt and empty.

"I wanted something you didn't have to give to me. I wanted . . ."

Lilly pulled Cora away, making sure to look into her sister's identical blue eyes. "You listen to me, I am here because I love you and I want to be. It doesn't matter what I provide you—there's no secret list of things owed. Anything, and I mean *anything,* is preferable to taking something from him. Anything."

Cora shuddered a little, but then she nodded. "I know you're right. That's why I got mad. I don't . . . want you to always be the one who's right."

"Oh, honey, not always." Always was such a burden to bear, and she hadn't borne it very well last night.

"So, we're okay?" Cora asked hopefully, and Lilly tried not to notice that her sister hadn't shed a tear.

"Yeah, we're good. I think you should talk to Dr.—"

"Yeah, definitely," Cora interrupted dismissively. Then she smiled. "So, did you sleep with the bearded hottie or what?"

Lilly couldn't match a smile, or anything other than a blank stare. "He's my boss, Cora," she finally managed.

Cora clucked her tongue and shook her head. "Such a pity. Such a waste of being rained into a cabin."

*Such a liar.* "Do you think you should talk to Micah?"

Cora looked at the computer, then back at Lilly. "Maybe we both should. Together. We're a team, right? The two of us." She held out her hand, an offering, a truce. Something.

Lilly took Cora's hand, forced herself to smile as she gave it a squeeze. "The three of us." Her, Cora, and Micah. That was Lilly's life, her focus, the reason she did everything.

She couldn't allow herself to try and shed that ever again.

# Chapter Seventeen

Three days since *that particular* morning, and Will had yet to say a peep about it. At least to Brandon. Not an offhand comment about Lilly, not a joke, or even one suggestive or snide comment.

Will acted like he hadn't walked in on exactly what he'd walked in on.

Brandon was growing considerably on edge about it. Surely his twin brother who never failed to skewer him over just about *anything* that might irritate or embarrass him wasn't just going to ignore what had happened. There was some bigger plan here, and Brandon was at the end of his rope waiting to see what it would be.

"So, this is it?" he demanded, doing a piss-poor job of hiding his frustration. "You're not going to say anything about the other day?"

Will casually loaded the dishwasher with his breakfast dishes and didn't even glance Brandon's way. "What about the other day?"

"You're not serious."

Will slowly turned to face Brandon. It wasn't often that Brandon noted the similarities in the way they looked. Usually Will left his hair longer, and his beard more fashionably trimmed. But Brandon hadn't shaved his head in a while, and Will was looking a little scraggly himself.

He was trying to pretend like the divorce didn't bother him at all, but Brandon had his doubts.

"What is it that you want me to say?" Will asked, sounding old and tired—two things he'd usually rather die than sound like.

"I don't *want* you to say anything. But silence and respecting each other's privacy is not our relationship. So, I'm sitting here wondering why the hell you haven't said anything."

Will cocked his head as if he were considering this. "The thing is, I know you, Brandon. I don't always understand you, but I know you. And I know more than anything else you don't want to be like Dad."

Brandon took a breath, steeled himself for the words that would come next. They would hurt. Maybe if he held himself tense enough, he could ward off the worst of the blow.

"So the fact that you slept with Lilly, who is an employee, means that it had to mean something. It means it wasn't a joke, or something I should give you a hard time about. Because if you did something like that, it's a pretty big deal."

Brandon's jaw went slack. That wasn't what he'd expected . . . at all. That nearly sounded like absolution. *Which you do not deserve.*

"I also happen to believe what happened has a lot more to do with Lilly, who I very much like, than it has to do with anything Dad would've done. Furthermore, I don't think I need to bother you about something you're going to self-flagellate yourself about for probably, what, years? Decades?"

"It shouldn't have happened," Brandon said, his

voice rusty, but something about *acknowledging it* instead of pretending it hadn't happened like he'd been doing with every damn one for the past three excruciating days, seemed . . . imperative.

"You say that with such finality, and yet for what, four or five or more years, you haven't been with anyone. Not just an employee, or someone from town. But anyone. I consider that none of my damn business, but let's be honest that it means something. It means something that Lilly was the one."

"You're putting a lot of emphasis on just a timing thing," he forced himself to say, wishing he could force himself to make it true.

"No, you're being a dumb ass."

"Will—"

He held up a hand and shook his head. "I'm not going to argue with you about this. These are my thoughts, these are my opinions, and you cannot change them. No matter what you say. I can't make you see or admit you're being a dumb ass. So, instead of arguing, let's do what we've always done, brother."

"Fume silently and then get drunk and joke it off?"

Will grinned at that. "Work, Brandon. Let's go to work."

Brandon wanted to argue. He wanted to rage. He wanted to explain himself and excuse himself a million times over, but he got the feeling that said something about the situation that he didn't want it to. And more, excuses and raging and explanations were something his father would have indulged in.

There were no excuses. There were no explanations. Brandon had acted rashly and irresponsibly, and it had been wonderful. But he did not deserve wonderful.

He had a town to save, hundreds of people's liveli-hoods teetering on his shoulders. So, he couldn't be that man. The man who put himself above all that. Too much was riding on him—on Mile High. Whether anyone else saw that or not.

Will headed out the door, and Brandon could only follow. Because their schedules varied so widely, they both had to drive their own vehicles down to the office. Will got in his Jeep, and Brandon stood next to his truck, giving himself a second to breathe in the thin air, crisper and pinier up here around their cabin. One built so much in the style of the office it was a wonder they hadn't just combined the two.

He let out the breath, tried to find his peace, his passion. The thing and belief that had driven him here during the darkest part of his life.

But no matter how he tried to ignore it, something was missing. He had a sneaking suspicion he knew what—or who—but thinking her name would only make it harder. Better to ignore it. Always better to ignore.

He got in his truck and drove the winding mountain road down to Mile High. This thing he'd built. This thing he'd poured his all into. Mile High and the town of Gracely, and nothing else for years upon years.

It had never felt like a burden he *resented* before. No, it had always been his due. The thing that drove him. A goal. *It still is, you're just a hard-up dick.*

The road was still uneven in parts, most of the repair work being done in town, where more people drove. But things were slowly getting back to normal. There was still more cleanup to do, especially on the trails and around the office building itself, but today Mile High was getting back to the business of excursions.

When Brandon pulled in to the parking lot, Lilly's car was already there, sitting like a gleaming, pretty little thing. Just like her. *Oh, man, you have really lost it.*

But there was another car there as well, which was awfully early for any of the excursions they had on the docket for today. Skeet never drove; he just sort of showed up every morning like magic. Brandon wouldn't be surprised to find out that he was a troll living under a tree in the back.

Maybe Lilly was meeting with someone at the office. That would actually be a good idea—to get some of the townspeople up here to see the ambience. To feel the air. Gracely was its own thing tucked in that looming shadow of the mountains. As much as he loved it, it wasn't the same as being up here. There was a way that things piled down on you in town. Even before the mining company had gone under, he'd felt a certain stifling pressure there.

Brandon got out of his car, and Will was standing next to his Jeep. "Car look familiar to you?" he asked, looking oddly . . . wary.

Brandon shook his head. They walked to the front door of the office and stepped inside. Skeet was at the front desk, and there was a woman standing in front of it with her back to them.

But because she was so out of place here this early, and because of the darker tone of her complexion, Brandon immediately knew this was the waitress from Gracely Café who had acted so weird to him.

She turned to face them, presumably because of the noise of the door opening. Her eyes went a little wide as she took in both of them.

Brandon noticed something that made him very, very, very uncomfortable. That thing that had nagged at him from the café, but he hadn't been able to place.

Her eyes were an awful lot like Will's. Which also meant his. That shade somewhere between brown and green.

But that was just . . . it was obviously too much going on in his head. Because it could mean anything. Except that she was here. In his office. After acting very, very strangely toward him.

With his father's eyes.

Skeet was standing at the desk, scowling. "This girl was sniffing around when I got here, and now she's refusing to tell me what the hell she was up to."

The girl glanced back at Skeet. "I wasn't sniffing. I was just looking."

"Looking for what?" Will asked.

Her gaze turned back to the two of them, something edgy and jumpy in her expression, much like she'd been at the restaurant. "I-I wasn't doing anything wrong."

"Technically, trespassing on private property is doing something wrong," Will returned. "Who are you and what are you doing?"

She only blinked in return.

"You're the waitress from the café, right? Hayley?" Brandon said, trying to infuse some gentleness in his tone to offset the hardness in Will's.

She stiffened, and Brandon wondered if there was anything but fear under all this girl's weirdness. Without answering his question, she darted toward the door, but without even talking about it, he and Will moved to block her.

Brandon felt badly that she looked scared, but this was too weird. "We don't mean you any harm, Hayley, but you have to admit this looks really weird. So, just tell us what you're doing, so we can all move on."

She pawed at her back for a second, pulling her phone forward. "If you don't get out of my way, I-I'm going to call the police." She waved the phone, trying to look threatening.

She failed so badly, but that didn't ease the crushing

pressure in Brandon's chest. Something was going on here, and it wasn't just the Evans family being her personal childhood boogeymen. Whatever this was, it was bigger.

Will folded his arms across his chest. "And we'll tell them that we found you here sniffing around."

"I-I was just looking. Everyone's talking about this place and I wanted to get a glimpse of it."

"And this has nothing to do with the fact that you look like and have the same last name as the woman who was our father's secretary twenty some years ago?"

She paled a little at that, her mouth going slack. "H-how do you know my last name?"

Brandon tried to keep his voice even, reasonable. She looked like she was about to jump out a window, given the opportunity to escape. "Whatever this is about, whatever you're doing here, if you'll be up-front with us . . ."

"What? Maybe you'll pay me off like your dad paid off my mom?" It was her turn to fold her arms across her chest, to arch her eyebrow and look wholly condescending, though there was an odd sheen of tears to her eyes.

Brandon tried to act as though his heart weren't trying to beat out of his chest. "I don't know what you're talking about, but if you'd like to come sit down and tell us about it, we'd really like to understand."

Her eyes narrowed suspiciously. "You're not like how I thought you'd be."

"How did you think we'd be?" Will asked, his demeanor much harsher than Brandon's, which was a rare turn of events.

"Do you know?" she asked cryptically.

"Know what?" Will returned, matching her stance.

"Do you know how we're related?" she asked, clearly

trying to act brave and in charge, but a vulnerability all but pulsed from the slim twenty-something.

Brandon swallowed at the hard stone of fear that settled itself in his throat. "We're related?"

"I'm supposed to believe that you guys don't know? I'm supposed to believe that your dad never crowed about his conquests? That he never bragged about how he paid off his poor black secretary so that she wouldn't claim her child as his, even though I was." Her lips quavered, but no tears escaped her steely gaze.

Brandon had to close his eyes. He'd known about the affairs. There'd been too many whispers after everything with Evans went down to avoid knowing his father was that kind of man. He'd had to believe everything bad about his father, one blow after another.

He'd thought the blows had to be over. Dad and Evans had been gone for over five years. He'd been certain he knew every lurid detail of his father's misdeeds. But paying off a pregnant secretary . . . denouncing his own child. No, he'd thought these things would have to be over by now.

How could a man do this? Pay someone off and pretend that his own flesh and blood didn't exist?

"So you're saying that . . ." Will cleared his throat. "You're saying that your father is our father."

She lifted her chin and gave a sharp nod. "Yeah, that's what I'm saying. Aren't you going to argue with me?"

"No, Hayley. We won't argue with you." Brandon gestured toward the living room and the couches. "Why don't you come inside and tell us a little bit about all this?"

She shifted on her feet, looking from him to Will and then back again. "You really . . . just believe me? And I'm supposed to believe that you didn't know about me?"

"You have the right to believe whatever you want to believe, but we're telling you the God's honest truth when we say that we had no idea our father had any other children," Will said, his voice sounding as rough as Brandon felt.

But he had to speak too. "We've learned in the last few years just what kind of man our father was, so it's impossible not to believe you. And we'd like to hear your story."

She shook her head, edging for the door. A suspicious sheen to her eyes. "I . . . I shouldn't be here. I promised . . . I shouldn't be here."

"Hayley, please. Stay. Tell us—"

"I'm sorry. This is a mistake and I can't be here anymore. Now you know, and it doesn't really matter. It doesn't matter who I am or what I am. And I can't be here. So please let me go and don't follow me."

"You come in here and drop a bomb like that and expect us to just let it go?" Will demanded, taking a step toward her. Brandon hadn't realized until that moment he'd taken steps toward her as well.

"Please." Her voice broke and she looked like a scared little girl. Brandon didn't know how to push against that. Not right now. Not when she was that upset.

"All right. We won't force you to stay. But please know that whenever you're ready to talk about this, we would like to talk with you about it."

Her gaze flicked between both of them, and then once to Skeet, who was sitting quietly at his desk, taking it all in and thankfully not adding anything to the moment. Then Hayley backed out of the office, the door shutting quietly behind her.

"What the hell was that?" Will asked, scrubbing his hands over his face.

Brandon sank into the couch and covered his head with his hands. "I have no clue. But apparently . . ."

"Apparently we have a half sister."

Yeah, that's apparently what they had.

Lilly rubbed her temples to soothe the headache that had been pounding there for the past three days.

No amount of aspirin or water or attempted sleep could get rid of the dull ache.

She refused to attribute it to anything other than air pressure.

She slid off her chair and stretched, rolling her shoulders to try and get the kinks out. She'd been hunched over her computer all morning designing brochures, and working on the website. She needed to set up more meetings, but that would mean looking at the schedule and going outside and probably having to run into Brandon.

Three days and she'd done a rather excellent job of avoiding him. It couldn't last, but she still felt . . . vulnerable. Raw. Someday, soon hopefully, that little pain would harden up and she wouldn't feel it anymore. She would be able to look at him as a boss and a . . . friend-type person.

But she wasn't there yet. Still, she was going to go to the kitchenette and get some tea, and talk to Skeet about the schedule. Then, she would make sure that whatever meeting she scheduled next, only Will or Sam was available for it.

Oh, what a mess. She stepped into the hallway, all of her muscles going tight, tense. It was stupid, but she knew the minute she saw him . . . things would happen. She would feel things and remember things, and she didn't want any of that.

But she wasn't a coward. She stepped into the living room and stopped short. Will was sitting on the hearth of the fireplace, and Brandon was on the couch. They both had their hands dug in their hair, postures slumped, and Skeet was walking toward them with two steaming hot cups of what looked to be coffee.

Lilly immediately knew something bad had happened. "What is it?"

Will and Brandon jerked their gazes toward her; then they looked back at each other. Since Lilly had a sister of her own, she knew they were communicating in their own way—a way only siblings who'd grown up in each other's pockets could.

Whatever they had discussed in their nonverbal language, it must have been decided that Brandon would be the one to answer her. "Do you remember Hayley from the café?"

"Yes, the waitress who acted so oddly."

"Yeah, she was here when we got here this morning. Looking around for we don't know what. But in the end she told us . . ." He cleared his throat and looked up at the ceiling. "She told us that she's our half sister. Apparently our father had an affair with her mother and her mother was Dad's secretary at the time. Then he paid off Hayley's mother to never tell anyone that Hayley was his."

Lilly could only stare at the matter-of-fact way he delivered that story. It was . . . a little close to home all in all. Her father hadn't paid anyone to keep quiet about her or Cora, but they had always been the *other* family. All the grand promises and proclamations had never made her father leave his first family.

"Oh, that poor girl." And Lilly meant Hayley. Not herself, because that would be foolish.

"She told us, but then she left. We're not quite sure

how to handle it," Will said, looking as affected as she'd ever seen him.

But it was Brandon whom her eyes were drawn to, Brandon whom, for some inexplicable reason, she wanted to comfort. But as an employee, and even as a kind of friend, that was not her job. She could not go squeeze his shoulder or touch his cheek or promise him that things would be okay.

Why did it hurt? Didn't she have enough people to comfort and help in her life? Why should it hurt she wasn't supposed to comfort *him*?

"I . . . Look, I have to get ready for the excursion. We haven't checked on the canoes, and there are so many . . . things."

"Yeah, we've got a lot on our plate today," Brandon said, nodding his head toward Will in a way Lilly recognized. It was a nod she gave Cora whenever she was scared shitless and couldn't show it.

"Go ahead," Brandon was saying. "We'll talk about her later. I've got to get some of those bills paid and out the door. For right now, we'll focus on work, and later . . . later we'll try to make sense of . . . all that."

Will nodded, and when he got to his feet, he paused. He looked at Brandon for a second and Lilly thought maybe he was considering offering him some kind of physical gesture of comfort. That shoulder squeeze she'd been tempted to give him, or some sort of manly, brotherly offering that would be an act of commiseration. An act of "hey, we're in this together."

But in the end, Will simply walked out of the office building.

"I got that doctor's appointment," Skeet grumbled. "Only reason I even came in is I saw that girl's car on my way into town, but I got to go or those bastards will charge me for missing my appointment." Skeet's concerned gaze moved from Brandon to her. "Lilly, handle the phones while I'm gone?"

Lilly blinked at Skeet, but in the end she nodded because what else was there to do?

In just a few quick minutes, she and Brandon were alone in the office building again. She should probably go sit at the desk and keep herself busy with work, but Brandon just sat there looking . . . shell-shocked and miserable and, *God*, she wanted to hug him.

She couldn't. But that didn't mean she couldn't offer *some* comfort. Friendly, platonic comfort. "I'm so sorry, Brandon."

Brandon stood, and shook his head. "I'm sorry too. I'm sorry for her. I'm sorry that . . ." He scrubbed his hands over his face, then looked down at his palms. "He was my hero," Brandon said softly, so much emotion infusing his voice Lilly's chest ached. For him. For Hayley. For all of this.

"I thought he could do no wrong," Brandon continued, his voice a soft, painful rasp. "It was bad enough knowing it wasn't true. That he was a liar and a crook and a damn cheat. But this? Another thing I have to clean up." He laughed bitterly. "Another fucking thing of his I have to clean up. Because that's what I need. Another responsibility."

"Brandon—"

He shook his head. "No, I'm being an asshole. This isn't about me. It's about her and . . . she came here for a reason, and she left for a reason. Until Will and I have any idea what to do with that, I just need to . . ."

He looked at her, all of the pain and confusion and hurt in his hazel eyes, and she had to cross to him. She couldn't stay where she was because she had to ease that hurt somehow.

But before she got to him, he sidestepped the other

way around the couch. It was like someone had stabbed her right in the heart. She froze in place, pressing her palm to her chest where it had been sliced through as she watched him walk away.

"I'll be in my office working on bills," he said, his body disappearing purposefully down the hall.

She should be relieved. She should be happy.

But she couldn't bring herself to be either.

# Chapter Eighteen

The next few weeks seemed to be nothing but walking through a fog. At work, Brandon avoided Lilly, and just about everyone, because his mood was foul. Leading excursions was about the only thing that kept him sane, and that was only because somehow, outside, a few of those responsibilities melted away.

Even though it felt kind of sleazy, he and Will had found a private investigator to learn more about Hayley and her mother. If Hayley was going to keep her distance, if she wasn't going to explain herself, then they had to figure it out for themselves.

At least that's how he justified it to himself. Because it was something his father would have done. But the difference—or so he kept telling himself—was they were just trying to understand. They were just trying to find a way to reach out to her.

*They* did not want to erase her existence. If she was theirs . . . a sister. The half wouldn't matter. Not to him and Will.

So, he didn't have a choice when it came to figuring out what had happened or why she was here or what she wanted from them. It was a necessary evil.

"Hey, I printed out the private investigator's report," Will said, stepping into their office. He handed Brandon a stack of papers.

"Bottom-line summary, Ms. Winthrop moved to Aurora about six months before Hayley was born. Presumably on Dad's dime. Hayley was raised there, and when she was about six, her mother married. She has a stepbrother and stepfather, both of whom are police officers in Aurora. Hayley lived with them through her coursework at the University of Colorado, and moved here last year. She got the job at the café about two months after the move."

"So, presumably, she's here because of us," Brandon said flatly. He didn't like this, whatever it was. There was something too purposeful about the choices Hayley had made.

"I think that's an adequate conclusion to draw," Will replied, just as flatly.

They sat there in silence for a few moments. It might have been weeks, but neither of them was comfortable with this. It wasn't that they couldn't believe Dad was capable of something so despicable; it was just . . . hell, where did it end?

"What do we do, Bran? How do we handle this?"

He was the oldest, the one in charge. He was supposed to know, and he didn't have a damn clue.

"She came here, but she also left," Will said, pacing the room. "We haven't seen hide nor hair of her since. I called Patty the other day and asked if she'd still been coming to work and Patty said she had. But if there's a reason she's here, she's apparently not telling us. I don't get it. I just don't get it."

"There has to be a reason," Brandon replied, staring at the stack of papers. "There has to be a reason why she's here and why it's now. She has to want something.

Surely she has to want something." But she wasn't telling them what.

A knock sounded at the office door and Lilly peeked her head in. "Hi, I just wanted to talk to you guys about a few things. Are you busy?"

"Not busy, just . . . talking excursions," Brandon said, gesturing her inside. Will gave him an inscrutable look, but Brandon ignored it. As much as he had no problem sharing certain things with Lilly, sharing this and talking about all of this . . . the thought of doing that actually somehow physically hurt.

It hurt to discuss secrets and feelings and the roiling uncertainty inside of him, not because he didn't want to, but because he did. Because he wanted to confide in her in every single possible way. He wanted to tell her what he was thinking, what he was feeling, and he wanted her to step toward him like she'd done the day when he'd sidestepped her.

He wanted that comfort, and he couldn't have it. Because at the end of the day he wanted to be back in that room with her, lying next to her. It had been a moment like no other because he'd never felt that kind of contentment before. Except at the top of a mountain.

And it just couldn't happen. It could literally never happen again. Everything about Hayley's existence proved to him that he couldn't let slips like that happen. No, he would never pay away his own child, but he never wanted to be in the position where a child came along and upended all his carefully made plans.

"What did you want to run by us?" Brandon asked, wanting thoughts on work, wanting all discussion to be about the job he was paying her to do.

"Well, I think the advertising for the weekend camping trip really needs some work, but I haven't been on it—I've never even been camping. And you probably don't want to do an overnight camping trip right now. So, I thought maybe I could collaborate on . . ." Her words trailed off as she looked at the stack of papers on his desk.

"Does that say . . ." Her eyebrows drew together and her gaze lifted to his, something odd in her expression he couldn't read. "Did you hire a private investigator on that girl?" She looked horrified, and Brandon couldn't quite understand what she had to be horrified about.

"Yeah, we hired a private investigator. She showed up in our place of business and refused to explain herself."

"She explained herself. She told you who she was."

"She didn't tell us *why* she was here," Will said, and Lilly turned to look at him as though he'd grown an extra head.

"I can't believe . . . You can't possibly think . . . I can't believe you . . ." She looked between them like they were monsters. Brandon couldn't figure it out at all. He stood, needing to move somehow.

"Lilly, she showed up here out of the blue, told us that she's our *sister*, and then left. Without explaining why she came or what she wanted."

"Maybe she only *wanted* to tell you. Maybe it's none of your business why. Did you consider that she might not want to tell you because of some real actual reason that has absolutely nothing to do with you?"

"She opened herself up for this."

Lilly whirled on Will. "No, she didn't. You have no idea the power you have, do you?"

"Power?" Brandon scoffed. "She came here and dropped a bomb on us."

Very slowly, Lilly turned back to him, with some kind of fury in her expression that seemed completely out of place.

"Yes, and you still hold all the cards. She's just a girl!

You're these rich, powerful men and she's been paid not to exist and . . ." Lilly suddenly looked stricken and clamped her mouth shut. She blinked, looking away from him. "Anyway, you didn't ask me for my opinion, so I'll stop."

"I'm interested in how you *got* to that opinion." Because he didn't think this was about him, or even about Hayley.

"I have to go check on something else," Will said, backing away. Neither Brandon nor Lilly really noticed as he edged out of the room. They were too busy staring at each other like they were strangers.

"What was that all about?"

"It wasn't about anything," she said primly, somehow smoothing away all that emotion in her face. "I just think you don't always consider the effect things have on other people. That not everyone thinks like you or can think like you. She's young and she's scared, and she probably doesn't quite understand what your role in all of this is."

"But she came here. She came here and—"

"And didn't want anything to do with you. And didn't want to hear what you had to say. She told you." Lilly's cool mask faded second by second. "She told you and she left, and that was her choice. That's the end of it. I'm sorry if you're looking for my approval. I won't give it." She raised her chin. "I think secretly poking into her life is morally and ethically wrong, and I'm shocked someone so obsessed with ethics and morals doesn't see it that way."

He was surprised that the insult, the disdainful way she said "obsessed" could hurt as deeply as they did. Not because he'd been under the illusion that her opinion didn't matter, but because he'd thought she understood that facet of him.

She looked away, her dainty hands curling into fists. "She has rights too. To privacy, to living her life. I hope you'll think about that before poking any farther into her life."

"What about poking into your business?" he asked roughly, because there was something here. Something deeper than his investigating Hayley. "What happened to you that makes you so touchy about this?"

Her gaze snapped back to his, hard and uncompromising. "Nothing happened, Brandon. I just happen to have two eyes and a heart."

"Are you insinuating I don't have one of those?"

She blinked, and then swallowed. "No, I think you don't quite understand what women have to go through. I don't think you quite understand how big of a deal this is. If you're hoping to have some kind of relationship with her. If you're hoping for anything, this is a breach of trust."

"I don't even know her. How am I supposed to trust her?"

"You're in the place where you should be the one worried about earning *her* trust. Your father paid her mother off to conceal the truth. For his own purposes and his own gain. Can you really blame her for being suspicious? For being distrustful? Of course she's here. She's curious about a family that's rightly hers and yet she's been kept away because of something *your* father did."

"You of all people should know that I'm not—"

"It isn't about me, Brandon. It's about her. What I know, what you know, none of it matters. Think about what *she* knows. Consider that she knows there might be a price to pay for approaching you. A price her mother obviously had to pay."

He took a step toward her, because there was such

pain in her voice, and it wasn't this. It wasn't about him, and somehow he wanted to comfort her. To hold her and have her tell him who'd hurt her this way. "This isn't just coming from your experience as a person with two eyes and a heart. This is coming from *your* experience somewhere along the line. I want to know what. I want to know what happened to you."

He knew he'd messed up the words—they came out like a harsh demand. He should have gentled them; he should have touched her. He should have *asked* her so she understood he wanted to know. He wanted to know *her*, soothe *her*.

But she stepped back toward the door, and the slight look of panic she couldn't quite hide kept him from taking another step toward it. "You're my boss, Brandon. My friend, at best. My past has nothing to do with you."

He had to close his eyes against the slice of pain that went straight through him. Gutted, maybe unfairly so. "Well, I guess if we're friends at best, I don't really care what your opinion on Hayley is." Somehow lashing out at her did nothing to assuage his own hurt.

For the briefest of seconds, he thought guilt might have flashed in her expression. Or maybe that was wishful thinking that she could say all of that and not feel that pain, that loss.

"I think that's best," she said, her voice raw. Then she reached for the door, and maybe he should've let her go.

Maybe he should have fought the instinct to be a total asshole, but this hurt and he wanted her to hurt too. "I thought you had business to talk about."

"We can discuss it later."

"Oh, no. I think we should discuss it right now." Her gaze met his for one brief second. All flashing pain. He'd thought if she hurt enough it would somehow ease the hurt inside of him. But it didn't. All he felt was a roiling kind of guilt on top of that sharp pain of loss.

There had been a lot of things he'd felt after everything had gone down with his father. Betrayal and hurt and pain and grief. But he had never felt as though he were completely empty except for pain, except for missing and longing. Not until Lilly. Not until this.

She angled her chin and regally slid into the seat at his desk. "All right then. We'll start with the website."

Her colorfully painted nails tapped at the keyboard, and Brandon knew he deserved this. Both the pain and the longing. Yeah, it was just about his due.

Lilly had never dreaded going to work. Even sleeping with Brandon hadn't made her *dread* work. But yesterday . . .

She closed her eyes as she dried herself off. She kept trying to tell herself it was good. She'd seen what Brandon Evans was capable of. Hiring a private investigator and seeing absolutely *no* problem with it.

She wrapped her hair up in the towel, angry all over again. How could he not see what a gross invasion of privacy that was? How could he . . . ?

All of the things he and Will were just *okay* with, had felt completely justified in doing, were so close to things her father and Stephen had done.

Even now, Lilly couldn't believe they'd looked at her like *she'd* been the crazy one for thinking a private investigator was too much. For thinking Hayley had a right to privacy, a right to her own choices.

It was infuriating and hurtful, and she didn't know how to reconcile that piece of Brandon with the parts she liked so much. Had she really been that blind? To think he was a decent, driven, *good* person?

Feeling upset and hurt and teary all over again, she pulled on her underwear. There was no choice about work, so there was no use dwelling on all that horribleness.

She pulled on her bra, had trouble fastening it for some reason. She frowned. She certainly hadn't been gaining any weight. Maybe it had accidentally gone through the wash or something. She pawed through her underwear drawer and pulled out a different bra.

This one she could fasten easily enough, but her boobs were practically spilling over the cups. "What the hell?" she muttered.

A knock sounded on her bedroom door and Lilly peeked her head out of the bathroom to see Cora enter. "Do you want some eggs? I'm making some for Micah."

"Yeah, sure. Hey, do you have a bra I could borrow? For some bizarre reason, mine suddenly don't fit right."

Cora shrugged. "Sure, I'll grab you one. You know, the last time I had trouble with my bras, I found out I was pregnant with Micah about three days later," Cora said with a little laugh, walking away.

But each word hit Lilly like a bullet. No. It wasn't . . . it wasn't possible. She stepped out into her room, groping for the bed. Sure, she was a few days late, but her period wasn't the most reliable thing. She hadn't thought anything of it.

Cora's face popped back in the door, and their gazes met. "Oh. My. God." She took a few careful steps into the room, but Lilly couldn't move. She couldn't breathe.

"Lilly, are you . . ." Cora slapped her palms to the top of her head. "Oh my *God*, that night you got rained in. You *did* sleep with the bearded hottie."

"My boss," she corrected, then felt so stupid for correcting her in this particular instance.

"You slept with your boss. You're . . ." Cora's gaze dropped to her stomach, then her overflowing bra cups.

"We used a condom!" Lilly yelled, probably far too loudly considering Micah was presumably out in the kitchen.

Cora shook her head sadly. "Oh, honey."

"We did! We used a condom. How could—"

"You know condoms aren't one hundred percent effective. Pretty sure we cried over that episode of *Friends* together. I mean, really, there's like a million things that could have been wrong with it. Manufacturer error—like when there's a recall on stuff, or it could have been expired, or did he keep it in his wallet? Because you never know how long those have been there or—" Cora must have finally read her horrified look. "Okay, I'll shut up now."

Oh. God. She'd used a condom from a *bucket of leftover condoms* and thought that was a good idea? Thought that was enough to be safe? After all her lectures to Cora and . . .

Lilly sank onto the edge of her bed. "It can't be." This just had to be . . . coincidence. She could not have done this. Not her.

"Don't move," Cora said, disappearing again.

Lilly couldn't have moved if she'd wanted to. She was going to have to tell Brandon. She was going to have to tell her *mother*, if her mother ever deigned to answer the phone.

She was going to have to tell . . . everyone. Everyone would know.

*You don't know for sure yet. Stop freaking out. Be practical. This could all be . . . coincidence. A scare to remind you not to make mistakes.*

"Here. We can find out the truth right now," Cora said, entering the room with a small, slim box.

"Why do you have a pregnancy test?" Which was kind of beyond the point, but it helped center Lilly to try and think about . . . well, anything else.

Cora shrugged, having the decency to look a little abashed. "Okay, so a couple months ago, I slept with this guy a couple times, and we were totally safe every time, but after everything that happened with Micah I just wanted to make sure I had something on hand in case I was ever late. But, I never was. So. You're welcome."

She handed over the box, but Lilly could only stare at the swirly pink print and promise of super accuracy.

"Lilly, you know you have to take it."

She tore her gaze from the box, and managed to look up at Cora, fear and dread and some weird niggling thing that felt like excitement wrapping itself around her heart. "But . . ." Tears sprang to her eyes and she said something to Cora she had never once in her life said to her sister. "But, then what? What do I do then?" *What do I do?* She was the one with the answers. She was the one who always had to find them.

But Cora put her hand over Lilly's shaking one. "Take the test, and then we'll figure it out. Okay?"

Lilly stood on shaky legs. If the positions were reversed, as they once had been, and Cora had been the one sitting there freaking out about things, Lilly would tell her to do the same thing. To get up and find out and go from there. So, that was all that Lilly could do.

She was nearly thirty, not a scared seventeen-year-old with only her sister for support. Lilly could support herself. No matter what.

She walked into the bathroom, read the instructions

on the pregnancy test, and then followed them to the
letter.

For being incredibly calm in the moment, Cora was
even more impatient than she was, asking every five
seconds if the time was up yet. With every second that
passed, Lilly's heartbeat felt harder against her chest,
and it was harder to keep her breathing even.

A baby. If this was a baby, she would be a mother.
And Brandon would be a father. *The* father of her baby.

Why did that produce both terror and some kind of
horrible, misplaced joy?

Finally, when the timer she had set on her phone
went off, Lilly couldn't seem to get herself to look at the
test. "I can't do it."

"Of course you can. You're the strongest woman I
know. You've helped me through everything. You will
look at your test, and then we will figure out what the
next step in your course of action will be."

"Cora, I don't know if I can do this. If it's . . ."

Cora took her by the shoulders, certain blue eyes
looking into her own. "Doesn't matter what the test
says. You can do it. You got me through everything.
Everything. Whatever this is, whatever this becomes,
you can do it. You were born to do it, whatever it is, I
promise you."

Lilly nodded, her throat tight. Cora's words meant
more than Lilly would ever be able to express.

And it was all true. She'd done so much for herself,
for Cora; she had gotten them here. She'd raised Cora
when she'd been a girl herself, and she'd helped raise
Micah every step of the way. Whatever this was, she
could do it. She'd made Christmas happen the year
she was twelve and had a broken arm. She could be the
woman she had to be.

She *would* be the woman she had to be, because that was all she'd ever been.

With shaking hands, Lilly looked at the test. Whether there were two pink lines or one, she would survive.

And if there were two, she would raise that child. Because she knew how to do that. She would get through it. Just like she got through everything else.

But when she looked down and the two lines were completely and utterly, unashamedly there, Lilly could only cry.

# Chapter Nineteen

Brandon locked up the outdoor supply shed with a yawn. He smelled like campfire and had slept for shit on the overnight trip, but it had been good. Good to be away for the weekend. Breathe some fresh air and try to find his bearings.

Of course, that's all it felt like he'd been doing for months. Ever since Lilly Preston had swanned into his life, he'd been fucking recalibrating every damn day.

Today was no different because, as he hiked up to the house, he saw an unfamiliar car in the lot again, and as it was Monday morning, there were no excursions scheduled.

If it was another skeleton out of his father's closet, Brandon thought he really might lose it. But, after he stepped inside and gave a curt nod to Skeet, he turned to the living room and saw Patty standing there with Will.

She turned to him. "Good. You're here."

"Patty," Brandon greeted her, doing his best to turn on some semblance of his charm. "To what do we owe the pleasure?"

The old woman who'd once dolloped extra whipped cream onto his pancakes rolled her eyes at him. "Oh,

don't pull your fancy-schmancy bullshit with me, boys.
Is Lilly here?"

"She's in her office," Will offered.

"Well, go get her."

"You aren't even going to tell us what this is about?"
Brandon asked, feeling the dread dig deeper. Did this
have to do with Hayley? Did it have to do with the private
investigator? Did—

"I'll tell you what it's about when you're all together
in the same room. Now, one of you boys, go get Lilly."

"No need to get me," Lilly said, stepping out of the
hallway looking pressed and pretty. Like spring or sunrise or some other bullshit he couldn't seem to get out
of his head no matter how many times he thought
about the way she'd looked at him as though he were a
monster.

As though he were his father.

But she looked pale, and Brandon and Will had both
commented on her being distracted before he'd taken
the group of campers out. He'd been worried about
her, but he tried to talk himself out of that worry. Alone
in his tent last night, trying to sleep, he'd tried to shut
that worry down.

He was her boss, her friend at best, as she'd said, and
he didn't get to worry about her. She didn't want his
worry or his concern.

He wasn't bitter about that at all.

"I don't suppose that third random boy of yours
is around?" Patty asked, giving Skeet the suspicious
once-over.

"It's his day off."

"All right. Well, I don't know him or his people
anyway so . . ." Patty took a deep breath. "I've been
telling everybody who I think matters in person. It'll be
around town soon enough. I'm closing the Gracely

Café. I'm losing too much money and, quite frankly, it's just not worth it to me anymore to keep it going."

Brandon had no words. He could only stare. Gracely Café had survived the worst of times. Things were supposed to be getting better and she was . . . closing.

"Patty. I'm so sorry." Lilly was all compassion and concern. Brandon shouldn't be bitter that she'd beat him to it, that her concern was so genuine, but these days he couldn't seem to help but be bitter about everything that had to do with Lilly.

But this right here wasn't about Lilly. It was about Gracely. "There's nothing we can do to change your mind? Or help out?" Brandon asked. He'd eaten dinner in that diner more times than he could count. Breakfast with his grandparents. Dates when he'd been in high school and thought he was king of the world.

It was beyond strange to think it wouldn't be there anymore, like all the many other things that had left since the mining company had. All those places that had made up his childhood and adolescence . . . gone. No matter how hard he worked, most of those places just didn't or weren't going to exist anymore. He didn't know what to do, how to absorb another blow like this.

"No, I think it's time to go. You tried to make this town something that it's just never gonna be again. I can't keep waiting around for things to take off. I got grandkids in Denver and some in San Francisco. I've got a family and a life that I've been ignoring for the past fifteen years hoping that I could make Gracely Café something they'd want to come be a part of. But it's time to face facts, and it's time to leave." She said it resolutely, but there was a sheen to her eyes. A sadness.

"I wanted to tell you personally because I know you boys had some interest in me helping you out with your business, but that's just not going to happen. So, Lilly,

I'm sorry if I wasted your time the past few months. But I can't do this anymore."

"What about your employees?" Will asked gravely.

"They've been notified of my plans to close. I'm staying open for two more weeks to have a sort of grand finale celebration, but that's all I can afford. If I don't get out now, I'll never get out and I'll lose it anyway." Patty gave another resolute nod, firming her chin. "Anyway, I wanted to tell you boys in person. And, Lilly, I want to thank you for trying to help, and trying so hard with these two."

"Patty." Brandon found he didn't have the words. Nothing to say what he felt, to show his regret that he couldn't stop this before it happened. Patty only smiled and patted his shoulder before leaving.

"Good luck, Brandon. I really mean it."

Brandon wasn't sure how long he and Will and Lilly stood there in the living room. The only thing that punctuated the silence was the occasional ring of the phone and a grunt from Skeet as he answered it.

"Well, at least Corbin hasn't given up yet," Will said, trying to infuse some cheer into his voice. "We must have given him *some* business."

"Yet might be the operative word, I think," Brandon said. Something about Patty coming and telling them in person, about her wishing them luck. Something about the fact she obviously had at least partially changed her opinion about him and Will and this business made it feel all the more dire that she was leaving. That she was giving up.

"You remember Grandma getting those ridiculous pancakes and then yelling at Grandpa every time *he* did?" Will said, and as much happiness in that memory as there was, Brandon could hear the pain in his brother's voice at the memory.

The pain that they were gone and the café would be gone and Patty would be gone and so much was gone. All because of one man's greed. Or was it even *one* man's greed? Maybe the Evans family had slowly been killing this town from the beginning.

Maybe it was the domino effect of people he'd never met, but shared blood with. Not particularly great blood.

"Well, I guess I should call up Corbin and see what he has to say. We still could win over that furniture store, and maybe the bakery."

"I've been hearing that the bakery's going out," Will said. "It's a rumor, but if it's not going out soon, then I don't think it's going to last. People just can't support a good small business out here."

Lilly got that line between her eyebrows and Brandon couldn't let himself look at it or think about her worry because he was feeling too raw and too stupid to make good choices right now.

"But, you guys, your business is doing so well!" Lilly huffed. "I don't understand how they aren't seeing some kind of benefit from people coming here, then going to town. People *do* come here."

"But they come here. Whatever we're doing, it's not driving enough people down to Gracely like we thought it would. At least not enough people to make up for years of failure."

"Apparently it's just not enough," Brandon echoed Will. "Not enough." God, he felt that failure in his bones.

"Well, we'll make it enough." Lilly fisted her hands on her hips, looking between the two of them. "We just need to move a little faster. I've been falling behind because of the deals with Patty and Corbin. I'll push the pavement harder now. We're not going to stand here and sound defeated."

Brandon looked at Lilly, and noted that Will did too. Will's serious mouth slowly turned into a smile.

"Man, we got to you. We got to you hard."

Lilly straightened, brushing something nonexistent off the front of her shirt. "What do you mean?"

"He means you've taken on everything that we've been yapping about for however long."

"Well, I work with you. Of course I take it on. I wouldn't be here if I didn't believe in it."

"I don't know that that's true. I think you're the type of person who would do the work if it got you what you wanted, even if you didn't one hundred percent agree with what we're doing."

"Is that an insult?" She looked hurt and of course he'd screwed up again.

"No, Lilly. I'm only saying it isn't necessary to believe what we believe as passionately as you do. And you do."

"You're right. I do. I believe in your stupid business and that it's important and that we should save this, but I believe it for different reasons than you think."

"Does it matter?" *Yes, keep being a dick to this woman that you actually really fucking care about whether you want to or not.*

"It matters. To me, and I think it *should* matter to you. Because the more people believe, the more people adopt this, the more chance you have to save what's left. Because there are people, like me who believe in the myth, in the legend." Her eyes glittered with truth or tears, and both hurt to look at.

But he made himself look, because she had a point about . . . thinking more about what other people believed. About tapping in to what they felt and wanted.

"I believe in the hope of this town, even when everything falls apart. This, being here, it *does* heal. That isn't a magic wand or a cure, but it's a good place to be.

This is exactly where I want to r—" She stopped herself, blinking, then curling and uncurling her hand.

What the hell was going on with her lately? How much longer could he keep that worry from bubbling over?

"Anyway, losing Patty's café is certainly a blow, but this isn't dire enough to stand here . . . moping. We are going to work even harder to make sure that Gracely . . ." She pressed a hand to her stomach, closing her eyes. "Gracely is going to survive, one way or another."

"Are you all right? You're looking a little . . . sick."

"I just . . . must be coming down with something," Lilly said with a wave of her hand. "I need to go to the bathroom and then we'll discuss this further." She rushed off down the hall.

"She's been acting weird lately," Will offered.

Brandon was still watching where she'd disappeared. "Yeah, I know."

"You should talk to her."

Brandon looked at his brother and scowled. "Why?"

"Oh, I don't know, because you two like each other, care about each other?"

"Look, she made it very clear she doesn't want that kind of thing from me, okay? I'm her boss, friend at best—and I get the feeling lately things aren't *best*. She doesn't want my concern."

"I call bullshit."

"Why? She said that to me. I'm just listening to her. I'm respecting her boundaries, okay?" It really wasn't fucking okay, but he wasn't Dad. So.

"Well, whatever she said is crap. And I don't think it's okay, considering you two look at each other like you're fucking Romeo and Juliet."

"I think that might be a little bit of an exaggeration," Brandon replied dryly.

"Sure, but not that much of one. You should talk to her, Brandon."

"She made it very clear she does not want that from me."

"What about what you want?"

"What I want really, really doesn't matter," Brandon returned. Not for a long time had his wants really mattered. Not when there were so many wrongs to right.

"No one likes a martyr, Bran, and your act is getting old."

"You want to step up and take the reins?" Brandon snapped, knowing it was more than unfair. Apparently all he could do was be unfair and an ass.

Will shrugged. "Bring it on, big brother. And my first order of business as the fucking reins holder? Making you go talk to Lilly. Now."

Brandon scoffed, but Will raised his eyebrows and folded his arms across his chest. "You a coward?"

"No. I also don't have to listen to you."

"Mature."

"You're irritating the living piss out of me, Will."

"Ditto. Now, we can either have a fistfight, or you can go talk to her. What's it going to be?"

He was a little tempted to pick the fistfight. There was a lot of anger roiling inside of him, and he wouldn't mind letting it out on Will's face.

But Will didn't deserve it. "Fine," he muttered, stepping toward the hallway. He could talk to Lilly without it devolving into a fight or hurt looks. They had a lot of months and maybe even years ahead of being *just* coworkers. Surely they could move past this awkwardness.

Maybe it would even be funny in the future. *Oh, haha, remember that one time we slept together? Wasn't that a riot?*

The only way to get there was to . . . keep pushing. Wasn't that the motto of his life? And he wasn't a fucking coward. So, that was that.

Morning sickness was getting to be a bit of a pain in the butt, and more and more of a reminder she couldn't keep putting off talking to Brandon. She had to tell him—she knew she did.

It was just every time she steeled up her nerve, he looked at her and she melted, and she . . . she had to be strong. She had to tell him when she was strong enough to say her piece.

Strong enough to stand there and tell him it was best if he let her do this on her own. It would be simpler and easier for everyone involved. The whole thing with Hayley and the private investigator just steeled her resolve.

She didn't want manipulations. She didn't want complications. She didn't want this baby to have to worry about . . . anything. Anything ever. She would give it everything, and Brandon could only ever stand in the way of her accomplishing that.

He would want things his way; he would steamroll and manipulate and not see how he was wrong. She wasn't raising her child in the shadow of another complex relationship.

Which meant she'd have to find a new job. Just the prospect of it made her want to cry, but it was the way of things. First and foremost, though, she had to tell Brandon before he figured things out on his own. That was the next step.

She stared blankly at the mirror. She had her plan in place. She'd practiced her speech, written things out. Still, she dreaded and stalled. She wasn't strong enough yet, which she knew wasn't fair. But sometimes life wasn't about what was fair. Their whole situation wasn't fair.

"Lilly?"

Lilly stilled in the middle of washing her hands. She didn't want Brandon to ask if she was feeling okay, because then she would really have to tell him. She couldn't possibly lie to him about this. She could avoid it for a little while, but she couldn't lie.

On a deep breath, she dried her hands. Because the only way out was through the door and to hope like hell he just wanted something business related.

She stepped out of the bathroom and plastered a smile on her face. "All yours," she offered cheerfully, walking past him, hoping against hope he wouldn't continue.

So of course he continued. He followed her right into her office, closing the door behind them. So that he was looking at her with concerned hazel eyes, taking up all her space with that thick air that she'd only ever had to breathe through when it came to him.

Why did it have to be *him*? Why did this have to be so complicated? And why did her plan have to be so . . . cruel?

*Because you want the best for your child, regardless of what* you *want.* Right. Right. This was about the baby. Everything was about the baby.

"Will and I are worried about you. Is everything okay?"

"Everything's okay with me. Why wouldn't it be?" *Not fair, Lilly.*

"You haven't been acting like yourself lately."

"Just a little under the weather, but I'm fine." *And pregnant. You have to tell him you are pregnant. And waiting is no longer acceptable.*

"You know you don't have to come in to work sick?"

"Yes, Brandon. I know what I can and can't do. What I have to and don't have to do. You do not need to lecture me about . . ." Oh, she was being shrill and nasty, and it wasn't fair. She had no right to be angry with him, even if it was his stupid bucket of condoms that had gotten them into this mess.

Everything in her screamed that she had to tell him, and she flat-out didn't want to do that. *You have to, you have to. You know you have to.* "Brandon, there's something I do need to tell you," she managed to blurt.

Oh, God, and now she had to do it.

"Okay."

She swallowed, but that hardly helped the tightness in her throat. "I . . . it's about that night," she croaked. She was stepping up and doing this. Because she had to be the woman she had always known herself to be. She had to be the woman she'd expected Cora and her mother to be.

She had to do this. She had a plan in place, and it might involve being horrible, but if she had to be horrible to give this child everything . . . well, she would be.

All she had to do was tell Brandon she didn't need his help. She didn't *want* his help. She was fine raising this child on her own. Because all she could think about since she'd found out that she was pregnant was Brandon saying Hayley was the last thing he needed.

Another responsibility to worry about. Another wrong to right.

She wouldn't be another responsibility on his shoulders, something he had to make right. He didn't get to make her and this baby his martyrdom. She would not stand for it, and she would cut him off at the pass.

"Lilly, I . . . I don't think that night is something we really need to rehash. I think we've done a pretty good job of moving on and being fairly normal around each other. Let's just . . . leave it at that."

Move on? Wasn't that a joke? "Brandon, I'm afraid moving on isn't quite the option you'd like it to be," she said, mustering all her strength, all her certainty. She had to be the woman she'd determined to be—the *mother* she'd determined to be.

"What does that mean? You were on the same page as me not that long ago. If this is about—"

"Brandon, I really didn't know how to tell you this. I don't know how to *say* this. It's a shock, especially considering how careful we were. But . . ." Where were the words? The strong, certain words.

"How careful we were . . ." His eyes widened and he stepped toward her, all but reaching out. She made sure there was a chair between them.

"Brandon, I'm pregnant. I found out not too long ago. I've been to the doctor and she confirmed it. Obviously, you're the only one I've been with here, so you are the father."

"I . . ."

He stood there looking stricken, and she found she couldn't look at him. She'd want to comfort him, she'd want to allow him something, and she couldn't. She couldn't be weak.

"You don't need to say anything right now. In fact, you probably shouldn't. I've made lots of choices in the past two days. And really put into perspective what it is that I want. I am in a financial and emotional place where I am capable of taking care of this child, and so that is what I plan to do."

He tried to say something, but she had to plow over him. She had to get this out. "I know you'll feel some responsibility for this child. I know you'll have some sort of warped feelings about it based on what happened with your father. And everything that's going on with Hayley. But, in the end, this is about me. Not about you. I am the one who will be carrying this child and having this child. I think I should be the one who's raising this child."

There. She'd said it. Coolly and harshly and awfully.

Brandon only stared at her as if she hadn't spoken at all, and perhaps he was still in a little bit of shock.

"Obviously, if there's some sort of monetary assistance you'd like to offer, I will consider it. But it's certainly unnecessary." She wanted to cry. She sounded like . . . like . . . like a heartless monster.

"You're telling me you're pregnant," he said in a ragged voice.

When he didn't say anything after that, she nodded. "Yes, that is what I'm telling you." Her voice wanted to break. She wanted to cross to him and hold him and cry on his shoulder.

*Another thing I have to clean up. Another responsibility? Because that's what I need?* He'd said that about a grown woman who'd turned out to be his sister—how could he not think worse about a baby?

She had to be strong. He might be bowled over and hurt now, but she had to think about the future, and what her child would need.

"And you . . . you don't want me to have anything to do with a child I helped create," he said, each word a little dagger on her surety that this was the right tactic.

"I don't want your . . ." She knew she had to say this, because it was true. She didn't need his warped sense of martyrdom screwing her child out of a normal upbringing.

Brandon wasn't like her father. Not really. He'd never made a promise he couldn't keep, not to her. But he didn't see the world the same way she did. He didn't understand the way things could be harder for people like her. He had all this influence, and he only understood his own power. He didn't know what it was like not to have those things. He didn't even understand Gracely—what it was. He only understood what *he* wanted for it.

He would always be stepping over and getting in the way of her having a normal life, always blindly following his own way.

Especially since her feelings for him refused to disappear. Every time she looked at him, she felt that shivery, melting feeling deep inside of her. She couldn't have that in her head. She couldn't always look at him like her mother had looked at her father and think that something was going to change. Or that he'd suddenly understand.

Brandon was never going to understand her life. He was never going to understand the way she had to live. He was never going to give her an equal say. So, he had to not be involved in it and it wasn't fair. She knew it wasn't fair. Fair didn't matter. She had to do the best thing for her and for the child. Just like she'd done the best thing for Cora and Micah.

"I know you'd do everything in your power to somehow make up for your father's mistakes. I know you would try to make certain I wasn't treated the way that your father would've treated someone in this position."

"You mean the way my father *did* treat someone in this position," he said, his voice cold and . . . just . . . empty.

She couldn't be affected by that. This wasn't about him. It was about the future. "Brandon, you have a lot of baggage. I have a lot of my own baggage—"

"That you've never told me."

No, she hadn't, and she was glad of it. Glad he didn't

have that ammunition. "Maybe you can hire a private investigator to find it out." She had never hated herself more than she did in this moment. Never. *Necessary evil. You know it is.* "The bottom line is I don't think our baggage can . . . coexist in a way that is healthy for this child."

"Our child. *Ours.* How can you ignore that?"

"I'm not ignoring it. I'm being practical about it. I think once you've had some time to think, you'll understand that it's practical too." She stared at her shoes, because anything else would tear her apart, break her resolve.

"Practical? Practical? You want me to have nothing to do with my own child because it's fucking practical?"

"If you're going to fire me, do it right now." It was a nasty, vindictive thing to say, because she knew he wouldn't. Not in a million years, but she had to make him want this too. She had to make him get as close to hating her as possible.

"After everything I have done and said to you, I can't believe you just said that to me."

Oh, God, he wasn't even trying to hide the pain in his voice, in his expression. And she couldn't breathe past her own. He didn't deserve those terrible words; she'd known it all along. But she had to protect herself, and she had to protect her child. "I think I will head home for the afternoon. I'm not feeling very well."

Brandon stood blocking the door. "We're not done discussing this, Lilly."

She looked him straight in the eye. She had to. *You have to be the strong one. You cannot let this turn into something like Dad or Stephen. You are protecting everyone.* "I'm done discussing it, and that's all that matters."

"Do you have any clue how selfish you're being?"

Thank God for his accusing, for his getting angry.

Anger she could fight so much better than grief. "It's my life to be as I choose."

"This is not right, Lilly." His voice was shaking and she wanted to believe it was anger still, but she knew better. "I think deep down you know that this is not right."

"No, Brandon. What I know is that it isn't fair. I'm sorry that something not fair has to happen. But it does. This child has to mean more to us than anything, and that means we have to put our own stupidity out of the way. We can't do this to the child. We can't put him or her through the same stupid crap that our parents went through and put on our shoulders."

But he still didn't move, so she had to fight harder. Harder and harder until she finally won something.

"I won't have this baby living through your attempts to be the opposite of your father. This child doesn't need your guilt, and I don't want it seeing me . . ." She couldn't let him see all of that. She didn't need to give him all that.

He was the one who had sidestepped her comfort the other day. He was the one who made sure that this could never be a thing. And yeah, she'd accepted that pretty easily, but she couldn't be her mother. She couldn't. She would give her child everything, even if it hurt. She would make all the sacrifices. She wouldn't ask her child to make them for her.

So, she had to say the most horrible thing she could think of, the thing that would cut him off at the knees. After all, he'd said it himself. He'd moved on. There was no use rehashing, so there was no use putting another responsibility on his shoulders. "And what's more, I don't want this baby to grow up an Evans in this town where it's a mark against them."

She couldn't look at him—it was too much. She

couldn't live with herself if she saw what expression those words might have wrought. "Let me out, Brandon. Now."

There were a few beats of humming, angry silence before he finally moved out of the way of the door. "This conversation isn't over," he said, his tone a pained threat, his hands in fists.

She looked him straight in the eye, ignored all of the ways this hurt, ignored all of the ways that she was breaking his heart and hers. "It's the end of any discussion I will have with you about it. Good-bye."

And she walked out of the room so she could cry. Alone.

# Chapter Twenty

Brandon didn't know how long he'd sat in Lilly's office. He wasn't even sure when or how he'd gotten to his feet. He didn't say anything to Will or Skeet. He didn't say anything to anyone.

He just left. Something he hadn't done . . . ever. He'd never just left people, not telling them where he was, or where he'd be. Especially not when he had a business to run.

But, he didn't have words. He didn't have anything. He could only walk out of the office, get in his truck, and drive up the mountain. He had to be somewhere Lilly had never been, and about the only place that was the case was the cabin he and Will shared.

Maybe there, where she couldn't haunt him, he could figure out what the hell had just happened to his life. Maybe he could figure out what he'd done to make everything so fucking messed up.

He walked into the house he'd left only this morning, feeling like some kind of stranger. Who was he? He was a man who had thought for so long he had it all together. He'd thought he knew exactly where his life was going. And yet consistently, every so many years, his life flipped. It broke apart. This time, two gigantic soul-splitting things had been dropped on him by women he hadn't even known had existed six months ago.

How was he supposed to know what to do? How was he supposed to keep going forward when everything kept pushing him . . . pushing him. Into this universe he didn't know, and didn't understand.

He wandered through his house feeling like . . . hell if he knew what he felt like. What was this? What was this life that he had a sister and was going to have a child—his responsibilities, his failures?

And Lilly, the one woman who tested everything, the woman who had felt different in every way, the woman who he'd thought was able to see through him, had somehow stood there and said she wanted nothing from him, nothing from him for his child.

He pushed out onto the back porch, not realizing until his hands curled along the rough wood of the railing that he was shaking. Shaking apart, maybe. Every piece of himself he'd stitched together in the aftermath of the Evans disaster—losing the business, his father, his mother, his life—was tearing apart into something he didn't recognize.

He looked out over the mountains. Even though summer was creeping in, the air was crisp and cool. Not too much farther up the mountain, there were clumps of snow dotting the peaks and scraggly spruce and fir trees.

This was the view he had built his life's work on. It was supposed to heal; it was supposed to give. It was supposed to somehow make everything that had happened all right. It was supposed to be the cure, the fix.

He felt broken. He felt wounded. He felt the very fucking opposite of healed, and what the hell was he supposed to do? How was he supposed to . . .

He gripped the railing tighter and tried to find some sense of certainty. Some sense of knowing what to do. He had to know what to do. He *always* had to know what to do. He had to be the one to step up and find answers and solutions to multiple problems.

He stood there looking at the beautiful vista below him, breathing this air that so many times had given him the answers, but all he felt—all he saw—was nothing. He had no answer for this, no grand plan.

There was a half sister who apparently wanted nothing to do with them, or whatever she *did* want to have to do with them was something she wasn't going to tell the brothers. And there was a woman, a woman whom he'd thought had meant something. . . . And she'd effectively cut out his soul and his heart.

*I don't want this baby to grow up an Evans in this town where it's a mark against them.*

How could he argue with that? How could he wish that for his child? He couldn't even hate Lilly for saying it because she had seen, firsthand, Corbin and Patty and everyone looking at them like they were scum.

He could take it, but, no, it wouldn't be fair to ask a child to deal with things that had never had anything to do with him or her.

For five years, Brandon had gotten by based on his sheer force of purpose. He'd known exactly what he wanted to do. Make up for everything his father had screwed up. It was all he'd wanted, and all he worked for.

Now there were two women who would not let him do that. Who wanted nothing to do with the name that was still a curse word in town, no matter that he'd dedicated years to trying to make it mean something good again.

Lilly was trying to keep him from having anything to

do with their child. Their *child*. Because of this thing he couldn't escape, and couldn't seem to fix.

He didn't know what to do with all of the rage inside of him. He couldn't seem to let it out, and he couldn't seem to work through it. It just kept bubbling there, like a geyser. What was he supposed to do? Scream? Punch something? Cry? Because he felt like doing all three at the same time, but he didn't know how to start any of them.

"I am not him." Everything he'd ever worked for was that he was not his father. Lilly was trying to make him into that against his damn will. She was *blaming* him for not wanting to be that. It wasn't fair. This was crap. He wasn't going to stand for it.

That was it. He wasn't going to stand for this. He was going to find a way . . . he was going to find a way to make this right. No one could turn him into his father against his will. No one. Not even Lilly.

For some reason, it made him think of his mother. The woman who wouldn't talk to him because of the events he had put into motion. Just like this town—she had blamed him. Blamed him for the loss of Evans, for the loss of Dad. Everything bad that had happened had been heaped on his shoulders.

Brandon couldn't even argue with her. He might have been right, but the consequences weren't.

*But this is your life. Like everything else, this is your life and you have to deal with it.*

For the first time in his life, not only did he not know how to deal with it—he didn't *want* to. He wanted to pretend it didn't exist. He didn't want to be strong and he didn't want to fight. He wanted to be weak and he wanted someone else to take care of it.

Someone who knew what they were doing. Maybe Lilly was right. Maybe this was just . . . Maybe he should

just bow out. Let her take care of their child without it
ever knowing what a shit history it had handed down to
it. Maybe she was damn right to keep him away.

He sank onto the floor of the porch and buried his
head in his hands. A child. His child. How could he
have nothing to do with it? How could he accept this
and walk away? But how could he fight?

"Brandon? Where the hell are you?" Will's voice rang
out from the front, and then, after a few minutes,
Brandon heard Will coming up the steps of the porch,
coming up from the backyard.

"What the hell, dude? You disappeared and you . . ."
Will looked down at him, sitting on the porch. "What's
wrong?" he asked gravely.

Brandon looked up at his brother. His twin brother
who had never really had a care in the world. He'd
gotten to skate by, gotten to do whatever he wanted because he hadn't been the heir apparent. He'd gotten to
spend more time on the ski slopes than the classroom
in college, and then he'd gotten to marry a lingerie
model, for fuck's sake.

And Brandon had toiled and worked and taken
every fucking responsibility on his shoulders.

It wasn't Will's fault. That had always been the expec-
tation, and Brandon had *loved* it. He'd thrived on being
the one to take responsibility. He'd embraced being the
one who had all the answers, who made all the choices.
He was good at it. He had been bred to be good at it, to
be the head of a huge mining company. Only to have
it gone at his own damn hand.

"What is going on? What happened? Is someone
dead or—"

"Lilly's pregnant."

Will stood there, still as a statue. When he finally
spoke, his voice was hushed. "And you're here because?"

"She said she doesn't want me to have anything to do with it."

Everything in Will's usually loose and casual demeanor went tense and hard, something like fury glittering in his hazel eyes. "And you fucking listened?"

"Yeah, I listened."

"What the hell for?"

"Because she's pregnant and she asked me to?" He pushed to his feet. "Because she's carrying that baby and she gets to make the choices? Because I'm just the fucking failure who would *stain* that child's life if I dared give it my worthless fucking name?" Brandon smashed his hand against the side of the house, because he couldn't take it anymore.

Finally, *finally* something had broken inside of him and the anger and rage poured out. Because Will was standing there acting like he'd made a mistake? Like he'd failed at this. If he'd pushed, that would have been its own failure. Because there were no right answers.

Not one.

"Because if I push, I'm the rich asshole pushing my fucking *privilege*. And if I let her have what she wants, I'm the deadbeat stepping aside. So either way, I'm Dad. Why not embrace it?"

"You're too old and have done too damn much to sit there and feel sorry for yourself. Thinking you're Dad? Give me a damn break. You stood up to him. You ended him and that company because you had too much integrity. So don't be a crybaby about how you're like him. It's bullshit. It's always been bullshit, and now you finally have a reason to accept it."

"You only know part of the story," Brandon muttered, the truth eating him from deep in his soul.

"What the hell do you mean?"

"I mean it's part of the story. Did you ever wonder how long I knew before I said anything?"

Will didn't say anything. He didn't move. So Brandon stepped toward him, poking him in the chest so Will would *get* it. Once and for all.

"Because I wanted it, Will. I wanted to be him. I wanted to be Evans Mining Corporation president more than just about anything. So, there was a long-ass time where I ignored every shady deal, every sidestepping of a law, every hint at an affair or scandal. I pretended it didn't exist, because I wanted to *be* him. I wanted people to look at me like they looked at him. The only reason I ever stood up to him was because I knew innocent people were going to get killed if we didn't fix that mine. But I thought about it, Will. I wanted it."

"You think you're the only one with a shitty family secret, Brandon? The only one who kept their mouth shut to save their skin?"

It was Brandon's turn to still.

"I knew Dad had gotten someone pregnant. That summer before senior year when you went to that leadership camp or whatever and Dad made me work in the mail room. I overheard two secretaries talking about how he'd gotten another one of them pregnant years ago, and paid her a big sum of money to disappear."

"Will . . ."

"And I told Mom."

"Mom *knew*?"

"She slapped me. Right across the face." Will laughed bitterly, turning away. "She told me that I wouldn't be going to college and I'd be completely cut off if I told anyone. So, I didn't."

"I don't . . ."

"The bottom line is this family is a hundred kinds of fucked up, Brandon. But *you're* not. You did the right thing because you knew people would be hurt if you didn't. You have a kid. You and Lilly can disagree about a lot of things, but she can't take away the fact that it is partially *your* kid."

"And partially hers."

"Yeah, I get that, but she's holding Evans shit against you. That isn't you. You're not Dad. No matter how much you wanted that glittering Evans life, you have *never* been the sick, twisted son of a bitch he was. Not even when you wanted his life. You got that? You are the best fucking man I know, Bran. In the whole of my life, all I have seen you do is try to help. Everyone but yourself. Me, Sam, this godforsaken town that hates our guts."

"Because I *ruined* it."

"Bullshit. Dad ruined it. Grandpa Evans ruined it. The greedy, soulless men who came before ruined it. We're just the ones who have to deal with the fallout." Will took a step toward him, something was unexpected in his expression—something Brandon couldn't put a finger on.

"You're going to be a part of that kid's life—*your* kid. I love Lilly, I think she's great, and I think she's great *for* you, but if she's pushing you out, she's wrong. And you're wrong for letting her do it. That's your kid. You're going to have that kid."

"Why are you . . . Will, what is this?"

"You're my brother and I love you and I respect you and admire you and . . . a kid? Yours. I get that it's Lilly's too, but she can't just cut you out of the equation. Maybe she's got some good reason in her head. That doesn't mean that you don't have a good reason for being a part of this kid's life. It's your fucking kid." He raked his hands through his hair and Brandon felt shaken by the fact that . . .

There were a lot of big pieces of his brother that he didn't know. He hadn't known about Will telling Mom about a possible child, and he didn't know . . . what this was. "Why do I get the feeling this has something to do with you?"

Will looked out at the mountains and Brandon had a feeling this was going to be another blow. Another thing he didn't want to have to accept or deal with.

"Look, there are a lot of things that happened with me and Courtney that . . ." Will cleared his throat, shook his head.

"Tell me, Will. Tell me what this is."

"About a year ago . . . Courtney found out she was pregnant. And she didn't tell me. She got an abortion. Because she didn't want a baby interfering with her career."

Fuck. "Will." He reached out for his brother because as non-demonstrative as they were as a rule, this was . . .

"So the thing is you have this chance and you can't ignore it because she wants you to. You have a kid. *Have.* It's yours."

"You never told us."

"What the hell was there to tell you? My wife so much did not want to have my child that she got rid of it. But this isn't about me. It's about you, and the fact you have a kid. A *kid.*"

"It can be about both, Will. This can be about both." He squeezed his brother's shoulder, and he saw the way Will's throat worked as he tried to swallow. His eyes were sharp on the blue sky, and Brandon didn't know how long they stood there.

"Just trust me, this one time, I know what I'm talking about. I, for once, have the advice, and you need to take it. You have to talk to Lilly. Whether she wants you to be a part of that baby's life or not, you have to push yourself into it, because that child is *yours*."

"Don't you remember all the things she said about power and influence and understanding?"

"Yeah, I remember all that. I say who the fuck cares. It's bullshit. It's distancing bullshit meant to protect her. Just like every other damn thing we ever talk about. All we ever do is give excuses to protect ourselves from hurt, from disappointment. Everything about not being Dad, you're just trying to insulate yourself from failure. But life is . . . fucking full of them. You gotta accept it."

"I don't want to fail my kid."

"The only failure is not being there for it. For Lilly. God, you're both so hardheaded and rule-focused and determined to do the right thing . . . and you're letting that ruin everything. You're letting it break you. See, that's the thing. . . . Courtney and I never communicated. Never talked. We had crazy sex, and we went out and got drunk together. It was fun and it was great. But it wasn't love, and it wasn't a relationship. So when she found out she was pregnant, she didn't even think to tell me. She didn't think that it would hurt me. She didn't *think* because she didn't know *me*. She only knew herself. Do you know *why* Lilly doesn't want the baby to have the Evans name?"

"Because people hate us."

"But why would she think that? She who works for us and believes in us? What happened to *her* that made her think that would be an issue? You're thinking about you. You're thinking about your feelings and Dad."

It made him think of earlier. Of realizing they'd been thinking about the way to heal the town, without having ever asked anyone in town what they wanted. Maybe . . . maybe Will wasn't so far off.

He eyed his brother. "You do a very good impression of being a self-absorbed party boy a lot of the time."

"Yeah, I do." Will's smile was empty, but he didn't try to argue it wasn't an impression.

"You know what Courtney did wasn't a reflection on you, right? You believe that part you just said, that she didn't even think about *you*, because you two didn't know each other."

Will shrugged. "Sure, yeah. But it's done and it's over. Your life isn't."

Brandon realized his hand was still squeezing Will's shoulder, but he didn't let go. "Your life isn't either."

"Yeah, no, I know. The point is that . . . man, you have to stop trying so fucking hard not to be him, and just be you. Because Brandon Evans was never, ever like our father. Not even when you were sitting there considering not telling anyone about all the problems with Evans. Because he never would've questioned it, he never had any guilt over it. You aren't him. And you're never going to be happy until you admit that. What's more, Lilly is never going to see you as the man you are until you can let that go."

"It's been me forever. Being him, and then not. How do I let it go?"

"I don't have that answer. But you have to give her a piece of yourself, and I know how hard that is. I . . . I've never done that. I've run away from that." His gaze was still on those far-off mountains, but his voice was so full of pain. Brandon would have never guessed that. He would have never guessed any of this had happened, because Will kept it so buried.

Brandon kept all his shit buried too, under this

passion, under this determination not to be Dad. He buried all the feelings, all the . . . everything. They all did, and seemed to do it so they didn't have to communicate. Even Sam, they'd brought him here when his life had fallen apart, but they'd never talked about that.

They'd just kept moving forward, using Gracely and Mile High as this shield against all those hurts, all those insecurities.

Lilly had seen through parts of that, but the minute she had, he'd used Mile High and his being her boss and his not being his father as an excuse to make sure it didn't continue.

Brandon's hand dropped and he took a deep breath of mountain air, mountain air that *could* heal, if you actually let the healing in. "You're right, Will. You're right."

His mouth curved, but the smile was empty. "I don't think you've ever said that to me."

"I wouldn't get used to it." Brandon looked at his brother, and knew they had to be more than this. They had to be bigger than this. "I love you, brother. But what's more, I'm proud of the man you are. The fact you went through that and kept going and we never knew about it. . . . it says a lot about your inner strength."

"Or my determination not to feel."

"That too. Will, you're a good man."

"How the hell did we come out of those two people?"

"No clue. But let's make sure . . ." Brandon took a deep breath and let it out. "Let's make sure our kids never wonder the same thing."

"Your kid. I'm not going there again. I'm done with women."

Brandon snorted. "Yeah, sure."

"I am. I'm writing them off right now. Who needs sex?"

"Men. Men need sex, and women, too, I believe."

"Nah, I think my life goal is to turn into Skeet."

"Now I know you've lost it. You'll find someone and you'll get the family that you deserve."

Will drummed his fingers on the wood railing. "You really think we deserve that?"

"You're right. We don't deserve a damn thing." Brandon met his twin's gaze and forced himself to smile. "But we're going to get it."

"Yeah, sure."

Will might not believe it, but Brandon did. They were going to get what they wanted because they weren't their father, but they were Evanses. They might not run the world, but they were pretty good at wading through a lot of shit.

# Chapter Twenty-One

Lilly was exhausted. She'd come home and curled up on the couch, determined to get some work done even if she'd fled Mile High. But after hours of sitting here, she was merely gritty eyed and frustrated. She'd gotten nothing accomplished.

Except crying.

Every time she looked at work, she wanted to cry again, because it made her think of Brandon. His name, the thought of him, everything . . . it caused a searing pain of guilt and disgust at her own actions.

"I made dinner. You feeling good enough to eat?"

Lilly forced herself to smile at Cora. "No, thanks."

"You know, even if you don't really feel like eating, you should be getting something into your stomach. It helps, you know, the whole snacking-through-the-day thing."

"I'll try to eat something in a little bit."

Cora slid next to her on the couch. "This isn't just morning sickness. You're moping."

"Yeah, I know."

"Did you tell him?"

Oh, how she would like to not be so dang transparent. "Yeah."

"He didn't take it well?"

"I didn't give him a chance to take it well," Lilly muttered, pulling the unnecessary throw blanket up to her chin.

Cora frowned at her. "What does that mean?"

Lilly knew she could beg off and not tell her the details, but she didn't have the strength to be in-charge, big sister, *don't worry about it* Lilly right now. She was too busy having to be in-charge *future mother* right now. "I told him I didn't think he should have anything to do with the baby."

"What?" Cora screeched.

Lilly shrugged, determined to be unaffected. "It's in the baby's best interest."

"But, Lilly. Lil, you like him. I wouldn't be surprised if he liked you, too. Who wouldn't?"

"My feelings for Brandon are irrelevant. The point is that I have to put the baby's well-being and feelings before my own. I'm not going to . . ." She trailed off, because apparently her reign of terrible things said wasn't over yet.

"You're not going to be Mom or me."

"I only meant—"

"I don't care what you meant. It's stupidity. You're as different from me and Mom as possible. We're talking polar opposites here. You're always taking care of us. You've always been the one to step up and do everything. How could you even think you're anything like us?"

"I . . . I didn't mean it as an insult. I'm not saying I'm better, I just—"

"But you *are* better, Lilly. You always have been. You're the thing that kept any of us upright. Come on."

"You're wonderful. You're so upbeat and you always—"

"Stop," Cora snapped, her voice commanding and surprisingly acidic. "Don't dig yourself out of that hole now. You're better. That's a fact."

"I'm . . . *different.*"

"No." Cora shook her head emphatically. "Mom let a married guy impregnate her twice and make a million promises to us he'd never keep. I let an abusive asshole keep me and my son under lock and key and fist. You've never let anyone have that kind of power over you. Good for you."

"It's not a contest," Lilly replied, feeling small and selfish and like such an awful bitch. Hell, maybe this child would be better off with Brandon, not her.

She placed a hand over her stomach. It was hard to believe something was growing in there, even with the uneasy, constant seasick feeling that dogged her. But just the thought . . . just the thought of giving this up . . .

No, she'd never be *that* strong. Even if it would be best. She couldn't let this go. This was hers.

*What about Brandon?* She squeezed her eyes shut. "I'm just tired. Can we talk about this later?" When her certainty didn't feel so fragile.

"No, because right here, right now, you need to understand that not only are you not like me and Mom, but that guy isn't like Stephen. He would have called you stupid or hit you or something by now if he was like him."

"No, he isn't . . . he isn't like Stephen, but that doesn't mean you're stupid, honey. He manipulated you. He knew just how to make you—"

"Yes, I know. It was all his fault, he's terrible and I'm great. Rah, rah, therapy. But this is about *you.* That guy isn't like Stephen, which I think is one of the worst things a father can be like. He also didn't make you a bunch of promises he was never going to keep, did he? He didn't use you or manipulate you."

"No."

"So, not Dad either. Lilly . . . come on, I saw the way you talked about that guy. I've seen how much it's weighed on you *not* to be with him, and if he wasn't at least half this determined, rule-following person you are, he wouldn't have felt the same as you did. So. Why should a man you *like*, like really, really like, have nothing to do with your baby?"

"He doesn't . . . he doesn't have those same feelings back, Cora. Not really." She wasn't sure where those words came from. She hadn't allowed herself much time to think about what Brandon might feel, but she was certain . . .

That day she'd stepped toward him to offer him comfort, he'd sidestepped her and walked away. When she'd been about to tell him about the baby, he'd said he'd moved on . . . He didn't have those feelings back.

"Why not? You're fantastic."

"I . . . He's just not . . ." Lilly didn't know this weird coiling fear inside of her. "He doesn't." If she focused on that, this was doable. Because . . . he didn't. What was she to him?

"Lilly? Why would you think he doesn't have feelings for you? Everything you told me about him makes me think that if he slept with you, he has some serious feelings."

Lilly felt short of breath and she didn't know why she wanted to cry, or why she felt . . . worthless. She felt worthless. Thinking about Brandon having the same feelings . . .

He couldn't. How could he? "He doesn't need me. He has money and influence and strength and power— why would he need me? Men like that don't need us."

She tried to stand up, but Cora's hand clamped on her arm.

"Lil, need and love are two *very* different things."

"Not for me they're not." She didn't know how it slipped out. That wasn't what she'd meant to say. She hadn't meant . . . that.

"Lilly—"

"Let me go, please."

"Hell to the no, sister. Tell me what you mean by that."

"I don't mean anything. It's just . . . Come on, you know me and my life. The only people who love me are the people who need me. So, that's . . . that." She couldn't look at Cora's face. She couldn't look at anything.

It sounded so warped when she said it out loud. Sad. But sad or warped, it was *true*. People who didn't need her had never loved her. Her father, the small pool of boyfriends she'd had. Friends had come and gone, and the only people who stayed were those who needed her.

No one had ever loved her unless they had needed something from her. End of sad, pathetic story.

"Well, I know I've always needed you. You've made yourself this thing I can't live without. But I don't think that was super healthy for either of us," Cora said in a hushed voice. "But you're right, I do need you, and I do love you. But they're not . . . not the same. I would never stop loving you. Even if I got my shit together and didn't need you anymore. You're my sister and I owe so much to you."

"Yes, see. You owe me. You need me."

"It's not the same. Love is a separate issue."

"How so? Who walks away? If I don't make myself indispensable, *everyone* walks away." And it might sound pathetic, but it was true. How could Cora not see it was true? "Every friend I've ever had, every boyfriend I've ever had, our own father. The only people who stuck in my life are you and Mom, and that is because you need me. Mom left us the second she had a husband and had an excuse to ditch us both. She didn't need us anymore."

"She left because I was pregnant."

"No, Cora, she left us because she didn't need to handle anything anymore. She didn't need me, because she'd replaced me with a husband."

Cora was quiet for a few humming seconds, but she didn't let Lilly go. "Don't you love Micah?" Cora asked, her voice a low, trembling thing.

"Of course I love Micah."

"You don't need him. In fact, he's probably more of a responsibility. But you love him. And you love me, right?"

"Of course. I have always loved you."

"You love us without needing us. That's love."

"For me. But . . . Cora, no one's ever loved *me* who didn't have to." Because this wasn't about love or other people. It was about her. Some fundamental lacking in her, because no matter how hard she'd tried . . . her parents had never loved her. The people who'd created her.

How could she believe anyone could?

"I could say the same thing, Lilly. I know I'm no one to talk. I seem to mistake love for being treated like a stupid piece of shit, but that's the thing about having a kid that you're going to find out. No, that's not even right. You raised me—you already know it. Because it isn't magical biology. It's just being a caretaker. When you have to care for someone, their every need, you learn what love is in a different way than you've ever known it before. You already know that, deep down I know you do."

Cora squeezed her hand, her eyes full of tears but her voice steady and strong and somehow comforting. "And they do need you, and that is so scary. I don't know how you did it when you were so little, knowing I needed you. But, Lilly, love and need are not the same thing, I promise you that. I don't know a lot of things, but because of *you* and your selflessness when it came to *me*, I know what love is. And it's bigger than need or responsibility."

"Maybe . . ." Lilly swallowed. She'd never shown Cora so much of her insecurity before, but hell, they were both adults, weren't they? Cora had a ten-year-old— surely she could handle some of Lilly's not-so-perfect thoughts. "Maybe it's me. Maybe there's just something fundamentally . . . wrong with—"

"Stop that right now, or I'll make *you* an appointment with the therapist. There is nothing wrong with you. You are one of the most wonderful people I've ever known, and I think you've lost sight of that because you've tried to be strong for so long. But you don't have to be strong for us. Not anymore. We're all standing on our own two feet, and we'll be strong for each other. For this baby. Because that's the family *we've* made. Out of *love*, more than need."

Lilly hadn't realized she was crying until Cora reached out and wiped a tear off her face. "When did you get to be so smart?"

"Well, I fucked up enough for twenty people. You'd think I'd pick up something."

Lilly managed a watery laugh.

"Look, about Brandon . . ."

Lilly took a deep breath and shook her head. "I get what you're saying, but . . . it's complicated."

"Yeah, life is a bitch that way." Cora laced her hands with hers. "You've got to give him a chance. Just because our dad and Micah's dad are crap doesn't mean he'll be. You love him, don't you?"

It was like a piercing pain, that question. Because she thought she shouldn't. That it was all too quick, and surely you had to sleep with someone more than a few times over the course of an evening when you were locked in a cabin together. You had to date and get to know them and . . .

But no matter how she tried to rationalize it away, she . . . couldn't seem to fight the fact that she did. She did love him, and honestly, that scared her more than anything else. Because . . . maybe love and need weren't the same things, but no one had stayed without need, and she didn't want her child . . . losing.

"Lilly. Come on. You can't just shut him out."

"But if he doesn't need me, how do I guarantee he doesn't leave?" How did she make certain he didn't break her heart *and* her child's?

"You can't. That's the thing about life—there is no guarantee."

"That's terrible." She needed guarantees. Not for herself. She could deal with anything, but she didn't want her child to have to deal with . . . anything. She wanted to give him or her all the love and happiness and carefree childhood she'd never had.

"Yeah, it is terrible. But it's life."

"I don't want this baby to have to go through what we went through. Did you want that for Micah?"

"There are worse things than what we went through. You know, like knowing your father is an abusive asshole?"

"Cora—"

"I did bad for him. I mean, Stephen did that, but I

allowed it. You know I allowed it. I made all sorts of mistakes, and I never get to make up for them. Except by giving him all I think he deserves now."

"That's why we're here."

"Exactly. So, Lilly, if you believe Brandon is a good man. The kind of man who'd make a good father—and I don't mean a perfect father. He'll make mistakes and you'll make mistakes, and that's the hardest thing about being a mother for me. Knowing I'm making mistakes that will hurt him, but there's no choice sometimes. We all make mistakes and we can only do our best."

"But if I try really—"

Cora squeezed her hand. "You'll still make mistakes. You made mistakes with me, and God knows at your age you had a right, but I'm just saying . . . life is never perfect. It's never ordered and easy. It's not all happiness and light. I'm getting there, to understand that, and some days are better than others, but the point here and now is—if Brandon is the kind of man that will do his best for your child, then turning him away isn't helping your child. It's trying to protect your heart. And you'll regret that. I know you'll regret that. You need to talk to Brandon and find a way that you can make this right."

"I don't want my child to be miserable."

"Having two parents who love them couldn't possibly be miserable for your child. It's a luxury I don't think anyone in this family has ever had yet."

"It's too selfish to want to not be miserable myself?" Of course it was. Of course it was selfish to push Brandon away because he scared her, because she was scared of what she felt for him. But was it wrong if it kept her from believing something that couldn't be true?

"Selfish is the wrong word. Sometimes being a parent requires some selfishness. And sometimes it requires being selfless. You've always been selfless with me. You've always given me more than I deserve. Just maybe you could learn from my life experience and . . . not let that warped view of love ruin it for you. You could give them *both* everything you've given me and Micah. And I think you'd be so happy."

"I . . ." Give Brandon what she'd given her sister? Unconditional love and bending over backward to make her safe and happy? But he didn't *need* that from her. And she didn't want to . . . give all of herself anymore. It cost too much.

"You need to talk to him. You need to explain to him."

Lilly pulled her hand from Cora's grasp and managed to stand up. Cora had said a lot of true things, and maybe Lilly's view of love *was* warped, but that didn't change that it was her reality. "I explained everything that I had to explain. I don't want his crap affecting my kid and I don't want my crap affecting my kid. So, he can't be a part of it. He just can't. I'm sorry you don't understand that, but you're wrong. I'm not going to change my mind about that."

"Oh, well, by all means, be hardheaded about this. That's the answer."

"I'm going to sleep." And to cry, and to . . . convince herself she was right. Because of course she was. She always had been, hadn't she?

How could she possibly be wrong when everything important was on the line? So. End of story.

# Chapter Twenty-Two

For the better part of the evening, Brandon had planned on marching over to Lilly's little house on the corner of Aspen and Hope and laying out how things would be. He would be involved in his child's life, but more than that—they were going to get married. End of story.

They liked each other well enough. The sex was amazing—even if it had only been one night. They both cared about Mile High. They were people who wouldn't cheat on each other, out of principle even if not out of feeling. It only made sense to get married and give this child a *whole* family.

He'd imagined that, been halfway to his car at least ten times, but something stopped him every time.

It wasn't what she wanted.

When Lilly had found out about the private investigator they'd hired, she'd thought about how *Hayley* would feel. When Patty came to tell them about the café closing, Lilly had offered sympathy over *Patty's* feelings.

Lilly routinely put other people's feelings first. She thought about what *they* would want. With the very painful exception of that morning, when she'd told him she wanted him to have nothing to do with their child.

But Lilly usually put herself in other people's shoes, and he never did. He'd been *convinced* he'd been doing everything for Gracely. For Evans. But in hearing Will's secrets, in seeing firsthand everyone leave Gracely . . . he realized he'd only been doing what *he* thought was right.

Not what was best. Certainly not what was best for anyone. He'd viewed himself as selfless, but he'd been blind and unerringly selfish.

If he was going to convince Lilly he deserved a chance with their child, if *they* deserved a chance at the thing that had *always* been between them, from those first moments of arguing, then he needed to think about what *she* would want.

Fuck it all.

How on earth did a person go about knowing what someone else wanted? How did he go about solving the puzzle that was Lilly Preston?

He knew she was good at her job, that she took her responsibilities seriously. She saw a problem to solve rather than an impossible, unclimbable mountain when faced with a challenge

She liked color. Silly and completely nonfunctional footwear. She always looked so polished because she liked feeling like she was in control, and because she simply *liked* feeling pretty.

She loved her sister and nephew most of all. She was . . . someone who took care of people. But not in the way he'd always considered himself a caretaker.

He . . . moved people forward. He could sweep them away from their problems, like he'd done with Sam. But he didn't . . . take care. He acted.

Lilly felt. When he'd said all those things about his

father that, until yesterday with Will, he'd never spoken aloud to anyone, she reached out to him. To soothe. To comfort. She was a woman who gave those things without doubt or reservation.

Which meant, he knew exactly what she would need from him. He knew exactly what he would have to give her to make her realize how wrong she was.

He would have to give her the scariest thing of all: his feelings. He'd have to communicate them, like Will had talked about failing to do in his marriage.

He would have to tell her all of those . . . confusing things inside of him. He would have to explain to her how he knew her, why he cared about her.

And Lilly wouldn't want to get married. Not yet. She didn't act as a way to solve problems; she sought to find the root of them and fix them from there.

So, no *insistence* on marriage. Just . . . his feelings. His openness to the possibility. For their child, yes, but because he knew being married to her would be a partnership

He paced the porch outside as the sun began to rise. Surely there had to be something . . . more. Something more than the idiotic things his heart whispered to him when his brain was otherwise engaged.

But a gift would be meaningless to Lilly. Even a thoughtful one wouldn't matter to her without the feelings behind it.

Damn it.

Giving her feelings, giving her pieces of himself he'd spent most of his life pretending didn't exist, was so much harder than blindly moving forward. It was so much harder to look someone in the eye and *tell* them what his feelings meant, how they'd hurt, and how they'd soothed than give them something, than *do* something with them.

Words, for him, were the hardest thing, which of course meant they were what he needed to give her. No shoulds, no rules, no demands. Simply, all those things he pushed down . . . poured in front of her and turned into words.

He felt sick.

The door to the porch opened and Will stepped out. It appeared as though he'd just rolled out of bed. He yawned and stretched, his eyes first seeking the riot of colors that was the sunrise before returning to Brandon.

"You're going, aren't you?"

"Yeah. Just . . . waiting for a reasonable hour."

"I'd say you're good to go. Want some coffee in a thermos?"

"No, I think my nerves will get me pretty damn far."

"For what it's worth . . ." Brandon waited, but Will didn't speak until Brandon turned to face him. "Even if it doesn't go all smoothly and perfectly, you're making the right step here. In my humble failed-marriage-behind-me opinion."

"Well, believe it or not, it's an opinion I value." Brandon looked out over the sky, the way the colors changed and melted into each other, the way the world didn't change so much as light up, shining on everything that was there, always there.

Lilly would like this, she'd like watching the sun rise over the mountains, especially from the deck of his house, where she could sip her tea and not have to fall down a mountain to get there.

Thinking about her here, in this little cabin he and Will had built. With a baby. "I think . . . I'm in love with her," he forced himself to say, for practice, to be sure.

"No shit, Sherlock. And drop the 'I think' when you tell her. I don't think women particularly care for that. Especially when it's bullshit."

"But . . . I just don't get . . . how . . . I don't even know why she acted the way she did, what happened to her. It's only been a few months, and there was only one night."

"Second thoughts?"

"Hell, no. I'm just working out my nerves. How do you . . . know? There doesn't seem to be a right answer. How do you *know*?"

Will shrugged. "I can't answer that. I didn't exactly choose love when I got married on a whim."

"What did you choose?"

"Fun with a lingerie model and not having to talk about my feelings."

"And what was the alternative?"

Will rolled his eyes. "Good luck, brother. Don't let the door hit you on the way out." And then he disappeared back inside.

Later, when he was a little more recovered from *his* feelings ordeal, he'd press on that. But today, even if it was still a little early, the most important thing was Lilly. And their child.

And somehow letting feelings triumph over rules and responsibility. Because no matter what kind of responsibilities a baby and Lilly were, the bottom line wasn't that. It wasn't doing the right thing or following the rules or not being his father.

It was love. Plain and simple, and he had to be brave enough to give that to her, or he certainly didn't deserve it in return.

It was a strange thing to know a baby was growing inside of her, but to see no effects of it. Her clothes still fit, with the exception of her bras. She could still wear her cute dresses and colorful tights and heels and feel . . . just as she'd always felt with her polished armor in place.

*Except* . . . She pressed a hand to her stomach. She was always thinking about the baby, what size it might be, if she was doing everything right so that it would develop well.

It hadn't been too terribly long, but already the baby took up so much of her thoughts. Which was much preferred to the other thing that kept occupying her thoughts against her will.

She'd had her heart broken enough times to know that's what this was. It was just that no one had ever . . . It had always been someone she'd loved for so long. How had Brandon wormed his way into her heart enough to break it?

She wanted to believe she didn't really know him, that his hiring the private investigator *proved* that, but . . . there was something about working with someone, talking about the thing they loved and gave their whole heart and soul to, *witnessing* them do that thing. . . .

It was hard to convince herself she had made the right decision. Especially with Cora's words about need and love . . .

But, why would she take advice about love from *Cora*? As much as she loved her sister, judgment was not one of her finest attributes. Judgment was not something that came naturally to any of them.

She had to trust reason over feeling, and considering she'd spent her entire life putting someone else's needs above her own without too much sacrifice, this shouldn't feel any different.

She pulled the brush through her hair with an irritated tug, then focused on putting on her makeup. Focused on putting on her armor, because she was going to get to work early. She was going to face the day, and Brandon.

If she gave in to the impulse to call in sick today, she'd never go back. She may need to start looking for a new job to start after the baby was born, because, God, she couldn't work for him and have his baby and keep them apart, but for the time being, she still had work to do at Evans.

She wouldn't be a coward. For herself, for the baby. For Cora and Micah. She was the sole provider here, and she would . . . continue to be. That was fine.

There was that damn stock word. *Fine.* Fine, if fine was wanting to cry, and doubting every choice she made, and just . . . wishing things were easier. Simple. Clear.

She didn't know how to deal with a complex issue. She didn't know how to maneuver something morally ambiguous. She was a black-and-white-type of girl. Things were right or wrong. Every problem had a solution, every question had answers, everything could be accomplished with enough determination and hard work. Good things were supposed to be happy, bad things were supposed to be sad.

What utter bullshit that was turning out to be. It turned out good was as hard as bad, happy as much work as sad.

She stomped out of the bathroom, wishing she could pummel something. Or some*one*. But Cora was blearily shuffling down the hall.

"What are you doing up so early?" Lilly asked, doing her best not to sound snappish.

Cora rubbed a hand over her sleep-tousled hair. "Oh, I have some errands to run after I drop off Micah. Wanted to look presentable."

"What kind of errands?"

Cora blew out a breath, looked up at the ceiling. "Don't get your hopes up, okay?"

"Hopes up about what?"

"I have a job interview."

"Cora!"

"No hopes up. Okay? It's in Benson, and I'm not qualified in the least. It's a total pipe dream."

"But you're going to *try*."

Cora's mouth quirked a little. "Yeah." She reached forward and gave Lilly's stomach a little pat. "It's far past my time to do a little trying. For you, and my niece."

Lilly put her hand next to Cora's. Still so strange this was real. Strange to be somehow overjoyed and terrified and frustrated. "Or nephew."

"Oh, it's going to be a girl. We need a little princess around here to spoil. Now, I have to get—"

Someone knocked on the door. Lilly frowned. She'd been in the bathroom a while, but it couldn't be later than seven.

Cora crossed over to the little hall window that overlooked the front yard. "Oh."

"Oh, what?" Lilly looked too, her heart catching in her throat when she saw Brandon's truck. "Oh."

"Can you see him?"

"No, just the truck."

Cora got on her tiptoes. "Yeah, me too. Why do you think he's here?"

"Oh, to bulldoze me into letting him be a part of his child's life, no doubt." Lilly brushed her hands over the front of her dress to straighten it and squared her shoulders. "And he's going to be disappointed."

"Lil . . ."

Lilly gave Cora a sharp look. "It's for the best. This is all for the best."

"I know you think that. . . ." Cora muttered, her gaze

returning to the window. But Lilly didn't wait around to hear anything else.

She had no doubt Brandon had gotten over the shock and had now worked his way to anger. He'd barge in and make demands, tell her how things were going to be.

And she was going to be strong. She was going to stand her ground. Because it was the right ground. The only choice.

*Only? Really?*

She shook the doubts away and got to the bottom of the stairs. She straightened her dress one more time, bracing herself for Brandon on a determined tear, and opened the door.

He didn't say anything. He didn't even look particularly angry. He looked at her with soulful eyes and said, "Good morning."

"Good morning," she repeated, habit more than anything prompting those words.

He tried to smile, but it died long before there was any curving of his mouth. "I was hoping we could talk."

"And by talk you mean you're going to barge in here and tell me what to do? What the right thing to do is? How things are going to be?" She crossed her arms over her chest, ready to fight against each and every thing.

"That might have been my first impulse."

Oh, damn him, she wanted to laugh. She wanted to soften. This . . . this was the Brandon she'd fallen in love with, unfortunately. The man he'd been at the lake, in the office that night. All those times they'd been alone and he'd let some of that hard shell . . . soften.

*The real him,* an insidious voice in her head whispered.

"But, I think it'd be better if we took a little drive and had a discussion somewhere . . . neutral."

"Are you looking to off me?"

"Lilly."

"Somewhere neutral sounds like . . . secluded and inevitable mysterious disappearance."

"I just want to talk." He looked her right in the eye, all . . . soft sincerity. "Please."

She opened her mouth to tell him no. To tell him they couldn't do this and there was nothing more to talk about. She had to. That was the solution to this problem, and there was no way *talking* was going to help.

So, she should tell him to go to hell. Had to. But his expression was so *grave*, and his demeanor surprisingly . . . not pushy, and—

Two hands pushed her from behind so that she stumbled into Brandon. Warm, piney, all too strong Brandon. She glared back at her sister, who was standing there, arms crossed over her chest.

"Go."

"Cora," she hissed, stepping as far away from Brandon as she could, but Cora blocked her reentrance.

"You owe it to yourself to have a peaceful conversation. He said please. He's not barging. Go." Lilly opened her mouth to argue, but Cora drew her fingers across her mouth like she was zipping them—a gesture Lilly had done to Cora too many times to count.

"Get the hell out of here. You cannot come back until you've had a calm, rational conversation with him."

"Thank you, Cora."

Cora glared at Brandon. "And if she comes back here shedding so much as one sad tear, I will personally cause lingering damage to your family jewels, if you know what I mean."

"Yes, I think that comes across loud and clear."

The door slammed and Lilly jumped. "I don't have

my purse, or my ph—" The door reopened and Cora
shoved a bag at Lilly.

"Phone and keys. No need to come back till you're
finished. And I put a granola bar in there in case you
start feeling bad." The door slammed again and Lilly
could only stare at her purse.

"She's . . . taking care of me," she mumbled to herself, so shocked and moved and . . .

"I'm glad."

She glanced up at Brandon and . . . this was going to
end badly. She was going to have to get meaner, nastier.
Make a break so deep he couldn't possibly want to
bridge it.

*You could hear him out first.*

But if she heard him out, she'd be . . . steamrolled,
wouldn't she? *Are you really that weak?*

She was beginning to wonder.

"It's just a short drive, and then we can talk. If, after
I've said my piece, you still want me to have nothing to
do with this . . ."

She waited.

"No, it's my kid. As much as yours. I'm sorry, Lilly.
You won't get rid of me. Not today, not tomorrow, certainly not in nine months. But this isn't about that."

"Then what is it about?"

"Us."

She closed her eyes against that word, leaning
against the door behind her. Because that was the absolute last thing she wanted to think about, let alone
talk about. Them.

"There was an 'us' for all of one night, Brandon."

"I don't think that's true, and I don't think *you* think
that's true either. Or you wouldn't be afraid to come
with me."

She glared at him, temper straining—and she had none of the reserves to rein it in. "I am not afraid."

"Then, your carriage awaits," he said, making a gesture toward his truck.

She moved her glare from him to it. She was not afraid. Because fear meant she thought she was wrong, and she refused to believe that. She could stand up to him. She would *have* to if she was going to give her child the life she'd never had.

So, she would go. She would face him, and she'd make sure she ripped out both of their hearts in the process.

# Chapter Twenty-Three

Lilly didn't say anything on the drive, and Brandon was glad for it. He'd been more than ready to walk up to her door, to tell her they needed to talk. He'd had it all planned out. He'd even known she'd resist.

He just hadn't counted on that making him so fucking pissed. He drove the bumpy, gravel road up to his destination, knowing he should feel a little guilty for making a pregnant woman hold on so tight to the door her knuckles were white.

But she should trust him. And she shouldn't be treating him like he was some kind of . . . evil monster set out to hurt her. This hadn't been one sided. This hadn't been . . .

He took a deep breath, trying to loosen his death grip on the steering wheel. He loved this woman, he was almost certain of it, and yet . . . she drove him absolutely insane. Wasn't love supposed to be an easy thing? Something comfortable and certain?

Which made him wonder about Will's marriage. There was so much he didn't know, but it had always looked easy. Will had said himself they had fun . . . but they didn't communicate.

Why the hell was *talking* so damn difficult?

He pulled to a stop on the little patch of rock next to the overlook. It was an often overlooked county property that few people seemed to know about, plus it would give them the opposite view of Solace Falls.

Right from the top.

"Is this your someplace neutral?" She peered out the window, those pale, perfectly arched eyebrows drawn together in concern and confusion.

"It is." He grabbed the thick blanket he'd put in the back when he'd left his cabin this morning, then stepped out of the truck. He skirted the back, then opened her door for her.

She was still buckled, that line between her eyebrows as prominent as ever. "What are you doing?"

"I'm going to show you something." He patted the blanket. "Then we're going to sit down and talk." He held out his hand to help her down.

She frowned at it, but she unbuckled her seat belt. She never took his outstretched hand—instead, she slid around it, hopping out of the truck all on her own.

He tried not to sigh, didn't want to show just how frustrated he was, but she glanced at him and he knew she'd caught it.

This walking-on-eggshells shit was crap. He should have barged in. He should have told her exactly what was going to happen.

She picked across the little lot on her completely-unsuitable-for-walking-any-length-of-distance heels, and then looked over the railing of the outlook.

"Oh." Her eyes widened and she looked back at him. "Is this Solace Falls?"

"The top of it."

"Why do people bother hiking it if you can drive

up here?" But even as she peered down at the roaring waterfall, she seemed to relax, soften.

She wasn't the outdoorsy type exactly. She'd never be as interested as he was in hiking and pushing her body to its physical limits in the middle of a forest or at the top of a mountain. But it spoke to her, the same way it spoke to him. "Some people like a challenge, Lilly."

She leveled him with a look that reminded him of those first few weeks. That cool disapproval. But that was better than the pained certainty she'd faced him with in her office when she'd dropped the bomb.

"Lilly, I . . ." He could have said it. Far more easily than he'd imagined, the words "love you" were on the tip of his tongue, swelling up from some part of himself he tried to ignore. But it was there, and looking at her here . . . he had no doubt.

But he knew she would.

He nodded toward a little patch of grass where they'd be able to see the top of the waterfall cascade over the craggy mountain of rock. He laid out the blanket so she wouldn't get her prissy clothes all ruined.

She stared at it, her lip faintly curled. So, he took a seat at one edge, and waited patiently for her to join him.

After a few minutes, she rolled her eyes and slipped out of her heels. When she took a seat on the blanket, she demurely curled her legs to the side since she was wearing a skirt. She had these bright pink tights on her legs, and he couldn't help but linger there. The smooth line of her calf, the way her skirt inched up thighs he'd once—

She scrambled onto her knees, pulling her skirt down as far as it would go.

It was Brandon's turn to roll his eyes. "I can imagine all of that just fine."

"Well, imagine away, but you don't get firsthand viewing anymore."

"Why is that?"

She blinked at him, as if taken aback by the question. "You chose that path, Brandon."

"No, Lilly, *we* chose that path. We agreed. We stepped away from each other because it was the right thing to do."

She looked away, over at the falls, her expression a mix of sadness and hurt. "Can you say your piece so I can get to work? Because, as you recall, you employ me."

"I need you to tell me why this is how you're dealing with things. Because I know you too well to honestly think . . . You're too kind, and too *caring* to cut me out like this without having a reason. I want to know it."

"So you can argue against it?"

"Hell yes, so I can argue against it. Maybe your estimation of me is somehow lower than mine of you, but why do you think I would ever allow you to just cut me out? I've spent the past few weeks trying to reconcile my father paying someone to keep quiet about *his* child, about how he could send her away. I already thought pretty poorly of my father, but I don't know how anyone just . . . doesn't acknowledge their own. That child is part of me—you don't get to choose otherwise."

She sucked in a breath, and looked as though she might cry. But she held her shoulders back, her chin up. Always so . . . strong. Immeasurably strong.

"Lilly, I meant it when I said I didn't want to talk about the baby right now. I want to talk about us. Because baby talk is irrelevant. That child is partially mine, and I will be a part of his or her life. No matter how much I care for you, you cannot shut me out of that. I won't let you."

She met his gaze with that same look she'd employed

when she'd told him. Detached—not just cold, but cool. As if . . . as if she simply *had* to say it, far more than she felt it. "It doesn't bother you what you'd be condemning them to?"

Maybe it was simply wishful thinking to want her not to mean it, but he knew her too well. He'd seen her be too . . . compassionate. There was something bigger at play here. "No, because I will protect that child with everything I am, everything I have. And as you love to tell me, I have a lot."

Something like . . . fear took over her features. He didn't think it was fear of him. No, he thought . . . He thought, much like he had been, she was trying to protect herself, trying to insulate herself from failure or hurt.

They were painfully alike in that way. Trying so hard to make things right for other people, failing miserably to make things right for themselves.

But, before he could expect her to give him anything, he had to be the one to give. He had to do the . . . communicating. Damn it all to hell.

"I think I was wrong to . . . I *was* wrong to think that we had to . . ." Christ, where the hell were all those words he'd practiced? All those feelings he'd put into clearly designed sentences and paragraphs and carefully organized arguments—jumbled. "People should be more important than . . . codes. Rules we hold for ourselves."

"But sometimes rules are all we have. Codes. They keep everyone . . ."

He raised an eyebrow at her, because what had codes and rules done for them? In the end, they hadn't mattered at all.

"If we hadn't . . . if we hadn't let those go, we wouldn't be here."

"Is here such a terrible place to be?"

She blinked. "It wasn't planned. It's not . . ." She frowned and looked down at her lap.

"Lilly . . . I don't regret it. Even with this unplanned thing, this responsibility, this part of me, I don't regret it. I have a *very* strong ability to deny feelings I don't want, but . . . I could never deny what I felt for you. It was killing me, day by day. I've struggled with a lot of ambiguous moral shit, but you . . . you were the biggest struggle. I wanted you. I . . . Stepping away from you that day you reached out, you remember? In the living room and I—"

"I remember."

It helped that she did. If she remembered so easily, that meant it mattered. "It was the hardest thing I've ever done. Harder than standing up to my father when I didn't want to, because at least then I knew lives were on the line. When I stepped away from you, the only thing on the line was my heart—and somehow that made it all that much harder."

His heart. That was what it boiled down to. Having one, and not being able to deny it. He'd tried—oh, he'd tried—but it always boiled down to this. Not being able to deny the thing that beat inside of him.

"So, I don't regret being with you. I don't regret it in the least, regardless of the outcome. Do you?"

She studied the hands clasped on her lap for a very long time. Only the rushing sounds of the falls on their great descent to the lake interrupted the silence. He watched her, noted the way the clasped hands in her lap pulled in, so that she was touching her stomach.

Where their child grew. *Theirs.* She had to see. . . .

"I was supposed to be better," she said, on little more than a raspy whisper. "Mom always told me I had to be better than her. But I always failed. Cora got pregnant, and I failed. Mom left us. Now . . ." She took a deep if shaky breath. "And I can't even regret it. How could I? I was supposed to be smarter—she said I had to be. . . . And I can't even be smart enough to regret it."

A tear slid down her cheek and then another. He would have ignored them. Any other time in his life, he would have looked away, given her privacy, let her have that moment of sadness alone. Oh, sure, he might have suggested a canoe trip, as he'd done the day she'd been upset over her sister losing her job, but he never would have . . . reached out.

But today, in *this* moment, he couldn't avoid it. He couldn't sit back and let her hurt, grieve, cry. He reached forward, brushed the tears off her cheek, and pulled her into his embrace.

Lilly cried into his shoulder. She wished she could be stronger than this, but she wasn't. She just . . . wasn't. She knew her mother would expect her to regret it. Hell, even Cora would expect her to regret it, but his simple question had done more to dismantle what she *should* do than anything else in her life.

No, strike that. He was always dismantling. Always . . . breaking her down to some part of herself she couldn't control. He was the only *person* she'd ever met who could upend this ordered world she'd created for herself.

She'd faced a million hard things, but Brandon was the hardest because he was a choice. Believing in him, giving in to him, accepting that she loved him—those were all choices, all in all.

But he'd felled her with that question because . . . she couldn't regret this child. She couldn't regret her night with Brandon. They were too big and too precious of things to obliterate with regret. What was wrong with her?

She couldn't neatly plan this. She couldn't order it to suit her. She couldn't manage him like she managed Cora, or her job. She couldn't ensure that she was indispensable to him, because he was his own capable, formidable force of nature.

*Except when it comes to you. Just like he was your "except when it comes to him."*

Maybe if she hadn't been crying into his shoulder, she might have found some strength, that strength that had lashed out at him. Maybe, if he weren't rubbing a soothing palm up and down her back, she could have pulled herself together.

But he was *comforting her.* After she'd . . . she'd been awful to him. Had to be. She *knew* she had to be, so how could he be so caring?

"Why are you being nice to me?" she asked with a sniffle. "I was awful. I plan on still being awful. I have to . . ." *Protect myself from you.*

Oh, God. It was true. He'd stripped it all down to what he'd do for the baby, to rules and codes not being as important as people, to having no regrets.

She pulled away from him, knowing somehow he'd won this battle. He'd erased all of her sturdy assurance she was doing this for the baby. With his calm, earnest honesty, he was making her face the fact she wasn't keeping him separate to give a certain kind of sturdy life to her child. She'd wanted to cut him out because she knew Brandon could hurt her, devastate her.

*Oh, Lilly, you're such an idiot.*

"Like I've said . . ." Though she'd pulled away from his comforting embrace, he took her hand. "I know you too well to believe that's what you really want. I know it's what you think you have to do, but you wouldn't hurt *anyone* that way if you didn't have your reasons."

"And you want to know them," she said flatly, drawing her hand from his. He wanted to know all of those ugly, failed parts of her. The ways she'd been left time and time again, and how that had turned her into this selfish, terrified woman who wanted to cut him out.

Oh, God, she felt sick to her stomach and it wasn't the baby this time. It was her own stupidity.

Because if he knew everything, he'd have even more ammunition to hurt her with. If she laid it all out, he would have reasons to doubt her, to think less of her. He might . . . realize he should leave too.

"You don't need me," she choked out, because his words were wrapping around her heart and making her dumb. All his words would make her dumb, and she would wind up hurt and alone, because that's how this always worked for her.

*Because you've never put your heart and soul into trying?*

"Do you want me to need you? I bet I could work up some kind of need."

She hiccupped a laugh. How on earth was he making her laugh when she'd felt so awful for days? "It's just . . . the people in my life have always needed me. Otherwise . . ."

"Otherwise what?" he asked, his thumbs stroking her tears into her cheeks.

"They . . . leave. They disappear. I . . . don't want to be devastated again. I don't want to be empty."

"So, you'll just be empty and devastated in advance? And you'll put me through it so you don't have to go through it?"

"No, I . . ." She had no argument for that. The truth was, the past few weeks trying to avoid Brandon, to pretend they didn't . . . feel anything, well, it had been empty. It had . . . yes, it had hurt. But there'd been a reason for that, a reason for keeping those lines and rules in place.

What had they been again?

"I *want* you, Lilly. In my life. And that was true before all of this happened."

"Except you weren't *going* to be with me." She pushed his hands off her face. "And I wasn't going to be with you. How can we ignore that?"

"Well, who knows how long that would have lasted? We weren't even tested for a month."

"You're determined to be stubborn about this."

"I could say the same about you." His mouth curved, just slightly. "It's one of the things that so impresses me about you."

"Even when I'm stubbornly arguing with you?"

"Yes. Who wants easy?"

"Apparently neither of us," she grumbled, and she didn't fight it when his hands took hers, when he held them there between them. And when she lifted her gaze from their hands to his eyes, everything in her shivered and softened.

No, no one had ever stuck around who hadn't needed her, but no one had ever . . . fought for her either. Said they *wanted* her. Maybe . . . maybe want was even better than need? Maybe the choice was the difference.

"My father . . . had another family," she found herself saying. "My mother was his . . . what? Mistress, I guess. She knew he was married, that he had other kids, but he would make all these promises. Even after me and Cora came along. He'd come spend a few days with us, promise us all these big, glorious things, buy us extravagant gifts, and then he'd be gone. No him, no money to get us through the next month. He didn't need us, we were a . . . distraction. A bit of fun. But nothing to . . . stick around for. Nothing worth taking care of."

"Just because he didn't give it didn't mean you weren't all *worth* it, Lilly."

She glanced up at him then, saw something like . . . fury simmering in his gaze. Yes, he was the type of man who would find that wrong, wasn't he? He'd stood up to his own father, had this strict ethical code.

"Is that all?" he asked gently. He was also a man who didn't give up.

Damn him. "When Cora was seventeen, she got pregnant with Micah. The father refused to help at first, demanded paternity tests and was just . . . awful. He wanted her to get rid of it, and she refused. They fought . . . physically sometimes. And all Mom could do was . . ." Lilly swallowed, because this was the harder one, the deeper cut. Oh, she'd learned not to trust men and their easy promises, learned all that from her father. But her mother had cut out her heart with a blow Lilly had never seen coming. "She'd berate her. Tell her she was stupid and was going to be miserable, and Mom was seeing someone at the time and he wanted to marry her. So, she left."

"Left?"

"She said she was moving to Nevada and she didn't want to see us again, if Cora was going to be a useless idiot and I was going to stand by her. We'd never been anything but burdens anyway, good riddance, et cetera.

"I loved her. I . . . thought she'd worked all those jobs *for* us, and I'd worked so hard to make her proud. And she just . . . left, as though we didn't mean a thing. Everyone . . . does. Once they don't need me anymore."

He reached out, cupped her face with his hands, which were warm and rough and capable. "I'm not letting you go. *You.*"

She didn't know why nice words, caring words would slice through her. Why something so sweet and damn near *loving* made it feel like she'd been gutted—so gutted all she could do was sob. She couldn't fight away the tears or swallow them down. She broke down.

Not let her go? Everyone did. Her father, her mother, even Cora had gone the moment she had the chance, and the only reason she'd come back was to save Micah from Stephen. Every romantic relationship she'd tried to foster had faded away. Everyone let her go.

That was her truth, her life.

But somehow Brandon, this determined, forceful mountain of a man was standing there telling her he wouldn't let her go and she was having such a hard time erecting all the walls and rationalities and rules to keep herself from hoping that somehow, someway, the cycle would break.

"I didn't just *bend* my rules to be with you," he said, his voice a ragged whisper, his hands gentle on her face. "I shattered them with a damn ax. Only you, that's only ever happened with you. This isn't about having a baby. It couldn't be. Even me with my excellent, if I do say so myself, denial skills, can't ignore that this is about *us*. You and me."

"But—"

He still held her face and he tilted it so she had to look him in the eye. "Hell if I know what love is supposed to look like, but no matter how I try to talk myself out of it, tell myself I'm not capable because of my name or worthy because I wanted something wrong once upon a time or whatever other stupid shit I tell myself to avoid feeling, I *love* you."

"Bran." Love. *Love?* He . . . couldn't. How . . . ?

But he held her face and looked at her as if . . . as if

she were those mountains he was always seeking. She'd only ever seen him look at mountains this way.

"I'll probably screw it up a hundred ways, but I'll keep trying. I won't walk away. No, I don't need you, Lilly. But I love you, I want you in my life, and I would never, ever walk away from that."

"I'm just so afraid," she whispered, the admission costing every last inch of wall she'd built to ward him off. Now there was nothing to save or protect her, and maybe . . .

Maybe he would step in and do that. She'd always been afraid to believe someone could, that someone *would*, oh, but hell, if anyone could or would it was Brandon Evans.

So, she had to give him . . . what he'd given her. Not because she owed it to him, but because it was true. She loved him. She *chose* him. "I . . . did all the things. . . . Everything I've done, I did because I had to. I didn't have a choice, or I told myself I didn't. There's so much less chance of failure when you don't have a choice."

He stroked her hair and murmured his agreement. Comfort and understanding. What no one had ever given her. Cora had tried to for the past few days, and she'd managed to succeed somewhat, but this was different.

This was choice. Brandon was *choosing* her, and that was somehow . . . bigger than need. More important.

She wanted to choose him back. She'd always wanted that, but she'd let fear get in her way, let protecting herself be more important.

She had a lot to make up for. "You really . . . want to have a relationship, and try to raise this baby together? To work together . . . because you love *me*, not because of the baby?"

"Yes. If I didn't love you I would have gone with my

original plan and barged over to your house, insisted you marry me. Insisted I had the right way of it and that's what we would do. But . . . I care about you, Lilly. I care about what you want and feel, and you made me realize that's where I've been going wrong this whole time with Gracely. I wanted to absolve my guilt. I wanted to rebuild what *I'd* had. I wasn't worried about them or what they'd lost or even what they wanted to rebuild. I was focused on my own wrongs—you made me see that. Every step of the way, from giving Corbin a paper printout instead of using your tablet, to genuinely giving Patty your condolences. You cared about those people you barely knew, more than I'd ever cared about them my entire life. You humbled me. You still do."

Oh, God, he was going to kill her with words, she was nearly sure of it.

"I don't want to be that man anymore. I don't want to be so self-absorbed I don't care about anyone else. I want to build a life *with* you, not build a life and then shove you into it."

That was . . . everything she'd ever secretly wanted. Someone to build *with*. Someone who would take some of the responsibilities, but not all. She'd always been searching for a *partner* more than any fairy tale.

Somehow Brandon was a little bit of both.

She was still afraid—trembling with fear—but she was also brave. She'd come so far. Didn't she have faith in herself? All she'd accomplished? Didn't she deserve a chance at this? Didn't they both?

She placed a hand on her stomach. Didn't they all?

"I want that too," she said, forcing herself to keep being brave, to bring her gaze to his. To face down all those fears, all those whispers that she would only repeat her mother and sister's mistakes.

But Brandon wasn't those men, and maybe they

weren't even her mother or sister's mistakes. Maybe they'd been manipulated and hurt before they'd had their chance to find someone like Brandon.

"So, you'll . . ." He cleared his throat. "*We'll* talk about what that means, about what that looks like."

"Yes, talk. We're good at talking . . . on top of mountains and in the middle of lakes."

He laughed, tucking a strand of hair behind her ear. "Luckily that's exactly where we are, and where we work, and where I live."

"Brandon, I . . ." She wanted to tell him that she loved him, but she wanted it to be more. Bigger. A promise. A choice. She wanted to give him what he'd just given to her, the chance at something she'd been so afraid to reach out for and have.

"I think I fell a little bit in love with you in Corbin's office when you gave him that speech. A little more when you took me to the top of a mountain and I saw the man behind the . . . armor." Yes, he had armor just like she did—that was how she could recognize what she'd seen underneath it.

"You *think*?"

She smiled, couldn't help it. She wanted to . . . laugh and cry and smile and hold on for dear life. The emotion swamped her, but she had words to say. Promises to make. "And I *know* I fell in love with you when you threw me into a lake."

He laughed. "You're full of it."

"No, I did. No one's ever . . . *played* with me before. Done something fun and silly and childish. I was always looked at as the one in charge, the smart one, the rule follower. And I took it on a little too seriously, just like you. And so, everyone looked at me for that, but you . . . saw more.

"I don't think I could have slept with you if I didn't

love you. I told myself all sorts of lies about what it was, what it meant, but it wouldn't have hurt to walk away if it wasn't love. If it wasn't right."

"And yet you were so certain you had to cut me out."

She could hear the hurt there, and she knew she had a long way to go to make up for that. She deserved that long, hard road. But long, hard roads had never fazed her. "I told myself I was brave, because I did everything I could for Cora and Micah, but the truth is I was only brave when it came to them—never when it came to me."

Brandon looked out onto the falls, his expression grave. "I know how that goes. I think we both . . . have some changing to do."

"We'll help each other."

His mouth quirked, his fingers lacing with hers. "Yes, we will."

"Will you kiss me now?" Except his mouth was on hers before she even fully said the "now," his arm pulling her closer, his hand tightening around hers. It was like the first time, the way the need flowed up from her toes, the way the rightness soaked her like a pouring rain.

He pressed a kiss to the corner of her mouth, to her cheek. She clutched his shirt with her free hand, needing to hold on to something. Realizing she got to hold on to him. For a very long time.

"I've missed you," she murmured into his bearded jaw. "Every time I turned away. Every time you avoided eye contact, it *hurt*."

"It hurt me too." His mouth covered hers again, this time gentle, sweet. When he pulled away, his hazel gaze held hers.

"Would you consider marrying me?" he asked, not a proposal but something even bigger. A consideration.

A discussion of what their future might look like. Other women might need romance, pretty proposals and flashy rings, but to Lilly, nothing would ever be more romantic than him asking her to *consider* it.

"You don't have to take the Evans name, and neither does the baby. I don't want—"

"I'll consider it. We'll both consider it, and if we choose yes . . ." She already couldn't imagine not, but she wanted to take that time to consider. But that didn't mean she didn't know . . . "I'd be more than proud to take your name, Bran. Our child will be an Evans regardless."

"Even if it's a stai—"

"It's not," she said firmly. "It certainly won't be by the time we're done with it."

He visibly swallowed, touching her face again, that steady, *loving* gaze never leaving her face. "I love you, Lilly."

"I love you, too." And more, she was ready to believe. To choose. She was ready to give and take.

And so was he.

And now . . .


Read on for a preview of Sam's story
in the next Mile High Romance:

## MESS WITH ME

by
Nicole Helm


Available in September 2017
wherever books and eBooks are sold.

Sam Goodall knew an ambush was coming. He'd known it for approximately three days and had made himself exceedingly scarce. He appeared at the cabin that headquartered Mile High Adventures with just enough time before his assigned guides to get ready, and no time to have conversations with anyone.

He was a quick man, an agile man, and he'd spent the past almost five years putting nearly all his effort into being a silent partner in Mile High Adventures, taking on the riskiest and most challenging guides, and mostly staying out of the way. He could disappear easily and quickly and hoped his streak would continue until whatever was being planned for him fizzled out.

Five years ago, his best friends, Brandon and Will Evans, had lured him from a fishing boat in Alaska, back to his home state and their once-shared dream of this outdoor adventure company, but they hadn't lured him back to the land of normal.

That land had been demolished a long time ago.

"Sam!"

Sam winced at the feminine lilt of Lilly Preston's voice. He liked Lilly well enough, despite her ever-present grunt jar and chatter and questions, but this would be none of those things.

This was only the beginning of the ambush.

"On my way out," he grumbled, barely pausing in his quick retreat out the back. His Jeep was parked in the front, and all he needed to do was turn the corner and disappear and he'd be safe for another day.

"I'm really not feeling up to chasing after you, Sam."

He cursed under his breath. Though he had no qualms about running from a pregnant woman, he knew Lilly would have no qualms about following him, and if she did something stupid like trip and fall, Brandon would likely kill Sam where he stood.

Which actually might be better than whatever was waiting for him.

Still, he stopped. He slowly turned to face the bright pop of color that was Lilly, Mile High's public relations specialist. She was excellent at her job, a good fit for Brandon, and most of all, she usually let Sam keep to himself. He liked her.

He glowered down at her, arms crossed over his chest regardless of any like.

Lilly merely smiled serenely. "Have dinner with us."

"No."

She pursed her lips before responding through gritted teeth. "It wasn't an invitation."

"Still no."

She grunted, and his scowl loosened. "I believe that means you owe a dollar to the grunt jar."

Her hands curled into fists, her quicksilver blue eyes flashing with temper. "Sam Goodall, you are the most frustrating part of this business, and this business includes *Skeet* of all people."

"Thank you," he replied earnestly.

"You don't even know who I wanted you to come to dinner with, or why."

"Brandon and Will, so you three can ambush me with whatever you've been whispering and plotting all week."

Her mouth dropped open and she blinked. "For someone who's never here, you're remarkably astute."

"Good-bye, Lilly. I'll see you tomorrow." Or he'd avoid her tomorrow. Time would tell.

"Sam." She exhaled loudly as he began to walk away. "We need your help."

He didn't stop, didn't pause, didn't even hesitate. "No, you don't," he returned, and kept on walking.

When Sam woke up the next morning, he scowled. Something was off. He knew the sounds of the small clearing high on the mountain his self-made cabin had been built on, and something wasn't right.

The stillness of the air up here had been interrupted by something. The usual summer chatter of birds and animals had stopped. Sam blinked at the darkness outside his window. It was too early for much of anything to be an interruption.

Apparently the ambush had come to call.

He swung off the tiny mattress that was shoved into the corner of the big square room that was his home. The only other room in the cabin was a small bathroom off to the back, and it was also the only room with electricity or plumbing.

He didn't live primarily off the grid for any moral reasons, any grand desire to save the environment or live some authentic simple life that would bring him closer to spiritual enlightenment. He did it because it felt necessary, and because it kept people away, and probably for a few other reasons he refused to spend any time considering.

Throwing on a T-shirt, Sam grumbled to himself. He pulled on socks and shoved his feet into his boots, and when he stepped outside into the pearly dawn of a summer morning, he swore. Loudly.

"Good morning to you, too, sunshine," Will Evans greeted him cheerfully. He and Brandon stood leaning casually against Will's Jeep in the middle of Sam's yard.

Though the Evans brothers were twins, and looked remarkably alike, especially when sporting beards, the brothers were nothing short of opposites. Which Sam had always supposed kept them from killing each other.

Once upon a time, Sam had been the instigator of trouble in their little group, Will always the willing follower, Brandon frequently the voice of reason. But things had changed for Sam, and he'd only agreed to return to Colorado and start this business with his friends because Will and Brandon had accepted those changes.

"Go away," Sam grumbled, running his hands through his sleep-tangled hair. He needed a haircut, and a shave, but his unkempt appearance kept people at bay. Customers he guided tended not to ask too many questions of the hairy, grumpy Yeti. A nickname that bothered him not at all.

"Stop being a coward, Sam. We've got a favor to ask." Brandon's reasonable tone scraped against the peaceful quiet of dawn.

"I don't do favors."

Will rolled his eyes. "Yes, we know. You're very gruff and scary. Now stop being so damn difficult and hear us out."

"Why should I waste your time and mine? I've got things to do." Which wasn't a lie. He had a schedule.

Being primarily off the grid meant any time he wasn't working at Mile High, he was working at the complex task of living stripped of most modern conveniences. He had laundry to do by hand, firewood to chop for heat, and a mind to keep occupied in solitary, physical pursuits.

"You owe us. You know you do." Brandon's voice was quiet but tense and brooked no argument.

Sam gritted his teeth, hating to be reminded of just how much he owed the Evans brothers. They'd saved him, he had no doubt of that. He was just more than a little shocked they'd stoop so low as to use it against him. "Didn't expect that one to be thrown in my face."

"We didn't expect you to be such a dick about something so important, before you even know what it is," Will returned, an ease to his tone.

"You're alive because of us, Sam." Brandon was all edge and fury, in direct opposition to his brother.

"Who says I wanted to be kept alive?" he grumbled

"Yourself," Will replied simply. "You'd be dead if you wanted to be."

Just because it was the truth didn't mean Sam particularly wanted it pointed out to him. "Fine. Talk. But I've got work to do." He stomped toward the back, any reference to a past he'd rather forget poking at every angry, ungenerous, destructive impulse he'd ever had.

He'd had a hell of a lot of those. Brandon and Will followed him, and despite Will's calm demeanor, in contrast with Brandon's, when they'd spoken, tension and stress radiated off both men.

"We need you to act as an intermediary," Brandon said, wasting no time, as much because he wasn't a man to prevaricate as because Sam wouldn't stick around for any fluff.

"Between what and what?"

"We want to offer Hayley a position with Mile High," Will stated, obviously taking the role of explainer so Brandon's head didn't explode from trying not to demand something. "She refuses to talk with us. She's barred any attempt at speaking with her. But she's still here, in Gracely—that's got to mean something."

"What the hell do I have to do with your family drama?"

"We need an intermediary," Brandon repeated, the way he was grinding his teeth audible across the yard as Sam picked up a cord of wood that he'd take inside to heat his stove. God knew he'd need coffee after this.

"Between you and your half sister? I'm the last man to ask."

"No. You're the *only* man to ask. You're our partner."

"Silent partner." Sam stalked back to the cabin's entrance. He had no time for this, no patience for this. Brandon and Will should know better than to try and manipulate him into *anything* that had to do with family, let alone sisters—even if the mysterious Hayley Winthrop was only their sister by half.

"You can be as silent as you want. After you offer her a job," Brandon said as if it were a foregone conclusion.

"And train her. If she takes it," Will added.

Sam whirled on them, and he knew the sizzling anger wasn't appropriate for the request, but they'd poked at every sore spot he had, long before he'd been ready to let it roll off his shoulders. What he owed, how he'd been saved, and worst of all, *family.* "No." He wasn't sure if he yelled it or if he growled it.

Brandon cursed and stalked to Will's Jeep, and Sam should have been relieved. He should have been happy it hadn't come to blows, but he found himself itching for a fight. Which was mostly due to this ambush, but at least a little part of the desire to fight stemmed from an edgy feeling that had been dogging him for weeks.

There wasn't enough work to keep his mind engaged lately, which didn't make any sense because it was the same work there always was, and summer was high season. He was busy and challenged, and yet something had been under his skin like a splinter for a while.

Yeah, a fight would have been nice. He wouldn't have had to think about that.

So, he glared at Will, but Will only shook his head sadly.

"It's beneath you, Sam. All of this."

"Right back at you, Will." He didn't even have to give Will a meaningful look for that barb to hit. No matter how close the three of them had once been, they all had their secrets. And they all had their no-go zones.

This "favor" was Sam's no-go zone, and Brandon and Will had both known it before they'd even set up this ambush. They couldn't be pissed that Sam had been an ass; they had to have known this would happen.

But no matter how much Sam tried to convince himself of that, he went through the rest of the day feeling like a complete and utter tool.

The tool feeling didn't magically dissipate that afternoon. Sam guided a kayaking group, getting irrationally irritated any time he had to repeat an instruction, just narrowly missing exploding at an idiot who overturned his kayak.

Normally, despite his lack of charm or cheer, he was a helpful and informative—if disinterested—guide. Calmness and distance had become something of Sam's hallmark. He fell into gruff and grumpy on occasion, but the kind that caused people to give him nicknames and develop elaborate, tragic backstories about him.

He was ninety-nine percent certain the customers on this expedition just thought he was an arrogant prick. Which was bad business and simply not the man he'd turned himself into.

He had to get his shit on straight, and the only way he knew how to do that was with physical activity. Since he had to get his shit straight with Brandon and Will, that could only mean one thing.

Once he'd returned from his guide and cleaned up after the outing, Sam collected three sets of climbing gear. It'd be pushing sunset even if they did one of the easier climbs, but he needed this edgy, destructive feeling inside of him *gone*.

So, he strode into the office of Mile High Adventures. Skeet, the old man who acted as something between troll and receptionist, greeted him with a grunt and Sam returned it, but he didn't pause. He headed straight for Brandon, Will, and Lilly who were huddled in the main room looking over brochures or pictures or something.

It was a cozy, homey place, full of dark woods and thick rugs. Even before Lilly had stamped her presence on everything, the walls had been decorated with mountain prints and cheerful sayings about the outdoors.

The furniture in the main room was all dark brown leather couches, situated around a giant fireplace that dominated the room. It wasn't lit today in the middle of summer, and Lilly had covered the entrance with a giant bouquet of wildflowers and greenery.

Brandon, Will, and Lilly looked like the picture-perfect family or group of friends, and Sam ignored the familiar pang that hadn't dogged him in a while.

He dropped the climbing equipment in front of the twins, waiting till three pairs of eyes were on him. "If you can both beat me to the top, you win."

Will and Brandon exchanged a look while Lilly stared at Sam as if he'd lost his mind. "Beat you to the top of what?" she asked.

"So, we both have to beat you?" Brandon demanded, always one to get the rules lined up before they did anything.

"Both of you."

"And who's the judge if it's close?"

"If it's that close, I'll forfeit." Because while Will and Brandon were adept climbers, Sam was usually the one to take those expeditions, which gave him more practice and more skill.

Brandon and Will began to stand, and Lilly all but spluttered. "What on earth . . . ? Explain this to me."

"Rock climbing. We'll just do, what, the south cliff face?" At Sam's nod, Brandon looked back toward his fiancée. "No big deal."

"No big deal?" Lilly fisted her hands on her hips, her eyebrows drawing together in two angry points. "You're not actually going to agree to that!"

Will and Brandon shrugged in tandem, and Lilly turned her glare to Sam. "You're going to risk your necks trying to climb the rock face of a *mountain* the fastest instead of just doing this favor like a good friend?"

Sam didn't say anything to Lilly's glare or accusation. He found that silence was almost always the most effective answer when it came to the force of nature that was Lilly.

"Bran . . ."

"It's tradition," Brandon replied before Lilly could

argue further. "And perfectly safe." He pressed a kiss to her temple before collecting one of the sets of gear Sam had dropped. "We should be back by dark."

"We'll wear headlamps just in case," Will joked, which helped Lilly's outrage not at all.

"You're going *now*?" she all but screeched, hopping to her feet. "Of all the pseudo-macho, irresponsible, foolish—"

"Just think, it'll give you carte blanche on finalizing the new brochures," Brandon offered.

Lilly whirled. "It'll give me carte blanche on your corpse," she grumbled, stalking down the hallway and then slamming the door to her office.

"I'm going to pay for that."

Will made an unmistakable whip sound and just narrowly ducked out of Brandon's reach and a punch to the gut.

"I'm going to kick both your asses," Brandon grumbled.

"Side wagers, then?" Will asked cheerfully. He and Brandon argued about a side bet while they loaded up Sam's Jeep with the climbing equipment and drove to the south cliff face, where they held most of their rock climbing training. It was an easy-to-moderate climb, good for teaching people on.

Or, in this case, good for a speed challenge.

They got out of the Jeep, Brandon and Will trading good-natured trash talk. It hit a little hard, all this . . . well, it was very much like those "old days" that Sam did his best to forget.

"It's been a while," Brandon murmured as they got into their gear.

Sam didn't meet Brandon's discerning gaze, and he

immediately regretted doing something from *before*, but . . .

It was an easier apology, this gesture, than an actual apology.

"All right, ready?" At everyone's assenting nod, Will counted off, and at his "go," they each took a different path up to the top of the cliff face.

The climb was steady and challenging without being overwhelming. Sam could have pushed harder, and he had no doubt he could have beat Brandon and Will if not easily, clearly. But . . . he didn't push. He was careful, overly so, and when both men reached the top before he did, he didn't even feel a twinge at the loss.

This hadn't been about competition, not really. He was pretty sure Brandon and Will had already known that, but if they hadn't, they certainly knew now. The three of them rappelled down in silence, and when they reached the bottom, they all sat on the ground for a few minutes to catch their breath.

"You let us win, didn't you?"

Sam watched the sky above him darken, took slow breaths as stars twinkled to life. He still didn't want to do the damn favor, sticking his nose in the tricky family business that was the half sister the Evans brothers had recently found out about. One who'd been the product of an extramarital affair, before the Evanses' father had paid off her mother to disappear.

Sam could think of few things he wanted to do less than this. But once upon a time, he'd had nothing except rock bottom, pain, and guilt. The Evans brothers had given him the tools to climb out of rock bottom. They'd put him on that fishing boat, then they'd brought him back to Colorado.

They couldn't fix what was really wrong with him.

No one could. But they'd kept him from complete self-destruction, and while he didn't know Hayley Winthrop at all, he thought a sister probably deserved to know her brothers when they were men as good as Will and Brandon.

*And maybe fixing one sibling relationship will—*

He couldn't let that thought go any farther so he got to his feet. "Let's head back so Lilly can relax, then you can tell me what you need me to do."

He didn't wait for the brothers to come up with any response to that. He grabbed his gear and walked to the Jeep.

He wasn't fixing anything. He was acting as a facilitator. Because he owed the Evans brothers. That was it. He would do what he had to, and then they would leave him in peace again.

Because peace was all he was after.

Read on for a preview of

## SO WRONG IT MUST BE RIGHT

by
Nicole Helm

Available now wherever eBooks are sold.

"You're not still emailing with that guy!"

Dinah looked up from her phone and blinked at her cousin. It took a minute to get her bearings and remember that Kayla was waiting on her to get started.

"Actually, I was reading up on Trask. I found an article that might explain his reluctance to sell."

Kayla snatched her phone away, then frowned at the screen. "It is sick that you get the same look on your face reading those pervy emails as you do reading stuff for work."

"I don't know what you're talking about," Dinah replied primly. Okay, maybe she did know what Kayla meant, and maybe it was a little sick, but Gallagher's Tap Room was Dinah's blood. The Gallagher family had moved to St. Louis over a century ago, and built a little pub on the very land beneath the concrete floor under her feet. It was everything to her, and if she got a little excited about that? It was fine.

Kayla gestured toward the back door and Dinah stood to follow. Meeting with Trask was going to be it. The moment she finally proved to Uncle Craig and the board she was ready to take over as director of operations.

Being Uncle Craig's "special assistant" had turned out to mean little more than being his bitch, and while she'd worked to be the best damn bitch she could be, she was ready for tradition to take over. From the very beginning, the eldest Gallagher in every generation took over. These days, the title was director of operations, but it was all the same.

She was the eldest Gallagher of the eldest Gallagher. She'd been told her whole life that this would be hers when her father retired, or, as it turned out to be with Dad, abandoned everyone and everything in the pursuit of his mid-life crisis.

It was time. Dinah was ready, and getting some crazy urban farmer to sell his land next to Gallagher's for the expansion was going to be the final point in her favor. No one would be able to deny she was ready.

Director of operations was everything she'd been dreaming about since she'd been old enough to understand what the job required. Long after she'd understood what Gallagher's meant to her family, and to her.

"So, you finally stopped emailing creepy Internet dude?"

Dinah walked with Kayla down the hallway to the back exit. "He's not creepy." The guy she'd somehow randomly started emailing with after she'd tipsily commented on his Tumblr page one night wasn't creepy. He was kind of amazing.

"Dinah."

"I'm sorry. No way I'm giving that guy up. It's some of the hottest sex I've ever had."

Dinah thought wistfully over how he'd ended his last email. *And when you're at the point you don't think you can come again, I'll make sure that you do.* It might be only through a computer, but it was far superior to anything any other guy had ever said to her.

"It's fictional."

"So?"

"He's probably like a sixty-year-old perv. Or a woman if he's really as good as you say he is."

"As you pointed out, it's fictional. Who cares?"

They stepped out into the lingering warmth of late September. The urban landscape around Gallagher's was a mix of old and new, crumbling and modern. Soon, Gallagher's was going to make sure the entire block was a testament to a city that could reinvent itself.

"What does he do, send you pictures of models? Oh, baby, check out my six-pack. Then suddenly he's claiming to be David Gandy."

"We don't trade pictures of each other or any personal information that might identify us. I mean, he knows I have freckles. I know he has a birthmark on his inner thigh, but that's about it. It is pure, harmless, sexy, sexy words."

"Geez." Kayla waved her phone in front of Dinah's face, the screen displaying a myriad of apps. "Not even Snapchat?"

"Nope. It's all very old-fashioned. Like Jane Austen. Or *You've Got Mail*. Only with sex stuff."

"Go have some real sex, Dinah."

"I do that too!" Although admittedly less and less. Maybe not for six months or so. Trying to prove herself to Uncle Craig was eating her life away, and the nice thing about a sexy email was she could read it whenever she wanted and didn't have to remember its birthday or cook it dinner. It was perfect really, except the whole do-it-yourself aspect.

But do-it-yourself had been instilled on her from a

young age, no matter how false the message rang in her adulthood.

The tract of land behind Gallagher's that Uncle Craig wanted to buy was a strange sight in downtown St. Louis. Between one empty lot Uncle Craig had already bought, and an aging home with a scraggly yard that Craig was also after, a land of green emerged.

Not even green grass, but huge plants, archways covered in leaves, rows and rows of produce-bearing stems. So much green stuff the crumbling brick exterior of the old house behind it all was barely visible from where they stood in front of the chain-link fence that enclosed the property.

"It's cute. Kind of funny we're trying to get him to sell it so we can pave over it and then have a farmer's market."

Dinah had waged her own personal battle over the seemingly ironic or at the very least incongruous business plan her uncle had put forth, but being the black sheep of the family thanks to her dad screwing just about everything up meant Dinah didn't have a say. Even Kayla adding her opinion as sustainability manager had done nothing to sway Craig.

So, Dinah would find a way to get Mr. Hippie Urban Farmer to sell his land, and with any luck, convince him she was doing *him* a favor and sign him up for a booth for next year's market, which Kayla would be in charge of. The Gallagher & Ivy Farmer's Market would be a success one way or another.

"Look, apparently, from what I can tell, he grew up on a real farm and his family left that one, then he worked on some other family member's farm and they sold to a developer or something. This place was his grandmother's house, and over the course of the past four years, he's turned it into this. So, that may explain his refusing Gallagher's initial offer."

"What makes you think we can get through to him if my dad couldn't?"

"His family has a history of selling land. He should be well versed in the benefits. Surely a guy like him wants a bigger space, and the money we're offering will allow him that. Besides, we have a soul and decency on our side."

Kayla snorted. "No offense, but I'm a little glad your dad went off the deep end and I'm not the only one with a soulless Gallagher as a father."

"Gee, thanks," Dinah muttered, trying to ignore the little stab of pain. She couldn't be offended at the attack on her dad. It was warranted. They'd spent plenty of their childhood complaining about Kayla's dad being a douche. But, still, it hurt. It wasn't supposed to be this way.

Oh well, what could she do? She and Kayla stepped under the archway of green tendrils and the sign that read FRONT YARD FARM. The place *was* cute. Weird, no doubt, but cute.

Before they could make it past the first hurdle of beanstalks or whatever, the door to the brick house creaked open and a man stepped onto the porch. Dinah stopped mid-step, barely registering that Kayla did too.

He was tall and lanky and wearing loose-fitting khaki-colored pants covered in dirt and a flannel shirt with sleeves rolled to the elbows over a faded T-shirt. It was the face, though, that really caught her attention. Sharp and angular. Fierce. Only softened by the slight curl to his dark hair, his beard obscuring his jaw line. Something about the way he moved was pure grace, and everything about his looks made Dinah's attraction hum to attention.

"He's like every hipster fantasy I've ever had come to life," Dinah whispered, clutching Kayla's arm briefly.

"Lord, yes."

The man on the stoop, with the hoe, and the flannel, and the beard—sweet Lord—stared at them suspiciously. "Can I help you two?"

Dinah exchanged a glance with her cousin, who was valiantly trying to pretend they hadn't been drooling.

"Mr. Trask?"

"Yeah."

"Hi, I'm Dinah Gallagher and this is Kayla Gallagher. We're from Gallagher's Ta—"

"Nope."

The door slammed so emphatically, Dinah jerked back. She'd barely registered the guy moving inside before he was completely gone behind that slammed door.

"Well."

"What were you saying about human decency and souls making a difference?"

Dinah started picking her way across the narrow and uneven brick path to the door. "He hasn't had a chance to see it yet. Maybe the meeting with your dad ended poorly. We'll have to mend a few fences."

"Before we buy them all," Kayla muttered. "Remember when we were kids and thought we'd be calling the shots?"

"We still will be. Just need another decade." Or two. That was how family business worked. She wasn't going to abandon it just because it was harder than she'd expected or taking longer than she'd anticipated. No, she was going to fight.

And should Kayla ever get married, Dinah would not

follow in her father's footsteps and sleep with her best friend and family member's spouse.

Dinah reached the door and knocked. She didn't entertain thoughts of failing because it simply wasn't an option. Failing Gallagher's was never going to be an option.

The door remained closed. Dinah pursed her lips. This was *not* going the way she'd planned.

"Okay. Well. I won't be deterred."

"Come on, Dinah. Let's go." Kayla stood in the yard, hands shoved into the pockets of her dress. "Call him. Write him an email. I don't want him calling the cops on us. Oh, maybe you can accidentally write him one of your sex emails. That'll get his attention." She sighed, loud enough to be heard across the yard. "I would so not mind getting that guy's attention."

"I'm going to pick something." Dinah surveyed the plants surrounding her. She didn't know a lot about farmers or farming, but if he was so dead set on not selling, he obviously cared deeply about this yard of produce. So, she'd lure him out that way.

"Don't! He'll call the cops."

Dinah waved her off. "I'll pick something ripe and give it back to him. I'm doing him a favor, really."

Kayla muttered something, but Dinah ignored her. She surveyed the arches of green and splashes of color—squash maybe.

Something about it all looked very familiar. Like she'd seen it . . . somewhere. Somewhere. Well, she didn't have time to dwell on that. She had to find something ripe to pick.

And since she had no idea what she was doing, that was going to be a challenge.

\* \* \*

Carter was not falling for this dirty trick. He wasn't. If he was grinding his teeth and clenching his fists in his pockets, it was only because . . .

Aw, fuck it. She was winning. Touching his plants, his stuff, picking a damn unripe squash. He couldn't let it go even if he knew that was her plan all along.

He threw open the window, pushing his face close to the screen. "I'm calling the cops," he shouted.

"Oh, I wish you wouldn't," the brunette returned, just as casual as you please. "I only want to have a civil conversation."

"Hell to the no, lady. I know what Gallagher means by civil, and it's 'screw me six ways to Sunday and then expect me to thank him for it.'"

"As you can see, *Mr.* Gallagher isn't here."

"Just because you have breasts doesn't mean I'm more inclined to talk to you." Even if they were rather distracting when she was kneeling facing his window. From his higher vantage point, he could see down the gap between fabric and skin. Dark lace against very pale skin. A few freckles across her chest and cheeks. He briefly thought of his last email from D.

*Maybe we couldn't wait, and I unbutton and unzip your pants right there on your front porch.*

He couldn't think about the rest of that email and maintain his irritation, so he forced it out of his mind and focused on the offending party.

Her hair was a fashionable tangle of rich reddish waves. Her face was all made up with hues of pink, and the heels of her shoes sank into the mud next to his zucchini. When she stood, wrinkling her freckled nose at him, he could see that she had long, lean legs, probably as pale and freckly as her chest, but black tights obscured them. Which was good. This was one attraction he had no interest in pursuing. A Gallagher for fuck's sake. Of course she was gorgeous. She probably paid a lot of money to be. Her family was rolling in it.

"I'm calling the cops," he threatened again.

"Don't you think they have better things to do?"

"Listen, lady—"

"All I want is ten minutes of your time, Mr. Trask. That's all. Much easier than getting the police involved."

# Connect with Us

Visit us online at
**KensingtonBooks.com**
to read more from your favorite authors, see books
by series, view reading group guides, and more.

for sneak peeks, chances to win books and prize packs,
and to share your thoughts with other readers.

facebook.com/kensingtonpublishing
twitter.com/kensingtonbooks

## Tell us what you think!

To share your thoughts, submit a review,
or sign up for our eNewsletters, please visit:
**KensingtonBooks.com/TellUs.**

# Books by Bestselling Author
# Fern Michaels

| | | |
|---|---|---|
| ___**The Jury** | 0-8217-7878-1 | $6.99US/$9.99CAN |
| ___**Sweet Revenge** | 0-8217-7879-X | $6.99US/$9.99CAN |
| ___**Lethal Justice** | 0-8217-7880-3 | $6.99US/$9.99CAN |
| ___**Free Fall** | 0-8217-7881-1 | $6.99US/$9.99CAN |
| ___**Fool Me Once** | 0-8217-8071-9 | $7.99US/$10.99CAN |
| ___**Vegas Rich** | 0-8217-8112-X | $7.99US/$10.99CAN |
| ___**Hide and Seek** | 1-4201-0184-6 | $6.99US/$9.99CAN |
| ___**Hokus Pokus** | 1-4201-0185-4 | $6.99US/$9.99CAN |
| ___**Fast Track** | 1-4201-0186-2 | $6.99US/$9.99CAN |
| ___**Collateral Damage** | 1-4201-0187-0 | $6.99US/$9.99CAN |
| ___**Final Justice** | 1-4201-0188-9 | $6.99US/$9.99CAN |
| ___**Up Close and Personal** | 0-8217-7956-7 | $7.99US/$9.99CAN |
| ___**Under the Radar** | 1-4201-0683-X | $6.99US/$9.99CAN |
| ___**Razor Sharp** | 1-4201-0684-8 | $7.99US/$10.99CAN |
| ___**Yesterday** | 1-4201-1494-8 | $5.99US/$6.99CAN |
| ___**Vanishing Act** | 1-4201-0685-6 | $7.99US/$10.99CAN |
| ___**Sara's Song** | 1-4201-1493-X | $5.99US/$6.99CAN |
| ___**Deadly Deals** | 1-4201-0686-4 | $7.99US/$10.99CAN |
| ___**Game Over** | 1-4201-0687-2 | $7.99US/$10.99CAN |
| ___**Sins of Omission** | 1-4201-1153-1 | $7.99US/$10.99CAN |
| ___**Sins of the Flesh** | 1-4201-1154-X | $7.99US/$10.99CAN |
| ___**Cross Roads** | 1-4201-1192-2 | $7.99US/$10.99CAN |

*Available Wherever Books Are Sold!*
Check out our website at **www.kensingtonbooks.com**

# More by Bestselling Author
# Hannah Howell